OPPORTUNITY KNOX

(THE UNDERDOG SERIES #3)

BREA BROWN

WAYZGOOSE PRESS

CONTENTS

Edited by Maggie Sokolik

Cover design by Keri Knutson at alchemybookcovers.com

(Note: An earlier, slightly modified edition of this novel, with the same title, was originally published in 2018, 9781982997144).

To the four greatest "opportunities" in my life.
You've made me a better person.

ONE

GRACE

Our phones chime: "Touchdown!" for Jet; a bar from the *Lord of the Rings* score for me. Jet tosses aside the playbook he's trying to study, and I abandon my adult coloring book as we scramble to see the updates on our screens. As we read the latest, Jet yelps, our pampered Bichon Frise, Torzi, lifts his head from his paws, and I utter a soft "Yaaaaaay." I'm elated, but too tired to show it sincerely.

Another text immediately arrives from Cyndi's phone, but presumably from her birthing partner, since I doubt my sister-in-law has been live-texting the birth:

Video chat in ten minutes. We're almost settled in a room.

I suppress my objection. It's nearly two in the morning. But I suppose it won't kill me to wait ten more minutes. It's hardly going to be a long call. And I have to admit, after waiting up this long, it'd be a shame to go to bed without seeing the little cherub's face. Work will be Hell tomorrow, but what else is new? Maybe I can catch a nap in my car on my lunch break.

I stretch on the couch, and my coloring book falls to the floor with a slap. Jet picks it up and sets it on top of his playbook, stacking both of them on the coffee table. Closing the lid on my tin of pencils, I place it on the small pile of books and stifle a yawn.

Jet pulls me into an unexpected hug that makes the leather couch squeak under us and Torzi vacate the room, clearly miffed by our shenanigans. "She's here!" he says gleefully into my hair.

I laugh. "Yep. She is. Finally."

"Oh, I can't wait to see her! I wonder if she looks like Mikey."

The mention of his clone reminds me that our three-year old nephew, who's staying with us, is going to wake us up in a distressingly short amount of time. And we'll be expected to be responsible adults when he does.

"If she's lucky, she looks like Cyndi."

His grip loosens slightly. "Hey! What are you saying? I'd be a cute girl."

"You're delirious. And speaking of..." I push away from him and stand. "Did you prep the coffee and set the timer on the machine? We're going to need some major caffeine in a few hours."

"Yeah. It's all set." He rises and moans. "Oh, shit. I sat too long."

"Stiff?"

He nods, kicking out his feet to warm up his knees. I avert my face to hide my worried eyes. It's going to be a long season.

Before I can contemplate too much on the ramifications of playing at least fourteen more games on joints that probably could have used surgical intervention rather than simple physical therapy in the off-season, Jet's phone bloops to notify us of an incoming video call. I lunge for the TV remote to turn it on and make sure it's on the right input while Jet pushes the button to cast his phone to the larger screen and sets the device on the mantle to frame up a steady shot of us.

Cyndi's face appears. "Hey, guys!"

I bump the volume down. The last thing we need is for Mikey to hear her in surround sound and come running, refreshed from his five hours of sleep and ready to go. "Hey, darlin'," Jet replies. "Are you sure you just had a baby? You look great!"

"Adrenaline," she explains. "I'll collapse here in a minute, but before that, we wanted to show off our newest teammate. Meet Grace, or Gracie, as we've already started calling her."

She picks up the phone and sends us on a stomach-rolling spin around the dim room as she points the camera toward the person sitting on the tiny sofa by the windows. I blink while she zooms in and focuses on a familiar person, who's grinning sheepishly.

"Colin?"

"Cheers," he says softly, bouncing the bundle in his arms when she startles at his voice.

"You're Cyndi's mystery birthing partner?" Jet blurts, suddenly oblivious to the baby.

I nudge him. "Jet!"

"What?" He glances down at me but quickly at the screen again.

"I think they're more than birthing partners," I mutter from the corner of my mouth.

Jet's jaw drops. "But— I mean…"

"Congratulations, you two," I say, picking up the social slack. "She's beautiful."

"Can't say I had anything to do with that," Colin says with a chuckle and a modest blush. "But I have to agree with you, Lady Maura." He peels back the blanket and walks closer to the camera to give us a close-up of her face.

She's a newborn, all right. Red, swollen, and indistinguishable from every other newborn I've ever seen. Still, I reiterate, "She's gorgeous."

"Isn't she?" He perches on the side of the bed so Cyndi can set the phone down on its stand once more. As soon as the device is settled, she turns her attention to her daughter and kisses the top of her head. Colin gazes down at both of them in a way I've never seen him look at anyone. Ever.

Feeling like we're intruding on a private moment, I clear my throat and say, "Well. This is... What a happy occasion! But you two must be exhausted. We'll let you—"

"Wait!"

I startle at Jet's near-shout. "Shhh!" I rest my hand in the crook of his elbow, but he shrugs me off.

"You two are... You're friends, right?"

Cyndi sighs but smiles patiently at her brother. "Yes. And then some."

"But you— And he's—" We all wait for him to finish the thought, but he doesn't seem to know how to do it, so he finally says, "Right. Okay. I thought you'd tell us about something like that, that's all."

"We are. Right now."

Colin shifts. "Sorry, mate. We wanted to say something, but things were a bit unsettled, what with the divorce still going through and—"

"That was months ago."

"—the baby expected any day. We wanted to keep stress down for baby and mum and figured this would be a better time to tell everyone."

"Everyone," meaning Gloria, the inimitable, formidable Knox matriarch. I totally get it. Wait until she's too enthralled and distracted with the baby to criticize the timing of Cyndi's new relationship. I doubt that's going to work, but good for them for trying. Mama Knox is going to have a much different take on all of this than Jet and I do.

Confident he doesn't have the balls to shrug me off twice, I pull on Jet's elbow again. "Come on. Let's all get some rest."

He smiles shakily. "Yeah. Um, okay. Yeah." To Cyndi and Colin, he says, "I'm happy for you guys. She's great. You're great. Super-great. We'll, uh, come by tomorrow to see you, bring Mikey. All that stuff. It'll be great."

With orders to kiss the toddler in our charge, we disconnect.

As Jet pockets his phone, he turns to face me and into my stunned silence says, "Well, screw me."

"Not tonight, Champ," I answer drolly. "It's late, and I'm way too tired." Chuckling at myself, I pat his shoulder on my way past him to the stairs. "Beddy-bye time."

He follows listlessly, and we slog up the stairs. "Do you think—"

"Yes."

"But what about—"

"That, too."

"And they—"

"Yep."

"Oh, man!"

"Best not to think too much about it right now." I fall into bed while he dutifully brushes his teeth and washes and moisturizes his face—gotta stay pretty for the cameras, right? Occasionally, as I drift off, I hear him mutter another curse word as more and more pieces fall into place for him. Then... oblivion.

TWO

LEGACY

Everything's changing. Rapidly. It's fitting that even something as steady as my friendship with Colin is shifting and transforming before me. Nothing stays the same. Ever. Especially "temporary" careers.

In a couple of weeks, I'll be jobless. This is how it has to be, though. What's hard to see from the outside is that the professional football lifestyle is as high-maintenance as its principle players. It's all-consuming, even for a fringe participant, like me. Trying to squeeze in my comparatively scant responsibilities to the NFL around my day job has been an exhausting exercise. When I'm at work, my phone buzzes and bings in my desk all day during appointments with clients. It doesn't matter that I ignore it until I have a free minute (usually on the toilet, if I'm being honest); I'm rarely mentally one hundred percent present, which is unfair to both my co-workers and my clients.

Under this current arrangement, Jet and I also don't get any time off together during the season. He's usually traveling —or sequestered—on Saturdays. Sundays (and sometimes

Mondays and Thursdays) are game days. I'm at work on Tuesday, the one day of the week he supposedly has "off." In both the regular season and the off-season, I attend charitable events with him and try to squeeze in other public appearances around my work schedule. I don't have enough vacation time to cover all the time off I need to do this thing right.

Something's gotta give. I can't do it all. And since I made an unbreakable vow with the bleating, beeping, and buzzing device in my desk drawer—or at least the person usually on the other side of those communiqués—it looks like this permanently temporary day job of mine is the giver.

My mother-in-law might have been right when she said that being Jet's wife is a full-time job in itself. Ew. I hate when she's right.

The blazing autumn trees provide a clichéd metaphor for my life right now. Their leaves look so vibrant, but they're at the end of their life-cycle. And like the soon-to-be-barren trees, I'll be aimless and idle in a matter of weeks. Also like them, I'll be expected to bear fruit again—eventually.

It's not all doom and gloom, though. After all, quitting my day job while still having the financial freedom to do things I'm truly passionate about (whatever those things are) is what I've always wanted. In my silliest daydreams, that is. Facing it in reality is something else, surprisingly.

On the surface, I'm all excitement and effusiveness. "It's going to be great! I finally get to be the lady of leisure I've always dreamed of being!" and, "What do I have planned? Watching all the award-winning movies I've missed and reading the books they're based on, to see which is better," and, "Heck yeah, I'll be traveling around the country to every football stadium the Chiefs visit. Duh!"

In my quietest moments, however, the soundtrack to my

thoughts is two repeating, ominous chords reminiscent of *Jaws*. The Career Center is the first place in the "real" world I've ever found a niche. It's scary to raise my head above the edge of the trench and crawl out in the open, where I'll be exposed. What if I never find another trench? What if I'm left out in the open, wandering, until someone shoots and puts me out of my misery?

Melodramatic mixed movie metaphors aside, I don't have a choice now. I have to trust that decisions made in more lucid, logical moments will hold, and my more recent, frequent fever dreams of doubt are simply the result of human nature's resistance to change, no matter how positive it may be. Instead of feeling threatened by the seemingly endless opportunity out there, I should feel challenged and invigorated.

Until I can get to that point, I have plenty to keep me occupied at work. With everything going on in my personal life, the Career Center, with its predictable routines, has been a veritable sanctuary. My final job fair coincides with my last day, and it's going to be a doozy.

For starters, I'll be transforming the tent into the Shire of Tolkien's imagination, with each employer's booth background resembling brightly colored round doors. A framed scroll-shaped piece of yellowed parchment will bear the label for each booth in the calligraphy made instantly recognizable by two film trilogies. I've hired another company to treat the concrete patio under the tent with a washable paint to resemble worn dirt paths and grass. And instead of boring cookies, I'll serve scones made to look like elven *lembas* bread, the stuff of lore that supposedly can satisfy a man for an entire day—or in Jet's case, an hour. An easel at the entrance of the tent will declare there's...

"One job to rule them all."

That's right—I'm going full Hobbit-slash-nerd on this place.

Needless to say, I'm sparing no expense. When I proposed this theme to my boss, Cynthia, she predictably balked. "There's no way this will stay within budget."

I waved her off. "A private donor has generously agreed to make up the shortfall."

With her signature bark-giggle, she showed me all of her chins while looking down her nose at me—a feat I've yet to figure out, considering I'm several inches taller than she is—and smirked. "And is this 'private donor' willing to sustain his support after you're gone, ensuring we can maintain the public's expectations of such detailed themes?"

After thinking about it for two seconds, I shrugged and said, "Sure. *She'd* be glad to do that."

Eff her and her assumptions. This is *my* legacy, not Jet's. (Not to mention, it'll be another nice tax write-off each year.)

Oh, gosh... I'm turning into... my brother!

Nevertheless, it was satisfying to leave Cynthia's office with that retort, which wiped the smirk from her face. She better watch it, or this private donor will change her mind, and The Career Center will be back to serving boring pre-packaged cookies and watery Kool-Aid at lackluster events that only attract the most basic employers and ordinary job seekers.

Better, more entertaining job fairs aren't my only legacy, though, I hope. I'm determined to place some of my heretofore most challenging candidates in permanent positions. I've already succeeded with Colin, who's happily ensconced at the University of Missouri-Kansas City's admissions department, what he calls his "big boy job." How grown-up and domestic he's become! That should have been my first sign that he had a woman—other than me—in his life.

But Colin's career commitment-phobia was charming compared to some of my other clients' issues. A few of them are downright unemployable, for a myriad of reasons. They suffer from chronic absenteeism and tardiness; they clash with co-workers; they find fault with everything and everyone. And in the case of Nina, her tender sensibilities result in her rarely lasting past her probationary period at any placement.

She's accused countless companies of everything from sexism to ageism. She's complained about poor ergonomics, co-workers' tasteless jokes, and working on religious holidays that have nothing to do with her personal faith. She's claimed employers are insensitive to her needs as a single mother. She's blamed physical and mental problems on bullying bosses. It's gotten to the point that I feel guilty subjecting any more businesses to this woman. But she keeps coming back, and it's my job to find her job after job, despite suspecting she'll never fit in anywhere.

Today, though... Today, I'm ready for her.

As soon as she sits down, I hand a referral across the desk to her. "All right, Nina. Here's the deal."

My uncharacteristically no-nonsense tone quickly garners her attention. She perches on the edge of her chair, her posture rigid, her eyes blinking rapidly. "Yes?"

"This is it, girl."

"What's it?"

"This. This is it."

"I don't understand."

"This is my last shot at finding you your dream job."

"It is?"

I nod. "It is."

She gulps. "Oh. You mean, if this doesn't work out, I can't come back here? Like, I'm banned? Because that's not fair, is it? It's not my fault all those places were so—"

I hold up a hand to silence her. "I can't ban you. I wouldn't ban you. In fact, I respect the heck out of you for trying again and again, no matter how hopeless it seems." She grins proudly, but before she can get too comfortable, I continue, "The thing is, I'm out of here in two weeks."

"What happened? Did someone sexually harass you? I can get you in touch with this lawyer I know. You'd be amazed how rampant misconduct in the workplace is."

"Nobody sexually harassed me. I'm... pursuing new opportunities."

"They're forcing you out, aren't they? It's always the nice ones who get walked all over."

I sigh. "Nina, listen to me. Nobody's forcing me to do anything. It's time for me to focus on other aspects of my life, that's all."

She sits back and winks. "Oh, I see."

"You do?"

"Yes." Again, she closes one eye and smiles knowingly.

"Why are you winking?"

She picks a piece of lint from her trousers. "Well, it's inappropriate to talk about it in this setting, but I know a little about your personal life—everyone does. I've read the stories."

"The stories?" I sit forward in my chair and lean nearly all of my weight onto my elbows on my desk. "What stories?"

"You know... About the..." With her arms, she mimes a huge bubble in the air front of her midriff and whispers, "...bump."

I clench my jaw.

"I'm sorry! You know what? Forget I said anything. It was completely out of line. If you ban me now, I'd totally understand. I wouldn't tolerate being talked to like that, that's for sure. I— The thing is— You know, it's easy to forget we don't know each other better than we do, because I see you all over the place with *him*. You two are in the paper and on the news constantly. When do you sleep or have time to make... bumps?" She blushes. "Too personal again. Sorry."

Slumping in my chair, I roll my eyes. For someone so sensitive, she, herself, is remarkably socially inept. "There's no 'bump.'"

"Oh." She eyes my gut, which I suck in. "But that's one of the new 'opportunities' you'll be pursuing?"

"No. I don't know. Not right away. Nina?"

"What?"

"Focus. This isn't about me. It's about you. Your future. Your success. I want this to be the last time I ever see you. No offense."

She chuckles. "None taken."

"And I mean that in the nicest way possible. But I'm all in." Channeling Jet, I dredge up a good sports metaphor. "This is my Hail Mary."

Nodding, she bites her lower lip and maintains earnest eye contact with me.

"At some point, you're going to have to stop playing the victim everywhere you go."

"I don't—"

"Yes, you do. And you're teaching your kids how to be victims."

"Hey!"

"It's true. You know I'm right. So, I want you to look long and hard at the referral in your hand and think of it as your last chance to get it right. This is the perfect opportunity for you. As soon as it came in, I thought of you. And I've vetted this employer with you in mind. If you can't make this work, you're not going to be able to make anything work."

"Well!" She puffs out her chest. "I don't think it's appropriate—"

"Of course, it's not. But you can trust I'm being honest with you. I'll never see you again, so I can afford to be frank."

Blinking at the card in her hand, she takes that in. "Gosh. That's a lot of pressure to put on me. That's a lot of pressure to put on yourself."

"The pressure's on, Nina. We can either prevail or choke."

She worries a hangnail on her thumb. "Okay. Tell me about this place."

I clear my throat and pick up my copy of the referral on my desk. "You'd be the executive assistant to the vice president of operations at the corporate headquarters of a pet supply chain."

"Sounds important."

"It is. The woman who would be your boss is a lot like you. She's in her mid-forties, a single parent, and incredibly driven. The difference is, she's never allowed anyone to make her a victim. Ever."

"How do you know that about her? Do you know her, personally?"

I shake my head. "No. But I told you, I vetted her more closely than I normally do, so that I could prepare you for the type of person you'd be dealing with. I did my research. She's been interviewed several times over the years in local publications. She was a 'Fifty Under Fifty' for three years in a row. She means business."

"Okay. I like the sound of that."

"She doesn't suffer fools, either, Nina."

"Meaning…?"

"Meaning petty gripes and complaints will get you nowhere with her. At the same time, she'd never ask you to do more than she'd be willing to do." Punctuating each point with a tap on my desk, I say, "She understands work-life balance; she respects her employees' rights to their personal lives; and she expects you to respect her for it and not take advantage of her good nature. By all accounts, she's tough but fair. She demands good, consistent work from herself and those around her."

"Reasonable enough."

"This is perfect for you. You're perfect for this."

"I am?"

"Yes. Go out there and prove me right." I stand and extend my arm over my desk, waiting for my final (I hope) handshake with my most challenging client.

She stands, too, and pumps my hand. "I will. I'll try, that is. No promises, of course. I don't tolerate misbehavior. Not in my kids, not in my co-workers, not in my bosses. Right is right, after all."

I release her from my grip. "Nobody's asking you to compromise your values. Your integrity and grit are your best attributes."

With a determined smile, my problem child folds the referral and places it in the inside pocket of her smart suit jacket, the one she's worn to every appointment with me. "Thanks, Maura. And you know, good luck with all of your new opportunities, whatever they are."

"If you hear what they are, could you let me know?" I half-joke.

She giggles. "You got it."

THREE

RIVALS

I'm not going to lie; I'm feeling pretty darn proud of myself after giving that pep talk to Nina. Jet always says that I should consider a career as a locker room motivational speaker, but I'm not sure I'd be able to concentrate with all those half-naked (and all-naked) guys around. Plus, from the videos I've seen, he and Coach Bauer do a pretty good job of pumping up the team before games and celebrating after wins. They don't need me.

But I have a good feeling about Nina's chances on this job. I'm hopeful she can make this work. At least, I hope she can last long enough that I'm gone before she comes back here looking for something else. Then I can believe whatever I want to believe.

While I'm looking for my lunch in the stuffed break room fridge, a voice startles me from behind. "I think we have a lunch thief."

Considering my bento box isn't on the shelf where I left it a few hours ago, I turn to face fellow job counselor, Derek Duggan, and say, "I think you're right."

"I know I am. My roast beef on rye went missing yesterday."

"Who does that?"

He shrugs. "A hungry person?"

"Well, they stole my food *and* my bento box."

Laughing, he reaches past me for his wax paper-wrapped sandwich, something not as appealing today, apparently, as my sushi. "However will you afford a new one?"

"It's not about the money!" I plop at one of the tables and plunk my cheek against my hand. "I'm hungry. And I liked that bento box."

"Are you in third grade, or something?" After purchasing an iced tea from the vending machine, he sits across the table from me and unwraps his lunch, what appears—and smells—to be tuna salad on wheatberry. A nice person would offer half to me. He bites into the top center of the sandwich and scouts the location of his next bite.

Packing the food into his cheek, he muffles, "If it matters that much to you, you should go around to everyone's desks and find the culprit."

I wave my hand. "It's not worth the confrontation."

"That's what I thought. Plus, it would look pathetic if someone of your means begrudged someone a free lunch."

Blushing, I sputter, "That's not— If they really needed it— It's stealing to take it without asking!"

He shrugs and takes another huge bite. "Are you really in a position to lecture someone about entitlement, though?"

Fed up with his holier-than-thou attitude, I rise from the table and head toward the door, planning to grab my purse from my office and walk my aggression off to the nearest food truck.

"Hey, Maura."

I stop in the doorway.

"We still set for a 'training session' later?" The air quotes in his smug tone put me on edge, but I try to pretend I don't notice them.

"Yeah. I blocked out a half-hour at two o'clock. Does that still work?"

He nods while chewing and swallowing. Then, iced tea bottle to his lips, he says, "I've been looking forward to it all day."

Oh, brother... Maybe my time would be better spent napping. Either way, sleep-deprived or hangry, I have a feeling my meeting with Derek is going to be painful. It's a no-win.

———

It seems like only yesterday I was freaking out about having to take over job fairs from the retiring Arnold. Now I *am* Arnold, complete with pooching gut but minus the male pattern baldness and halitosis. And at the tender age of thirty, I'm retiring. From mainstream life.

I shake my head at my desk to clear from it any more anxiety-causing thoughts like that. *Focus, Maura.*

Derek's rise from receptionist to counselor to soon-to-be-most-senior job counselor has been much more meteoric than mine was, thanks to high turnover and his relentless brown-nosing. The Giggler loves him. Often uses him in staff meetings as a "prime example" when making a point about how we should all do things, from making coffee to gently steering applicants to more realistic job choices.

If I were a pettier person, I'd make all kinds of assumptions about her relationship with the young, fit metrosexual. But I'm a professional, so I pretend figurative butt-kissing is the closest Derek's lips have come to Cynthia's nethers. It's too disturbing to contemplate, anyway, and none of my business.

My protégé will be here for his training session shortly, as soon as he's finished with the client I saw him leading past my office door a few minutes ago. And what am I going to tell him?

My predecessor was much more hands-on about passing the torch than I've been. Okay, that's an understatement, like calling Gloria Knox "hands-on" when it comes to her kids. Arnold had been organizing job fairs for decades, though. It made sense that his way of doing things was more entrenched, and he wanted to make sure he was leaving the task in capable hands.

I've only been doing this a few cycles, and I sweat when I imagine someone else planning a boring flop of an event, but I don't have a tried and true formula for success to pass along to someone. I'm a pantser. I wait for inspiration and hope it hits while I still have time to execute the plan. You can't exactly "teach" that.

Derek's a smart guy, though. (Just ask him.) All he needs from me is the template—budget, schedule, and contact lists —and he'll figure out the rest. With everything else I have to worry about, I don't need to add this phantom problem. He's capable, he's eager to take on more responsibility, and he's going to be working with a lot more money for these events than I was, thanks to *moi*.

So what if he's a dick? Not everyone can possess my charming, winsome personality. And his not-so-pleasant demeanor won't be my problem for long.

He knocks on my door with all four knuckles, startling me from my unfocused stare at the notes on my desk. "Wake up!"

I blush. "Oh, hey. Sorry. I was... thinking." *Thinking about how one of the perks of no longer working here will be saying goodbye to you.*

"Don't hurt yourself." He pulls up the chair on the other side of my desk and looks around the office. After a low whistle, he places his hands behind his head, his elbows spread so that it feels like he's taking up the entire room. "This'll be all mine soon, huh?"

"Yep. For what it's worth."

"This office is about twice the size of my itty bitty closet. And you have a window!"

I glance behind me at the narrow slit of foggy glass that I suppose qualifies as a window but barely affords a peek at the current weather conditions. Otherwise, it's mainly a view of another brick wall in the building next door. "I guess I do."

"Something like that is easy to take for granted when you've always had it, but it's going to be a huge upgrade for me. I feel like Harry Potter under the stairs most days."

I smile at his movie reference. *Maybe this guy's not as bad as I thought.*

"This was the office that was open when I was promoted to job counselor. Mere chance that it's the biggest one and has *a* window. But it's nice that you'll appreciate it."

Something on the wall catches his attention, and he hops from the chair and crosses to it. At eye level with my diploma, he reads, "'Film studies.' At UMKC. Who'da thunk that?"

"It was a popular program."

"I'm sure. Popular with slackers who wanted an easy 'A.' And kind of irrelevant here. But I guess it's better than nothing."

I flap the paper on my desk to return his focus to our real purpose here. "Anyway..."

His head snaps my way, and he jabs his thumb at the frame on the wall. "That's not going to leave an outline, is it?"

"I haven't been here that long!"

"It doesn't take long. And I'm just saying... I don't want the walls marked up."

"Do you mind if we talk about job fairs? I—" I catch myself before I spill that I'm leaving early to drop by the hospital for a visit with Cyndi, Colin, and company. I redirect with, "We don't have a ton of time."

"How long can it possibly take to go through this? I've read the CBA." Despite his protests, he returns to his seat, resuming his power stance. He sits back as far as he can and rests his left ankle on his right knee.

I slide my admittedly scant notes across the desk toward him, not surprised when he doesn't sit forward to look at them, much less pick them up. "Actually, the Current Best Approaches are slightly out-of-date. Nothing too huge, but the budget's bigger, and the approval process for budget increases will also be different than in the past, because... Well, we'll get to that in a second." I tuck my hair behind my ears, my brain scrambling to put my talking points back in order.

Before I can get there, he chuckles. "Look at you. All business."

"Uh..."

"I get it. You have to justify the last however many years you've been occupying this prime office space, and you have a ton of territory to cover before you go, but you have to realize, I remember you B.C."

"'B.C.?'"

"Before Celebrity." He grins, proud of his cleverness.

I bite back a retort about his daily ginkgo smoothie paying

off and instead say, "It wasn't that long ago, and I don't think it's changed me that much, either."

He leans forward, dropping his hands and bracing his elbows on his knees. "Ha! I knew you back when you came in here every day, put in your eight hours—no more, no less— skated by doing the bare minimum, and had more 'appointments' with your little English buddy than with legit clients."

"Colin is—*was*—a legit client."

"Okay, I'll give you that one, but he was a bigger constant at this place than some of the receptionists."

"Not anymore. He has a permanent placement, and—"

"Congratulations. After *years*, you were able to place a fully-qualified white male. Bravo." He smirks. "How's it going with that Nina chick? I saw she was here—again—today. Eightieth time is the charm?"

My blood pressure rises to the point that I can feel it in my eyeballs, but I will myself not to raise my voice or otherwise react to give him the satisfaction of knowing he's hit a nerve. "Some clients are more challenging than others. You'll have your own repeat clients, and you'll learn not to take it personally. I will tell you, though, that when they finally do find that permanent placement, it feels pretty damn good."

"Whatever." He waves off my defense. "You can drop the act. You're the Queen of Career Counseling like I'm the quarterback of the Chiefs."

Seething, I nevertheless take a deep breath and say through clenched teeth, "Back on-topic..." I relax my jaw and rub my temples. *Oh, man. I'm too tired for this.* "We hold two job fairs every year, one in late May, after college graduations, and the other in the early fall—"

"You only started caring about this job to impress your man and to make yourself look less lame next to him."

"Hey!"

He raises his hands in surrender before tucking them in his armpits. After we stare each other down for longer than is comfortable, he sits up and grabs his copy of my notes. "Sorry. I call it like I see it." Glancing down at the paper, he appears to skim its contents then dismiss them by folding the sheet into fourths and jamming it into his inside suit jacket pocket. "Excuse me if I don't feel like hearing your spiel about something I could do in my sleep, since, you know, I actually want to be here, and I take my job seriously, not like some silly hobby that gets me out of the mansion five days a week so I can show off my expensive clothes and flashy cars."

"That's not—"

He rises. "Whatever. Update the CBA. If I have any questions, I'll refer to that."

———

What an asshole! I've been marinating in my righteous indignation since Derek's departure, thinking up witty comebacks I'll never use, because at this point, they would sound pathetic. Plus, he's right; I never cared about this job until it was the only thing separating me from a life of luxury I've had no part in earning and, therefore, don't deserve.

It's not like I have a passion for job counseling. Sure, I'm good at it, but I've always seen it as "just a job." I mostly wanted to hold onto it because I couldn't, and it sucks to have the choice taken away from me. But what sucks harder is realizing how much I stupidly sought Jet's approval when I did put forth any effort in my work—and how transparent those efforts apparently have been. Being smart, creative, and useful makes him proud of me, like I'm proud of him every time he steps on the field, despite my terror

I do care about the people I see every day, though. I do want them to find jobs. Mostly so I don't have to see them again, sure. But also because it means they've found where they belong. Belonging somewhere is important.

Jet has that with the NFL. And this job has been the closest I've ever been to having that, too. When I give it up, where will I belong? More importantly, what will I be? My identity will be entirely wrapped up in my marriage. One half of "Jetaura." I need more than that.

At 3:30, I shut everything down and try to ignore my paranoia at leaving early on a Friday, despite having earned this time off. As I say goodnight to co-workers and wish them good weekends, I wonder if they see me the same way Derek does. It's not as though I'm shirking my duties; I don't have many duties anymore. Which, come to think of it, would probably piss me off if I were in their shoes. But it's not my fault. This is what Cynthia wanted when I announced I was resigning. Through her nervous giggles, she asked me to stay long enough to organize one final job fair, and I agreed, figuring it was the least I could do.

I didn't anticipate this awkward transitional period where that's the bulk of my responsibilities, and it doesn't quite fill a forty-hour work week. I've offered to cut back to part-time, but Cynthia muttered something about HR and benefits and said it would be less complicated if I remained on the way I've always been. The whole point of waiting until after this job fair was to make everything as easy and seamless as possible, so it seemed silly to argue. Maybe if I were doing a more thorough job of training Derek, I'd be busier, but he doesn't want or need my guidance.

Now, as I slink from the office, I'm relieved to see he's not around to witness my early departure.

I breathe easier when my feet hit the parking lot. Fall has officially arrived, in all of its crisp-skied splendor, which means the whole city has come alive. Even people like me, relatively apathetic to the outdoor experience, are shaking off their summer lethargy, emerging from their air conditioned caves, and blinking into the breeze.

Adding to the excitement is home opener Red Friday, when everyone sports their crimson clothes to show support for the team ahead of their first Arrowhead game of the regular season. We have a tough opponent Sunday in the Patriots, who are already the favorites to win the Super Bowl, a championship title we're vigorously defending this year. People are pumped.

I'm rendezvousing with Jet downtown later for the season opener pep rally. First, though, I have a cuddle date at the hospital with my new niece. Jet visited this morning and dropped off Mikey before he had to report for practice and meetings. Both of us are going to be dead on our feet by the time we meet up later. Last night was a bad night to miss out on sleep. Gracie sure knows how to make her entrance felt. (Cyndi might agree.)

As it is, I feel like I'm walking through molasses just to get to my "flashy" car in the enormous parking lot reserved for the office park that contains The Career Center.

Since when is a Mini Cooper "flashy," anyway? Cute, sure. But "flashy"? Hardly. Cyndi needed a car, and she wouldn't let Jet buy her a new one, so I gave her the Honda I'd had since college. I figured I'd use one of the other cars Jet already owned, but he insisted I choose something brand new. The Mini was the first model that sprang to mind. And I like it.

But it's still just a car. Owning this one hasn't turned me into a motorhead overnight. Chrome and glass and plastic don't turn me on. This thing gets me from Point A to Point B. The end.

Jet hates my car. After we bought it, he read something about Minis being about as safe to drive as a PowerWheels Barbie Jeep, so he keeps hassling me about trading it in for something sturdier (a.k.a., "more expensive and grown-up). Each evening when I return from work, I'm surprised to open the garage to an empty stall. Any day now, he's going to lose patience with me and take matters into his own hands. The only thing stopping him is that he knows I'll never drive it, and even Jet Knox doesn't toss money into the wind.

"Dashing home for some early Friday fun?"

I flinch like a bad actress playing an abuse victim in a made-for-TV movie. My finger slips off the "unlock" button on my key fob and hits the red one, instead, setting off the panic alarm. While I fumble to silence it, Derek smirks, sucking on that ridiculous vaping contraption of his. I forgot he's not allowed to use it indoors anymore.

As soon as the car stops squealing at me, I snap, "City ordinance harshing your mellow?"

"No. Ironically, the one thing I missed about real cigarettes was the fresh air. When the weather is nice."

"And the extra fifteen-minute breaks away from your desk."

"Rich, coming from someone who's bugging out two hours early."

"One and a half hours. And I'm using vacation time that I've *earned*."

He snorts and inhales more fruity-smelling vapor.

I yank open my door. "I don't have to explain myself to you."

Finishing his latest smoke ring, he replies laconically, "Nobody said you did. You obviously feel the need to, because you care what people think. That must be a tough character trait to have when everyone on the Internet has an opinion about everything, especially celebrities' wives." He sucks in, then exhales a plume of white smoke. "By the way, I didn't think the dress you wore to that hospital wing opening was 'frumpy.' It was a step up from what you wear to the office every day, that's for sure. You keep doing you, girl." He detaches the drained pod of nicotine syrup from the device and places it in one pocket. The pipe goes in his other one.

I silently hope he gets mouth lesions, then say to his dig, "I didn't realize you were so into fashion. Or trashy Internet gossip sites."

"It wasn't a gossip site. It was the *Star*."

"I didn't realize they were fashion critics now, too."

"Everyone's a critic." He pushes off his car, a fairly new but admittedly un-"flashy" domestic model. "You should know that by now."

I narrow my eyes at him as he trots his pert butt back into the building, noticing for the first time that he's quite the natty dresser, and if he wasn't such an asshole, I might ask him for some tips for tonight's pep rally appearance. As it is, though, I'd rather show up in a white trash bag.

On second thought, make that a black trash bag. We're past Labor Day, and I could use something more slimming.

FOUR

SHAMELESS

My funny friend has tried every conversation starter from movies to amusing stories about his academic co-workers, but I can't muster any decent responses to anything. I'm too busy trying to formulate a zinger back in that parking lot with Derek. Two hours later.

Around Colin and me, people bustle through the hospital lobby. The automatic revolving door sucks them in and spits them out, each face a tableau of emotion, some worried, some sad, many happy, depending on the reason for their visit. As they traverse the gleaming floor, some of them nod to the statue of the Virgin Mary in the center of the room. Others pause by the water feature and contemplate—or pray—while sucking in the oxygen provided by the indoor plants. A few stand or pace, occasionally glancing at their phones or watches. Still others head straight to the information desk to consult with the volunteers as to where they can find certain departments or patients.

Everyone here seems to be on a mission. I bet none of them care what a cocky co-worker thinks about them. I bet none of them would stand in the presence of a stone saint and a treasured friend, wishing they'd said this or that... or nothing at all.

Why can't I ever simply keep quiet? Sometimes silence is the best retort. It says, "You're not worth the breath or thought or words it would require to reply," even if it typically means, "I have no witty retort." It's so much better to make someone guess than to confirm you have no comeback by stuttering something lame.

Nearby, a man's tense expression relaxes as a woman with a kid on each hip shoots through the revolving door at a jog. She greets him with a guilty smile and a "Sorry we're late," before handing off one of the children to him, and they all walk together to the elevators. I watch them for a while, a sweet family here to visit someone—presumably. Maybe a sick grandparent or a friend or family member with a newborn. There were so many babies in the nursery! So many families celebrating brand new lives and welcoming warm, cuddly bundles into the world. Just like Colin and Cyndi.

Colin and Cyndi. That's still so odd, like I've fallen through a wormhole into an alternate reality. Yesterday, literally, my British buddy was single, widowed, and childless—to me. Today, he has a partner and two kids, like some stranger I've been observing in a hospital lobby. Only he's not a stranger. He's Colin. Lord Merrydo. Change that to Lord Honeydo now, I suppose.

What the hell is happening? And why is it all happening so fast?

"Oi! Lady Maura!"

I blink and focus on my friend's furrowed brow. "What? Sorry. I was— I was..."

"In the Twilight Zone? Yes. You've been there all afternoon. What's up?"

"Nothing." I look around the sparkling lobby while I try to remember what we were talking about, but I can't. I'm officially the worst friend ever.

Misinterpreting my distracted behavior, Colin asks quietly, "You're not terribly cross are you? About Cyndi and me?"

"No! I think it's great. Really. I'm mad at myself for not figuring it out sooner."

"We were extremely careful."

"Obviously."

"Not even Mikey knew. Couldn't risk him grassing us up."

"Doing what?"

"Tattling."

"Ah. Yes. Children can be real blabbermouths."

More than once, Mikey has innocently repeated to Gloria a juicy nugget he's overheard me saying about her in his presence. And in case anyone isn't sure where he's heard something, he religiously credits his sources.

"Anyway," I say too brightly, peering through the occasional gaps in the slowly spinning door at the waning sunlight beckoning beyond, "this weather is gorgeous, isn't it? I adore fa—"

"Jet's quite angry, isn't he?"

"Jet? Angry?" I stall, adjusting my infinity scarf. "I don't think so. Not that he's told me. Did he *seem* angry earlier today, when he was here?"

"He was quiet. Basically spoke to us through Mikey. Didn't stay long, either. Held the baby and made his excuses."

I gulp. "Well, he did have practice today. Big game day after tomorrow."

"Yes, I understand, but—"

"And neither of us got much sleep. He was probably tired."

"I s'pose."

Now I smile reassuringly. "He'll be okay. Eventually."

"So he *is* cross."

Too exhausted to continue lying, I shrug. "Maybe. 'Hurt' might be a better description."

"He's not going to beat me up, is he? He already would have done, right?"

I laugh.

"There. The first laugh I've gotten from you all afternoon. Which is how I know something's not right with you, either."

"But you've always known that," I try to joke, digging my keys from my purse.

"If you don't tell me what it is, I'll have to assume it's to do with me."

"It's not you. I promise."

"Then tell me. Would you like me to begin guessing?" He folds his arms over his chest.

"No!"

Cupping his hand over his ear, he leans toward me. "What was that? A 'yes'? All right. Here goes…"

I grab his shoulder and, giggling, shake him. "Colin, no!"

"Gloria's announced she's moving to Kansas City. Better yet, she's moving in with you and Jet!"

"Not funny."

His face darkens. "No, it's not. For either of us. Let's hope that never happens. I know!" His eyes twinkle, and he grins mischievously. "You're up the duff!"

"What does that even mean?"

"Preggers!" He flaps his hands and jogs in place while I look around, hoping none of the other visitors entering and exiting the hospital witness his display.

"Get ahold of yourself. I'm not ducked up, or whatever the heck you called it."

Bracing himself against the Blessed Mother, he wheezes at my deliberate botch job of his idiom. My mostly feigned annoyance cracks while I observe him inadvertently rest his palm against the statue's crotch. He soon realizes his inappropriate stance and flinches away, reddening from the roots of his hair all the way down his neck. "Oh, dear. Blimey. Pardon me, Matron." He nods at a disapproving volunteer across the way and wiggles his fingers. "Pardon."

I look down at my feet, bite my lip, and wait out his theatrics.

After a few seconds, he wipes the sweat from his upper lip. "Seriously, though, you and Jet have been such wonderful mates. If there's anything I can do—anything—to make up for keeping you in the dark about Cyndi and me..." He wrings his hands and lowers his voice conspiratorially. "You don't know how many times I wanted to tell you. We both did! But we knew it would cause such a fuss if Gloria found out and more of a problem if she were the *last* to find out, so—"

I cover his hands with mine and squeeze. "Colin. Sweetie. You never have to explain yourself with me, especially when it comes to *her*. I get it. I will always get it. You're talking to someone who basically ran away from home to avoid the wedding of my nightmares because I was so terrified of that woman."

He chuckles. "She is terribly scary. Cyndi and I have been summoned to California as soon as the baby is old enough to travel."

"Ohmygosh."

"That bad?"

"It's a nice house," I hedge.

"Oh, dear. That bad."

"I couldn't tell you the last time I talked to her. I'm such a coward that I've feigned illness, bad cell reception, work emergencies, and kitchen accidents to avoid her calls. Hell, I'm getting to the point where I'd stage my own kidnapping or fake my own death, because all she ever wants to talk about is how soon I'll be shooting out kids, now that I'm about to be unemployed."

With a wince, he looks down at his feet. "And here I am, adding to the chorus, with all of my talk of being up the duff —or what did you call it? 'Ducked up'? Yes, I'll have to remember that one. Classic, that."

"Happy to amuse."

"Sorry."

I pat his knuckles. "Don't worry about it." A quick check of the time on my phone confirms I'm behind schedule. I still have to run home to change, so there's almost no way I'm going to make it to the pep rally on time. "I gotta get movin'. You sure you don't want me to take Mikey? He'd love the parade."

He shakes his head. "I promised him some one-on-one time with Geezer this evening."

I laugh at the toddler's nickname for Colin. "All right. But you'll still be dropping him by later, to spend the night, right?"

"Of course. Thank you, again, for all of your help with this. I realize it hasn't been the most convenient timing."

"Stop thanking me, and stop apologizing."

"Right-o, Lady Maura." He salutes me and backs toward the elevators. "Don't forget, any time you'd like free birth control, I now have *two* delightful kippers I can rent out to you for an evening or weekend."

I giggle and edge toward the scary, whooshing door. "Oh, you're too kind, Lord Merrydo. Too, too kind."

The parade was as crazy as expected, but this introvert had more fun than she planned. The fans are so proud of their team and so ready to kick butt for the second season in a row that their fervor is palpable. Despite knowing how nearly impossible it is to win one Super Bowl, much less two in a row, I truly believe we can do it after that pep rally. We have the best team and the best fans in the NFL. The two wins away to start the season have only boosted our confidence that much more.

Still flushed and giddy, I gush about it all to Jet later as I remove my red, white, and yellow scarf and black leather jacket. In my red tee and black jeans, I follow Jet into the closet, where I hang up my outerwear, then hop on one foot at a time to remove my black booties. He grins at my excitement.

"And War Paint! He's used to noise, and he's well trained, but he's not used to being so close to the crowd. He did so well!"

Jet laughs as he pulls up his baggy athletic shorts and ties the drawstring. "Okay, I gotta stop you there. You're complimenting the horse now? What's next? The mascot?"

"He's a great horse. And we have an awesome mascot."

"I agree. But you've never been all that jazzed about either of them. How many ciders did you have?"

"I'm just happy tonight. Giving credit where credit is due."

Shirtless, he moves closer to me and pulls me against his chest. "What about me? Did you like my pep talk?"

I smile and trail a finger between his pecs. "I already told you I did. You were magnificent."

"Oooh... 'Magnificent.'" He backs me up. We clear the closet doorway and keep going. A few steps later, the backs of my legs hit the bed, and I let him push me down onto the mattress. Hovering over me, his weight braced on his hands on either side of my shoulders, he says, mouth close enough to mine that I can feel the heat from his lips, "You were magnificent."

I laugh. "All I did was stand there! And somehow managed not to fall off the float."

"You clapped and cheered."

"Oh, big whoop."

"It was hot."

I bite my lower lip to keep from laughing again. Then something serious pulses against my leg as he lowers his weight gently onto me. I close my eyes and suppress a moan when he covers my mouth with his. I don't want to make any noises that will distract him or remind him he's two days away from an important game. I don't want him to stop.

He peels off my t-shirt, unclasps my bra, and kisses each breast. I lift my hips and grind against him. He quickly unbuttons and unzips my jeans and yanks them and my panties in one go to a spot barely below my knees. Then he slides down my body until he's kneeling next to the bed. For the next several minutes, nothing exists for me except that talented tongue of his.

I'm still quivering inside when he rejoins me on the mattress, collapsing on his back next to me. With great effort, I roll to my side, untie his shorts with one swift motion, and slide my hand beneath the waistband.

He sucks in a breath and covers my hand with his, on the outside of his shorts. "Maura..."

"Let me," I whisper.

He says through clenched teeth, "I can't."

"Yes, you can. You want it."

"Yes."

"You deserve it."

Suddenly possessed, he sits up and bounces to his knees, simultaneously pulling down his shorts and underwear. With one thrust, he's exactly where he should be.

Afterward, sated, he buries his face in my neck. I bring one arm down and rake my fingers through his hair as he shudders on top of me, moaning my name over and over. His eyelashes tickle my throat when his eyes flutter open, then closed again, and he grunts the one word that most colorfully describes what we've done.

"I'll say," I pant back, kicking free of my jeans and panties.

He coughs out a dismayed chuckle. "That wasn't supposed to happen."

"I beg to differ." I trail my hand down his back and stroke his butt.

He withdraws, rolling slowly onto his back and pulling up his shorts. "That was... amazing."

"I agree."

"But so bad."

"That's why it was so good. And you have all day tomorrow to recover, so it wasn't all that naughty."

"Yeah, but..."

I flip on top of him and press my finger against his lips. "Shhhh... We needed that."

"Like a hole in the head. If this is what it's going to be like this season..."

"Then what?" I say, when he doesn't finish.

His enormous exhale ends on a tortured laugh. "I'm in trouble."

Good. It's time we both caused some trouble. Before I can say something to that effect, however, our first spot of it arrives.

"Hewwo?" we hear from below, accompanied by the thundering of clumsy feet (and sometimes slapping hands) on the stairs. "Unca Jet? Aunt Mo-Mo?"

Colin's chagrined voice follows. "Mikey! Chap! You can't just barge in, mate! Come back here!"

I scramble for the closet while Jet calmly retrieves a t-shirt from the dresser and meets his nephew out in the hallway.

"Mikey, my man!" I hear as he closes the bedroom door softly behind him. "How's that little sister of yours? Are you taking good care of her, showing her all your best tricks?"

He continues to talk to Mikey down the hall until I can't hear them anymore, which reminds me of what Colin said earlier at the hospital—"*He was quiet. Basically spoke to us through Mikey.*"

Sounds like he's doing it again. I'll have to get to the bottom of that eventually, I suppose. Probably should have been, rather than letting him see to the bottom of *me.*

Then again, I have no regrets.

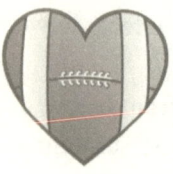

FIVE

INVASION

Finding a good time for serious conversation proves nearly impossible the next couple of weeks. While it was true that Jet behaved more coldly than usual toward Colin when our friend dropped off Mikey, I never got a chance to address it. We had our hands full with a super-charged toddler, high on his newfound big-brother powers and responsibilities. By the time Mikey collapsed, I was too exhausted for any discussion past, "Goodnight."

The next day, once Jet and I were finally alone again, it was time for him to pack up to go on the road. Plus, he was in game mode already, headphones on for total focus. Interrupting that is a major no-no.

Win or lose, after the game on Sunday would not have been appropriate timing, either. If they'd lost, he would have been in a funk and not at all receptive to probing questions about his feelings on anything, much less his sister's new relationship. Since they won (yay us!), he was in too good a mood for those aforementioned probing questions, and I sure as hell wasn't going to play the spoiler.

Since then, he's had to prep for a Sunday night game against Oakland, which is always intense and all-consuming. We've hardly seen each other—awake, that is—at all. He leaves the house before I wake each morning and returns home after I've already nodded off in bed, watching whatever's airing on my favorite classic movie channel. I usually wake up briefly when he turns off the TV, but by the time he finishes getting ready for bed, I'm asleep again.

That's okay, because I've been preoccupied with some last-minute details added to my Tolkien job fair. It's officially out of control. But that's another story.

The biggest news event of the week, though, has been yesterday's arrival of Mama Knox, plus Ned and pretty much everyone else, sans kids, to visit the newest member of the clan, Gracie. Fort Knox has become The Knox Hotel (and restaurant, bar, fitness center, and cinema). Work has been a fabulous—and legit—excuse for escape. Jet and I extended the invitation for them to stay here, with the caveat that neither one of us would be around much. Fortunately—or unfortunately—everyone's made themselves quite at home, so our absence hasn't affected their stay.

The only worse time for them to descend on us would have been next week, on the day of the actual job fair—and my last day. Both Jet and I will also be prepping to travel then, as he and the team go on the road to play the Houston Texans, and I begin full-time NFL wifedom.

Being a more active participant in the Wives and Girlfriends Club is going to be a huge adjustment, one I'm approaching with dreadful excitement. It's a disconcerting feeling, so unfamiliar that I've not allowed myself to think too much about it yet, for fear it will overwhelm me. I have too much to think about and do between now and then to get caught up in any future worries.

Plenty of present worries vie for my attention. Like dinner tonight. Jet is late from practice, so I've had to go it alone—with Beau, of course. Mostly I've run interference between him and Gloria, keeping her out of the kitchen as much as possible to avoid a) her backseat cooking and b) her murder at the hands of our personal chef.

"But surf and turf is my specialty!" she says as I shoo her once again, this time pressing another stiff drink against her palm. "You have to get the scallops just right."

Like a recalcitrant child, she lets me lead her back to her chair in the living room. "It won't be as good as yours," I lie, "but let Beau take care of it. You relax. Jet will be home any minute."

Any minute. Jet *will* be home. I chant this to myself on my way back to the kitchen while I text him again to get an estimated time of arrival.

Instead of a dinging response, I get the true article, waltzing through the door as if he doesn't have a care in the world and is in no rush. After dropping his bag of sweaty clothes on top of the washer, he goes straight for the fridge and pulls out the recovery smoothie waiting for him. Lifting it to Beau in a toast, he says, "Thanks, man," and turns his attention to me.

My stormy expression amuses, rather than intimidates. "Yikes. What's wrong with you?" Before I can answer, he places a peck on my forehead and gulps down half the smoothie. "Agh! Brain freeze!" He grimaces, rubbing the back of his tongue against his soft palate.

During this entire one-man show, I merely stare, one foot

tapping. Finally, when I have his full attention, I ask, "Didn't you get my texts?"

He clears his throat and avoids my eyes by holding up his glass and gazing into the depths of his blended beverage. "I was driving. The car read them to me, but I couldn't respond. Sounds like it's been kind of hairy around here. Where is everyone?"

"Your mom will be back in here any second," Beau mutters behind me, almost eliciting a laugh from me. Almost.

Fortunately, Jet doesn't hear him, and I rush ahead with an answer before a fed-up Beau decides to rectify that. "Colin, Cyndi, and the kids aren't here yet. Your siblings are all in their rooms, doing... whatever."

"Let's call it, 'getting ready for dinner,'" Jet suggests with a wrinkled nose before taking his next, more moderate drink.

"Agreed. And as for your parents, your dad's reading outside on the patio, and your mom's..."

...driving Beau and me crazy.

...getting drunk, I hope.

...practicing her best jabs to use on Cyndi and me.

He raises his eyebrows expectantly over the rim of his glass.

"...relaxing with a pre-dinner drink in the living room. You should go hang out with her."

He smiles. "Driving you nuts, huh?"

My shoulders slump. "You have no idea."

"No idea," Beau seconds.

This time, Jet does hear him and leans over to look around me. "Sorry, dude. I tried to get here as fast as I could."

So Beau gets an apology, but I get a peck on the forehead and knowing smiles?

Without turning away from the stove, the chef lifts his tongs in a conciliatory wave. "You're a busy guy."

Jet finishes off his smoothie with a satisfied, "Ahhh!" He rinses the glass and places it in the sink. "Off I go, then, if you two have everything covered in here."

"Go!" we both say together. I underscore the word with a gentle push against his shoulder toward the door.

"I'm going, I'm going! Sheesh…"

Left alone, Beau and I finish our preparations in record time, and I'm standing back to admire the beautifully set table when I hear Jet answer the door to Cyndi and her brood. Gidget, David, Keith, and their spouses emerge soon after, everyone fawning over the baby.

As I fill the wineglasses, I hear Gloria and Ned arrive in the foyer, and Gloria immediately says, "Oh, my! She's the spitting image of Justin, isn't she?"

Beau places the last dish on the table—a heaping pan of foil-wrapped baked potatoes—and mouths to me, *"Have fun,"* before disappearing for the night.

"Coward!" I hiss at his cackling escape.

———

Learning from past meals, I've devised the optimal seating arrangement for tonight. Gloria and Ned occupy the ends of the long table. Then, going clockwise from Ned, sit Cyndi, Colin, and Mikey, myself, Jet, and Gracie sleeping peacefully— for now— in her carrier between Jet and Gloria. We face Gidget and Rick, David and Tammy, and Lucy and Keith across the table. It's perfect.

Or so I thought.

I haven't taken my first sip of wine before Gloria, color

high from my generous pre-dinner pours, lines me up in her crosshairs and shoots. "What an exciting time for you, Maura. We have so much to discuss."

"W-we do?" I respond, nearly dropping the platter of steaks I'm passing to Jet. His cat-like reflexes and big hands save us from a disastrous fumble.

"Oh, yes." Gloria takes her time looking through the steaks as Jet holds the platter for her, his arm stretched in front of Gracie's "place." The matriarch leaves me to wonder and worry while she mutters something about each fillet, deeming every one either under- or overcooked. She finally settles on one, despite declaring it too fatty. "I've been meaning to ask you if you're all set for the next phase of your life, considering your 'career' ends next week." As intended, I'm sure, the quotes around the word, "career," are obvious and designed to elicit a response from me.

I deny her the satisfaction and ignore them altogether. "Well..." I select the first lobster tail on top of the plate and pass it to Jet. "I have a few ideas."

Lies, all lies!

"I figured you'd already made a decision and laid the groundwork. Unless, of course, you and Jet are ready to start your family."

I glance at the squirming sperm donor in the conversation, who pretends like tonight's lobster tail is the most important choice of his life. When it's obvious he's not going to chime in, I smile tightly. "I'm still concentrating on work. There's been a lot going on."

"Such as...?"

"I have the job fair to oversee."

She tuts down at the crustaceans. "Oh, dear. I think I'll

pass. There's something wrong about eating seafood so far away from the ocean. It can't possibly be fresh."

"Mom!" Gidget admonishes.

"More for me, then," David, the Minnesotan, says, rubbing his hands in anticipation.

Glad to change the subject, I reassure everyone the lobster, shrimp, crab, and scallops were flown in this morning specifically for this meal, but Gloria waves off my explanation. "Back to this job fair that has you too busy to think about your future—or properly host us this week. Haven't you already done several of these? Surely you have the hang of it by now. You'd think they'd practically organize themselves at this point."

Oh, buh-rother.

"They're much bigger events now than they were when I first took over. And this time, I went all out with the theme."

"Which is?"

I lift my chin and will myself not to blush when I reply, "Hobbits."

She blinks rapidly at me. "Hobbies?"

"Hobbits," Cyndi enunciates. "As in, short barefoot creatures of the Shire."

Directing her glare down the table at her youngest daughter, as if she'd forgotten she was there, Gloria says dully, "Oh. I see. And what do Hobbits have to do with jobs?"

Jet pipes up in a terrible Irish accent, "Hobbits love jobbits."

I giggle nervously, and Jet laughs at himself when the rest of the table cracks up, too.

His mom doesn't seem amused.

"It's actually a Tolkien theme, not just Hobbits," I say when the laughter dies down.

"I'm still not understanding the connection." Gloria passes yet another tray of seafood to Gidget without taking any.

I stifle a sigh. "There isn't one, strictly speaking. It's fun, that's all. You know, 'One job to rule them all,' and stuff."

She waves off my apparently annoying eccentricity and allows me to hope the topic is dead as she concentrates on loading up her baked potato with butter, sour cream, bacon crumbles, and cheese. But alas, after everyone has heaped their plates with food and has started to tuck in, she says while cutting her steak, "I read *The Hobbit* eons ago in school, but I've never understood the fascination with the movies."

"Oh. Well, I guess they're not for everyone," I say. "There was a lot of material to mine for a theme, though, so I went with it."

"Half of your job seekers aren't going to get the references."

"You think?" I tell myself not to let her get into my head, but her declaration nevertheless triggers a flurry of self-doubt.

Jet grabs my hand under the table and squeezes it. "Mom, I'm pretty sure you're in the minority. Even people who don't know the films frontward and backward will recognize the theme and get the idea."

"Seems too niche to me."

David shrugs. "I love them, and so do the kids. We watch them all the time. Milo loves to pretend he's Smeagol."

"Mikey does, as well," Colin says. "Do your 'Smeagol,' mate."

"'My precious!'" Mikey says to the large shrimp in his hands before biting it away from its tail.

I grin down at him while the rest of the table's occupants laugh. "Good job. Scary."

Keith swallows a massive mouthful of steak and says, "The

movies are kind of nerdy, but the special effects are impressive."

"Classic works of literature, too," Colin says.

Gloria snorts, reminding me of the time Rae pointed out her "horsey" appearance.

Cyndi drains her first glass of wine and pours another. "Maura's shown me some plans, and it's going to be super-cool."

"Ooh, I want to see!" Gidget says. "Do you have anything on your phone?"

"I'll show you later," I promise.

Gloria piles a bite of potato on her fork, then stabs a chunk of meat. "Well, I stand corrected, then, I suppose. It still seems like a stretch, theme-wise." With that, she pops the food into her mouth and chews.

"That's why Maura's so good at what she does. She's clever," Jet declares proudly his arm around my shoulders. "Her fairs always get written up in the paper and online."

"Because I'm married to you."

"No, because they're cool. And visual. They make for great photo ops."

"Okay, you can stop now. You're embarrassing me. Ow!" I recoil from the fork Mikey pokes into my forearm while hissing, "Hobbitses is tasty!"

Colin confiscates the utensil and mumbles a mild correction at the boy, waiting for a promise from him to cease stabbing people before giving it back.

Jet bends over his plate, shoveling food into his mouth. Between bites and swallows, he says, "You have vision. And sometimes it's hard to see where you're going with something or how it's going to work—I was pretty stumped about the

Oscars thing, to be honest—but when I see your plans in action, they always blow me away."

Colin winks around Mikey at me. "I'd like to point out that I played a part in making that Oscars theme work."

Cyndi mock-glares at him. "You might not want to remind everyone *why* you played such a pivotal role in that particular effort. Or Mikey's first haircut."

He grins sheepishly. "Right. Never mind. Carry on."

Lucy plunks her elbows on the table and leans forward. "Maura, your job sounds like so much fun! Remind us again why you're quittin'?"

I grasp for all of the reasons, which are definitely there and legitimate, but I can't quite verbalize them.

Jet clears his throat. "It's hard during the season. There never seem to be enough coinciding days off for us to be together on the few days I do get, and I'm always pestering her at work about stuff at home."

"Stop doing that, then," Gidget says. "You're a big boy; you don't need someone to hold your hand all day."

"It's not that. But there are things that have to be decided or done that I can't do, because I'm out of town, or my phone's in my locker, or whatever. Plus, it's not like she needs to work because we need the money."

The women—save Gloria—erupt at that statement.

He waves a hand at us. "You know what I'm saying!"

His mom shushes everyone. "He has a point, you know."

"It's not about the money!" Cyndi says.

"Yeah," Lucy says. "Seems like you're excellent, Maura, at what you do, and that you like it."

"I don't like it *that* much," I say. "I would like to explore other things. I simply haven't figured out what yet. I have to find something that combines my interests with something philanthropic. When I do, I'll be golden."

"You'll figure it out," Colin says, like he has a million times before. "You simply need some time to think. With no pressure."

"Yeah. Exactly." Since now is definitely not the time or the place to voice my doubts about that, I pivot. "Anyway, enough about me. There are much more interesting people at this table tonight." A mischievous twinkle in my eye, I look pointedly at Cyndi and Colin.

Okay, so that wasn't very nice, but whatever. A girl can only take so much heat. I've been such the center of attention up till now that it's felt more like a roast than a dinner to celebrate new family members. To atone, I quickly redirect again. "Look at that Gracie. Is she something else, or what?"

While everyone else repeats their earlier compliments, I smile down the table at Cyndi. She mouths, *"Thank you,"* and finishes her second glass of wine.

I hope she's bottle-feeding that kid tonight.

SIX

HEADACHE

I've underestimated how tense things are between Cyndi and Gloria.

While I make more coffee (because that's what we all need —caffeine jitters and insomnia), Cyndi corners me in the kitchen under the guise of heating a bottle for Gracie. Someone should inform her that breast milk doesn't need to be shaken that vigorously. It's about to become whipped cream.

"She's driving me insane," she says, needing no further specifications.

I take the bottle from her and set it on the counter next to us. Gently, I pull her into a hug. "Listen. I know she's being a bitch lately about everything, but she's *our* bitch. So, we have to love her."

"You don't know the half of it."

"Okay. Maybe I don't. I know enough, though."

"And Jet's still mad at me for not telling him about Colin and me."

"He's not mad!"

"Don't lie for him. I can tell by how nice he's being that he's pissed off. It's his 'talking-to-the-media-after-a-loss' voice. Ugh. I never thought he'd use it on me." She pushes away from me and grasps my hands. "I'm sorry. We're sorry. We just— We didn't want to make a big deal about it. There was so much else going on: your wedding, your *canceled* wedding, being so sick those first few months of my pregnancy, my divorce..."

"Like I've said to you guys a million times, I get it."

"I wish Jet did. Colin's a nervous wreck."

"There's no need for that. Jet will get over it."

She squeaks. "Oh, gosh. He *is* mad."

"He's still getting used to the whole idea, that's all. And with the season kicking off, he's had a lot on his mind. You know he can't multi-task."

She giggles at the truth. "I realize you guys are dealing with your own stuff, and it's not all about me. But..." She gestures toward the living room. "...if a certain someone asks one more time when Colin and I are getting married..."

I emit what I hope sounds like a sympathetic hum and try not to feel too guilty for being glad the marriage pressure is keeping the baby pressure off me—for now.

What it all boils down to is that Gloria thinks it "looks bad" that Cyndi is already involved with someone else. Appearances are always my mother-in-law's main concern. Last night, while looking ahead to tonight's dinner, Gloria said with a shiver, "I'm not sure how I'm going to keep quiet about them shacking up together. It's unseemly!"

Later, I asked Jet privately why his mom had no objections to us living together before we were married. If I've learned nothing else this week, it's that she definitely would have made those objections known if she'd had them, yet she never said Word One about it. He turned off the overhead light and set its remote on his bedside table, then burrowed under the covers on his side. "I dunno. You shouldn't try to figure out why my mom thinks and feels the way she does about anything. There's usually no logic."

But in this case, there is logic. And it sucks. For whatever reason, Cyndi seems to be Gloria's whipping girl. In contrast, until recently, Jet could do no wrong. Now that he's married to me, though, that's changed.

I return my attention to the coffee while Cyndi resumes her bottle-shaking. "Welcome to my world," I mutter about her threatened sanity, courtesy of Gloria. "It'll all settle down eventually, though. I promise."

"You sound like Jet."

"'Talking-to-the-media' Jet?"

She laughs. "No! Real Jet. Who's nice. I miss him."

Pouring the coffee into mugs, I say quietly, "He's right out there. He wants things to go back to normal too, you know."

"I'm afraid this *is* the new normal."

"Not where he's concerned. You know how he is. He has to pout it out. Then he shakes it off. Like an Etch-a-Sketch."

The bottle nearly slips from her hands as she wheezes at my description of her brother's selective memory. While we titter over the mugs, she rests her head against my upper arm. "Oh, Maura. I love you."

Warm and tingly with sisterhood, I squeeze her to my side. "I love you, too. We'll get through this. All of it."

"Yeah, well... You might have to hold me back if Mom doesn't stop with her digs out there."

"Let's make sure she's always holding the baby. That'll protect her from your wrath."

"Good luck prying Gracie away from Jet."

"Good point. Let's go. Feed that baby, make your excuses, and run home."

———

Things only worsen after Cyndi leaves and Gloria's truly free to speak her mind. She still hasn't forgiven her youngest child for "abandoning" her first husband, an airman stationed in Germany. She also objects to the swiftness with which Cyndi has jumped into another relationship following her divorce and dismisses Colin as Cyndi's rebound fling, which Gloria finds unbecoming of a single mother.

Cyndi's ex, Justin, has been elevated to fresh sainthood, too. Not only is he a patriot, serving in the military, but he was always so polite and fit in so well with the rest of the family. Either Cyndi hasn't told her mother everything she's told us (admittedly likely), or Gloria's conveniently forgetting a few things. I never personally met the guy, but based on some things my sister-in-law has told me about her former marriage, I can honestly say I don't ever *want* to meet him. He sounds like a sexist bully. But that's probably a-okay with Gloria, come to think of it.

Since I don't have firsthand experience with him, and it's not my place to contradict the narrative Gloria may have been given by Cyndi, I grind my teeth and take frequent bathroom breaks.

Finally, after the third soliloquy about St. Justin, Gidget says, "Ma. Give it a rest. It's over. Cyndi's obviously moved on, and Colin is nice. She seems happy. Isn't that all that matters?"

Examining her fingernails, Gloria says, "I suppose... But a foreigner? Really?"

I snap from my bored doze next to Jet on the couch. He tenses. Laughing tightly, he asks, "What does that have to do with anything?"

Gloria shrugs. "I dunno. It just does."

Digging my elbow into Jet's side, I wait for him to jump to our friend's defense, preferably in a more diplomatic way than I will if forced to speak. But he merely scoffs at her xenophobia and tries to change the subject.

Before he can get out two words about something else, though, I say, "Hang on a minute."

Jet grabs my hand and mutters, "It's not worth it, Babe."

I shake off his hand. "Yeah. Actually, it is. I'm not going to sit by and listen to anyone badmouth Colin."

Gloria bristles. "I'm not badmouthing him. I'm merely stating a fact. He's not American."

Keith lifts his head from the floor, where he's stretched out like a bear-skin rug. "He told me he was a U.S. citizen."

I nod. "He *is* a naturalized U.S. citizen. Has been for years."

"That's not the same, though, is it?" Gloria asks, faux regret dripping from ever word.

Fuming, I turn to Jet. "Wow. You never told me you were Native American."

"Maura…"

"No. I want to hear this. I want to hear how much *more* American all of us are in this room than Colin is." Nobody says a word during their extensive study of the ceiling. "That's what I thought."

Tammy recovers first, her Midwestern manners taking over. "If you want to get all technical about it, there wouldn't be a United States, as we know it, if it weren't for 'his' people."

David clears his throat. "Good point, Hon."

Ned, the historian, grabs hold of that and treats us to a short lesson about colonial America.

As soon as he winds down, I say, "My point is, if you have a problem with Colin, keep it to yourself when you're around me. I love that guy, and I'll take down anyone who speaks against him. Or doesn't defend him when someone else speaks against him." I say this last part while making uncomfortable eye contact with my husband. He looks away first.

"Now, if you'll excuse me, I need to use the bathroom."

On my way up the stairs, I hear Gloria say something about Beau's cooking not agreeing with me. Her nervous chuckle fizzles into the awkward silence I've left behind.

Once in the bedroom, I close the door and crawl into the bed, putting myself in time-out. Under the covers on my back, I stare at the sparkling chandelier above and wonder what the hell is happening. Did the Knoxes travel here—thousands of miles, in some cases—to show their support for Cyndi, or to vet Colin and stage an intervention? In fairness to the siblings, they're being pulled along, as usual, by the undertow that is Gloria. At some point, though, don't you need to grow up and stand up to someone like her? They each try, in their own jokey ways, but subtlety is never going to work with her. She's about as self-aware as an avocado.

And Jet. What the hell is his deal? I kick off the blankets, wishing for the umpteenth time that aesthetics had ruled a bit less in this room, enough that the designers would have consented to put in a nice, ugly ceiling fan. I reach over and flick on the small personal fan Jet sometimes uses for white noise. Pointing it directly at me, I re-settle against the pillows and close my eyes, relishing the cool breeze against my arms.

My thoughts return to my husband and his stunned silence

in the face of his mother's audacity. He's always been Cyndi's champion. It's almost cruel for him to withdraw now, simply because she hurt his feelings. That is, it would be cruel if it were intentional. He likely has no clue he's doing it, though. He's always the last one to realize he's pouting, and I usually have to be the one to undertake the odious task of pointing it out to him. Unfortunately, I never found the opportunity to do so before this visit, and now I'm kicking myself.

Fifteen minutes later, I open my eyes and inhale deeply, preparing to return downstairs to make nice-nice. Before I can force myself to move, however, a text arrives from Rae.

How're things in Knox Landing?

I laugh at her typical snark and tap back:

About as dramatic as an 80s soap opera

Is Jet wearing his shoulder pads around the house again?

Gloria's here

Ohhhh nuff said. Never mind, then. I was going to see if you wanted to meet up for a drink, but since you're hosting company...

Where and when? I'm there

Wow. If you're sure.

I'm sure

Close to you?

Don't care. Will travel

After a slight pause, she names a place I've never heard of that's not far from the stadium down the road. I program the address into my phone for navigational purposes later and agree to meet her within a half hour. I simply need to devise a legitimate-sounding reason to leave the house for an hour or two. Or twenty-four.

With that promising reprieve in my future, I rejoin the rest of the group.

"Are you all right, Maura?" Gloria asks as soon as I step down into the living room.

"I'm fine," I say shortly.

"You seem..." She widens her eyes innocently. Something that's supposed to approximate concern enters them, but I see it for what it really is—hope—when she finishes, "irritable. And you've disappeared to the bathroom several times now for long stretches. Are you feeling all right?"

Jet waits expectantly for my answer, suddenly looking worried.

Hardly believing she could be so obtuse but not wanting to resurrect an uncomfortable topic for the sake of reminding her what led to my most recent departure, I merely repeat, "I'm fine," but more forcefully.

"You and Jet wouldn't happen to have any news to share with us, would you?"

"No!" he and I say at the same time.

His siblings and their spouses laugh, half of them believing us, half of them supposing we protest too much.

Waving off everyone's speculations, I say, "If you must know, I'm on my period."

"Oh, gross," Keith grumbles.

Gloria wrinkles her nose. "Really, Maura. You don't have to be graphic about it. A simple, 'I'm fine,' would suffice."

Jet barks a disbelieving laugh. "She said it twice!"

Rather than react defensively, I look for an angle to work this to my advantage. "Sorry," I say magnanimously. "I have cramps and a headache. Is that better?"

"Did you take something?" Jet asks.

And there it is. The out I need. Bless that man.

"No. I'm, uh, out of the stuff I usually take. I'm going to pop out to get some."

He hops from the couch and pats his pocket to make sure he has his wallet. "I can go."

"No!"

He blinks at my vehemence.

I chuckle at myself. "I mean, it's okay. The fresh air will do me good. I'll drink some water and see if that helps before I go."

Yet another escape, this time into the kitchen.

Jet follows me. I pretend not to care that he stares at me while I fill a glass of water from the fridge door and power it down in a few gulps. I refill and repeat, ensuring I'll need the bathroom again soon.

"You don't have to lie."

I whirl on him.

He laughs at my wide eyes. "What Mom said about Colin was awful. And I'm sorry I didn't stick up for him faster. I didn't want it to turn into an ugly... thing."

Transitioning from "guilty" to "sheepish," I look down into my glass. "You got me. I do have a headache, though. Hormones, you know."

He takes my glass and sets it in the sink, then cradles my face in his hands, stroking my forehead with his thumbs. "I'm sorry."

"Not your fault."

I step back from him and edge toward the mud room. "I'll be back soon. Gonna run to the store, take a short drive to clear my head and let the medicine kick in, and I'll be good as new."

I grab my purse from its hook in the mud room and dig out my keys. After a detour to the powder room to tuck into my purse the medication I normally take and is supposed to be gone, I re-emerge, only to find Jet still standing where I left him, at the threshold to the kitchen.

I smile reassuringly. "I'll be fine. Don't have too much fun without me."

He listlessly receives my peck on his lips and watches me go. I try not to think about how long he'll stand there, staring after me.

———

Smelling like a bar isn't the best way to come home from "running to the pharmacy." Unfortunately, I didn't factor that into my stupid—and completely unnecessary, in hindsight—decision to lie about my escape destination. Leave it to Rae to find the one watering hole around here that still stinks like it's 1990. There's been no smoking inside Kansas City restaurants or bars for ages, but something tells me that entire lot would still reek of cigarettes and cigars if the place were razed and its rubble doused with a Febreze fire hose.

Now, back home and dying to de-stink, I try not to allow Jet's hurt expression, complete with tilted head and slack mouth, affect me. I could continue the deception and say Rae called me while I was out, so I swung by for a quick drink on my way home, but who does that when they have a booming headache, like I supposedly do (or did)? Not this girl. And he knows it. It's time to come clean, literally and figuratively.

I step into the shower under his scrutiny and mutter, "I'm sorry. I had to get out of here."

"That's all you had to say. I would have understood."

"*You* would have. But everyone else would have read too much into it."

"That you don't like them and will make up any excuse to get away from them?"

I blush under the hot stream of water and wave the smoky steam from my face. Perhaps it's time for a distraction.

"Why don't you come in here with me and let me make it up to you?"

He snorts. "Being lied to doesn't exactly put me in the mood. And no offense, but you smell nasty. Where the heck did you go, anyway? To a casino?"

Lathering my hair with twice as much shampoo as usual, I scrub with my head tilted back to keep the suds from running down my face and into my eyes and mouth. "You know that crap-hole past the mobile home park on Raytown Road?"

He looks up toward his forehead, as if trying to picture what I'm describing. "No."

"Neither did I. But it's there."

"Why there?"

"I dunno. Rae picked it. Because it was close to here, I guess." After a pause, during which I focus on the water beating on my scalp and the clean, spearmint-scented shampoo eradicating my stench, I take a deep breath and, with eyes still closed, say, "I had to get out of here, not because I don't like your family, but because I was reaching the point that I wouldn't have been able to filter myself."

"I said I was sorry about the Colin thing."

"I accept your apology. And if that was the only thing upsetting me, I'd consider myself lucky."

"What else is wrong?"

Do I really want to go there? Hasn't it been a long enough evening? My brain tells me I definitely don't, and that it definitely has been, and I should definitely shut up. Now that I smell better, I should try to lure Jet in here again. Brain says, "Shut up while you're ahead." Something much, much lower says, "I could eat."

My mouth overrides everything else, though, and blurts, "I don't like how your mom practically licks her lips and rubs her hands every time my womb and I enter a room. She's obsessed. Every conversation leads back to that. I long for the days when she was planning our wedding." When Jet pulls a face, I say, "Uh, yeah. I know. I'm *that* over it. It'd be different if you were her only child, and whatever shot out of my vagina would be her only grandchild, but she's up to her ears in offspring and babies. Therefore, I can only conclude that she's purposely torturing me. Which sucks."

"I'm sorry, Baby."

"Don't 'Baby' me. Ugh! In fact, I wish we could ban that damn word from this house." I slap the controls to turn off the water and grab my folded-up towel from the nearby bench.

As I shake it open, Jet appears in the doorway to the shower. "She just wants us to be happy and have a family, and—"

"We are happy! We do have a family! You, me, Torzi..."

He laughs but quickly stops when he realizes I'm serious, and I direct a glare at him to underscore it. "Ahem. Right. Well. Yeah, but..."

I vigorously dry myself, then wrap the towel around my torso and tuck in the end near my armpit to hold it up. My tousled wet hair probably makes me look as crazy as I feel. "And we're surrounded by extended family, too. All the time. Nieces and nephews on all sides. Isn't that enough?"

"Yes, but—"

"There was a point earlier, when you were holding Gracie, and your mom was getting all starry-eyed, as usual..."

"I can't help that I'm adorable."

"...and she pointed out for the eleventy billionth time what a natural you are, and that you always had more babysitting jobs than Cyndi did when you were teenagers, and I wanted to scream at her transparency."

"I did get more jobs than Cyndi did, though. Kids like me."

"You got more jobs because the moms didn't have to worry about their husbands checking out your ass. Meanwhile, I'm sure the moms—and a few of their husbands, come to think of it—quite enjoyed it."

He pulls a face. "Ew. They were old. I was a kid!"

Since the conversation is veering into territory I'd rather it not go, I steer it back. "I wish you'd tell your mom to shut up about all the baby stuff."

"I'm not going to say that to her!"

"Maybe not in so many words."

"What's the point, anyway? She doesn't listen."

"It would still be nice if you'd stick up for me. Like I've stuck up for you with your sister and Colin and Rae and countless other people, even your mom." I edge closer to him, but not because I want to. "Move."

He steps aside so I can wipe my feet on the bath mat. "Rae? What has Rae said to make you stick up for me?"

All body parts agree that I don't want to go *there* tonight. I cross to the vanity and drag a comb through my unruly locks. "Not anything specifically from today," I fib. "In general, over the course of our relationship."

"Oh. And Colin and Cyndi?"

"You need to stop pouting, stop acting weird, and let them know you're happy for them. I can't keep covering for you."

Into the mirror he asks, "Covering for me? Who asked you to do that?"

"You don't have to ask. And I'm not doing it for your bene-fit, either. I'm doing it to spare their feelings."

"From what? I'm not being a dick. I'm busy. I'm under a

shit-ton of pressure, and I haven't had time to throw them a love parade. Excuse the hell out of me."

"That's what I've told them. Multiple times. Nicer, of course. But fewer jokes from you about Colin taking advantage of your vulnerable sister would be nice."

"He knows I'm kidding! That's how guys talk!"

"Not that guy."

"Oh, for crying out— I can't win lately!"

I slap the comb onto the granite counter and spin to face him. "It would be a huge win, in my book, if you'd stand up to your mom the next time she starts prattling on about us having babies."

"I honestly don't hear her anymore when she goes on about it. I've tuned it out."

"That must be nice. Some of us can't escape to Lala Land at will."

"Instead, you lie about your period and headaches and escape to seedy bars."

"Hey, that lie about my period was funny, and it shut your mom up about... other stuff."

"What you did was still crappy."

"It was one time! And how is it any crappier than what you do, escaping into your head? Because I have to physically leave the premises, it makes it worse?"

"The lying makes it worse."

Ah, the moral high road. How I hate thee. With no defense against it, I merely stare at his chest and try to think less murderous thoughts.

Before I arrive even close to a place where I can speak civilly, he says gently, "Let's get through the rest of the visit, huh? I'll teach you some meditation tricks, so you can tune her out, too."

I roll my eyes and leave the bathroom only to slip into our closet, which I close behind me.

While I'm riffling through my shelves of yoga pants and hoodies, Jet says through the wood, "Are you going to come downstairs? Mom and Dad wanted to play Yahtzee."

I grit my teeth and make him wait while I pull on my clothes and grapple for a reply that won't re-heat our simmering argument. Finally, I pull open the door and say, quite honestly now, unfortunately, "No. I have a headache."

———

Burning.

My nose figures out the danger first and urges the rest of my body into a sitting position while the rest of sleepy me protests the interruption in my blissful slumber.

Something's burning. Or burnt. Or something.

I blink into the dim room, relieved when I don't see smoke, but that smell... It's getting stronger. Charred something. "Jet?" I mumble, fumbling for the remote on my bedside table to raise the blinds or turn on the light. Anything so I can see what's happening.

"Aw, you woke up before I was ready."

"What?"

The mattress shifts next to me while I continue to push buttons on the device in my hand. The TV on the opposite wall clicks to life, blaring rock music. Giving up, I drop the remote and cover my ears with my hands. Jet places a tray in my lap, and the charred smell intensifies, but the music stops as he turns off the TV.

"What the hell is happening?" I moan, dropping my hands

and grabbing the tray's handles before its contents topple sideways onto the bed from my wobbly thighs.

Finally, the chandelier above us fades up to half-brightness so I can more clearly see Jet's face and the items in my lap and put everything into context. That's when he provides the now-unnecessary explanation, "I made you breakfast in bed. Sort of."

I examine the scorched bagel, pot of cream cheese, glass of orange juice, and mug of coffee before me. "Oh. I see."

"There was bacon, but I ruined it. The bagel's a little crispy too, but only on the edges."

If this is "a little crispy," I can only imagine what the bacon had to look like for him to deem it inedible. Still, my heart, now returning to a normal rate, softens. "Wow. You didn't have to do this."

"I wanted to."

"Well, thanks." I surreptitiously scrape at the black fringe of my bagel, then decide cream cheese covers all manner of sins and give up on my repair efforts. I like burnt marshmallows; why should an "everything" bagel be any different?

A couple of bites later, I realize they are different, but under Jet's proud, expectant watch, I power through. Mind over matter. "Delicious," I muffle with one hand in front of my mouth, so I don't spray him with seeds and onion bits.

"It's not anything close to what Beau would make, but his day off happened to fall on a morning when I needed to kiss butt, big-time. And anyway, I wanted it to come from me."

I wash down my latest bite with orange juice, chased by coffee, then run my tongue over my teeth to make sure no cream cheese, seeds, or onions have been left behind. "You don't have to kiss butt."

"I am sorry, though."

"I am, too. I shouldn't have lied to you. I guess I didn't want to put you in a position to lie to your family, so I kept you in the dark. It was stupid."

"I get it, though. And I promise, I'll be more present and try to keep my mom in check when she goes off on her tangents."

"Thank you."

I pucker my lips for a kiss, but he doesn't see, since he's directed his gaze to the bedspread, which he pinches and picks as he mutters, "You know how important honesty is to me."

Willing myself to resist defensiveness or extreme contrition, I set the tray on the bedside table and tap his knee... hard. He noticeably blanches and looks up at me.

"That's what I thought," I say with a pointed look that conveys I'm no longer speaking about his intolerance toward dishonesty.

His cheeks pale, then flush.

"When were you going to tell me, Mr. Honesty? Lies of omission are still lies, you know." I say it gently, teasing, careful not to start an argument. The last thing I want is for him to clam up.

He swallows loudly. "There's nothing to worry about."

"Try again. When were you going to tell me?"

"Soon." His evading shrug says otherwise, though. "I haven't known long."

"Bullshit. Rae told me she broke the news to you weeks ago, after the first game, when you could hardly walk."

Irritation flashes in his green eyes. "She's exaggerating, as usual. I could walk just fine!"

"After you sat in an ice bath and got cortisone injections."

"What happened to patient confidentiality?"

In spite of my irritation and worry, I laugh. "She's a trainer, not a doctor."

"Yeah, and Doc was too chickenshit to tell me about the surgery himself, so she did."

I cringe at the s-word.

"It can wait until after the season, though," Jet says.

"Is that wise?"

"Probably not. But that's what I'm going to shoot for."

"Both knees?"

His only answer is a nod.

"That's... That's a big deal, isn't it?"

Picking at a hangnail, he mumbles, "Not really. They're scopes, not replacements, or anything."

"Bilateral arthroscopy," I say, calling it the official name Rae used.

"That makes it sound more serious than it is."

"It's more serious than you want it to be, I think."

"Guys have it done all the time in the off-season. It's not a big deal. As long as I'm good about physical therapy, I'll be ready in time for next season, good as new."

"And this season?"

"I tough it out. Like all of us do all the time."

"Couldn't you do more damage, in the meantime? You have thirteen more games!"

His shrug confirms what I've already learned from Rae, but mothering isn't my style, so I grab his hand. "All right, then. They're your knees; it's your career."

"My career will be fine." Determination setting his features, he says quietly, fiercely, "I have to do this. I have no choice. My contract is up at the end of the year. Sitting out this season for a couple of sore knees would screw me over, big-time."

"And playing, possibly poorly, in pain is going to help your cause?"

He withdraws his hand from mine. "That won't happen. I'm going to play lights-out this season and prove I'm irreplaceable."

"Jet...."

"I've never let pain stop me before, and I'm not going to let it stop me now. Mind over matter."

If anyone can do it, it's him. I absolutely believe that. But just because he can doesn't mean he should.

SEVEN

HOBBITS

Today is *the* day. The *final* day. The *final* job fair.

It's all so anticlimactic (like the finale to *The Hobbit* trilogy, in my opinion). So far, however, the employer participants seem impressed and delighted with the theme. Let's hope the job seekers are equally enthralled. And, of course, the main goal is that today's events result in a decrease in the area's unemployment rate. To stave off panic, I'm operating under the assumption that my apathy is a result of my immersion in the details all these months.

We're thirty minutes away from go-time. I don't know what to do with myself, so I keep straightening and re-straightening the bowls of pretzel rings and plates of scones on the snack table and lamenting that the lemonade-and-orange-drink I mixed with clear soda and sherbet for my fake mead came out looking more like foamy transmission fluid. Should have used more lemonade. Next batch, that's what I'll—

"Hello, my Precious," someone whispers right next to my ear.

I whirl on a laughing Jet.

"Your face!" he says, dodging my slaps to his chest.

"You're a creep."

"Speaking of, who's that clown at the entrance? Shortest Gandalf I've ever seen."

"That's Derek. My, uh, my replacement."

"Would have made a better Hobbit."

"I thought so, too, but I only gave him two choices, and he had a problem with hairy feet and capri overalls."

"You're a meanie."

Derek wasn't thrilled with the gray robe and pointy hat, either, but I told him the pipe would help with his oral fixation and make him miss vaping less. He didn't think I was funny, especially when he found out I'd be attending the job fair as "Galadriel. In a business suit." He grumbled something about wishing I looked like Cate Blanchett, to which I mentally gave him the middle finger and called him an insufferable twerp.

Obviously, he and I have gotten along swimmingly in my final days here.

Jet snickers. "I guess that explains the attitude, then. He almost didn't let me in. Pulled out the old, 'You shall not pass!' line. Which I kind of respected, actually. Nice callback."

"Then you asked him, 'Do you know who I am?'"

He snorts. "No, I knelt down and said, 'Go get Maura, please,' and I guess it seemed like more work than it was worth, so he let me through."

"He and I are staying out of each other's way."

"What's the story there?"

I shrug. "Nothing." I haven't told Jet anything about the minor annoyance that is Derek, and I don't plan to do it now, minutes before the fair opens. "A personality clash. I don't think he likes to be told what to do."

"By a woman, no less."

"No. He doesn't have a problem with Cynthia. Just me."

Jet pulls his chin back. "That's weird."

"Like I said, it's a personality thing. And it's about to be a historical issue, so..." I smile up into his face and gesture to the tent around us. "What do you think?"

He takes in the painted path meandering from booth to booth, the multi-colored, round "wooden" doors on the backdrops behind each table, and the mingling Career Center part-timers dressed in costumes ranging from elves to Hobbits to dwarfs. Rubbing his chin, he grins. "It's... different."

"Different, as in bad, or..."

"Fun. You've outdone yourself. I'm a little disappointed, though."

My stomach knots. "Why? What did I forget?"

He grasps my upper arms and rubs them. "Why aren't you in character?" He wiggles his eyebrows. "You'd be a sexy elf princess."

Relieved, I laugh. Then, assuming a more serious air, I say, "I'm the director of this production. The director doesn't dress up."

"Sometimes they make cameos. Mel Brooks, Rob Reiner... Heck, Woody Allen casts himself as the star most of the time. Of course, you're too tall and sexy to be Bilbo or Frodo."

"I'm not that type of director. I'm more of a Nora Ephron or Nancy Meyers."

"No fun."

A human resources rep from the Highway Patrol booth waves me over.

I nod an acknowledgment and turn back to Jet. "Gotta go. I

am, technically, at work, you know. You showing up here is like me hanging out in the locker room or on the sideline before the coin toss."

He winces. "Sorry. That *would* be distracting. I just wanted to stop by before the team meeting and see the setup before everyone stomps through and messes it up." He glances behind me at the snack table. "Can I have one of those cookie things?"

"Are you looking for a job?"

"Maybe. We'll have to see how this season goes, right?"

"You're four-and-oh so far against some first-class opponents. You've got this." I tiptoe and kiss his cheek.

"No cookie?"

"They're scones. And no. They're for job seekers."

"Aww!"

Backing away from him, I laugh. "Scram, Knox."

"Fine. Save one for me, then. When's this thing over? Five o'clock?"

"Yep."

"I'll be here to help with cleanup. Good luck, Beautiful."

I blow him a kiss and pivot to cross the tent to the beckoning employer. With a last glance over my shoulder, I catch Jet snatching one of the scones and scrambling for the exit.

Typical. Sees what he wants and doesn't take "no" for an answer.

Damn, I love that guy.

———

Robes flapping, Derek rushes up to me about thirty minutes before the close of the fair. My feet and legs are killing me, like they always do at the end of one of these days, and my face aches from holding such an unnatural smile all day, so the last thing I want is for him to tell me anything that accompanies that peeved expression.

"What is it?" I ask with more exasperation than I intended.

"The snack table is empty."

"Seriously, Derek? That's what you came over here to tell me?"

"And a reporter from *The Star* is here to talk to you."

My mouth dries. "Oh."

"I already gave her the basics about the event."

"You what?"

He shrugs. "I guess she assumed that since I was so authentically dressed, I was in charge."

"And you didn't think to disabuse her of that assumption."

"I answered some simple questions. Sheesh. It's not like I took credit for this insanity." He waves his arm, nearly whacking a job seeker in the face in the process. "Sorry," he mumbles to the person, who bows dramatically at him. As soon as we're relatively alone again, he grouses, "Shit. It's like Comic Con in here. I signed an autograph earlier!"

I stifle my giggles and try to return to our original conversation. "Where is this reporter, then?" Rising on screaming toes, I scan the tent for someone with press credentials around his or her neck and eventually spot her in the corner, by the empty snack table. "Oh. I see. Thanks, Derek."

He mutters something at my back as I leave him to presumably return to the task I assigned him: mingling in the crowd and asking wise questions to efficiently direct people to the booths that would best suit their interests and qualifications.

At the table, I stick out my hand toward the reporter—a Kendra Johnson, based on the badge hanging from her lanyard

—and say, "Sorry to disappoint, but demand greatly outpaced supply in the food department today."

She smiles and shakes my hand. "That's okay. I don't need it. I have a nasty habit of eating when I'm bored."

I wait for her to backtrack on her mildly insulting statement, but she merely skims her notes and says, "I spoke to some little dude dressed up like a wizard... Derek Duggan?"

"Yes. Derek's one of the job counselors at The Career Center."

"Right. But my assignment editor specifically told me to talk to you. Maura Knox."

"That makes sense. I organize the job fairs. Twice a year: spring and fall. Well, 'organized,' past tense, I guess, now that this one is in the books, for the most part."

She blinks up at me. "Okay. Anyway. Derek covered the general 'who,' 'what,' 'where,' and 'when,' plus the official 'why,' so that leaves you to answer the 'how' and explain in detail your reasons for..." She looks around us as if she's found herself in a parallel dimension. "...*this*."

I chuckle nervously. "I guess I don't understand your question."

"How did you come up with this idea, and why did it seem like a good fit for a community job fair?"

I'm tempted to give her Jet's "Hobbits love jobbits" line and wish her a lovely evening, but I've made it this far. It would be a shame to be fired on my last day. So, I regurgitate the answer I gave Gloria at dinner last week, something about fun, and I end with, "I admit it's somewhat gimmicky, but the goal is to connect as many job seekers with as many employers as possible, and it's been my experience in the past few years of doing this that themes bring in bigger crowds."

Again, she consults her notes. "It somewhat begs the question, though, considering who you are: is this partly a matter of a celebrity's bored wife filling her days?"

I resist throat-punching her and simply answer, "No."

"But being married to Jet Knox helps in the publicity department, right?"

Chewing the inside of my cheek, I compose myself enough to say, "Since you're the first and only reporter I've talked to today, and we're about to wrap this one up, I'd hardly call it a successful publicity stunt."

"You're disappointed in the turnout?"

"Not at all. As you can see, there are still several applicants here, and this is the slowest it's been all day. It's been a successful fair."

"Derek Duggan said, and I quote, 'Themes are great, but as Maura's replacement, I'll be dialing back the flash and bringing the focus back to substance and results.'"

I grit my teeth. That little shit...

"And a second ago, you said you '"organized," past tense' these events. Is your departure voluntary, or have you been replaced?"

I almost laugh at the lifestyle peon reporter trying to get a juicier scoop on the dull story she's been assigned, but I don't want to be flippant to the point of defensive, so I reply, "Today is my last day with The Career Center, by choice. I'm moving on to new things."

"Such as?"

I look around the tent as if realizing for the first time how today's event relates to me. "I don't know. I, uh, guess I should have brought my resume with me."

She laughs politely but quickly sobers. "Seriously. What *is* next for one half of Kansas City's favorite power couple?"

"I don't know. You'd have to ask that person."

"Starting a family? Travel? Any pet projects or charities you'd like us to know about? Now's your chance to get in a free plug for it."

"Nothing specific in mind yet. But I'm excited about whatever it ends up being."

She looks down at her notebook and screws her mouth to the side, skepticism rolling off her in waves.

"What I'm most excited about today, though, is completing another successful job fair. I'm sure Derek will be happy to pass along the stats from today—total attendance, positions filled by attendees, and all that stuff—in a few weeks, if you'd like to do a follow-up report."

"Hmph." Her eyes dull as she shakes my hand one more time and announces she's going to walk around and snap a few pictures. Then she brightens considerably at something over my shoulder, and I can tell before I turn to look that Jet has arrived.

"Well, well, well," she says with a smirk. "Looks like I have one more interview. Want to get the complete story, after all."

"Oh, Jet's not—"

"Hey! How'd it go?" He arrives next to me and plants a kiss on my lips, then grins at Kendra and winks. "I see the paps are here."

She tucks a strand of hair behind her ear. "Can I get a picture of the two of you?"

Before I can refuse, she snaps one with her phone and gives it a cursory glance to make sure it took but doesn't offer to let me approve it. "Care to say a few words about your wife —or the job fair—to add some color to the story?"

Jet practically bounces on his feet. "You bet! I could brag on her all day. What do you want to know? Let's see... Did I have any idea she was this into Tolkien's Middle Earth? No.

No clue. Like, we've watched the movies—she's a huge movie buff and has a ginormous collection of films and screenplays—but I had no idea she had this... this hidden nerd inside of her."

Kendra giggles.

I smile tightly at both of them. "What can I say?"

"There's nothing to apologize for. I mean, look at this place! It's awesome. Didn't she do a great job, Kendra?"

The reporter nods. "For sure. I was gushing to her about how amazing everything is. So creative!"

He gazes down at me and says to me, about me, "She's incredible."

"That's me," I mutter, blushing.

"See how humble she is, too?"

"Very. In fact, I can't for the life of me drag out of her what her next big triumph is going to be."

Jet squeezes me to his side. "The sky's the limit, right? She can do anything. It's her choice."

"Lucky girl."

"I don't know about that. She's married to me, after all. Has to put up with all of my crap."

"I'm sure it's a pleasure."

"You don't know many professional athletes, do you?"

"You're the first one I've ever met."

He blows on his fingernails and pretends to buff them on his t-shirt sleeve. "Try not to be too impressed."

I shrug his arm off my shoulders and say brightly to the two of them, "Well, this has been so much fun! But I have to make my final rounds. Kendra, good luck on your story and, please, thank your editor for sending you to cover this event. We do appreciate the exposure."

With barely a glance at me, she mutters, "Yeah, sure.

Whatever," then focuses her adoring attention on the real star. "So, Jet, who's the biggest diva in the locker room? Off the record, of course."

As I walk away, I hear him laugh and say, "You're crazy if you think I'm going to answer that question, even off the record. To be honest, it's probably me."

"No! I don't believe it!"

No, *I* don't believe *this*.

EIGHT

ADRIFT

As usual, this morning Jet's acre of the bed is empty when I blink awake from the doze I fell into after my final trip to the bathroom, around five o'clock. As if to punish me for my lying about her to Gloria last weekend, Mother Nature's been wringing my uterus in her gnarled hands all night, to the point that the poor organ feels like it's trying to secede from the rest of my body. Popping out some kids suddenly seems like an attractive option, if it will garner several months of relief from this. But Rae swears exercise relieves menstrual cramps, so I'll try that slightly less extreme solution first, I suppose. If nothing else, the activity will induce cramping in other muscles, and I won't notice the ones in my lady parts as much.

Plus, new life, new me. Maybe I can make exercise part of my daily routine for the first time ever. Yes! I'll wear one of those activity trackers, count calories, and get in shape so I can be the arm candy my NFL star husband deserves. Barf.

That reminds me...

I grab my phone and navigate to Kendra's write-up of the

job fair in *The Star*. To my dismay, there's only a tiny blurb about the actual event, which she describes as "quirky" and "quaint." The first mention of my name glows blue, signifying a hyperlink to something else, so I click on it. It takes me to a much longer story on the society pages.

My irritation quickly spreads to horror as the photo of Jet and me pops onto my screen. He, of course, looks amazing, smiling proudly down at me. My side of the picture is every bit as unflattering as I figured it would be—and then some—considering how unprepared I was when she snapped it. Eyes half closed and mouth agape, as if I'm in the middle of saying something, I submit to Jet's one-armed squeeze, all of my chubbiest bits on display as my clothes bunch and pull in the embrace.

The caption on the photo doesn't disappoint, either: "'The sky's the limit,' Chiefs QB Knox says of his wife's life after retirement from The Career Center. 'She can do anything. It's her choice.'" The article proceeds to portray me as an aimless moron, content to hole myself up in my mansion and spend my husband's money while watching movies and stuffing my face with popcorn. (Okay, I added the "popcorn" part myself.) My favorite excerpt, which I will memorize, of course, and play on a loop in my head on my worst days, says this:

Maura Knox is brimming with humility but seems empty of ideas. It's ironic that someone whose career was devoted to finding people's vocations would retire into idleness or retreat to her extensive private movie collection. However, the woman who's often been described as 'colorless' next to her personality-full husband, Jet Knox, is in no rush to reveal what's next in the power couple's personal life. We'd say, "Watch this space," but it might be like watching paint dry.

Screw her.

I toss my phone into the dent left by Jet's head on his

pillow and spring from the bed so quickly it brings on vertigo. When my vision clears, I roughly don leggings, a sports bra I didn't realize I owned, and a long, baggy t-shirt and stuff my hair into a messy bun. On my way downstairs, I detour through the kitchen to fill a water bottle and try not to let the enticing aromas of coffee and Beau's breakfast waylay me.

Downstairs, clinking metal shortens my purposeful strides as I approach the gym, and I pause outside the door for a split second to adjust my grumpy attitude. Who cares what a celebrity-chaser wannabe says? If it makes her feel better to dog me, fine. Who has Jet Knox? *This* girl. Sure, he comes with some not-so-great baggage (Gloria, public scrutiny, Gloria, frequent absences, Gloria, memory loss, Gloria, Type A personality, and—don't forget—Gloria), but he's mine for as long as we both live. And I'd take him in sickness and in health, for richer or for poorer, in good times and in bad, with or without—ah, yes—his mother. So Kendra Johnson can shove her judgments and speculations up her perky little ass.

My smile is mostly genuine by the time I enter the gym.

Jet's surprise at my entrance *is* genuine and would be comical if I weren't so cranky. He sits up on the bench press machine and wipes his sweaty forehead on the towel he keeps tucked into his waistband. "'Morning, Beautiful! What're you — Oh, I see what happened. Keep goin'. The theater's farther down the hall."

I nestle my water bottle into the holder on the elliptical's console and step onto the paddle-like pedals. "You're funny." I pump my legs to get the machine going. "I won't be bothering you, will I?"

He snorts. "No. I'm finished. Will it bother *you* if I sit here and watch you?"

I glance over my shoulder at him and take in his twinkly

eyes. "Yes. Creepy." With a flirty air kiss, I return my attention to my task before I lose my balance and fall. Momentum starts to do some of the work to keep the equipment moving, so I relax into a rhythm.

A few seconds later, Jet sidles up to my elbow and says barely loud enough for me to hear over my quickening breath and the whirring flywheel, "You don't come around here often."

Concentrating on my pace—and stifling my laughter—I say nothing.

"Because there'd be no forgetting you."

"Shut up. I'm exercising."

"That's the thing—you look like someone who's much more at home in bed this time of day."

"And you smell like someone who should be in the shower."

He reaches behind me and pinches my butt, pushing me forward.

I grab the handrail at the last second. "Hey! You tryin' to kill me?"

He backs toward the door with his hands raised at shoulder level, palms out. "My bad. You're no good to me dead."

I narrow my eyes at his retreating form.

After barely clearing the threshold, he boomerangs, holding onto the frame. "I'll be in the shower, if you, uh"—he wiggles his eyebrows at me—"want me."

Laughing, I yell after him, "Not likely!"

My inaugural visit to the gym doesn't last long, though, and since he's still in the shower when I drag myself upstairs on rubbery legs, I take him up on his offer to partake in an activity that burns calories in a much more enjoyable way.

As we dry off, he hits the dimmer switch on my afterglow by asking, "What's on the agenda on your first day as a retiree?"

Initially, I intend to answer as curtly as possible and stifle my irritated response, but after the short, "I don't know," I add, "You're not going to ask me that every day, are you? That'll get really old, really fast."

He pauses with the towel against his head. "I was just making conversation. I don't care if you lay in bed all day and masturbate, if that's how you want to pass the time."

"Typical guy fantasy."

He laughs tightly. "No judgment here. I ask because I care about *you*, not because I care about what you do all day."

"I'll find ways to stay busy. And when I get bored, I'll find other things to do. Like have babies."

He laughs. "Something tells me you'll have to be super-duper bored to get to that point."

I shrug. "You never know."

He drops his towel on the floor for Helen to pick up later, but I grab it and hang it on the rack. What are we, animals? After wrapping my hair, I follow him into our closet, where we silently pick out our clothing and dress for the day, him in active wear for practice, me in lounge wear for binge-watching, uterine cramping, and brooding.

Finally, he says, "The pool guy's gonna be here later to try to figure out what's wrong with the pump. I replaced that thing last spring, so it better still be under warranty. You'll have to dig for the paperwork. I'm sure I filed it... somewhere."

"Okay. I'll deal with it."

"And do you mind calling someone to come out and fix the windshield on the 'Vette? Freaking semi pinged me with gravel on I-70 last week. Thought it was going to be a chip, but I hit a pothole on my way home last night, and the crack started to spread. I'll text you the number of the place I want to use."

"Yeah, yeah."

"Do you mind?"

"No."

"I don't want you to feel like my personal assistant."

"It's fine. That's what I'm here for. Apparently."

"Never mind. I'll call during a break."

"No! That's stupid. I'm here, and I don't have anything else going on. The least I can do is make a couple of phone call for you."

He pulls me, half-dressed, against him and looks down into my face. "Thank you. I'd like to get those two things taken care of before I leave for Houston Saturday."

"I understand. And you're welcome."

"Are you excited about traveling to the games this season?"

"More excited about California next weekend than Houston, but being in the same place with you will be a nice change."

Removing the towel from my head, he fingers my wild, damp hair. "Stop worrying so much about everything. Enjoy this time for what it is—relaxing."

I close my eyes. "I'll try. I never imagined it would be a challenge for me."

He presses his lips against my forehead then releases me. "That's what I love about you, though. You're full of surprises and still learning things about yourself." As he exits the closet, he drops my towel.

I sigh and pick it up.

NINE

WAGS

There's no better place than southern California in the fall. It's gorgeous. Green palm trees against spotless blue skies, warm breezes, beautiful people with bright white smiles and sun-kissed skin... It's like a sci-fi utopia. This isn't exclusive to autumn, though; it's like this year-round. If it weren't so close to Gloria, I could totally get behind moving here and becoming one of the pale, ugly minority. After Jet's retirement, that is. If he ever considers playing for the Chargers, it's Splitsville. That's a deal-breaker.

Kidding.

Sort of.

Another player's wife, Keela Jackson, says something similar to me about Denver as we watch the game below, and I laugh. "WAGs do get caught up in the rivalries, don't we?"

"It's our job," she replies in our own defense. "Remember Wendy Marshall?"

I shake my head regretfully, although I do remember her husband. He was an amazing wide receiver, and it was a shock when he was released a few off-seasons ago, when I was still just an anonymous fan.

"Before your time, I guess. Anyway, when Teandre was picked up by the Raiders, she refused to go with him."

"No. Come on. All kidding aside…"

"Seriously. They're still married, barely. He has a girlfriend and a new baby out in Oakland, but he's promised to stay married to Wendy until their kids are out of school. She lives down the street from me. Her kids go to school with mine."

"Wow."

"Works for them, I guess."

While I imagine agreeing to a similar arrangement with Jet, my face must convey the horror it spawns in me, because Keela giggles. "Oh, girl. You're funny. More WAGs than not live separately from their husbands. It's probably saved a bunch of marriages." When I relax my face and try to pretend I already knew that and that it's no biggie, she says, "Being a Florida girl, I wasn't all that thrilled about movin' to KC, but we were newlyweds without kids yet, and the thought of living separately was too depressing. Plus, I knew it could be worse, and I wanted to save any protests for the really crappy trades. Can you imagine having to relocate to Buffalo? Or Cleveland?" She shudders.

"I guess I'd consider that the 'worse' in 'for better or worse.'"

Nudging my shoulder, she laughs again. "Y'all are still young."

"That doesn't—"

"It matters. Trust me. Let's be clear: I'm not that much older than you are, age-wise, and I don't mean to sound like a cynical, old-fart know-it-all, but y'all's relationship is still young. When the kids come along, you won't want to be city-hoppin' every other year. And the time apart won't be that big of a deal anymore. You'll be too busy—and tired—to care."

"How old are your kids?" I ask, keeping a close eye on Jet as he scrambles out of the pocket and throws away the ball for what seems like the hundredth time this game. The offense isn't clicking today, and I can tell he's beyond frustrated. That's when he tends to take risks he shouldn't, running and sliding with the ball for the sake of getting yardage. Any yardage.

Keela clicks her tongue at another busted play, then answers, "Ten, twelve, and fourteen."

"Wow. You have your hands full."

"Why do you think I'm here?" She chuckles. "My mom lives with us and watches the kids so I can go to the conference away games."

"That's nice."

As the sides switch out, she turns to me. "I'm glad you're here, too. Our husbands are such good friends, but I've never had a chance to really talk to you. It'll be good to debunk some of the mystique around you." She wiggles her fingers in the direction of my head, as if mimicking sparkles—or possible dust motes.

Snorting at the idea there's any "mystique" about me, I swig my beer and tap my wedding ring against the glass bottle.

"You laugh, but people talk. Some of the other WAGs think you're— Well, never mind."

I stiffen. My lips come away from the bottle with a squeak. "Some of the other WAGs think I'm what?" I chuckle in an effort to act like negative gossip doesn't bother me.

It works, because she readily replies, "Snotty. Standoffish-like."

"Mmm." I nod, not trusting myself to say anything else.

"But Demarcus says you're nice. And we had a great time at your place last summer. Y'all know how to throw a party now! I've tried to tell the others you're just shy."

"I am. Sort of. Introverted. Stuff like this"—I gesture to the full suite behind us, bustling with WAGs and team muckety-mucks—"intimidates me. I'm still not used to it all. I can fake it in small groups, but big crowds like this…"

"You'll get there."

When I raise a skeptical eyebrow, she says, "Or not. Whatever. Who cares what they think?"

Problem is, I do. I want not to, but I do. Seems like I'm destined to be an oddball.

In high school, I was "that tall girl with the mean lesbian friend." In college, I didn't fit in with the other film studies majors, eccentric types who all fancied themselves the next Tarantino, Scorsese, or Jolie. I simply liked movies. In Jet's family, I'm the quiet observer who can't keep up with their boisterous conversations and relentless teasing and has to excuse herself regularly to recharge her introvert batteries. And now, with full-time WAGdom looming, I won't fit into that club, either. I don't have a favorite "cause." I don't have—or want—a herd of children. I don't view spending money as a competitive sport. I'm not a social butterfly.

I do love my husband and football, in that order. I guess that's a start. For the first time in my relationship with Jet, I'm going to be at nearly every game, home and away, so I need to be more sociable, no matter how uncomfortable it makes me. I get this, logically. I'd already vowed to start at the next home game, where I'll be in slightly more familiar territory. But I was relieved when Keela approached me today and started a conversation.

When I say nothing to her somewhat rhetorical question, she inhales a contented breath and says brightly, "Anyway, you had a career before, right? I'm convinced they were jealous that Jet didn't make you give up everything that was yours when y'all got married. Now that you're in the same boat as the rest of us, they don't have to feel so inferior."

Before I can unpack all of that and respond, she stands and claps at a huge stop by her husband. "Yeah, Demarcus! Now, let's force a turnover, Baby! Get somethin' started!"

TEN

REST

While I spent the majority of the next three months "debunking the mystique" around me in luxury suites all over the country, Jet and the team had their hands full eking out hard—and some not-so-hard—wins and suffering a few disappointing losses. By the end of the season, with an eleven and five record, everyone was fairly confident of another trip to the Super Bowl. Therefore, it was a shock—to the fans, anyway—when the Steelers sent us packing in the first round of the playoffs.

Jet was surprisingly Zen about it. "Pittsburgh had our number this season."

"And your knees defected."

"If our plays had worked, it wouldn't have mattered."

Still, I'll be holding a grudge against those traitorous joints for a while, no matter how illogical that is. They've given all they have—and then some—and have taken more abuse than any body parts should be asked to take. I should be angry with the jerks who low-tackle and rough the passer. And I am. I'm plenty honked off at them, too. But they were only doing what they were paid to do. And they're not here.

Jet wasn't himself out there on the field this season, either. He hardly ever ran with the ball, despite having many clear openings to do so. In those rare instances when he did make a break for it, he more often than not hobbled to the sideline soon afterward. His limping became so familiar to me that I almost forgot what his normal stride looked like. He spent every post-game day with huge, dripping ice packs shrink-wrapped to his knees. Most disturbingly, he almost seemed relieved when the season was over, a full month earlier than everyone had hoped.

Not that I blamed him or disagreed. However, it was disconcerting for him to be so chipper after such an early departure from the post-season.

I'm torn. Staggering through the season only to lose in the first round of the playoffs doesn't put Jet in the strongest position to negotiate his new contract in the off-season. Obviously, I don't care about the money, but big contracts are an unfortunate indicator of a player's worth to the team. If Jet doesn't pull in a bigger contract than the one he already has, it will send a message to the entire League that he's not an elite player. And he is. He deserves the recognition.

In the grand scheme of things, it's all bullshit, fueled by pride and big egos. But it's our life. Resisting it won't change it. We're in it for the long haul, and that means we have to continue to play along or get out.

Trust me, getting out is a major temptation. I long for the days when football was fun, when I was aware of—but not affected by—the political maneuvering and could enjoy the game without thinking about what every single one of the guys on the field had sacrificed to entertain me each week.

Health, marriages, time with family and friends—money can't get any of those things back. People might say, "They chose that life, and they live like kings." But many of them don't live like kings. And one could argue that some of the guys *didn't* have a choice. Football was all they knew, all they could do, all they were ever good at. They poured everything into it, seeing it as their only chance at a financially stable life.

They still don't warrant pity, and the ones who squander their talent and go off the rails when they let the celebrity go to their heads are idiots, but I've witnessed firsthand that playing pro football isn't always the magical dream fans might think it is. I've seen guys say goodbye to their families in airports, the kids clinging to them and crying. Sure, the players aren't going off to war—they're leaving to play a *game* —but their children don't know the difference. Absence is all the same to them.

The sea before me seems to be mirroring my thoughts, with its endless water as far as the eye can see, capped by roiling waves, churning and beating the white sand that has no other desire but to lie there peacefully.

The occasional coconut-scented breeze soothes me, though. The unnaturally pink, fizzy drink in my hand helps, too. After weeks of a roller-coaster season, followed by an exhausting but fun Pro Bowl week in Hawaii, I've earned these measly two days on the beach before we have to fly back home. All I'm thinking about right now is this pink drink and what I'm going to do later with that snoozing guy next to me. He better sleep up.

I startle from my naughty daydream when my husband, the napper, suddenly says, "This is so nice. Let's run away here. Open a trinket shop and change our identities."

Licking sloshed stickiness from my hand, I say, "I'm okay

with the first part, but we need to capitalize on your celebrity. And the souvenir market is saturated here."

He sits up more fully and flicks sand from his arms. "Okay, smarty. What's your idea, then?"

"A sports memorabilia hut. Owned by Super Bowl MVP and All-Pro quarterback, Number Fourteen, Jet Knox. Plaster your cheesy smile all over billboards and on the sides of buses..."

"Hey! My smile's not cheesy."

I laugh. "And make you autograph every single thing in the store, especially stuff that makes no sense. Like a Chiefs toaster."

"You mean one that burns the team logo into your bread?"

With my thumb and forefinger in a gun shape, I shoot him. "Bingo."

"We have one of those somewhere at home still in the box."

"And we don't use it every day?"

He chuckles. "We can if you want to."

"I can't believe you have to ask."

"The one I have isn't autographed, but that can be fixed." He smiles un-cheesily over at me and grabs my hand while pushing his sunglasses to the top of his head. His green eyes crinkle as his smile fades. "You okay over there? That sports gear hut idea seemed pretty detailed. Like you've been thinking about it for a while, or something."

Thankful for my own sunglasses, which are staying put for now, I grin back at him. "Fine! Excellent. This was a great idea."

He taps his temple. "I still have a few good non-football-related plays up here. Anyway, I knew we'd both need this, and there's no huge rush to get back, right? It's amazing here now that most of the other Pro-Bowlers and their families have left for home. I wish we could stay longer."

We both know we can't, though. He has an appearance to make in the Super Bowl pre-game show next Sunday in Atlanta. Then... I don't want to think past that. Suffice it to say this off-season isn't going to be one long extended honeymoon, like last year's.

Aware of the other sunbathers, swimmers, and castle-building children around us, I nevertheless set down my drink and transfer myself to Jet's chair, stretching out next to him.

He wraps his arm behind my neck and around my shoulder and shifts to make more room for me. "Hello there."

I nestle against his sun-warmed chest. "Hey." As I look down our bodies, my eyes linger on his hairy knees for a beat before I force them lower, to our playful feet and beyond, at the water.

If I'm tempted to dwell on more serious things, Jet has an antidote to that. He tickles the arch of my foot with his big toe and says, "You're giving me a boner, Mrs. Knox."

Laughing, I reach over, grab the arrowhead-emblazoned beach towel from my chair, and drop it in his lap. "There are kids around here!"

"They're not our kids."

"Bigger reason for you to behave, pervert."

"You started it, rubbing against me and playing footsie with me."

"I just wanted to cuddle."

"That's how it always starts. My body is conditioned to respond one way to cuddling. Like when I hear the whistle on the field. Show time."

"You get a boner every time you hear the ref's whistle? That's weird."

"No! I have *an* immediate physical response. Not *that* physical response."

"Oh. Glad you clarified. I was starting to worry. You could hurt yourself on the field if you fell on a stiffie."

He laughs so hard he nearly tumbles off the other side of the chair.

I tighten my hug. "Careful!"

When he recovers, he says, "A six-inch spill isn't gonna kill me, as long as I land dick-up."

"You gotta protect that thing. I'm pretty fond of it. Not to mention, I have big plans for it later."

"Later? How about now?" Releasing me, he swings both legs over the side of his lounger and starts collecting our stuff. "Let's go."

"You might want to wrap that towel around your waist for the trip back to the hotel, Champ."

He looks down and blushes through his tan. "Oh, geez." Quickly turning his back on most of the beach, he fashions a terry cloth sarong and shakes his legs, one at a time, before setting off without me.

"Hey! Wait up!"

ELEVEN

DISTRACTION

Reading to sick kids at the hospital. Ladling soup at the home-less shelter. Flea bathing dogs at the no-kill shelter. This is what I do now. And it's rewarding, important work, but it's so not me. Unpacking an introvert and tossing her into the extro-verted world on a regular basis could be viewed as a form of torture.

It's worked, though, to get me out there more, socializing with the WAGs and the rest of the community. I wouldn't say I've made any great friends, although I do enjoy spending time with people like Keela Jackson, but that wasn't the objective, anyway. The point was to make a difference in the community. It's a bonus that I'm continuing to prove I'm not a stuck-up snob.

I've pulled Rae in on some of my activism, too. "I don't do sick kids or animal shelters," she said when I proposed my three beta projects. "The kids make me cry, and I'd bring home every single dog from that shelter."

"Aw, you old softy. You try to act all tough, but you're just a big—"

"Shut it. I'll go with you to the homeless shelter."

She's cried after leaving there a few times, too. We both have. Privilege guilt sucks. I come home to my big, clean house with my stocked fridge and pantry, my unlimited access to clean water, soap, and comfortable clothes, and my warm, cozy bed and feel repulsed by it all. How did I end up here, while they ended up there? It's not all about choices, as some would have us believe so that we can sleep at night. Much of it is luck—or lack thereof. And luck is a fickle bitch. It'll turn on you.

Jet hates "homeless shelter Wednesdays," as he calls them. He usually returns home from his own obligations to a half-empty closet. Or a weeping wife. Or, after the first time, both. Scared the daylights out of him. "Why are you crying in the bathtub, and where are all of our clothes?"

"We still have plenty. More than enough. More than we need or could ever use."

He groaned. "You worked at the homeless shelter today, didn't you?"

I covered my face with my wet hands and nodded.

Sitting on the edge of the tub, he patted my shoulder. "Babe, are you going to be okay? Maybe that's not the best fit for you."

"Why?" I dropped my hands and shrugged off his touch. "Because I shouldn't have to see how terrible other people's lives are?"

"No. Because you're going to feel like shit every time you do see it."

"I deserve it."

He sighed. "This is why I volunteer at the hospital. Less guilt. I can't control disease, and I'm not responsible for it. But Maura, we can't control poverty, either. We can try to help, but you're not going to solve much by giving away all of our stuff and crying in the bathtub. Maybe you should stick with the flea-bitten dogs and the sick kids."

The sick kids upset me, too, though. Jet and I leave the hospital on Tuesday afternoons and, more times than not, we drive immediately to Cyndi's house to snuggle Mikey and Gracie. Jet entertains the kids while I try to hide the fact that I'm one baby-shampoo-scented sniff away from blubbering all over them. Or I call my brother on the way home and schedule a play date with Meleah so I can smother her in kisses and whisper frantic prayers over her. Now that Deirdre's pregnant again, I fret a fair bit about the baby boy still incubating inside her, too.

I'm not much better with the dogs and cats. Like Rae, I want to rescue them all. My first day, before I left the house, Jet grasped my upper arms and looked me in the eye after kissing me goodbye. "I love animals, and I love Torzi. But some players have five, six dogs. And all of them sleep in bed with them. These guys have lost all control of their lives. Please, don't bring home a bunch of dogs—or cats. Match them to other people. Share the love."

A few weeks into this, I have it down. Mostly. I still cry about the sick kids and the homeless people, but I haven't brought home a single animal, and I'm toughening up. Or learning to get it out of my system before Jet gets home.

Most importantly, my experiences have provided an emotional education that no movie, not even the grittiest documentary, could have done on its own. I'm also discovering what I *don't* want to do with my influence on a permanent basis. Unfortunately, I still stress about never figuring it out. That's only going to get worse, too, now that the season is over, and I'm no longer constantly on the move.

My solution to that: overseeing extensive renovations on the main floor of our obscene house. Hey, if it's going to give me privilege guilt, it might as well be worth it.

We've hired the same company that overhauled our bedroom and transformed the basement "craft room" into my dream in-home cinema. Husband-wife dynamic duo Carl and Sarah, and their enormous, unnaturally polite crew have taken my inspiration pictures and run with them, blending mine and Jet's seemingly contradictory requests in a design that will make this dark, rambling place feel more like home for both of us.

When I dragged Jet into the empty front room that runs the entire length of the front of the house, between the foyer and dining room, and told him I was ready to give it a purpose, he'd laughed. "Like what? A skating rink? A bowling alley? The space is so long; that's why I've never done anything with it. That, and I couldn't think of anything else I needed."

"I'm envisioning two areas: a desk and some shelving and cabinets over there..." I nudged my thumb behind us at the corner near the first front window. "...and a sitting-slash-reading area right here, by the fireplace. Built-in bookcases. A library, I guess you could call it."

"Oh."

"You sound disappointed."

"It's kind of boring. And pretentious." In an accent supposedly English but sounding *not* English, he fluttered his eyelids and droned, "Let's retire to the lib'ry, shall we?"

Ignoring his criticism, I said, "It'll look nice. Peaceful and cozy. But also cheerful. I want to go with a pale gray on the walls, white trim, built-ins for pictures and accents and books. Replace those stuffy French doors with something funkier and more private, like sliding panels. Bamboo floors and cute rugs. Pops of yellow. Pillows and stuff."

He wrinkled his nose. "Yellow? Like penalty flags?"

"Pale yellow."

"Oh. Okay. Have you been watching HGTV?"

I clenched my jaw. Because the truth was, *"Yes. Obsessively."* But that was beside the point. And I didn't appreciate his condescending tone. "It's interesting that you have no ideas of your own, but when I tell you my vision, you wrinkle your nose. I guess if it's not your idea, forget it."

"I don't mean to sound like that."

"Well, you do. Not being in control kills you."

He grabbed my hand and brought my knuckles to his lips, saying against them, "I'm sorry. I'm sure the room'll look nice when you're done."

I seethed. "Don't patronize me, all right?"

"I'm not. I can tell you've thought a lot about it already. Maybe you can show me some pictures, and it'll make more sense to me."

"I can do that."

"Don't be mad."

"I'm not. At all."

"You seem mad."

Of course, I was. A smidge. But I'd rather die than admit I'd let a petty disagreement about a room renovation anger me. Talk about the ultimate first-world problem. Instead, I used his contrition to my advantage, proposing my ideas to make the living room "less leathery."

On this topic, though, Jet had much more specific demands. He was especially vocal when I started talking about knocking down walls, namely the one between the kitchen and living room.

"Whoa, whoa, whoa! I'm pretty sure that wall is load-bearing. Unless you want our bedroom and bathroom to fall into the kitchen and mud room, you better slow your roll."

"There are solutions for that. Supporting beams and columns and... stuff."

He shook his head. "I like the layout of the house the way it is now."

"It's so choppy!"

"Maybe, and I realize open floor plans are all the rage, but I don't want to smell fish the whole time I'm watching Sports Center on Taco Tuesdays. And I don't want to feel like we're putting on some lame reality show when you and I are hanging out in the living room, and Beau's fixing dinner. Or Helen's folding clothes in the mud room."

Considering I want to overhaul the kitchen next, I decided to capitulate on the floor plan issue and leave Fort Knox's layout alone. "Fine."

"And my leather chair stays."

"What are you, eighty?"

"No, but I like that chair. It has good memories." He wiggled his eyebrows at me.

I blushed and promised, "We'll design the whole room around it."

I've stayed true to my word, too. Like a nice wife—and to Sarah's obvious consternation and frustration—I've repeatedly rebuffed beguiling suggestions of lam beams and archways. All of the walls are staying up. In contrast, the designer was thrilled about keeping the chair.

"It'll be a great juxtaposition to the rest of the room, will make it seem less matchy-matchy. There's nothing worse than a living room that doesn't look lived-in," she gushed.

I pretended that's exactly what Jet had in mind.

Volunteer work and renovations. That's what my life has become. I'm officially *that* person. It fits about as well as a Victorian corset. All I need to add to the equation is shopping, fad dieting, liquid lunches, mani-pedis, massages, blowouts with "the girls," and a convoy of kids cared for by a nanny, and I'll be the ultimate cliché.

"What does your wife do?"

"Oh… stuff. She answers my texts really fast."

I've given myself until the house's completion to choose a true purpose. This life of leisure is *not* going to get its hooks into me.

———

Every year, the NFL parades its surviving Super Bowl MVPs in front of the current championship audience. It's a tradition I've always liked—until now, when it inconveniences me.

While Jet packs to leave for Atlanta, I say, close to a whine, "What's the deal with the cheesy pomp and circumstance? We have to disrupt our lives so you can grant some interviews, pose for some pictures, and walk onto the field for five minutes before a game you'd rather be playing in? Way to rub your nose in it. 'Hey, remember when you won the whole shebang? Well, that's not this year, but stand here, so we can stare at you.' Dumb."

He laughs. "I'll be back by early afternoon Monday."

"What am I supposed to do all weekend?"

As soon as the words are out, I want to drag them back. I'm not some bubblehead who depends on my husband to entertain me. Then again, I've been left to my own devices, often in strange cities and stadiums, nearly every weekend for the past four months, so I'm ready to have him back. Is that too much to ask?

"Hang out with Rae," he suggests. "I'm sure you two have some catching up to do."

"She and Ana Paula are in Vegas for their post-season vacation."

"What about your brother? Get some quality time in with sweet Meleah."

"And be around Greg and Deirdre while they're in the throes of another first trimester of pregnancy? No thanks."

"Your parents?"

"Hiking through the Mayan ruins. Would be a long commute for me."

"Colin, Cyndi, and the kids?"

I shrug noncommittally.

"I'd keep throwing out suggestions for you to poop on, but I have a plane to catch. Call you later?"

Grudgingly, I tilt my cheek toward him, but he pulls my chin toward him with a finger and kisses me properly on the lips, then says, "It's my job, you know."

"Yep."

"And being named MVP was a dream come true."

"I know that, too."

"The least I can do is show up when and where they tell me to."

"You worked hard—and sacrificed brain cells and body parts—to win that title, though. Nobody *gave* it to you."

"Still… Every day in the NFL is a privilege."

I manage not to convey my disdain for that party line. I'm glad he feels that way and loves his life, but every time he says it, he sounds like a brainwashed cult member. Like Commissioner Tallmadge is feeding lines into an implanted receiver in his ear.

"Have a good time," I finally say while he zips his rolling suitcase and extends its handle for the trip down the hall.

"You know, you could have come with me."

After all of the travel of the past few months, the thought of sleeping in another hotel bed—even with Jet—makes me want to weep. And I have absolutely no desire to witness in person Drew McKnight and company win *another* Super Bowl.

"It's fine. Don't mind me. A quiet weekend with Torzi is exactly what I need."

"Atta girl. Remember, Mom and Dad will be here on Wednesday. Enjoy the peace while you can."

Like he has to remind me. Yet another visit, this one their usual post-season stay. I tried, to no avail, to persuade Jet to discourage them from coming, considering what a mess the "library" still is, but he said, "Nobody ever goes in that room, anyway. As long as the living room is finished, it'll be fine. I promised Mom she could see me before my procedure so she'd stop bugging me about having the surgery out in California."

His surgery. Ugh. Of course, he had to bring that up. I assume the doctors and surgeons know what they're doing, and Jet's confident he'll have plenty of time to recover before the next season starts. Good enough. I'll be the bandage changer and ice fetcher and keep my mouth shut and my doubts to myself.

For public relations purposes, we're not supposed to talk about it, anyway, so it's best that I don't want to. Of course, we're allowed to discuss it privately, but it's easier to remember not to mention it publicly if I never mention it, full-stop. That's what I tell myself, anyway.

Call me a coward, but it sickens me to think about the procedure, much less listen to Jet describe what they're going to do next week when they slice open his knees. The words "scope," "scrape," and "trim" come up often in these conversations and more than adequately feed my imagination. I'll tune in when the surgeon tells me what I need to do to keep the dressing clean afterward, but I don't care to know the gory details of the operation itself.

I quickly change the subject by drawing his attention to the time and reminding him he has a plane to catch. He mutters an oath and hurries down the hall, tossing a hasty, "Love you!" behind him.

It takes me approximately three minutes in the now-silent house to decide to call Colin to see if he and Cyndi mind an extra person tagging along on whatever winter weekend activities they have planned. For someone who used to take such delight in her own company, I've become socially needy—disturbingly so—in the past few months. Hanging out with personality-rich women like Keela Jackson converted me in a hurry. Now, the thought of spending an entire weekend alone fills me with dread.

"Uh-yeah," Colin answers, then immediately says, too loudly, "Oh, blimey. The bowl's right there, mate! How'd you miss that? Sorry, Lady Maura. Can I ring you back in a mo? We've a situation here. Bye."

The phone chirps in my ear to let me know I've been well and truly dropped. Five minutes stretch into ten, then twenty, then forty.

In the meantime, I shower, dress, and formulate Plan B: some uncharacteristic retail therapy. My destinations and routes are almost fully mapped out in my head when the phone in my sweater pocket buzzes.

"Hey, dude. What happened?"

Colin sighs. "Crikey, it's a mess here. Literally. Both of the children are sick, and Cyndi's not feeling so great either, although I think she merely has sympathy nausea."

"Ew."

"Quite."

"Then never mind. I was going to see what you all had planned for the day and ask to tag along, but…"

"Actually, I'm going minivan shopping."

The thought of Colin behind the wheel of a mom-bus produces uncontrollable giggles.

"Laugh all you want, but they're remarkably fuel-efficient, roomy, and safe."

"You've already read the pamphlets."

"Of course. I'm not going in unprepared. It's stressful enough having to haggle over cost; keeping all of the features for the various models straight in my head would be a nightmare. Today's mission is to test drive them all."

"And Cyndi doesn't want to take part in that?"

He snorts. "I'm convinced part of her stomach upset is at the prospect of such a venture. So, I'm taking one for the team, as they say."

"I'll come with you," I impulsively offer, surprising myself as much as him.

"That would be fantastic."

"Pick you up in…" I calculate how long it will take to eat some breakfast and traverse the city. "…forty minutes?"

A harmony of cries and moans from Grace and Mikey ring through the earpiece. The higher part of the duet becomes louder, as I assume Colin picks up the baby and soothes her.

"Better make it an hour," he replies wearily.

———

In our third van, I remark how similar all vehicles are to people like Colin and me, who are not all that turned on by cars. They all have the same functions, albeit in somewhat different configurations of buttons and knobs and switches, so that each ride starts with a scavenger hunt of sorts to figure out where the essentials are. This one has a push-button start and a dashboard dial rather than the gearshift handle on the steering wheel we've seen in the previous two.

"Fancy," Colin says in his poshest Queen's English.

"It's like piloting a spaceship," I observe, as he jabs buttons and twists knobs to get the thing out of the parking space. A camera shows us a fish-eye view from the back bumper while we reverse.

"It's almost too fun," he says, maneuvering carefully through the tight car lot and waving to the salesperson who holds copies of our identification in case we abscond with the merchandise. "I'm worried the children will think it's a toy and accidentally put the thing in gear."

"Won't they need the key fob to turn it on, much less do anything crazy?"

He considers for a second. "Oh. Yes. Right. See? I told you it was a nightmare keeping all of this straight."

"I only know, because mine has a push-button start. Took me a long time to get used to it."

"And here, I've been making do with turning a key in an ignition my whole driving life."

"Luddite."

Colin navigates through city streets, headed toward the highway to test out the van's ride at higher speeds. I poke at the touch-screen radio and open all of the hidey-holes, where

I'm sure things like lip balm, gum, spare change, extra napkins, tissues, and the odd toy will secrete themselves. It's definitely a mobile command center, reminiscent of the USS Enterprise or similar.

I'm exploring a pop-out cup holder when Colin says, merging into traffic on the interstate, "I think this is the one."

"It's pretty bad-ass, for a minivan." The cup holder folds back in with a click.

"The true test will be the cargo area. How easily do those third-row seats fold down? Because that first one was bonkers. One shouldn't need a degree in engineering to make room for football gear or groceries."

It suddenly hits me how domesticated we are. I flash back to a few short years ago when Colin and I would stroll through the bookstore to people watch or meet at the pub for after-work drinks. Two confirmed singletons, content—if not thrilled—to be navigating life independently, never in a million years foreseeing a Saturday outing like this. The contrast between us then and us now elicits a stunned grunt from my side of the cockpit.

He glances my way. "Not feeling carsick, I hope."

I shake my head. "No. I just... I... How did we get here?"

Returning his attention to the road, he answers, "I took Metcalf to Shawnee Mission Parkway to—"

"No, no. I mean, *here*. In life. Test-driving a minivan. For *you*. And your *family*."

He chuckles. "Life is a bit bizarre, isn't it?"

"Yes! And it got that way so quickly! Like, overnight!"

"Not quite for me. Maybe it's because Cyndi and I felt the need to be so discreet for so long, but the past year feels like an age."

Struggling to put the feeling into words, I finally say,

"You're right that it seems like life has been like this for forever now, but at the same time, it seems like just yesterday, it wasn't like this. I was a job counselor, and you were a... Well, you were something different every other month. And it didn't matter. Neither one of us needed a job title to tell us who we were."

"Nah. I had that in the UK. 'Copper.' It was a pretty heavy title, at that."

"And now you're 'Geezer.'"

"I like that one a lot better. Much more fun. Although the pension's crap."

I laugh at him but soon fall pensive once again.

"Meanwhile you," Colin continues, his voice suspiciously light, "refuse to be categorized."

"That's a nice way of saying I'm nothing."

He tuts. "Oh, come now. I'm not even going to dignify that blatant cry for a compliment." He veers onto the next exit, beginning our loop back to the dealership.

"I'm not fishing for compliments. My statement is an easily verifiable fact."

"Aren't you the CEO of the Jet Knox brand?"

"I *will* kill you and stuff you in the cargo hold of this thing." My tough talking earns a hearty laugh, and I can't help but smile at our banter. Continuing the theme, I say, "Oh, you know me. I'm 'brimming with humility but empty of ideas' about what I want to do with the rest of my life."

"You're not seriously still stewing about that twit's story in the *Star*!"

I shrug. "She's been proven correct, hasn't she? And she's not the only one with that opinion. Gloria—"

"Is a jealous cow."

"Colin!"

"Oh, please. Don't act like you haven't thought the same thing a thousand times."

"Of course, *I* have. I didn't expect that from you, though."

"Why not? I despise the way she treats you and Cyndi, just because the two of you don't bend to her every whim. It's quite obvious and disgusting. I wish someone with a bit more leverage and standing in the family would call her out on it in front of everyone. Just once. I'd pay to see her face."

"Jet's been close."

"Close doesn't cut it." I open my mouth to defend my husband, but Colin cuts in. "You know I love the bloke, but he has serious mummy issues."

"No arguments there."

"He's really the only one who would be able to get away with telling her off, too. But he tiptoes just as much as the rest of them." He sighs. "I'm sorry. I don't mean to slag off your husband. That's not on."

"You're not saying anything I don't already know. And you're not 'slagging him off'; you're pointing out the obvious."

He taps the steering wheel with his thumb while we wait at a light. "Thing is, I'm lashing out at Jet here, because I know I'm a hypocrite."

I laugh incredulously. "You're too new to the family dynamic to be the one to say something to her. She'd dismiss it and play the victim. Trust me, I know how it goes."

"No, not that. I don't have it in me to tell anyone off, much less the matriarch of a family like the Knoxes, and I don't think of it as my responsibility, anyway."

"Then why are you a hypocrite, pray tell?"

He glances sideways at me, color rising in his fair cheeks.

"Uh, well... The thing is... There's a reason for the urgency in this vehicle purchasing venture..."

I giggle. "Yes...?"

Clearing his throat, he says, "The visit next week. I want to prove to Gloria that I *am* in this for the long haul. A long haul in a minivan, if need be."

"For a second, I thought you were going to say Cyndi was 'ducked up' again."

"Good God, no."

"So basically what you're saying is you're not immune to Gloria's pressures? You're human, like the rest of us?" I press my fist against his shoulder in more of a push than a punch.

He leans into it and smiles wryly. "Indeed."

"That's actually kind of reassuring." Returning both hands to my lap, I stare out the window and say distractedly, "Ah, well. You're in good company, if it makes you feel better."

His only reply is an ambiguous snort-chuckle that I choose to interpret as agreement.

I wish proving my worth were as simple as buying a minivan.

———

Colin drove off the lot with the spaceship minivan and a new monthly car payment, leaving me to what was left of my Saturday while he "scuppered" back to the sick house. Not eager to return to my Jet-less abode, I revived my earlier plan to boost the local economy, visiting some boutiques I've always been curious about but haven't had the time—or desperation—to explore.

In one, a mixologist custom-blended my own shampoo, based on my chemistry and personality. About halfway through the process, I panicked that it might come out smelling like farts, but when she finished, I was pleasantly surprised by its simple, clean aroma with citrus undertones. I paid her handsomely for three bottles and ordered a matching perfume to be bottled and shipped to me later.

Next door, the stationery shop beckoned. Now that I'm a lady (loosely defined) of leisure, maybe I'll be one of those people who hand-writes special greetings—or cries for help—on monogrammed note cards to my closest friends and family. Deep down, I know this will never happen, but I bought the cards and a set of hand-carved wooden pens, anyway.

Followed by new bedding, towels, his-n-her robes, some fuzzy slippers, and enough feather pillows to stock a hotel.

I hated myself for the blatant, senseless consumerism, so I silently vowed to go online later to donate a matching amount to a charity. (Because that will make it *all* better.)

Eventually, it was time to go home, despite my urge to avoid it.

My tiny duplex never seemed so oppressively empty when I lived alone. Big houses, however, foster loneliness and toxic introspection. The ticking clocks, groaning plumbing, settling beams, and whooshing ventilation echo so loudly, they become like annoying roommates who never shut up, yet also never add anything valuable to the conversation. Rather, their senseless noise leaves you shaking your head and wishing the person you were missing was there, instead.

Big houses under renovation exhibit their own quirks. Sounds that used to be absorbed by carpeted floors now echo off bare subflooring. Plastic tarps flap, and idle tools somehow seem louder in their uncharacteristic silence than they do when performing their normal functions. Primer, paint, and sawdust camouflage the smell of "home" and overpower any lingering scent memories of people not immediately present. And in the case of the new living room, its radically changed appearance tricks the mind into thinking that all of those major life events and wonderful memories happened elsewhere.

As much as I disliked the living room's former decor and couldn't wait to change it, now that it's been transformed, I stand in the middle of it, close my eyes, and picture its former bachelor-pad glory and everything that occurred here. Jet down on one knee, proposing to me officially, in person, after his dramatic on-camera proposal—and my eventual agreement. Countless viewings of football games, sometimes alone, sometimes surrounded by friends and family, always with Torzi. Jet dancing, prancing, and twerking when an unexpected loss by a rival team resulted in a surprise berth in the playoffs, which eventually led to the most unlikely of championship wins. My long-winded analyses of films while Jet sat captivated, listening (or doing a great job of pretending to be interested). Snuggling on the couch. Making love right there. And over there. And there. (We've had sex in here almost as much as our bedroom, now that I think of it.)

That thought snaps me back to the present, and I open my eyes, almost shocked to the point of disorientation at the current sight before me. Where walls and built-in shelves used to be, now windows tower, providing a view of the glowing pool and dark backyard beyond. The moonlight brightens the room now more than the sun ever did during the day with the old setup. In daylight, this room practically glows with natural light, even on the cloudiest afternoon. No more seasonal affect disorder for this girl!

We've switched out most of the furniture, as well. Gone are the hulking leather couches that squeaked and squawked with every movement. In their places sit deep, cream-colored sofas with massive cushions and cuddly throw pillows. Jet's chair, currently occupied by Torzi, squats between them like a cocky athlete flanked by two cheerleaders. Its slightly worn surfaces boast of a proud history. If I didn't know better, I'd say it was smirking at its survival. But I'm glad Jet insisted that it stay. Sarah was right—it lends a coziness to the room that would otherwise be missing among the shiny new pieces.

There's balance elsewhere, too. Dark wood beams and flooring juxtapose with the white window frames and light walls and ceiling. Strategically placed sconces, lamps, and recessed spotlights add sparkle and shine to the glass and metal accents scattered throughout the room.

It's perfect.

But it's not "home." Yet.

I finish my woolgathering and redirect myself toward the kitchen, which remains, for now, the same as always. Torzi deigns to open his eyes but doesn't move from his napping spot.

"Don't get up," I tell him. He predictably obeys but rolls onto his side to present his belly for the rub he assumes is his due for holding down Fort Knox all day.

Of course, I oblige. Because he owns me.

"How was your day, Torzi-boy?"

He grunts and yawns.

"Maybe you can teach *me* a few things about being a loafing free-loader."

I'm off to a good start with all that shopping.

When the dog jumps down from the chair and noses impatiently at the back door, I open it to let him out. "Yeah, yeah," I say to his retreating butt. "Go pee on a rose bush. I'll be

here, trying to figure out what I'm going to do with my life."
Or, more immediately, the rest of my weekend.

Gloria would say there's an easy way to fill this house, make new memories, and cure my loneliness when Jet's away, but there are few worse reasons than sheer boredom to have children. One being in order to sell them on the black market for illicit drugs. And... okay, that might be the only worse reason.

I pad barefoot through the kitchen and pull out the Saturday-labeled container that Beau left for me. Prying up the corner of the lid, I peer warily at the contents. Chicken pot pie, no peas. The man's a saint. While my dinner rotates in the microwave, I stare into the illuminated appliance.

Despite my determination to stop using food as an emotional crutch, I can't seem to give up comfort foods like pot pie. Hence, the "bump" the entire city seems to be obsessed with discussing, and I'm trying to shrink. I'm sure Beau doctored my dinner tonight to make it less "comfort," more "fuel." But as long as he holds the peas and makes his other super-secret nutritional ingredients undetectable, he can have at it.

After my pot pie has been devoured, I rinse my plate, place my dirty dishes in the dishwasher, and stand in the back door to summon Torzi. He shoots through the doggy door in the "guest" cottage, where Jake, the dog/house sitter lives. The dog skids to a stop on the stamped patio.

Hands on my hips, I say down to him, "Up for a movie marathon weekend, Bud?"

He answers by trotting into the house, leading the way down to the home theater in the basement.

I'm thinking we'll start with *Must Love Dogs*.

TWELVE

REPAIRS

I survived another week with Gloria, but there's no time to recharge or congratulate myself. We shepherded her and Ned onto a plane yesterday and spent the rest of the day preparing for this: surgery day. Jet followed the pre-op instructions to the letter, and I stayed out of the way and tried not to nag or ask too many questions. Mainly, my job is to be present.

It's all I can do to keep my anxiety in check. I've packed a tote of things to keep me occupied while I wait. Books, magazines, phone and charger, tablet. I also tucked some coloring books and colored pencils into the bag, just in case. Thank goodness I did, too, because it's the only thing that's calmed me so far.

My older brother would claim that coloring is yet another symptom of my stunted maturity, but I'm not the only WAG who does it. Keela Jackson confessed it keeps her sane some games. She swears by the activity's calming effect and laughed when I admitted it's one of my crutches, too. Then she said, "Coloring beats drugs."

It hasn't quite worked *that* well, but it's helped. It's definitely saved our televisions from irreparable damage in a couple of instances. While I'm not sure of the exact science behind the phenomenon, coloring in shapes and pictures slows my heart rate. My shoulders relax. I can filter out most minor annoyances.

But I've never done this outside of my house, in plain view of other people. I'm getting plenty of strange looks over here at the table in the corner but pretend the other folks waiting for their loved ones are jealous they didn't bring their own coloring books.

One person's surreptitious glances hold no judgment, only longing. A little girl with messy blonde pigtails fidgets in the chair next to a man I assume is her dad, whose leg bounces while he bites his fingernails and occasionally checks his phone. When he's not looking at his phone, he stares at the pager that's supposed to light up and vibrate when his patient is in recovery, and the surgeon wants to conduct the post-op consultation.

My pager sits under the cover of my coloring book. I don't want to see the hypnotic blinking LED that seems to be saying, "Not yet, not yet, not yet."

The pigtailed girl says to the nervous man, "When is Mommy coming back?"

He mutters something and asks her for about the thirtieth time to be still.

"I'm bored!"

I observe this cycle a few more go-rounds, then, heart thumping, break my own cardinal rule of public behavior, one I've followed since I was that girl's age (*Don't talk to strangers*), by clearing my throat and saying to the father, "Excuse me."

He turns his wary attention to me after shushing his daughter once again. "Yeah?"

The other waiting room occupants openly stare at the scene about to go down. After all, as the weirdo adult coloring in the corner, I'm unpredictable.

I blush, despite having nothing to be embarrassed about... yet. "If it's okay with you, your little girl can come over here and color. If she wants to."

She doesn't wait for her dad's okay before saying, "Yes!" and scampering to the table.

He doesn't object but moves to a chair closer to us.

"My name is Maura," I tell my new playmate.

She grins to expose a lack of so many teeth I wonder—not for the first time—how anyone her age manages to eat. "I'm Kaitlynn, with two n's."

"Nice to meet you, Kaitlynn-with-two-n's. Which book do you want to color in?"

She surveys her choices and carefully considers, but when I notice her eyes repeatedly roaming to the one under my hand, the one that features lush forests and ornate castles, I slide it over to her. "You want this one?"

For the first time, she displays a sense of shyness by merely nodding.

"That's cool. I'll finish this picture later and start a different one now." I shift my attention to a book of mandalas that lends itself more to mind wandering, anyway. Sliding the flat, square tin of pencils so it's between us on the laminate surface, I act like this is something I do every day.

After a few minutes of her not-so-neatly filling in one of the largest, most complicated pictures in the book, she stops to admire her work and seek my opinion.

"It's great," I say in that fake tone that adults always use with kids when they're being diplomatic. I immediately kick myself for being that person and try to relax.

"Purple is my mom's favorite color."

More sincerely, I say, "It's a pretty color. What's yours?"

"Yellow."

"I like that one, too. It's happy."

"Yes. Like in *Inside Out*. Joy is yellow. With blue hair. Joy is a remotion."

Thanks to Mikey, I'm familiar with the film, so this is something I can actually speak intelligently about. Whew. "Yes. Joy is a super-nice 'remotion.'"

"I like Disgust, too. She's funny. And she doesn't like broccoli. But I do. It gives me the toots, though."

I laugh. "It has a way of doing that."

"Kaity," her dad says, his leg jiggling in triple time now.

I can relate only too well. Last night, plagued by insomnia and a nervous tummy that had nothing to do with broccoli, unfortunately, I lay awake, sweating, staring through the dark at the shape of my clothes on the chair next to the window. It felt like the night before the first day of school. New clothes and school supplies at the ready. Will I like my teachers? Will I be able to find all of my classes and have enough time between bells to get there? Will I be able to remember my locker combination? Will Rae and I have the same lunch shift, so I'll have someone to sit with?

"It's only a knee scope... or two," I whispered to myself. "He'll be fine; he'll be fine."

I wasn't worried about the actual operation, though. What I've been dreading is watching Jet suffer through the pain of recovery; seeing him struggle with physical therapy; knowing he's wondering if he'll ever be the same again on the field and how that will affect his contract negotiations. *That's* what's been keeping me up at night.

The patient-to-be sighed in his sleep and stirred until he

was pressed against my damp back, his nose at the nape of my neck. His knees nudged behind mine through the fabric separating us. His arm flopped over my side, hand resting heavily on my breast next to the mattress. A subtle squeeze pulled me more firmly backward until my bottom nestled against his abs. My stomach full of nervous gas, I prayed he didn't hold me any tighter.

He mumbled something, his lips tickling the sensitive skin on my neck. I lay there, chanting, "He'll be fine," to myself through two on-and-off cycles of the whooshing heating system.

A few minutes later, Jet groused, lowered his head, and rubbed his face between my shoulder blades. I froze, waiting for him to go back to sleep, but he said, "What's the matter?"

"Nothing. I can't sleep. Thinking about tomorrow."

"Think quieter."

I chuckled. "I will. Sorry."

He backed away from me. "Dang. You're sweaty." He sniffed. "And did you—"

"Sorry. My stomach is killing me."

"Stop worrying."

"I can't help it."

"Then go fart and worry in a different bed."

I flipped over to face him and slapped playfully at his chest. Eyes closed again, he smiled. "Just kidding. Don't leave me."

"I won't. I'm not."

Before I could say anything else, he drifted off to sleep again, his mouth slackening, his breathing deepening.

Now, to avoid further trouble with Kaitlynn's dad, I resist the urge to commiserate with her about "toots" and smoothly transition to something else we have in common, our reasons for being here. I decide to tread lightly, though, since medical issues can be sensitive topics. "I brought my coloring books today, because I don't like being bored. My husband is having his knees fixed, and I don't know how long it will take."

"Did he broked them?"

I focus on finding all of the similar trapezoidal shapes in my picture and coloring them the same deep green. "Uh, sort of. No, not really. You know how sometimes if you cut yourself, and it's really deep, the skin is kind of white and shiny—scarred—after it heals?"

"Yeah. Like the bad guy in *The Lion King*. His name is Scar." She nods solemnly and chooses a bright green to scribble in the ivy on her castle's walls.

"Exactly. Well, my husband has those on the *inside* of his knees."

"Ew." She wrinkles her nose. "How did he cutted up the insides of his knees? I scraped my knees when I falled on my bike. Did he fall down on his bike?"

"Your knee scrapes won't give you scars inside your knees, though. He, uh..." I glance around, hoping everyone's returned to their magazines and phones and that nobody's eavesdropping. Of course, her dad is listening—or should be, considering a complete stranger is talking to his kid. But he seems preoccupied with a random spot in the middle of the room's carpeting. "He plays football."

"Oh. My dad plays football, too. On the XBox. And watches it on TV. He yells at the TV sometimes."

"I do, too."

"You do? I don't like yelling."

"Sometimes I can't help it. I get excited."

"Daddy gets mad. He says, 'Stupid idiots!' and then he turns the channel to a movie."

The excitable football fan clears his throat. "Kaity, that's enough."

"Well, you do."

That seals it; I won't be dropping Jet's name around that guy. Not that I'd planned to, anyway, but I'm going to make doubly sure I don't.

Casually, Kaitlynn chooses her next color for a turret-topping flag and says, "My mommy broked her foot falling down the stairs. It hurted real bad. The doctors have to put it back together again."

"Ouch."

"But after this, we get to have ice cream."

"That should make her feel better."

"I'm gonna get sprinkles."

"Ice cream isn't the same without them."

"But I'll be careful not to drip."

"Good plan."

Quite unexpectedly, my coloring book buzzes. My hand slips, causing my shading to stray outside the lines. When I realize the vibration is due to the pager under the front cover, the slip turns to a shake.

"Ooh! Your thingy is going off!" Kaitlynn jumps from her chair and runs to her father. "Is our thingy buzzing, too?"

Her dad shakes his head and shows her the quiet device. Shoulders slumped, she returns to the table, where I'm hastily packing up my toys, only one thing in mind—reporting to the desk so I can meet with the surgeon and, eventually, reunite with Jet.

"Awww!" Kaitlynn grumbles when I put the lid on the tin of pencils. "Not fair! You get to leave."

In spite of my nerves, I laugh. "You will, too. Soon, I bet."

She crosses her arms over her chest and pooches her lower lip. "This place is so boring!"

"Kaity, tell the nice lady 'thank you,' and come here." Her dad pats his lap. "I'll find a game on my phone for you."

"Thank you, Maura," she grumbles toward her chest.

"You're welcome, Sweetie. I hope your mom's foot feels better soon." Then, my hand hovering over her book, still open to her messy castle picture, I pause. Without giving it much thought, I nudge the pencil tin toward her. "Here. You keep all this."

"For realsies?"

"That's not nec—" her dad interjects.

"For realsies," I insist.

"Those are nice things, Miss. She'll just ruin 'em."

"But Dad!"

The last thing I want to do is cause a scene. The second-to-last thing I want is to waste any more time arguing with this guy. My final statement is to simply leave the coloring supplies where they are and pack up the rest of my stuff. On my way past Kaitlynn, vibrating pager clutched in one hand, tote bag in the other, I wink at her. "Don't forget to take those home. And don't drip ice cream on them."

"I won't! Thank you!"

"Thanks," the guy mutters, reminded by his daughter of his manners.

I mumble my own "Nice to meet you" and scurry for the front desk, where I wait for the receptionist to finish her phone call and acknowledge me. Suddenly, I'm hit from behind with considerable force. My knees buckle forward and hit the front of the desk, giving me a taste of what Jet must feel on a regular basis during the season.

"What the—"

A pair of tiny arms encircle my thighs before they're yanked away. I half-turn to find the maroon-faced dad lifting Kaitlynn to his hip. "I'm so sorry, Miss. She's— Normally, I'm more on top of things, but I'm distracted, and she got away from me…"

I smile at both of them, lingering on Kaitlynn, who looks like she's about to burst into tears. "It's okay!" Admittedly, this isn't my normal experience in public, and my knees are still singing from the impact on the metal and wood counter, but she didn't mean it, and she was only trying to show her appreciation. I set down my tote bag and pat the little girl's back. "Thanks for coloring with me."

Suddenly shy, she nods into her dad's neck. To him, I say, "Really. It's okay. She's a sweet girl. I hope she's not in trouble."

He shakes his head. "Are you okay?"

"Yes. Of course, I am."

"Then she's not in trouble." For the first time, he smiles, revealing laugh lines around his mouth and eyes. This is obviously not his natural element or his usual demeanor. I can relate.

"Mrs. Knox?" the receptionist says behind me.

The guy's smile slides from his face, which whitens considerably.

Before he can say anything else, I mutter, "Excuse me," give Kaitlynn's back one more pat, and nod once more at her dad. Then I turn and ask what I'm dying to know: "How is he?"

How is Jet? The answer is: full of it. In more ways than one.

As usual, his reaction to painkillers is comical. I wish I could focus more on the hilarity, but I'm preoccupied with saving him from himself. He's like a two-hundred-fifty-pound stoned toddler, complete with short attention span. When I think I've secured him in one location so I can tend to something a few feet away, he moves on me.

While I was signing him out at the surgical center, for example, he rolled himself into the waiting room to look out the window at the parking lot below. Like, with his nose pressed to the glass. It caused quite the stir in there when he was recognized.

That led to me standing behind him for thirty minutes while he signed autographs that looked nothing like his signature. My eyes connected with Kaitlynn's dad's in the middle of that, and I think we shared a moment. *See? I get it. You turn your back for a second...*

Now at home and on slightly weaker drugs, he's been more physically subdued but still a handful. Propped in bed with pillows jammed under his abused knees, he demands I stay with him and keep him entertained. We've watched TV, shopped online, napped, and played Yahtzee on a TV tray.

Then the inevitable: the drugs nauseated him, like they always do. There's no "rushing" anywhere in his condition, so I held the bathroom trash can—and my breath—and closed my eyes. Soon, he'll be crabby as hell because he can't poop. Glamor, glamor, glamor all the time here.

This may be our first surgery together, but the rest is all disturbingly familiar territory by now. A major thumb injury, several minor concussions, one big one, and multiple sprains to various muscles since the beginning of our relationship have indoctrinated me well into the religion of pain management and its various side effects.

My favorite part of the routine, Jet's drug dependency paranoia, arrives the morning following his procedure, when I'm helping him downstairs—at his insistence—for breakfast. ("Real breakfast. None of this lame breakfast-in-bed shit.") Halfway down the stairs, he pauses at the small landing to catch his breath. I adjust my grip on his waist. His nostrils flare and his breath whistles through his teeth as he grimaces while holding onto the banister.

I pat my robe pocket and feel the pill bottle nestled there. "As soon as you get something in your stomach, it'll be time for a re-dose of your pain meds."

He shakes his head. "No. I'm fine." Sweat pops on his upper lip and brow.

"Don't be ridiculous. You're hurting."

"I'll take some ibuprofen, or something. Acetaminophen. Both. But no more of the heavy stuff."

"It's silly to be a tough guy."

"It'll be fine now that I've gotten through the first night. Let's keep going."

He drapes one arm around my shoulders and keeps a firm hold on the railing. With a massive amount of concentration that seems to include willing his knees to function the way they were designed, he lifts his right foot and shuffles it down to the next step. His left quickly follows to bring both feet to the same level and limit the amount of time either of his knees must hold his full weight. It reminds me of how Mikey goes down stairs—step, together; step, together—now that he thinks he's too big to descend on his bottom. Maybe I should suggest to Jet that he sit and scoot for the final eight stairs.

At the bottom, he hobbles to the waiting wheelchair.

I stand before him and smile. "Good job. Not bad at all."

He flashes a crooked grin through his panting. "Pathetic.

But it'll get better fast. Get those crutches ready, because I won't use this stupid wheelchair after today."

To get to the dining room, I push him through the nearly-finished library, hoping to distract both of us while he continues to recover. "Look: a few more touches to add, and I need to get those boxes of books on the shelves, but we're almost there."

"It looks great, Babe. Sorry I doubted you."

"I knew it would work; that's all that matters."

When he doesn't laugh, I lean around him to get a peek at his face. Still sweating, he grimaces.

"You should take another heavy-hitter with your breakfast."

"No."

"Just one more to get you through the first full twenty-four hours."

"I don't want to, and I don't want to fucking argue about it! Okay?"

Pulling back as if I've been physically slapped, I blink away my hurt tears. "Okay! Sorry. I was only—"

"Well, don't."

He grips the wheels and stops our momentum, then strokes forward with his arms to "drive" himself. Rather than be pulled along, I let go of the handles and stare after him. Through the doorway, I watch him navigate the dining room, banging his feet on the chairs and cursing. He eventually gets close enough to grab one and yank it out of the way. It teeters on two legs for a few seconds, then crashes to the floor.

Beau comes running from the kitchen. "You okay, man?" he asks, righting the chair and setting it out of the way in a corner.

"I'm fine. Starving."

"I can help you with that. I can scoot you closer to the table, too, if you—"

"This is good enough. I have long arms."

The personal chef leaves it at that and returns to the kitchen, where I assume he's plating the food I can smell. Gritting my teeth, I continue forward and edge between the wall and Jet, planning to regain my composure while I pour coffee and orange juice.

Jet demonstrates his reach by snagging my hand on my way past.

I stare down at our fingers, too emotional to look him in the eyes.

"I'm sorry, Maura."

With my free hand, I sweep tears from my cheeks. "You're forgiven," I mumble. "I'm sorry I annoyed you."

"I'm tired. And hungry. I promise I'll be less of a jerk after I eat."

Throat tight, I nod and pull my hand from his.

Strike "nurse" from my list of possible callings.

THIRTEEN

PURPOSE

This Valentine's Day is not going at all like it should—and normally would—under different conditions.

Even these circumstances aren't panning out like I thought they would. It's like Jet doesn't need me at all. True to his word, after he ate, he was much more pleasant that first post-op day. And independent. I haven't had to change a single bandage.

On the second post-op day, he ditched the wheelchair and hobbled around on crutches, his knees tightly wrapped for extra support. He's surprisingly nimble on those things, too. Years of practice, I guess. Once or twice, he asked me for help with a closed door or an item he needed me to carry, since he had no free hands. Other than that, I was as useless as a light switch in an electrical outage.

Day three, he's relied solely on his fancy knee braces for support. I figured that would mean he'd need to lean on me when walking. Nope. Turns out, he can cruise from one piece of furniture to another like a boss. More like a toddler, but either way, he regularly makes it to his destination before I realize he's up. At this point, I've resigned myself to being superfluous. He goes up and down the stairs by himself, and even his bathroom issues have been resolved (not that I was ever a help in that department, anyway).

That would be fine—more than fine—if it meant we could spend time together like a normal couple on the one day a year devoted to lurve. But with his newfound freedom, he seems to have other priorities, some of which aren't necessarily his choice. Like physical therapy.

As he prepares to leave for his session, I ask, "How much pain are you still in?"

He drops his shoes on the floor in front of him and sits on the bench at the foot of the bed. "A little. Not bad. Mostly twinge-y. And only when I do certain things. I'm fine."

"Do you want me to take you to P.T.?"

He frowns while considering it, but replies, "Nah. Beau's got it. He wants to observe the exercises, so we can do them here at home, too."

"How do your incisions look?"

"Like they're supposed to look."

"Do you want me to double-check?"

"I want you to stop worrying about me."

"I'm more worried about how much you haven't needed me at all than I am about you. You're all over this." What I tried to say lightly comes out brittle and sharp.

"It goes with the territory," he says with a grunt as he ties his shoes.

"For some reason, I thought you'd be more… helpless."

He laughs. "Sorry to disappoint you, Madame."

"I'm not disappointed." My churlish tone says otherwise.

He looks over his shoulder at me. "What's your deal?"

I shake my head, unable to speak for the moment. Then,

plopping on the edge of the mattress, I finally give into my funk.

He shuffles to my side and sits, rubbing my back.

Eventually, I manage, "Part of me is glad this has been easier than I expected, but another part of me keeps thinking how useless I am."

"Oh, c'mon."

"I am! These past few days have sealed it. You don't need me to help you after surgery. You don't like my suggestions for renovating the house. You don't want to talk to me about contract negotiations. When it finally does come down to it, it won't surprise me at all if you figure out a way to have kids without me, too. 'Looky there! I spooged in this potted plant, and a baby came out!'"

Although I wasn't trying to be funny, I'm relieved when he cracks up at the idea—and my vulgar word choice. His laughter is contagious, too, so I smile and shake off my mopes.

Kissing his tilted cheek, I stand. "Never mind. This is dumb. What's worse than a spoiled, bored wife? A spoiled, bored wife who complains about how boring her life is."

Sobering, he looks up at me. "It's not dumb. This is important. It's obviously bugging you. And if you feel useless and unhappy, it's going to be a major problem that only gets worse the longer you feel that way. We'll figure it out and find something you care about."

"No, *I'll* figure it out." I pull him to his feet and kiss his chin. "Sorry to be such a downer."

He grins. "You keep things interesting, that's for sure."

"'Interesting.' Is that code for 'annoying'?"

Pulling me closer, he brushes his lips against mine. "It's code for 'I love you.'" He deepens his kiss, then pulls away right as I'm getting into it. "I need you." Another, longer kiss, then separation. "I want you to be happy. And we'll figure it out together. Because we're a team." His eyes search mine.

I nod, for once not minding his obsession with sports-themed metaphors. We are a team. That's what keeps me going most days.

Right before a final spine-tingling kiss, he murmurs, "I'll see you after a bit."

Following him down the hall, I watch him reach the bottom of the stairs, where he gives me a silly thumbs-up. Then I return to our bedroom and plop into the chair by the window that overlooks the backyard. It won't do any good to pout—and that's Jet's specialty, anyway—so I grab my phone and dial one of the only numbers I have memorized and can punch in faster than I can navigate menus.

When Rae answers, I say, "Happy Valentine's Day!"

There's a pause, and she replies, "Is this the part where you declare your unrequited love for me, having only come to the realization that you're a lesbian after years of sex with selfish male partners, like Jet Knox?"

I laugh. "No! Jet's not—"

"I don't want to know."

"You brought it up."

"And I'm instantly regretting it. Anyway, you definitely aren't a lesbian."

"Really? You don't say."

"No, if anything, you'd be bi- or pansexual."

"Pansexuals have all the fun."

"That's what they say. But guys are gross, so I disagree."

"Does it ever concern you that you haven't matured past the 'boys are gross' phase in your personal development?"

"Nope. I prefer to see it as holding a piece of knowledge

that frees up brain space for other, more important information."

"Well, guys aren't gr— Okay, *some* guys can be gross at times, but your blanket statement is unfair."

She snorts. "You just thought of a prime example of Knox being gross, mid-sentence, didn't you?"

Yesterday, Jet went into the bathroom and came out with fresh, clean wraps on his knees, and I was like, "I thought you were in there trying to poop."

"I was. Figured I might as well re-wrap while I was sitting there, waiting for nothing to happen."

I'd rather contemplate how unsanitary it is to expose healing incisions to fecal matter than admit to Rae that happened, though, so I change the subject back to my call's original purpose. "Anyway, I just wanted to wish you a happy Valentine's Day."

"Which we haven't done since we were in college and pretended like it didn't matter we weren't getting laid."

"And ask how your Vegas trip with Ana Paula went."

"Oh, that. Yeah. That was…" She pauses, searching for the right word. "Well, you know, it was Vegas. Pretty dumb. But AP had never been, and she pestered me enough about it that I finally caved. It was as dumb as I remembered, but we got married—not by Elvis. By some dude in a bolo tie, though—so that was kinda crazy."

I sit up straighter in my chair. "Hang on a sec! Back up the train, you lead-burying psycho. You and AP got married?"

"Yeah. I mean, it's no big deal."

"You deserve the biggest punch in the ovaries right now. 'It's no big deal,' my ass. It's a huge deal!"

"See, I knew you'd be like this."

"And that's why you didn't live-stream that mother? I can't

believe you didn't tell me! Were you drunk? Tell me you were just too drunk to remember to call me. That would make it almost okay."

"No, but it was a spur-of-the-moment thing, and I didn't want to ruin it by messing with technology or hearing you squeal in my ear. Or crying. Or telling me we *had* to do this or that. We just did it."

Her accurate assessment of how I would have reacted makes it hard for me to argue. That doesn't mean I'm not hurt. I'm self-aware, but I still have feelings. "It was probably late at night, too, so I get it."

"No, it was late afternoon. And we were totally sober, thank you. Fun fact: you're not allowed to get married there if you're drunk. Supposedly. At the place we went, anyway, they even made us take Breathalyzers to prove we weren't blitzed. How nuts is that? Vegas…"

"Yeah, Vegas. I can't believe you eloped."

"Uh… Pot, meet Kettle."

"That was different! I was escaping Gloria and a mega-wedding that would have been…" I shudder at the thought. "How long ago was this, anyway?"

"Just a couple days," she says breezily. "Near the end of our trip."

I try not to let it bother me that she couldn't even be bothered to send me a text and a selfie to tell me about one of the most important days of her life. That's Rae for you; she's never been one to volunteer information without major questioning ahead of time.

"You and AP could have still had a quiet ceremony here, surrounded by a select few people, like me. And Jet. And your parents. Led by someone *not* wearing a bolo tie. No Breathalyzer, either."

"It was perfect. It's going to be a great memory. Quirky, like us. Anyway, it saved a lot of people the awkwardness of declining an invitation to a wedding they don't approve of."

My blood pressure soars. "Like who?"

"A lot of people. My parents, for starters."

"Bullshit. They love AP. They love you."

"They love pretending AP and I are 'special friends.' Attending a same-sex wedding isn't in their wheelhouse. At all."

Disappointment in the elder Lewisbergs pushes me back into a slump in my chair. How could I have not known this about two people who always seemed like a second set of parents to me?

While I'm still processing the hurt it must bring Rae, if it's this disheartening to me, she says, "They're not the only ones, either. Not by a long shot. A lot of people are okay with 'the gays' as long as we're okay with being second-class citizens. The minute we want to have the same rights as first-class heteros, we find out what people really think."

"Then screw 'em."

"Thing is, I'd rather not know. It's bad enough knowing my parents fall into that category. But they're old."

"You're their only child!"

"Yeah, and their only chance at grandchildren, which they'll never have, because I've 'chosen' this 'lifestyle.'"

"I just can't believe they think that."

"They do."

"Anyway, you and AP could always adopt."

"Could, but won't. We don't want children."

"That has nothing to do with your sexual orientation, though. You wouldn't want kids even if you were straight, right?"

"I don't know. Straight people are kind of obsessed with reproducing. Like you think the world isn't complete without your DNA continuing into perpetuity."

I laugh. "Not this straight person."

"What about the straight person you're married to?"

Staring at the steaming pool below and noting the sporadic snow flurries, I sigh. "Maybe not 'obsessed.' But yeah, I think that's still on his bucket list."

"I know it is. And you do, too. You may have talked him out of football-team-like numbers, but that doesn't mean 'zero.'"

"Hm."

"Is your uterus ready?"

"Shut up."

"Gloria would be happy to check." She laughs, and I join in.

"You're such a shitty friend."

"But you love me anyway."

"I do." Still grinning, I say, "That's all I wanted to say to you today. I love you, Rae Lewisberg. And I'm so happy for you and AP."

"Thank you." She clears her throat. "I guess I love you, too, you know. In a non-lesbian way."

After coercing a reluctant promise from her that she'll let Jet and me do something special for her and AP to celebrate their nuptials, I end the call.

The occasional snowflake turns into a swirling shower, which I watch until I hear Jet and Beau return from physical therapy.

By the time I arrive downstairs to tell Jet the big news about Rae and AP, he and Beau have already gone downstairs to the gym to figure out how to duplicate some of the exercises on our own equipment. They stay down there until just before lunch but talk more strategy in the kitchen while Beau prepares simple iceberg wedge salads.

Finally alone for a quiet lunch together, I say, "You'll never guess what Rae and AP did in Vegas."

Around a mouthful of salad, Jet says, "Got married?"

I tap my fork on the side of my plate as I count to ten to stifle my irritation.

He looks up from his food, swallows, and laughs. "Oh, sorry. I thought you wanted me to guess. Did I get it right?"

"Yes," I answer stiffly. "You did."

"That's awesome! Please tell me Elvis did it."

"No. A guy in a bolo tie."

"Lame."

"They had to take Breathalyzers to prove they were sober."

"How romantic!" He spears a chunk of lettuce, tomato, and avocado and sits back in his chair to chew.

"I told her we'd do something here to celebrate."

"Great idea."

"Rae didn't seem all that excited about it."

"I don't think Rae does 'excited,' does she?"

"I guess not."

After sawing and shoveling the rest of his salad in record time, he declares, "It'll be fun. Our wedding party was." He pats my shoulder, then uses it as leverage to stand. He leans down and kisses the top of my head. "Dang. I'm tired. I'm gonna take a nap, then walk some laps in the pool. If the snow stops." With that declaration, he leaves the table and starts his painstaking trek to the closest couch in the living room.

I poke at the rest of my salad in solitude while debating how to fill my own Valentine's Day afternoon. Eventually, I give up trying to figure out something fresh and retreat to the movie room, to dwell on my boredom with *Calendar Girls* playing in the background. Helen Mirren, Julie Walters, and the girls will make everything okay. They're women of action. Their characters are, anyway, and I'm assuming, considering who they are, they're fairly purposeful in real life, too.

The comedy that never fails to make me laugh out loud barely raises a smile today, though. I'm in the throes of a good and proper snit. And why shouldn't I be? My Valentine doesn't seem to even realize what day it is. Since sex is off the table for medical reasons, the observance doesn't exist for him, apparently. We don't go crazy on Hallmark holidays, but we typically go through the motions. He hasn't wished me a happy Valentine's Day, much less produced a gift. And I don't want to give him the smartwatch I got him if he's forgotten to get me something, because then he'll feel bad. I can save the watch for another occasion—or no special occasion at all.

It doesn't help that a certain intrepid girl reporter's words keep haunting me, no matter how many "Screw her" pep talks I've given myself.

"...brimming with humility but seems empty of ideas...."

"...colorless next to her personality-full husband..."

I defy anyone to have something like that written about her without a resultant complex. When people closest to me got wind of the article, they pooh-poohed it as a gossip reporter trying to pad her writing resume and snatch attention from popular celebrity blogs. But my brother and Deirdre probably agreed with Kendra's assessment. Gloria surely did.

And while I haven't brought it up again since mentioning it to Colin a couple of weeks ago (what's the point in making others dwell on it and repeatedly reassure me of its inaccuracy), here I sit, proving my critic(s) correct, my head empty of ideas as I "retreat" to my "extensive private movie collection."

Back when I was a typical middle-class person from a middle-class background with a middle-class education and a middle-class job, living in a middle-class duplex in a middle-class neighborhood, driving my middle-class car, doing my middle-class thing, day in and day out, I had no clue what it meant to be wealthy. To me, it meant you never had to worry about money. Period.

I scoffed at lottery winners who went public with their tales of post-win woe. "Having all this money ruined our lives." Buh-rother. I vowed if I ever won the lottery (if I ever decided to play, that is), I wouldn't eff it up. I'd do it right. I talked a big game about quitting my job and moving to an island, where I'd withdraw from society and happily become "that weird lady with her own IMAX screen." Anyone who lists "too much money" as one of their problems is a douche.

Then again, if I'd been asked five years ago, I wouldn't have thought I'd have a problem not having a job, either. Yet lately, I've complained a bunch about both of those things. Class-A Douche material.

To be fair to myself, I'm not really complaining. "Complaining" connotes a voicing of discontent, and I rarely dare say these ridiculous things out loud. But I do live with a near-constant discomfort due to my sudden position in a system of disproportionate wealth distribution.

After about an hour of staring at the screen without comprehending what I'm seeing or hearing, I acknowledge Torzi's entrance. He takes up his usual position on my lap, and I stroke his head, abandoning the movie altogether to

Google its prominent UK thespians and find out their pet causes.

Many of the usual charities pop up: childhood poverty, domestic violence, clean water in undeveloped nations, adoption, animal rights, environmental sustainability, medical research, affordable housing, blah, blah, blah.

Finally, my internal "blah, blah, blah" elicits a laugh. How cynical can I be? These people use their money and influence to effect change all over the world, for a myriad of causes. That's more than I can say right now.

And in most cases, they don't merely throw money at the problems. They get involved. They travel to remote, unsafe places. (Not my thing; I didn't inherit my parents' adventurous genes, unfortunately.) They—or their "people"—organize fundraisers and ask their richest friends to contribute. (Also not my thing; I couldn't even ask my family to buy cookie dough when I was trying to raise money for after-prom in high school.) They publish books, donating all of the royalties to charity. (I can't write and don't know any ghostwriters.) They design and sell calendars, like the ladies in this movie. (I don't want to compete with the Chiefs team or the cheerleaders' calendars. Plus... what the heck kind of calendar would I publish? A day-to-day guide to being idle?)

The point is, they use what they know and what they have to make the world a nicer, better place. What do I know? Job counseling and movies. More accurately, watching movies, not making them. *Making* movies would be useful. Unfortunately, I'm not rich enough to bankroll features that would shed light on important issues. I own some films that match that description, but sitting here watching them doesn't change anything, except to make me feel more insignificant and useless. And it's not like I can charge admission to my house to have people watch them with me, in an effort to raise awareness, thirty people at a time.

I sit up straighter in my seat at that last thought. Then more thoughts pop and bounce around my head, shifting and rearranging themselves into something that actually makes sense. I recognize this phenomenon. It's happened every time I've dragged myself from the edge of panic and despair, worried I've exhausted my lifetime quota of bright ideas.

It's thrilling.

It's magical.

It's inspired.

Torzi lifts his head and tilts it at me.

"This is going to sound crazy," I say to him, "but hear me out."

FOURTEEN

INSPIRATION

By the time Jet finishes his water walking, my kernel of an idea has exploded into an entire popcorn machine of fluffy, buttery goodness. Eager to share my brainstorm with someone slightly less hairy than the dog, I corner my husband in the mudroom, where he's shaking out his trunks and winter swim shirt and dropping them into the washing machine.

He looks up from pouring in the detergent and grins when I lean against the doorway. "Hey, there. What's kickin', chick—"

"I know what I'm going to do with my life."

Replacing the cap on the bottle of laundry soap, he pauses. "Okay. That's, um, great."

"It *is* great."

"Is it going to cost us a shit-ton of money?"

"Yes."

He inhales, holds his breath for a beat, exhales, and swallows. "Lay it on me."

"I want to start my own non-profit."

He places the detergent bottle in the cabinet above the washer, every one of his motions oddly deliberate and slow. "Go on."

"There are these restaurants where groups can take over the staffing for an evening, and all of the profits during their shift go to that organization."

"You want to open a restaurant?"

"Hell, no!"

His shoulders relax. "Oh, thank God. Because I've heard that's a nightmare. Sean Glitzenbock had that place out in Shawnee Mission, remember? One thing after another. If it wasn't personnel problems, it was health code and inspections. Overhead was nuts. Profits? Forget about it." He swings shut the washer hatch and presses some buttons to start the machine.

"I want to open a movie theater."

Leaning against the whooshing appliance, he crosses his arms over his chest, then shifts his weight and winces at the resultant discomfort. "I see."

Gesturing for him to join me on the flip-top bench that holds our rain gear, I wait for him to sit and settle comfortably. For the next ten minutes, I lay out the plan I've already rehearsed with Torzi.

"Charities can apply to staff the theater—ticket booth, concessions, janitorial, the whole works, with some basic oversight by a couple of permanent theater employees—for a movie's run. The non-profit organization can then pocket the profits from that run. With only one or two paid workers, overhead will be low. We'll play older films, so we won't have to pay first-run premiums. Concessions will be simple: boxed candy, bottled drinks, and popcorn. One screen to start, with the option to expand if the idea takes off like it has in other areas and industries. Marketing will be the biggest part of our budget, since we'll have to work hard to get the word out for each charity's benefit. Oh, and we can rent out the facility for private functions, too."

Other than a few strategically placed "Uh-huh"s and "Okay"s, Jet remains silent and contemplative during my pitch.

"The possibilities are endless," I say, finishing up. "But the point is, I'd be giving back to the community while sharing something I love: films."

He bends and straightens his legs to keep the muscles warm and loose. Finally, he says, "That sounds great, Maura."

Every one of my internal organs drops three inches when I recognize he's using the same tone he's used every time I've told him about a room redesign idea. "But?"

"No buts. Except..." He licks his lips, then wipes his mouth, grasping and tugging his lower lip in his closed hand before releasing it with a gush of air. "Maybe right now isn't the best time."

"Why not? When else?"

"Later. Soon."

I open my clenched fists and grip the front of the bench. "I'm dying here, Jet. It's been four months since I left my job, and we're only a couple of weeks into the off-season, but I'm climbing the walls. Not to mention, I feel like a useless waste of space." *As gossip reporters so helpfully like to point out.*

"I know, and I'm sorry. Maybe it was a mistake for you to quit your job." He scratches his eyebrow and finger-combs his damp hair.

And there it is. Jet's finally realized how embarrassing it will be to have a spouse who does nothing. My heart thunders against my breastbone.

A sneering face appears through a cloud of vape smoke. *"You only started caring about this job to impress your man and to make yourself look less lame next to him."*

Swallowing my panic, I say, "We agreed I'm too busy during the season to maintain a day job."

"You're too smart to sit around the house all day in the off-season, though."

"I don't just sit around the—" The prickle and choke of tears bring me up short.

He rubs the back of his neck. "Oh, man. I'm sorry. That came out wrong. I know you have your volunteer work and stuff. But that's not enough, is it? For you, I mean. I think it's plenty. But you're already bored."

Scrabbling my way back to the original topic, I say, desperation more obvious in my voice than I would like, "That's why this non-profit cinema idea is perfect. It'll be a real challenge, something I can immerse myself in. Plus I can get it up and running this spring and summer and have people in place to keep it going smoothly by the time next season starts."

He hums doubtfully.

"Why are you crapping on this idea?"

"I'm not crapping on it! I told you it's great."

"But not great enough to invest money in it."

"Not now."

"Oh, so we can afford a housekeeper, a personal chef-slash-trainer, and a... a friggin' dog minder who basically does *nothing* most of the time, but not this? We can afford vacations and the maintenance and taxes on your parents' house out in California, but not something that will benefit the community we live in? We've spent tens of thousands on remodeling projects on *this* stupid place, but I can't use any money on something that will make me much happier than a pretty room?"

"I'm not saying no."

"Good. Because I didn't realize I was asking permission. So much for all of that, 'My money is your money' bullshit."

"It's not bullshit. Maura, I— You just have to wait."

"I've already been waiting for what feels like forever to figure out what I wanted to do, and now that I have the perfect idea—"

"I'm not sure how much longer we're going to be here, all right?"

It's as if he's physically punched me with something merely stated. If I'm half as pale as I feel, I'm practically transparent when I ask, "What do you mean?"

"Now, don't panic, or anything. I'm only trying to explain myself. Tom submitted a contract proposal to the team, but we haven't gotten a counteroffer yet."

"What does this mean?"

"We don't know. It could mean nothing. It could mean they're exploring other options. It could mean everyone's on vacation at Disney World, and nobody's checked their email."

"Oh."

"Maybe not that last thing."

"Probably not."

"The point is, we've heard nothing, so we know nothing. I have to start preparing myself—and you—for the worst case scenario."

I process this information and all that it entails, then say quietly, "I thought you'd be a Chief forever."

"Me, too. I'd hoped, anyway." He smiles shakily. "Who knows? Maybe I will be. But until we know..."

"I get it."

He sits next to me and grabs my hand. "I love your movie theater idea, Maura."

"You do?"

"Yes. I do. It's perfect. And we'll definitely do it, no matter what, no matter where. Someday."

"In the meantime?"

"Dream, plan, research, go crazy. On paper. And..." He exhales. "Get Sarah and Carl back here to redo the kitchen. You're right—it's outdated. And if we're going to have to sell this place..."

How many times have I dreamed of unloading this behemoth? But not like this. Not in this context. Not because we *had* to. And not after I've finally been able to make it feel somewhat like home.

I nod. "Right. Okay."

He squeezes my hand. "I didn't want to say anything to you about this, especially so soon after we've gotten through the stress of my surgery."

I smile bravely at him. "It's fine. This is how it goes. I get that. But..."

When I pause, he prompts, "What?"

"Please don't accept a deal from Buffalo."

He laughs, but I'm totally serious. When he can talk again, he kisses my forehead and pulls me to his side in a hug. "Oh, Babe, we're nowhere near being forced to go to Buffalo. It's early days. I don't want to make any more huge decisions here, though, until we get this figured out."

"Fine. That makes sense. That's all you had to say."

As I'm helping him to his feet, the doorbell rings. He grins. "Oh, thank God. I thought it would never get here!"

I tilt my head, feeling like Torzi. "What have you done, Jet Knox?"

"Your Valentine's gift! I've been avoiding you all day, waiting for it."

I smack his chest. "You little— What is it?"

"Help me to the door, and you'll find out."

————

The good Valentine's Day news is that Jet didn't forget. And he ordered an amazing gift, a custom-made, hard-bound coloring book drawn from photos of us and our family and friends.

After I kiss him, carefully, so as not to upset his precarious balance, I run upstairs and back with his card and watch.

"Thanks! I've been wanting one of these."

"It's not romantic, but—"

"It's perfect." He straps it to his wrist and admires it for a few seconds, then returns his attention to me with a smirk. "You thought I forgot, didn't you?"

"Or didn't care."

His eyes bug out. "How could you think that?"

I shrug. "I thought maybe with everything else going on, it fell off your radar. It wasn't a big deal."

"An opportunity to show you how much I love you would never fall off my radar." Nuzzling my neck, he murmurs, "You know what I *really* want to do right now?"

"Hmmm. I can guess, but the doctor said—"

"Color!" He grabs me by the hand and limp-leads me back to the couch. Opening the book on the coffee table, he asks me to choose a page. I pick the one of us from Gracie's christening. The picture on the opposite page is the baby by herself. "Aw, look at that pretty darlin'!" he coos, snatching a brown marker and filling in her irises.

I color silently for a while, trying to figure out how to break the *bad* Valentine's Day news to him. Finally, keeping my focus on selecting the perfect shade for my dress, I drop as casually as possible, "So, uh, since it seemed like we weren't doing anything special for V-Day, I, uh… Well, I sort of made other plans with, uh, a slightly younger sweetheart."

He stops shading in the cherries on Gracie's romper and stares at my profile. "You did what?"

I clear my throat. "It's not a biggie. Greg and Deirdre's babysitter canceled last-minute, and since we didn't have anything going on, I told Greg we'd watch Meleah."

Jet whines, "Aw, Maura!"

"I thought you forgot!"

"What time are they going to drop her off?"

The doorbell rings, and I cringe at the perfectly imperfect timing. "Now o'clock?" I flutter my lashes at him and hop from the couch to answer the door. When the doorbell rang earlier, I thought it was my brother, and I nearly panicked that I hadn't had a chance to let Jet know we were babysitting. This is almost as bad. Almost.

It gets worse when I open the door to my brother, my screaming niece, and her ten tons of crap, including a plush toy entourage.

"Teething," Greg shouts over the baby's cries as he hands her to me. "Oh, and we're trying to wean her from the pacifier. There's one in her bag, but we'd prefer you didn't use it until bedtime."

I blink into her hot breath. As soon as her father no longer has hold of her, she ramps up the volume. I half-listen to his instructions about bedtime feeding, knowing there'll be a detailed, typed-out note in the diaper bag. As he backs toward the door, the impossible happens: Meleah cries louder.

Jet appears at the threshold between the living room and foyer, startling both Greg and me with his relatively stealthy arrival. "Who's pinching the baby?" he asks.

Greg winces. "Separation anxiety. She'll be fine once she can't see me anymore. See you guys later!"

But she isn't fine. At all. We've followed Deirdre and Greg's instructions about mouth pain relief; we've sung her favorite songs; we've (I've) walked her through the circle that is the library, dining room, kitchen, living room, and foyer; Jet's put on plushy plays. She's still crying. I tried feeding her some bedtime cereal and got a face full of it back, like something out of a cheesy movie about an inept caregiver—or a horror flick about exorcism. Now, while she lustily downs her bottle, I figure we have a ten-minute reprieve.

Feeling like an auctioneer, I rattle off to Jet, "What the hell is wrong with her?"

He shrugs. "I don't know. I guess it hurts like a mo-fo when they're getting teeth."

"Ya think? Sounds like a pain they should look into simulating to get information from terrorists."

Laughing, he says, "Or put them in a cell with a crying baby and tell them they can't come out until they're ready to talk." He taps his chin for a second, as if seriously considering his idea and crafting it for an eventual call to the CIA. "Actually, a recording would be better. No pauses. And safer for the baby, too."

Looking down into my usually sweet niece's tear-puffy face, I shake my head, feeling like a failure. "Maybe we should call Greg and Deirdre, tell them to come get her. She's miserable. She needs her mom and dad."

"I'll text Greg. Till then, what do we do?"

"What *can* we do?"

He taps an SOS to my brother and hits "send." "I don't know. Ride it out, I guess."

Meleah whimpers around the bottle's nipple as her eyelids droop.

"Oh, hang on. She's falling asleep," I whisper.

Jet slumps with relief. "Thank goodness."

Still, the dread builds as we watch the formula seep lower and lower, until only air wheezes through the nipple. As gently as possible, I pull it from Meleah's still-sucking mouth. As I'm making the decision not to risk waking her by burping her, her nose wrinkles, her eyes scrunch, and her chin wobbles.

"Hurry and get her pacifier," I say to Jet, forgetting his current capacity for "hurry" would frustrate a sloth.

He rocks to a standing position and lurches across the room to the diaper bag while Meleah warms up with some indignant sputtering and coughing.

I bounce and shush and placate as he rummages through the bag, muttering, "Where is the dang thing?"

"Try the side pocket."

"I already did."

"The front pocket."

"I've looked in all of the pockets!"

His raised voice startles the baby, whose cries nearly drown out the chime alerting us to an incoming text on Jet's phone. He pauses his search to read it, then snorts and pockets the device, redoubling his efforts to locate the one thing that might save us all from further misery.

"What did my brother say?"

"He said there's nothing to worry about; she's always fussy in the evenings. They'll be here in a couple of hours."

"A couple of *hours*?"

"Can you come over here and help me look? My knees are about to buckle."

I haul Meleah to my hip, trying to ignore that it places her cry hole right next to my ear hole. Jet plops into the nearest seat and places the diaper bag in his lap. I trade the screaming baby for the bag.

While I'm rummaging with my head basically in the bag, using my phone as a flashlight, he ruminates down at our niece's red face, "Remember when she was born, and she was the only baby in the nursery who wasn't crying? And we were like, 'Wow. What a sweet, content baby!'"

"Vaguely."

"What happened?"

Unfortunately, I can relate all too well to how a personality can change seemingly overnight. Environment matters. "She's lived with Greg and Deirdre for nearly a year now. That will wear on even the most laid-back dispositions."

He chuckles but quickly sobers. "Oh, geez. You don't think this is permanent, do you? I mean, I figured she was going through a phase, or something."

"Found it!" I pull the pacifier from the depths of the designer bag and aim it directly for the gaping hole near Jet's chest. Meleah resists at first but must realize it's close enough to what she wants and that it's the best I have to offer, so she takes it. A snot bubble erupts with her first exhale from her nose.

"Gross!"

Jet laughs. "I've seen worse come out of someone's mug."

At the risk of angering her all over again, I wipe her wet face, cooing down into it. "It's all right, sweet girl. We're so sorry you're sad."

Her shoulders jerk as her sobs turn to hiccups.

Lifting the child to my shoulder, I kiss her flushed cheek. She rests her head on my shoulder, turning both Jet and me to putty. Our simultaneous "Aww"s make us laugh at ourselves, but it's a laughter borne out of relief. The silence is our reward for a job sort-of-well-done.

"She looks good on you," Jet says, stroking the baby's fine hair in the same way you'd pet a dog or cat you're worried might turn on you and bite you at any second.

"She's a person, not an accessory."

"Still, you look so motherly. It's hot."

"Shhh. Don't make me laugh."

"Like, if it wasn't so wrong getting horny around a kid, I'd be totally turned on right now."

"The fact that 'motherly' is hot to you might be something you want to explore with a therapist."

"C'mon, Baby. Don't turn it into something perverted."

"Don't call me 'Baby' when I'm holding a baby. I don't know which one of us you're talking to."

He snickers.

"In fact, don't call me 'Baby' at all. You know how much I hate it."

"You hate how much you love it, you mean?"

"You are so lucky my hands are full and I can't raise my voice."

"The madder you get, the harder I get."

"That's twisted, too."

He covers his mouth to stifle his laughter.

"You wake up this kid, and you can forget getting laid for the rest of your life, Jet Knox."

His sparkling eyes betray his frown when he rises and says, "Now, that's serious. I'm gonna go find something quiet to do until Little Miss Priss goes home."

"You can't leave me here alone with her," I hiss as he limps toward the basement stairs.

He merely chuckles.

"And no working out without a spotter!"

Nagging in a whisper is highly ineffective.

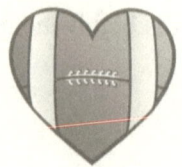

FIFTEEN

NEGOTIATIONS

That was two months ago, and I still have nightmares about it. Sometimes in these dreams, Jet and I wind up using the baby as a football and take her out to the backyard to toss her around until she stops crying. Other times, she multiplies into more and more crying babies every few minutes, the longer we can't figure out how to calm her.

Everyone says, "It's different when they're yours." Is it? Explain infanticide. Explain shaken babies. Explain men and women running away from their lives and disappearing into the Crazy Parent Protection Program.

I get that I don't love Meleah or Mikey or Gracie to the extent their parents do and that biology plays a huge role in unconditional love. (I guess? I have no idea what I'm talking about.) But I do love those kids, and I'd die for them or—less drastically—raise any of them as my own if something happened to their parents.

Please, God, don't let anything happen to those people. Begging.

Love only takes you so far, though. You can love someone to your core and still be driven mad by the things they do. I don't want to be driven mad. Not yet. I want to live a sane, happy life first. Madness can wait.

Fortunately, Jet's in perfect agreement with me. After each babysitting gig, he half-jokes, "Thank God we get to send them home," but after our first encounter with separation anxiety and teething screams, there was no amusement in his voice when he said, "I'd have surgery every day if it meant never having to go through that again."

He may not have been laughing, but it made me chuckle. You'd think someone who regularly works in a venue that boasts having the loudest crowd in the NFL would be able to tune out any noise. Guess not.

When I pointed out the inconsistency, he said, "Crowd noise fades into the background after a while. Even when fans are screaming, they're screaming together, and they're enjoying themselves. But what's so horrible about a crying baby is that it's one person, and she's suffering. And after you've tried everything you know to do, you realize there's nothing you *can* do about it. The helplessness is the worst."

"The suffering baby isn't the worst?"

He shot me a dirty look. "She won't remember it. But that sound will haunt my dreams."

Good. I hope he doesn't forget it anytime soon. It needs to inform our decisions. We both need a whole lot more patience —and I'll need a good meditation technique—before we'll be able to handle daily what we experienced that night with Meleah. And *we* definitely won't be adding to the world population anytime soon. For now, sex will stay firmly in the "for fun" column, where it belongs.

Jet props himself against a mountain of pillows, huffing and puffing and nickering like a contented horse. I laugh at the equine symphony while I smooth down my hair and snuggle into his warm flank.

"Man, that was awesome," Jet says.

"Wasn't it, though?"

"Yeah, but it's lame to sit here and brag about it, isn't it?"

I twirl the wispy hairs trailing down his tummy. "As long as we keep it between the two of us, it's okay." I yawn.

"You fallin' asleep on me?"

"Mmmm. Maybe."

"Don't make me tickle you."

I groan. "I'm tired. How come when you want to roll over and pass out, it's okay, but when I'm sleepy, you get all chatty?"

"I could win a Super Bowl right now."

"I could sleep for the rest of the weekend."

"Aw, c'mon. That's no fun. Wait! I know!" He moves to sit up.

"What? Hey! Stay still!"

He ignores my pleas and gently pushes against me. "Let's go swimming."

Wrapping my arms around his torso to keep him in bed and acting as my pillow, I say with my lips against his ribs, "No!"

"Yes! Skinny dipping is awesome."

"An awesome show for Jake. I swear, you enjoy parading in front of him."

"He's not home this weekend."

"He's not?"

"No. You really need to pay better attention to stuff."

Instead of defending my lack of awareness, I stick to the original argument. "It's too cold at night in April to swim, much less swim naked."

"The pool is a heavenly eighty-five degrees."

"You gotta get from the house to the pool. And back again, wet, when you're done. No thanks."

"Maura!" He scoots away from me.

"Jet!" I prop myself on my elbow, wide awake now and excited at the prospect. But it's more fun to make him think otherwise. And anyway, I'm never going to win the inevitable race downstairs if he's ready for me to make a run for it. Those knees of his are almost game-ready, thanks to his tireless rehab and sheer will.

He perches on the side of the bed. "Maybe I'll go out there by myself, then."

"Knock yourself out." I giggle. "No, don't. No more concussions."

"Har-har-har."

While he pouts with his back to me, I slide by inches toward the opposite edge of the mattress, closest to the door, keeping my face pointed at him, so he doesn't hear a change in my voice. "Only you would want to leave a perfectly warm, cozy bed to go swimming in the middle of the night." My foot lands on carpeting, and I sink to my knees on the floor, my chin right at mattress level. My tummy flutters as I anticipate breaking for the door.

Suddenly, Jet's head whips around. Eyes twinkling, grin flashing, he yells, "I knew it!" and streaks, naked, across the room. I follow him down the hall at a sprint, then have to slow down and hold a breast in each hand as I scamper down the stairs behind him.

"Ow, ow, ow."

"Last one in's a Raiders' fan!" He skips the last two steps and nearly lands in the living room with his mighty leap.

"Hey! Watch those knees!"

"You're not gonna catch me."

Sure enough, I'm still navigating the living room and its furniture as he crashes through the back door, cackling gleefully across the patio and launching himself into the saltwater pool with an ill-conceived, sloppy dive that doesn't quite make it to head-first.

I choose a more dainty entrance into the water—only slightly—by performing what I like to think is a cute cannonball. My naked skin barely has time to register the chilly spring night before warm, velvety water engulfs me. I swim to the surface and toward Jet's wavy figure.

He moans.

"What happened? Did you hurt yourself jumping off the stairs?"

Pinching water from his eyes, he rolls them at me and spouts into my face. "No. I busted my junk on that belly flop."

I laugh and splash him. "Serves you right. And stop spitting on me!"

"I need a hug. That'll make it better."

He pulls me to him, and I bob for a while in his arms, then wrap my legs around his waist.

Before he can make a joke—or I lose my nerve—I push a wet lock of hair from his forehead and say, "Contract negotiations."

He blinks. "What about them?"

I've exhibited great discipline by not bringing it up since our conversation on Valentine's Day. I can't resist any longer. My life is on hold as much as his is—if not more so—until he signs on that line.

"How's it going?" I press.

"Fine, I guess."

"You guess?"

He traces a drop of water down my shoulder into the water, between my breasts. "Slow."

"Isn't that normal, though?"

His eyes return to mine but quickly dart to a spot somewhere behind me, in the direction of the dormant, covered outdoor kitchen. "I don't know. Seems to me when you have a player who's committed himself to being the franchise quarterback you've claimed to always want, and he brings home the Lombardi trophy—busting his ass in the process—it should be a no-brainer to re-sign the guy."

"I agree. Then what's the hold-up? Are you asking for too much money?"

"My agent doesn't think so."

I laugh. "Well, Tom would ask for your own private jet for away games, if you let him."

"I gave him a figure that he told me was insulting and—what did he say?—'displayed a shocking lack of self-respect,' but it's more than what I made before. And I may look and sound dumb, but I understand the salary cap, and to be honest, I'd be okay with the team spending as much as it can on an O-line that can protect me. And my knees."

"Hear, hear!"

"But even the crappiest employee still gets a three percent raise once a year or so, right?"

Thinking back on my own experience, I have to admit, "Yeah. Usually."

"That's about all I was asking for."

I laugh. "But three percent of your salary is huge."

"I get that."

"They countered, then?"

"No. They still haven't said anything. It's like they're sitting on it so that when they finally do get back to me, they can offer me anything, and I'll take it, because I've had so much time to stress about being dropped."

"They're not going to drop you."

"They're looking toward the future, right? Like they have to. And what am I?"

"Still young. And still playing at the top of your game. And now you have like-new knees."

He snorts. "Yeah. We'll see how that goes. We can't do shit this early in off-season training, so I haven't had a chance to test my scrambling or sprint speed."

"You were pretty fast, just now. If I didn't know better, and someone told me you'd had surgery on both those knees two months ago, I'd accuse them of lying."

"They feel good. I mean, still not a hundred percent when it comes to what I'll need them to be able to do on the field, but they don't hurt all the time anymore. That's huge." He shifts his hands from around my waist to under my bottom, most likely in a bid to distract me as his fingertips brush against my inner thighs. "I was worried there for a while."

"You were? You hardly ever complained, and you acted like the surgery was an overreaction."

He tries to kiss me, but I dodge my head sideways, waiting to hear his response.

"Maybe I downplayed it all because I was freaked out. Like, your mind starts to go to bad places when you're in pain all the time."

"I'm sure. So…" I stare at the pulse in his throat. "…are you downplaying this whole contract thing with me, not talking about it, because you're freaked out?"

Staring hungrily at my lips, he says, "Nah. Tom tells me to be cool, to not let them psych me out with their head games. Anyway, I'd play here for next to nothin'."

"Shhh!" I cover his mouth. "Don't let anyone hear you say that!"

He laughs and tosses his head to free it from my grip. "You sound like Tom. It's true, though. I love this city. The fans are great. And this is our home."

"The only one I've ever known."

"They've got me. And they know it. Because I've never been shy about saying how much we love it here. It's not in my nature to be aloof."

I grin at his use of such an old-fashioned word.

"What?" he asks, swiping at his nose. "Do I have a booger?"

"No." I tighten my legs around him and kiss his chin. "I was thinking about how adorably un-aloof you are."

"It's mean to make people wonder where they stand with you."

"I agree." I peck his mouth, then place a series of lengthening kisses there and notice with smug satisfaction a twitching against me below the surface of the water.

He beams. "Oh, hey! Lookit here. I'm magically recovered from my injury."

"Junk is resilient."

"It sure is!"

―――――――

The blue glow from the pool competes with the stars above us as we hunker against each other, wrapped in a huge, puffy quilt, back to front, on a lounger. Nestled between Jet's legs, I close my eyes and inhale the scent of our salty skin. It transports me back to summers of my youth, hanging out at the beach on family vacations and hoping to catch a glimpse of that lifeguard I had a crush on. What was his name? I can't remember. Maybe I never knew. He never gave me a second glance. Probably wouldn't have, even if I'd been drowning. Beanpoles like me were never the first choice of young guys who had yet to hit their final growth spurts. It was emasculating to have to look up to a girl, or some such nonsense.

It wasn't until I was well into college that I dated anyone as tall as I am. And Jet was the first man I ever had to look up to.

Not having heard a peep from that tall guy in several minutes, I tilt my head back against his chest to get a look at him. His eyes are closed, and his lips are slightly parted. I stare at his stubbled jaw and the line of his nose (more like up his nostrils) and mouth and chin. He licks his lips occasionally, signifying he's awake... barely. After a few minutes of silence, I say, "Do you ever feel like you're not a real person?"

He lifts his head off the back of the chair and blinks blearily at me. "Huh?"

"Like, do you ever wonder if what you're experiencing and perceiving as life is a dream sequence, that it couldn't possibly be real, because if your life is real, that means there are hundreds of billions of other lives happening simultaneously, as well? And countless more that have already happened. How can that be possible? How can this planet sustain that many storylines? But you have to believe it's real, because how else do you explain it? Therefore, the only way you can prove your existence is by doing something to justify it, by making an impact on other people so that your storyline intertwines with as many other people's storylines and becomes so... so enmeshed that if you were to be erased from existence, other people's stories would no longer make sense."

Rubbing his jaw, he widens his eyes at me. "Uh, no. I can

honestly say I've never thought that. Have you been listening to TEDTalks in the car again?"

"If you must know, it was a podcast a couple of weeks ago. Some quantum physicists were discussing perceived reality, and I can't stop thinking about it."

"They said all that stuff, though?"

"No. They discussed concepts I could barely follow, but the part I did understand basically amounted to this: 'If a tree falls in the forest and nobody is around to hear or see it, does it really happen?'"

He scoffs. "I've never understood that question. Of course, it happens."

"Prove it."

"Well, it's on the ground, and trees don't start out that way, so it had to have fallen at some point."

"Right. But when? Why? What impact did it have on the other trees or the wildlife? If it can't be documented, then how can we be sure? And what if nobody ever sees this tree, upright or fallen? Does it exist at all? Is our existence completely dependent on being seen and having an effect on the world?"

He laugh-sobs. "It's too late to think about stuff this deep. Let's go back upstairs to bed."

Neither of us moves.

Lowering my voice to barely above a whisper, I say, "Sometimes I feel like we're all starring in our own movies. Movies that nobody will watch. And if nobody watches them, then what's the point?"

Jet laughs. "I think it's scarier to imagine that people *are* watching. Think of the things you do when you're alone. What if it turned out a bunch of people saw you do those things?" He shivers.

"What have *you* been doing when you're alone?"

"Nothing too crazy. But even everyday things we all do would be embarrassing for the whole world to see." After a slight hesitation, he confesses, "I fed one of my boogers to Torzi the other day."

"Jet!"

He laughs at my horror. "I wanted to see if he'd eat it. He did."

"I can't believe you. That is so disgusting! And mean."

"I gave him a biscuit right away, because I felt bad."

"Please stop talking about it."

"All right." He arches into a stretch, pressing his warm belly more firmly against my back. "Seriously, though. We need to get back to bed."

I'm fully uncooperative while he disentangles himself from me and rises from the lounger, taking the quilt with him. Without his support, I flop naked onto my back on the chair, then gaze up at him.

He laughs down at me and extends a hand. "Come on, my little philosopher."

Goosebumps forming all over my body, I allow him to pull me to a standing position and wrap the blanket around both of us for the walk inside.

Torzi, the literal booger-muncher, greets us inside the back door, like a ticked-off parent scolding a couple of kids breaking curfew. The three of us silently plod upstairs to bed.

SIXTEEN

BABYSITTING

The doorbell rings much too soon afterward. My eyes fly open, but I don't move. Jet blissfully snores on. I poke him in the ribs. The bell sounds again.

"Shit," I hiss.

Jet rolls over, pulling all of the covers with him, and grumbles into his pillow, "I'm naked."

"So am I!" I say, shivering and exposed.

"My balls hurt."

"That's not a legitimate reason to not answer the door!" I flounce from the bed, grabbing my robe from the bathroom door and swinging it around my shoulders. While I tie the belt, he cracks an eye at me and grins.

"You're a shit," I say, nevertheless returning his smile. "What if it's a door-to-door murderer?"

The doorbell rings again, followed by insistent knocking. Jet's phone buzzes on his nightstand. He grouches and rises on his elbows to grasp the device and check the notification from his security system app. I peep over his shoulder. Cyndi and Colin, kids in tow, wave at the camera.

"It's my sister," he announces, collapsing into his pillow again.

"Your sister? What's she...? Oh, shit!"

"And the word of the day, children, is..."

I swat his back, then rush to the door. "Shut up. Get up. We promised Colin and Cyndi a kid-free day."

"Why'd we do that?"

Probably because we thought they'd never take us up on it. But I say out loud, "Because we're nice. We scheduled this weeks ago, remember?"

"Vaguely. But remembering things isn't my thing."

I thunder down the stairs and do a final check of my robe to make sure everything's covered before pulling wide the front door. "Hey, guys!"

Cyndi looks me up and down. "Hey, yourself. Uh, did we catch you at a bad time?"

I smile sheepishly. "No. We overslept, that's all. Come in!"

Mikey pushes through the obstacle course of adult legs in the entryway and bolts for the stairs. "Hey, Mo-Mo. Where's Uncle Jet?"

"He's, uh, upstairs. He'll be down in a—"

But the three-year-old is already gone. I take a step toward the stairs but stop and shrug. Whatever. A few seconds later, we hear, "Whoa! Mikey! Where'd you come from?"

I turn back to my other three guests with a shaky smile that drops off my face when Cyndi plunks a seven-month-old into my unprepared arms and loops a massive diaper bag onto my shoulder.

"Everything you need is in the bag."

"And then some," Colin mutters.

Cyndi sticks out her tongue at him but says to me, "I

realize you're not as equipped here as you are when you babysit at our place."

"No, this is fine. This is good. Everything will be fine," I reassure the two of them over Gracie's fuzzy head. "We'll figure it out."

"Of course, you will." Cyndi pecks her daughter on the temple one last time and submits to Colin's hand-pulling.

As they edge away, I say, "You'll be back...?"

He shrugs. "Two? Three? You can reach us on our mobiles."

"Okay. Yeah. Whenever. But before dinner, right?"

"Definitely," Cyndi answers. "I didn't pack enough food for Gracie to eat dinner here, so you're safe."

My nervous chuckle chases them more quickly toward the door.

Mikey appears at the top of the stairs and yells into the echoing foyer, "Uncle Jet was nakey in bed!"

Colin laughs at my wince. "I say! We assumed it went without saying that today's activities—here, at least—weren't 'pants optional.'"

"Bye, guys! Have a good time!"

"Oh, we shall." He wiggles his eyebrows at me over his shoulder as he and Cyndi practically jog to her car.

I close the door and rest my back against it. "Buh-rother," I say before Gracie grabs a fistful of my salt-stiffened hair and yanks my head at an unnatural angle. "Ow!"

Mikey threads his legs through the spindles on the uppermost landing's banister. "I'm gonna wait for Uncle Jet."

"Why don't you come downstairs, and I'll make you breakfast?" I suggest instead.

He shakes his head. "Nah. I pwomised I'd wait right here." Wrapping his hands around the wrought iron bars, he pushes his face through the gap between two of them and swings his legs. "He said he'd be out 'in a minute.'"

Before I have a chance to wonder whether this is a football minute (including timeouts and clock stoppages) or an actual minute, Jet appears, ripping his nephew from his perch and swinging him, giggling, onto his shoulders for the commute downstairs.

"This little turd burglar got more than he bargained for, barging into our room without knocking."

I pry my hair from Gracie's fist and lead the way through the living room, where I dump the diaper bag onto the first couch I pass. "Serves you right for not getting up and putting on some clothes to answer the door."

Through his giggles, Mikey says, "I not a turd booger. Hey, Mo-Mo. I saw Uncle Jet's dingle. It's a biiiig dingle!"

I stumble and nearly drop the baby, but as I right myself, I laugh and say, "Well, I'm glad you chose not to mention that when your mom and Geezer were still here."

"I saw Geezer's dingle, too, in the baffroom. When am I gonna get a big dingle?"

"When you're older," I say simply, then add, "It grows with the rest of you," in case he thinks it's going to arrive under the tree one Christmas in the future.

Jet clears his throat and squeezes Mikey's legs. "Hey, little dude, why don't we talk about something else?"

"Why? I like dingles."

"I do, too," I say, earning a dirty look from Jet while I dig the portable high chair from a mudroom cabinet.

"They're great," Jet says agreeably while setting Mikey onto a stool at the island, "but it's weird to talk about all the ones you've seen."

"It would take Uncle Jet all day to do that," I choke out.

"Mo-Mo needs to shut up."

"Ummm! Uncle Jet, that's a bad word!"

"No, it's not. What do you want for breakfast?"

"I ate breffkist at home."

"Oh, so you don't want anything?"

"Yeah."

"You do want something?"

"No. I tol' you, I already ated."

Jet reels toward the coffeemaker, which I miraculously remembered to set last night to auto-brew. "I need coffee before I deal anymore with this kid."

"Pour me a cup, too, please," I say, struggling with my one free hand to strap and clip the booster to the chair next to Mikey's. I could let go of Gracie altogether, considering she has a death grip on my hair again, but knowing my luck, she'd let go at the same time, and I hear it's bad form to drop babies, especially when they don't belong to you. Finally, I'm forced to admit defeat. "A little help here?"

Jet turns with two steaming mugs and sets them down on the counter in front of Mikey, who rises on his knees to see into them and says, "That smells like butt."

"Well, I'm not offering any to you, so..." Jet bends over and snaps the plastic buckles together behind and underneath the chair, then tightens the nylon straps so hard I worry he's going to bend the metal bars on the chair's back.

"Easy, big guy."

"I want to make sure it's not going to fall."

"During an earthquake or hurricane?" I secure Gracie in the seat and scoot her up to the counter so she can slap the surface.

He snatches his mug from under Mikey's nose and slurps

his first sip. Then he asks, "What're we gonna do with these two all day?"

"We don't have to *do* anything, do we? We can just hang out."

"Bo-ring."

"Bo-ring!" Mikey parrots his hero.

"Cyndi didn't leave their car seats, so we're stuck here."

"The Hummer has car seats in it."

"Ugh. Not that tank."

"I wanna drive the tank!"

Jet ignores Mikey but says to me, "We can move the seats to a different car. Duh."

"And go where? Honestly, I'm not in the mood to wrangle two kids out in public. It's always such a spectacle."

Understatement of the year. In addition to the usual autograph-requesters and selfie-seekers, people come up to us and ask us if the kids are ours, and when we explain we're babysitting, they ask us when we'll have our own. Then, when they finally do wander off, they still stare at us, so every bone-headed mistake we make, which are many, considering what amateurs we are, is on display.

"It's supposed to be warm today. Let's hang out at the pool and have a picnic lunch in the pirate ship." I toss out desperately, knowing how much Mikey loves the huge play sets in the backyard.

Jet raises an eyebrow over his coffee at Mikey, seeking his approval. Mikey shrugs. "Ahright."

"Then what?" Jet asks me.

"Then N-A-P-S."

"What's enn-ay-pee-ess?" Mikey asks, looking from Jet to me and back again.

Jet avoids his nephew's eyes by focusing on the lowering

level of black liquid in his cup and mutters, "A super-fun game we're *all* going to play later." To underscore that, he yawns. Then, before Mikey can press him for more details, he rests his huge palm on top of Gracie's head and leans around to see the seven-month-old's reaction to the contact. She grins and drools up at him and kicks her feet. "You make a good hand rest, Gracie darlin'. Anyone ever told you that?"

She squeals her response.

"Well, you do."

I smile wearily at the two of them over the rim of my mug, then ask, "So did we decide what's for breakfast?"

"Pancakes!" Mikey shouts.

"You said you weren't hungry," Jet reminds him.

"I changed up my mind."

It's going to be a long day.

———

It *was* a long day. And the last thing I want to hear at the end of it is, "We need to go to California for Mother's Day."

"What? No! Why?"

Jet chuckles at my horrified, immediate reaction as he loads an impossible amount of plasticware into the dishwasher after his niece and nephew's departure. "Because."

"That's not a reason."

"Everyone's going to be there this year."

"If everyone else jumped off a—"

"Maura. C'mon. Even Cyndi agrees we're overdue for a visit to the Left Coast."

"She would. Send us as her emissary and—"

"She's coming, too. And Colin. And the kids." He closes the dishwasher and dries his hand on a towel that he then throws with impeccable form in the general direction of the laundry room door.

I collapse onto the counter and bury my face in my arms. "Why, though?"

He leans over and, rubbing my shoulders, says near my ear, "Because it's the right thing to do. It's the nice thing to do. And if we don't go, it'll look bad."

"Jet, please." I straighten and blink up at him, finding myself humiliatingly on the verge of tears. "Don't make me go."

His jaw tightens, but he says, "Fine. I can't make you, obviously."

"Thank you." I sniff.

"It'll be really weird, and her feelings will be hurt, so that will kind of ruin it for the rest of us, but if you're that against it…"

"Tell her I'm spending the weekend with my own mother."

"In Botswana? Sounds legit."

I bite my lower lip. "They know my parents are in Botswana?"

"Yep. Your mom sends them postcards."

"Damn." I tap my finger against my lip. "We could say I'm sick."

"Which will end one of two ways: she'll register us for baby stuff, *or* she'll research hospitals, convinced you have something seriously wrong with you, because you're *always* 'sick' when she's around."

"Oh, come on."

"It took everything I had to get her to stop Googling 'brain tumors' when you kept disappearing with your 'headaches' last fall."

I rub my temples, feeling one coming on now. "Fine. I'll go."

"It'll be fun."

"Liar."

"The weather's going to be awesome. We're going to cook out, maybe go hiking, fly kites on the beach…"

"Are we hanging out with your mom at all?"

He laughs. "Yes! It's Mother's Day."

"None of those things sound like Gloria's jam."

"Mom's game for anything when we're all together."

"*Everyone's* going to be there?"

"For the weekend, yes."

The last time we attempted that, Jet and I wound up sleeping on an inflatable mattress with a slow leak and found ourselves on the floor with two farting Great Danes halfway through the night. And when we tried to decamp to a hotel for the rest of our stay, Gloria turned on the waterworks and begged us not to "break up the family." Then she made Keith and Lucy trade places with us and blamed it on "Maura's sensitive back." Mortifying.

"We're going to fly all the way out there for a weekend?"

He snorts. "Hell no. Everyone else has to leave Monday morning, but we're going to stay the week."

This keeps getting better and better.

Resigned to making the trip but wanting to get at least one demand in, I stipulate, "We're sleeping at a hotel. No arguments."

"Uh, sure."

"Jet…" The warning in my tone conveys my seriousness.

He smiles. "Yeah, you're right. It's the easiest thing. I'll make the reservations, and it'll be a done deal before we touch down."

"Thank you."

"Come here." He opens his arms, and I walk into them, trying not to wonder what that damp, sour-smelling spot on his shoulder might be against my forehead.

"You're mean, springing this on me when I'm so exhausted after watching Mikey and Gracie all day."

He squeezes me. "I'm not 'springing it on you.' Cyndi and I *just* talked about it in the driveway while I was helping her and Colin get the kids in the car. I came in here and told you right away, because you'd be mad if I waited too long to tell you. Yet another no-win situation."

"You make me sound so unreasonable. I used to be easygoing, you know? It wasn't until I met you that I became this neurotic weirdo."

"You say that, but..."

I look up at him through narrowed eyes. "What?"

"Seems like I'm your scapegoat."

Pushing away from him, I cross the room, bending to retrieve his tossed towel and taking it into the mudroom. Our wet beach towels lie in a heap in the middle of the tile floor. I scoop them up and dump them into the washing machine with the dishrag. While I pour detergent into the dispenser, close the door, and press the buttons to start the machine, Jet appears in the doorway, his hands reaching up to the frame and grabbing it. His stretched pose and raised t-shirt afford me a glimpse of a good portion of his abs, which I work mightily to ignore.

"Anyway, you hate being part of the nitty-gritty decision-making. Don't you always say, 'Let me know what you decide, and I'll be there'?"

It's true that strategizing used to be the bane of my existence. I played everything by ear. The big, the small, the substantive, and the inconsequential were all the same to me. I never met a plan I liked. They're tedious and never turn out the way you envision, anyway, so it's silly to spend the energy and brainpower devising them. But that was when I was in control of every decision I made—or chose not to make. Now I have zero control over anything not related to my own reproductive system. That's an extremely small sphere of oversight.

I stare down at the gleaming white enamel of the washer and say, "It would have been nice to have been included in the conversation, that's all."

"You were inside! And I tossed it out there, like, 'Hey, why don't we go to California and surprise Mom for Mother's Day?' Cyndi and Colin ran with it. It wasn't like, 'Now that Maura's not here, let's plot.'"

"It was your idea?"

He releases the door frame. "If you want to know the truth, I figured Cyndi would be dead set against it, and she'd talk me out of it, but I'd still get credit for the thought."

"Well, that backfired."

He laughs. "Yeah. I guess they've been looking for an excuse to get out of town for a couple of days. And Colin's never been to Mom and Dad's, so..."

Oh, gosh. Better yet. Colin's inaugural visit to the mother ship.

"When do we leave?"

SEVENTEEN

OUTSIDERS

Gloria's still talking in a register three octaves higher than her normal voice, euphoric from the surprise of us—well, let's face it, *Jet*—walking through her front door. Nearly an hour later, the kids have been dismissed to play upstairs in one of the guest rooms, and the adults have found roosting places around the large, high-ceilinged living area. Gloria holds court in her oversized chair that's a hair smaller than a love seat, with Gracie nestled in her lap, two enormous dogs at her feet, and Jet perched at her right elbow.

The excitement is finally dying down, so my guard goes up. Jet quickly diffuses the first bomb, sleeping arrangements, much to Lucy and Keith's obvious relief. When Gloria tries to argue there's plenty of room for everyone—lies! All lies—Jet simply says, "Ma, we've already checked into the resort. It's settled. But we'll only go there to sleep. I promise we'll be here bright and early every morning, and we'll stay late."

"No, you won't," she chides, but with a smile. "Oh, I don't care. You're here! I'm so happy!" To my utter astonishment, she reaches up and pinches his cheek.

Standing near the windows with Colin, I glance to my right to exchange an incredulous look with him, relieved I'm no longer the newest outsider and that we have each other to help us endure times like these. He's too busy surveying his surroundings, though, to catch my non-verbal message.

Not that I blame him. The house *is* magnificent. Not imposing and massive like Fort Knox, but open, bright, airy, and impressive in its own right. Its floor-to-ceiling windows afford a one-hundred-eighty-degree view of its surroundings—mostly palm trees and a peek of the ocean a couple of blocks away—and its open layout is much more conducive to entertaining than our place is.

It's also worth a lot more per square foot than our house. While a quarter of the size, it's valued about the same. I know this, because I opened the real estate tax statement with the rest of the mail last December without realizing what it was. I would have felt bad about that, but I was too busy chasing my eyeballs across the mudroom floor after they'd dropped from their sockets at the figure on the paper in my hands. I also realized that I, technically, own this place now, so I suppose I have a right to know how much it's worth and how much we pay in taxes on it each year.

It was probably better that I didn't know. Now, every time we're here, I look around and think, *Holy crap. This house is costing us a fortune to maintain.*

If I were a different kind of person, I'd hold that over Gloria's head every chance I got. But I prefer to try to forget it's even true. Maybe I should start using it as leverage. *"Be nice, or we'll sell your house."*

I lean over and whisper to Colin, "Crazy, huh?"

"It's so Californian."

"Right?"

"The pink stucco, the floor-to-ceiling windows, the terra cotta tile roof And that back garden... er, that is, yard."

"It's pretty tiny."

"But what there is of it that's not covered by swimming pool is the greenest grass I've ever seen. It's like a carpet. Isn't there a drought on?"

"Rich people don't sacrifice their lawns. Brown grass—or pebbles—are for the plebs."

"Where do the dogs do their business?"

"They walk Ned multiple times per day."

"Explains his svelte build."

"They also have a climate-controlled pen around the side of the house that's nicer than my first house."

"The house I currently live in?"

"That'd be the one."

"Pampered pooches."

"Gloria needed something to spoil after all of her kids left home."

"That was ages ago, though. Those dogs don't look that old."

"They're her second set of 'Laurel and Hardy's."

"Which is which? When you call one, they both come."

"I have no idea."

"And she gave them the same name as a now-dead pair from before?"

"Yeppers. Like mascots. They have Roman numeral twos after their names on their papers, but—"

"Oh, they're registered?"

"Of course. Would you expect anything less?"

"What are you two whispering about over there?" Gloria asks, still smiling but having switched from her natural, genuinely happy expression to the pained, forced one she points so often my way.

Before I can answer, Colin says, "I was simply remarking to Lady Maura how beautiful your home is, how beautiful this whole area is."

She raises an eyebrow. "'Lady Maura'?"

Jet's siblings laugh too.

I blush and shrug. "A silly nickname."

"We had no idea we were in the presence of royalty," Keith says, mimicking a tea-drinker, extended pinkie and all.

Gidget snorts. "Knock it off, everyone. We still have to be nice to Colin, because he's new."

"Oh, don't act differently on my account."

"Damn!" David says. "That's the most polite way I've ever been scorched."

In the car on the way here, the four of us discussed the "game plan," what we would do when—not if—uncomfortable topics arose. When everyone's picking on Jet and me about babies, Cyndi and Colin are supposed to drag out cute stories about Mikey and Gracie. When everyone's picking on Cyndi and Colin about marriage, Jet's supposed to bring up the NFL draft, which is going on this weekend. But by some weird oversight, we failed to practice this most likely scenario: everyone picking on Colin and me. How dumb could we be?

Now, I appeal to Jet with widened eyes, begging him to say something distracting, but it's like he's scrambling with the playbook in his head, wishing he had one of those wrist cheat-sheets some quarterbacks use.

Cyndi's the first to recover and improvise. "Oh, my gosh. You guys. You won't believe what Mikey said this morning when we were getting ready to leave for the airport. It was early, and he was so tired—"

Gloria waves a hand at her youngest child to silence her. "I keep forgetting that you two go way back," she says to us newbs. "In fact, Maura, we have you to thank for introducing Colin to Cyndi, isn't that right?"

"Uh, yes. I guess so. He was Jet's friend too by then, though."

"And Mikey's friend," Jet chimes in, finally getting his conversational act together. "Cyndi was still pretty sick when Maura and I went to Belize to—" Too late, he realizes that sentence is a colossal mistake.

"When you and Maura *eloped*, leaving the rest of us to make your excuses to three hundred expected guests?" Gloria finishes.

He looks down at his hands. "Yeah, that."

I clear my throat. "Colin stepped up and made sure everything was okay with Cyndi and Mikey while we were gone."

Colin shrugged. "Simply did what any friend would do."

Keith chuckles. "Oh, I don't know. You did more than I'm willing to do for *my* friends."

From his chair in the corner, Ned's voice cuts through the raucous laughter. "Anyway! We're glad it worked out the way it did, and we're glad that you and Cyndi are happy."

For the first—and hopefully last—time ever, I have the urge to French kiss my father-in-law.

Since nobody could contradict him without looking like a major jerk, his classy statement serves as the final word on the topic (for now), and everyone tunes into Cyndi's cute Mikey story.

No longer scrutinized, Colin and I turn our backs to the room and pretend to gaze out at the pool and yard.

"Blimey. I forgot how intense they all are when they're together. It's brutal," he whispers.

"Pack mentality," I hiss back.

"They despise me."

"Nah. If they hated you, they'd be nice to you. The number one Knox family pastime: teasing. Nobody's safe. And the person who gets teased the most is the most-loved. Jet's usually the focus."

"Gloria didn't sound like she was teasing."

"Oh, no. She's absolutely serious. She tries to camouflage it with the rest of the good-natured jabs, but her comments are the real deal."

"She scares me."

"Because you're smart."

"I'm starting to think agreeing to come here this weekend is evidence to the contrary."

"At least we have each other."

"We have, haven't we?"

I'd wrap my arm around his shoulders, but I don't want to draw attention to us with any unnecessary movement, so I simply reply, "Absolutely. I've got your back, homey."

"Ditto."

———

In Gloria's house, we observe strict divisions of labor. Most hearken back to simpler (a.k.a. more misogynistic) times, when women cooked and cleaned and men were allowed to be boys—with one slightly more modern exception: the men are in charge of the kids. "They're still a bunch of kids at heart, anyway," Gloria says wryly with more pride than regret.

If you have a vagina, you *will* spend most of your time in the kitchen, because we can't trust the guys to provide fifteen thousand calories per person all day long. If you have a penis, you better like kids and the outdoors, because someone needs to take those crazy children into the backyard and wear them out. And you don't try to buck this system. Private parts dictate roles. Period.

Personally, I'm not a fan of kitchens *or* the outdoors, so either way, my genitalia does me no favors. (Story of my life.) If I were allowed to choose, however, between hanging out in the kitchen with Gloria and overseeing the chaos in the backyard with Jet, I'd pick the latter every time. Since "choice" isn't a concept my mother-in-law understands too well, I go where I'm sorted, based on what's in my underwear. And if any of my sisters-in-law feel the same way I do, they do a great job of hiding it. In fact, they act like this arrangement is thoroughly progressive, because it forces the men to change a diaper once in a while.

The only one who seems as uncertain about the situation as I am is Cyndi, who keeps stealing sly glances toward the windows looking out onto the post-dinner touch football game in the backyard.

Every touchdown results in both teams—and dogs— jumping into the pool as part of their celebration. Gloria tuts and mutters about the "kids" wearing their clothes and shoes in the pool and how she's going to have to have it shocked, but she can't keep the smile from the corners of her mouth. Giving her the opportunity to complain and nag is better than any Mother's Day gift money could buy.

For the most part, I've remained silent, trying to evade notice. I tossed the salad for dinner, and now I'm wiping down counters as part of the cleanup effort. The only time I've spoken was to deflect attention when Tammy asked when Cyndi and Colin were going to "make it official," and nobody liked Cyndi's frank answer about not rushing to marry again.

Since Gloria seemed about to stroke out, I decided to sacrifice my own safety and wellbeing by changing the subject to something I knew would be too irresistible for Gloria to dismiss: Jet.

It started innocently enough with my updating everyone on his physical progress post-surgery. Then it got murkier when Gloria asked about his contract negotiations, and I didn't have any satisfactory answers for her. And now... Is it hot in here, or is it that huge spotlight shining in my eyes while everyone grills me?

In her lilting Texas drawl, Lucy says, "Things seem to be comin' together. Jet's knees are almost back to normal. As soon as those contract details are hammered down—and I'm sure they will be, Honey; everyone knows Jet Knox *is* that team—y'all'll be all settled in to start that big family Jet's always wanted."

Cyndi's too busy staring wistfully into the backyard to come to my rescue. Or maybe she's analyzing the lexical enigma that is "ya'll'll," not to mention the grammatical nightmare of that entire sentence. Lord knows I've diagrammed it five ways in an effort to distract myself from responding to it.

Gloria tosses some flatware into the dishwasher with a clang. "I'm beginning to think that's never going to happen, especially with this new movie theater idea you and Jet are kicking around. The point of you quitting your job was so that you'd have more time, fewer distractions!"

Gidget focuses her eyes on drying the hand-washed stockpot that wouldn't fit into the dishwasher but murmurs, "Oh, Mom. Patience."

I shred the antibacterial wipe in my hand. "We're just not ready."

The veteran mothers, Cyndi included, laugh at my naïveté. Then Lucy says, "Nobody's ever ready, Sugar. You gotta do it anyway."

"But we *don't* have to do it. Yet. Or ever."

Tammy, Gidget, and Lucy rush to toss out their objections to such a bold, controversial statement. They talk at once, over each other, to the point that I can only hear a few words here and there. Things like "Babies!" and "Precious!" and "Daddy!" and "Amazing!" I can connect the dots and get the idea, though.

Finally, they wind down, and Gidget gets the last word, the only full sentence I catch. "You'll change your mind."

With a heavy sigh, Gloria looks at each of the other women in turn. "Their decision, girls. Nothing we say is going to make any bit of difference, except to make them dig their heels in more. It's USC all over again."

Everyone nods knowingly, and I'm willing to stay in the dark as long as it ends this conversation, but Gloria helpfully explains, "Jet had his pick of any school in the country with a great football program, but he was determined to go to Southern California."

I feel the need to defend teenager Jet. "It's an amazing school!"

Gloria takes the dry stockpot from Gidget and walks it to the cabinet where it belongs. "Of course it is. Nobody's debating that now, and we weren't debating it then. But countless 'amazing schools' offered him full scholarships. 'Amazing schools' in more visible athletic conferences to showcase his abilities, which would have led to more media exposure and, ultimately, landed him the Heisman. And a higher Draft selection. You have to keep in mind that when he went to school, the SEC was the king of college football. The

PAC-12 wasn't what it is today. USC has always been an athletic giant, but the other teams in the conference haven't been as strong, so it diminished the school's accomplishments."

"Okay." Fortunately, she doesn't make me wait too long to bring it back around to why Pac-12 history has anything to do with our current decision to abstain from procreating.

"Jet was a California boy, though, and he wanted to stay here. There was no convincing him. We made the big mistake of questioning that. If we'd let him think about it for a while, he probably would have come to the conclusion on his own that accepting that offer from Alabama was smarter. But we pushed. And pushed. And it made him all the more determined to have his way. 'It's my turn to start making some of my own choices.' I told him he'd get to make all the choices he wanted once he had that Heisman and was the number one Draft pick in his class, but he was in a hurry to be emancipated."

Imagine that.

Gidget laughs. "I'd almost forgotten that. He was so mad at you guys. Rick and I were newlyweds, and Jet would crash on our couch in that one-bedroom apartment we had—you know, the one over the Thai place?—after you guys would have another one of your arguments, and Rick and I would be like, 'So much for any romantic plans *we* had this evening.'"

Lucy giggles. "Clueless then, clueless now."

Gloria shakes her head and frowns. "Cost him the Heisman, too, I'm convinced. I never did say, 'I told you so,' though."

"Who won the Heisman that year?" I ask the group at large. "Who was the number one Draft pick in Jet's class?" When nobody, including myself, can answer (although I'm sure Jet could readily supply both names), I nod. "Mmm-hmm. So, who cares?"

Gloria waves a dishtowel at me. "My point is, we've been here before, and we're not going to make the same mistake. You two want to make a silly, selfish decision that you'll live to regret? Have at it. You can make that decision in peace."

Not sure how to respond to such backhanded benevolence, I mutter, "Uh, well, thanks. I guess."

"You're automatically going to want to do the opposite of what I want, anyway, to spite me. Does it break my heart that my baby boy may never know the joys of fatherhood? Yes. But heartbreak is a big part of being a mother. Lord willing, you'll find that out for yourself one day."

I gotta say, she sure knows how to sell something. Battles of wills with teenagers; heartbreak… add in the dirty diapers, sleepless nights, and temper tantrums, and I can't sign on the dotted line fast enough. I bite back my sarcasm, though, and merely reply, "I might someday. But that's a private decision, so I'm glad you're willing to…"

…*butt out of it.*

…*mind your own damn business.*

…*trust us with our own lives.*

"…let us make it ourselves, in our own time."

More cheers and splashes erupt outside, and Gidget shakes her head. "Those guys are going to be a mess. Now that the kitchen's clean, I'm going to round up some towels and get everyone dried off before it gets dark and cold out there."

Tammy and Lucy agree that's the best plan of action and file behind their sister-in-law up the stairs.

Gloria edges past me and follows. "I'll help."

As soon as they're gone, I turn to Cyndi and glower.

"Thanks for the backup there. Did you use up all of your Mikey and Gracie stories earlier?"

She shrugs sheepishly. "Sorry. I was legitimately curious about your answer. I've been wondering for a while what the plan is, but I didn't want to be the one to ask."

"Well, now you know. We have no plan."

"I hate to say this, and this is a real first, but... I agree with Mom." Before I can object, she rushes on, "It makes me sad, because you guys would be phenomenal parents, and I think you'd love it. Believe it or not, you'd love it more than sleeping in on Saturdays and doing whatever you want to do."

"Not you too."

She snaps a wet dishtowel at me. "Hey, misery loves company."

I grab the wet cloth Gidget abandoned and snap back, leaving a welt on Cyndi's leg, right below the hemline of her shorts. Mouth open and incredulous, she looks down at the mark and back up at me.

My strike wasn't intentional, but I pretend it was and smirk while winding up for another shot. "You want a piece of me?"

Eyes narrowed, she chuckles ruefully. "Oh-ho. You're in trouble now. I missed you on purpose before."

"Bring it, small-fry. I used to punish Greg daily in towel fights."

"And I grew up with *three* older brothers. Prepare to beg for mercy."

That's not happening. I don't beg for anything from anyone.

EIGHTEEN

DOUBTS

Three hours later, at the hotel, Jet gasps while flopping into bed when he sees the backs of my legs. "Holy shit! What the hell happened?"

Next to the nightstand on my side of the mattress, I dab aloe onto the welts and say, "Never mind. A score that had to be settled between Cyndi and me."

"Those look like— Hang on. Are those *towel lashes*?" He scoots closer, reaches out, and gently fingers one of the smaller marks behind my knee.

"This is nothing. You should see her." Capping the gel, I nudge him over, gingerly slide under the covers, and turn off the lamp. On the way to my pillow, I lean over and kiss his stunned lips. "Goodnight."

"No, wait." He stretches to turn on the lamp closest to him.

I blink in the light, then laugh at the concern etched on his face. "It's not a big deal. It wasn't a *real* fight or anything."

He relaxes and grins. "Okay, then what was it about?"

"Do you have to know *everything*?"

Before he can answer, the murmuring on the other side of the wall—in Colin and Cyndi's room—changes to more distinct sounds of passion.

"No, but we have to keep talking to drown *that* out." For good measure, he also turns on the television and bumps up the volume.

I giggle. "Sounds like someone's taking advantage of a kid-free night. It was nice of your dad to offer keep Mikey and Gracie for them." Gloria would disagree—she was furious when Ned suggested it. That's probably what makes it all the sweeter, in my book.

He jabs at the volume button when a loud, "Ohhhh…!" from his sister bleeds through the wall. "Yeah. Dad has a heart of gold."

"Like father, like son."

Rather than respond to my compliment, he pulls his pillow around his head. "Do they have to be so loud?" He raises his fist and moves to thump the wall, but I grab it in time.

"Don't you dare."

He harrumphs but settles back under the covers and adjusts the angle of his head on his pillows so he can see the television while he channel surfs.

Since she's not my little sister, and I'd be lying if I said I never imagined what it would be like to have sex with Colin—before I ever met Jet, of course—the amorous noises next door don't bother me. In fact, if I'm being completely honest, they arouse me, and I'm a wee bit jealous of the fun they're having.

When my own eavesdropping starts to disturb me, I turn my attention to Jet, who's abandoned all pretense of conversation in favor of focusing on the ESPN *30 for 30* rerun I'm pretty sure he's already seen more than once about the 1983 NFL quarterback draft class. While the documentary waxes poetic about Elway, Marino, and Montana, I cuddle up to my husband, who drops a distracted arm around my shoulders and turns up the volume another few more notches. It's practically blaring now, and I worry we're going to be reported by another guest.

"Champ," I say softly, then repeat more loudly when he doesn't hear me the first time.

"Mmmph?" he grunts, his face red with concentration, his eyes glued to the screen.

I pluck the remote from his hand and, ignoring his protests, return the program to a more reasonable decibel level, then set the device on the bedside table nearest to me, where he'd have to work hard to reach it. "What are you doing?" he whines, finally looking at me.

"Distracting you," I reply, running my hand down his chest, under the covers, and over the front of his underwear. Nothing happens.

He swallows and says miserably, bobbing his head toward the wall, "I can't. Not with *that* going on."

"Oh, come on," I cajole, rubbing harder.

"Ow."

I stop and collapse onto my back. "Wow."

His chest smashing against my face, he reaches over me and regains possession of the remote. The volume goes back up, and he practically yells, "Sorry! It's just too distracting. And gross."

"How is it gross? They're two adults who love each other."

"What?!" He leans closer so I can repeat myself louder.

"NEVER MIND!"

I flounce onto my side, facing away from him, and make a big show of fluffing my pillow and burrowing under the covers. Still stewing several minutes later, I'm startled by the silence when Jet mutes the TV. He waits a few seconds to be sure of the all-clear, then sighs with relief and turns off the television, plunging us into darkness.

"Finally," he says, yanking at the covers. "I thought they'd never finish. Geez."

"You are such a child," I spit.

"If you heard Deirdre and your brother going at it, you'd feel the same way."

He has a point, but I'm not ready to concede it—ever. "Your reaction is what's childish."

"Are you pissed at me?" He scoots across the mattress, cups my shoulder, and tries to pull me onto my back to look at him. I tense and resist. "Maura. Seriously. Are you pissed?"

"Annoyed."

He kisses my upper arm. "Awww. Don't be like that."

"Don't tell me how to be. You have no right, after your display just now."

"Display? It wasn't a 'display.' I was totally grossed out."

"Whatever."

"Is this because I didn't want to—*couldn't*—have sex with you with that going on in the background?"

"No. Don't be dumb."

This time, he pulls hard enough that my puny muscles have no chance of defying him. So I close my eyes.

He snorts. "Who's immature now? Look at me."

"No."

For a few seconds, he says and does nothing but breathe over me. Then he kisses my eyelids in turn. I squeeze them more tightly shut. "Maura, please. I'm sorry. Please, look at me."

I crack one lid and laugh at the comically hangdog expression he's wearing. He flutters his lashes, then laughs, too. Making myself less plank-like, I relax against his weight.

"I love you," he whispers, brushing his lips against mine.

"I love you, too," I reply.

Our kisses deepen, our hands explore, and our clothes disappear, but my mind stays on one worry, something that won't let me fully enjoy what's about to happen.

I pull my head back and say up into Jet's quizzical face, "What if I never want to have babies?"

Blinking, as if waking from a deep sleep, he struggles to form a response, so I narrow down my question, to make his response easier—I hope.

"Will you still love me? Will you stay with me?"

He smiles sadly. "Of course. How can you even ask that?"

"I just know you—"

Resting a finger against my lips, he says, "You don't know anything about me, if you really think I'd be able to leave you — for any reason. You're my everything." He buries his face in my neck and kisses a trail from there down my torso.

With that pesky issue out of the way, bliss awaits. My eyes drift shut again, pushing the puddling tears down the side of my face, into my ears. I bury my fingers in his hair and surrender to him.

————

After brunch the next day, the younger kids nap, the older ones scamper down to the beach with Jet, Ned, and the dogs to fly kites, the mothers relax in the living room, and the fathers clean up the kitchen.

I'm prepared to hang out with the guys, like I've done all day, but Gloria surprises me by motioning me to join the ladies. "We've hardly had a second to chat, since you've been so busy cooking."

I wait for a "thank you" that never comes. She seems more intent on making a point—"If you'd only pop out a kid, you too could relax on Mother's Day"—than giving me credit for my service. Maybe if the conversation in the kitchen had gone differently yesterday, if I had backed down and agreed to have Jet knock me up ASAP, that very night, even, I would have been allowed to suck down mimosas while the guys prepared the meal.

But no, I was relegated to the kitchen with the other adult "non-mothers," where I was supposed to oversee the men's culinary efforts. I was in my element. Not because I like cooking or I'm good at it (we burnt the bacon and toast, and the breakfast casserole came out runny), but I had a much better time in there discussing football and everyone's favorite binge-worthy shows than I've ever had in my mother-in-law's presence.

Since it would seem odd, though, to want to assist with cleanup duty, I accept Gloria's invitation to join the women, grab a fresh glass of orange juice and champagne, and follow the moms. Once in the living room, I raise a toast to the others. "Happy Mother's Day, everyone."

"Happy Mother's Day!" they echo.

Next to me, Gloria says, under her breath, obviously only for my benefit, "Well… not *everyone*."

I freeze. Hardly taking a sip, I set down my champagne flute on the nearest surface with quiet precision. All eyes follow me as I cross to the back door and announce, "On second thought, I'm going to… go fly a kite." I say those last four words while holding Gloria's eye contact. Unimpressed by my not-so-subtle message, she drains the rest of her mimosa and reaches for the pitcher on the coffee table to pour herself a refill.

I yank open the door and exit. Without hesitation, I trek down the sandy path to the beach.

During the two-minute walk through the dunes, I consider my strategy for getting through the rest of the week. Gloria's is obvious: every time Jet leaves me alone with her, she's going to get her digs in. Jab, jab, jab. Her end game? That's what I'm not sure about. Does she think harping will cause me to cave? Or is she interested in something more radical? Is she trying to drive me completely away? I wouldn't put it past her.

The first time we met, she said I was perfect for Jet. She said it when I wasn't yet sure of it myself, and it freaked me the hell out. How long ago that seems! Maybe she thought I was "perfect" for *her*, though. If her first impression of me was some easy-going, aimless airhead, she surely thought I'd be another family member to manipulate and control. As she's gotten to know me better, she's realized I'm a much less malleable addition to her minions than she originally thought I'd be. It's not that I've changed, either; she merely misread me. And she can't stand that she was wrong.

Her patience is finally paying off, though—or so she thinks. She sees the chaos of our current situation as an opportunity. She knows that the NFL life and its culture of consumption and excess isn't my natural habitat and hasn't afforded me more confidence; if anything, I'm more out of place than ever! Most of all, she recognizes that this frustrating holding pattern we're in, waiting for Jet's next career move to determine what I can do and where and when I can do it, is driving me batty. I'm floundering right now, vulnerable, desperate to find my practical place. And she thinks if she applies enough pressure during this time of uncertainty, she can force her will on me.

She's wrong.

But if she wants to waste her energy trying, okay. I'll even make it a fair fight and keep Jet in the dark about her passive- and not-so-passive-aggressive campaign to wear me down. At least for this week. Why ruin his visit? When we get home, I'll mention in passing how relentless she's become, and with the perspective distance grants, we'll figure out how to avoid situations like this in the future. Blowup: avoided. Now, I just have to get through the rest of this week.

Before rounding the last dune and coming into view of the shouting and laughing and barking group, I pause to collect myself. I pat my hot cheeks with my cool hands, dab the pesky rogue tear or two that's splashed off my lashes, sniff deeply of the salty sea air, and run my hands through my hair. My forced smile becomes genuine and spreads to my chest as soon as Jet sees me and waves.

"Hey!" he calls.

"Hey!" Ricky, Gidget's son, says when Jet's sudden inattention causes him to lose control of the kite his uncle was helping him fly.

"Oops! Hang on there, Tigger!" Jet instructs.

"I can't! It's too strong!"

Jet returns his full attention to the flapping plastic Spider Man on the end of the nylon string, but it's no use. The wind has seen its chance and capitalizes on it. The kite dives to the sand with a sick crunch. Ricky bounces down the beach to inspect the damage, yelling back gleefully at us, "It's okay!"

"Awesome! We'll get it back up in a sec, okay, Tig? Wind up the line a little bit for me." Jet stomps through the loose sand and stands before me, squinting into the wind and sun, hands on his hips. "Hey, pretty lady. What brings you down here with us kids?"

"I was excused from cleanup duty, but I'm not a mom, so I didn't quite fit in with that group, either." I say it lightly while tossing my sandals on the pile with the others' flip flops and slides, so as not to hint at any bitterness or conflict.

It works. He grins and grabs my hands. "Awesome. C'mon. You can help Brianna."

I glance over at Gidget's oldest child, who already has commanding control of her Wonder Woman kite, which soars about twice as high as her brother's did before it bit the dust. "She looks fine to me."

Jet laughs. "Yeah. Just like her mom. Little Miss Independent. Always has been." Raising his voice, he calls into the wind, "You still okay over there, Miss Thing?"

She nods but keeps both hands on her line, her eyes on her Amazonian hero.

Keith's kids, Patience and Gage, have abandoned kite-flying altogether in favor of exploring the various tide pools scattered around the beach. Sitting back on their haunches, they poke and prod the creatures that form microcosms in the sand while waiting for the next high tide to whisk them out to sea again.

The dogs pull Ned over to us. He quietly tells them to sit, and they do, one on either side of him. He hands the retractable double-lead to Jet. "Here. Trade me. I'll work with Ricky."

"Thanks, Dad." Clicking his tongue at the dogs, Jet leads all of us to the chairs and umbrella he and his dad lugged down here with the naïve hope they'd have a chance to use them. When we're all settled in the shade, Jet loops the handle of the leash around his wrist. I reach over and thread my fingers through his. We both dig our feet into the sand.

"Look at them," he says, nodding to the four kids, each engrossed in their play.

"They're something else," I reply noncommittally, not sure what I'm supposed to be seeing.

He pulls the bottom hem of his t-shirt up to wipe the fine sheen of sweat from his forehead, nose, and upper lip. "They're constantly moving, constantly exploring, constantly everything."

I laugh. "Yep."

"Don't get me wrong. They're great. But it's like… you get them past that baby stage where you have to do everything for them, and you think it's time to coast, but no. There are new things to think about and do. Like keeping them entertained with something besides phones and tablets." He shakes his head. "Gosh, it was a freaking chore getting Ricky to even come down here. The others bitched and moaned, too."

"They seem happy enough."

"Yeah, now. The first ten minutes were awful. 'It's hot!' 'I'm thirsty!' 'This is boring.' 'I can't do it!' 'Can we go back now?'" He sighs. "I mean, when I was a kid—"

"Watch it. You're about to sound like a seriously old fart."

He grins. "No, but really. When I was a kid, I would have *loved* to have access to a beach like this. But look around." I do. "What do you notice?"

"Uh…" My eyes roam from the waves to the brown-sugar packed sand to the dunes and the waving grasses. "It's empty."

"Exactly. Nobody's down here. It's a gorgeous day, but everyone's in their air-conditioned houses, surfing social media on their phones or binge-watching shows."

"You don't know that. They could be at the zoo. Or out to eat. Or at Disneyland."

"I doubt it."

"It's Mother's Day."

"All the more reason to get outside and give Mom some peace and quiet. When *this*"—he motions to the ocean in front of us—"is at your back door…"

"It's at their back door every day, though."

"I've never seen anyone else down here."

Not sure why I'm defending a bunch of strangers, other than that I feel an affinity for folks who don't have a pressing need to be out in nature all the time, I merely say, "Hmm," and wait for him to get to his point, if he has one.

When I've decided he doesn't have one—or has forgotten what it was—he pipes back up. "We had video games when we were kids. We're not *that* old."

"Correct."

"But we didn't play them all day."

"We would have, if our parents had let us, and if we'd had the unlimited selection available nowadays, at the click of a button."

He laughs. "Fair enough. Still, though…"

I squeeze his fingers. "Don't be a curmudgeon."

"I'm not!"

"You kind of are." I smile over at him. "It's cute."

"I'm just saying that kids these days—"

I toss my head back and roar at the inevitable three words that brand him a grumpy old man.

His jaw twitches, but he chuckles along like a good sport and waits for me to stop laughing before continuing. "They act like they're allergic to the sun and fresh air."

"Little vampires."

"It's sad."

"Oh, there are so many more important things to be sad about, Champ."

"You know what I mean, though."

"Yeah, I do. Things have changed since we were kids. It doesn't mean things are worse; they're just different."

"I think they're worse."

"Because you're looking back on your childhood with nostalgia, through the eyes of a weary adult, bogged down by grown-up problems."

"Maybe."

"Definitely." Scrambling for an example, I say, "Remember... Remember... Did your parents ever *make* you stay outside in the summer, like, *forbid* you to come in except for meals and emergencies?"

He thinks about it, then admits, "Yeah. It drove Mom nuts if we came in and out of the house a hundred times. But there were five of us, so I totally get that."

"My parents did that, too, though. And there were only two of us. They didn't want to have to deal with us during the summer. So we'd sweat our guts out in the backyard or on our bikes. If we were lucky, we'd be allowed to go to the neighborhood pool with friends who had older siblings. I hit the jackpot when Rae moved to the neighborhood, and her parents let us hang out in their house."

"Spoiled only child," Jet says mock-scornfully.

"You're not remembering all of the bad parts of being a kid in the summer, before parents could rely on tablets and phones to keep kids occupied."

He grumbles something that sounds like, "You're right," even if they're not those exact words.

I nod at the little people scattered before us. "So cut them

—and their parents—some slack. We don't really know what it's like, do we? We're just the fun aunt and uncle who get to play with them and laugh at all of their quirky personalities, then give them back to their parents when they get hungry or tired or bored."

He pulls his feet from the sand, arches his back, and yawns. "It's a pretty sweet gig, when you describe it that way."

We watch as Brianna gives Wonder Woman a mighty tug to disturb her smooth flight pattern and bring her down into the bubbling surf. "Oops!" she says, making both Jet and me laugh at her performance.

"We know you did that on purpose, Miss Thing!" he shouts with his hand curled around his mouth to amplify his words.

Grinning sheepishly, she retrieves her kite and runs it and its tangled line up to us. I take the mess from her and begin the tedious task of winding the string.

"Can we get ice cream now?" she asks her uncle, folding her hands under her chin and batting her eyelashes at him.

As if choreographed, the three other youngsters scamper from their spots to join Brianna in a chorus of "Pleeeeeeeeeease"s.

Slightly out of breath, Ned catches up and dumps the kites he's picked up from the beach into a heap on the sand, presumably to wind their strings later for storage. Jet stands and hands the now-fidgeting dogs to his dad.

"Yeah, we'll get ice cream. But we're walking. Get your shoes."

"Awwwwww!"

"It's not that far! We can all use the exercise."

Gage whines, "I already exercised with my kite!"

"For two minutes," Jet says. "Now, come on. If we go back to the house to get cars, the little kids will wake up and want ice cream, too."

"They don't deserve it!" Patience says with a petulant pout.

Jet shoots her with his thumb and forefinger. "Bingo. They've been lazing around, taking naps."

I laugh. "They're babies."

He wrinkles his nose. "So?"

Ned edges toward the path back to the house. "I'm with the babies. I'd rather take a nap than eat ice cream."

"Toss-up for me," I say.

Gesturing to the chairs and kites, my father-in-law says, "I'll come back for these after putting the dogs up." Of the restless throng about to mutiny, he asks me, "You guys have this?"

I wave him off. "We're good."

Jet pats his shorts pocket to make sure he has his wallet. "All right, ye scurvy cusses," he says in his best pirate voice. "Off ye go. Our treasure awaits thataway!" He points to a gap between two massive houses that hides a sandy boardwalk. From there, it's about a three-block walk out of the neighborhood to a sidewalk-lined avenue with businesses, including a frozen yogurt shop. "No complaining, me hearties, or ye'll be tossed in the hold!"

Walking backwards, Ricky asks, "Will you throw me in 'the drink' when we get back to Gigi's?"

"I wanna walk the plank!" Gage shouts. "That's the diving board at Gigi's pool," he explains to me.

Jet sighs and, in his normal voice, says, "Those are supposed to be bad things, guys."

"Not when *you* do it," Brianna says.

"Yeah, it's fun!" Patience chimes in.

As they all run a little bit ahead of us, excited to eat their sweet treats and convene back at Gloria's for pirate swimming, I loop my arm through my husband's and smile up at him. "Everything's fun with Uncle Jet."

He returns my grin and winks. "Aye. Every day's a parrrrty."

NINETEEN

INQUISITIONS

As planned, the majority of the Knox clan traipsed back to their Gloria-free homes first thing Monday morning, leaving Jet and me alone with his parents. The good news is, with less chaos, Gloria will have fewer opportunities to harass me. The bad news is, Jet and I are now her sole target for the usual nagging.

My stomach rumbles and mouth waters while I ogle my mother- and father-in-law and Jet as they eat a luscious, full breakfast that would constitute my entire caloric budget for the day. I sit and sip my fourth cup of coffee and try not to make it too obvious how lustfully I'm eyeing those fluffy scrambled eggs, the ones where Gloria adds a tiny bit of heavy cream and chives.

"Sure you don't want some of this?" Jet asks while scooping the last of the eggs—his *third* helping—from the large skillet.

"Oh, I guess I could eat a few bites," I reply, my willpower dissolving like butter in a hot pan.

With a knowing smile, Jet halves the portion on his plate

and scrapes it onto a clean dish that he slides in front of me. "That's what I thought. Woman can't live on fruit alone."

"Plus," Gloria says from across the table, "good prenatal health starts with diet and exercise long before pregnancy begins."

I stab at the eggs on my plate and try not to think too much about the ones inside my body.

"Mom."

"What? It's true!" she says to her son's long-suffering tone. Returning her attention to me, she leans closer. "You're taking pre-natal vitamins, right?"

Jet clears his throat. "It's not even ten o'clock yet. Let's pace ourselves on the baby mania."

Ned chuckles behind his newspaper.

Gloria's face falls, and she sniffs before sipping her coffee, but she mercifully respects her son's wishes.

In an effort to change the subject, Jet asks, "So, what do you guys want to do today?"

Neither of his parents say anything at first. After an awkward pause, Gloria fake-flinches. "Oh, you're asking me? Am I allowed to speak now?"

I whimper through my mouthful of eggs. Maybe they'll think it was one of the dogs. Looking up from my plate, I smile, chagrined to see they all know it was me. Ned has forsaken his newspaper for the show he suspects he's about to witness.

I swallow my eggs and clear my throat. "Excuse me."

"Problems, dear?" Gloria inquires, her lashes fluttering.

"Me? No. Egg stuck... in my throat." I pick up my mug and drain its dregs.

Jet rushes ahead. "We could walk on the beach."

"No more walking, Jet-honey," Gloria pleads. "This girl is worn out from the weekend. I'm not young like you guys."

He reaches over and pats her hand. "You're not old, either. But okay. Something more relaxed. Hanging out by the pool?"

"We're supposed to get some rain today. It's been all over the news."

Grabbing the coffee carafe, I pour myself a refill. Only in SoCal is rain the top headline.

It's bad news for me, though. The thought of being stuck indoors all day with nothing but conversation to keep us busy makes the eggs stick in my throat for real. I wash them down while I mentally panic and frantically think of what else we can do. I don't know the area well enough, however, to plot a decent diversion.

Fortunately, or otherwise, Gloria already has an idea. "There's a play at one of the local community colleges, and it sounded fascinating. I read it on the line."

"'Online,'" Jet corrects automatically through a mouthful of bacon.

"Whatever. I'd love to go see it." She places her bifocals on the tip of her nose and picks up her phone, ostensibly to use "The Google" to find it.

Jet and Ned groan.

"I'll go by myself, if I have to!"

While she taps and swipes at her screen, Jet looks up from his plate and across the table at me. He widens his eyes.

What does that mean? Oh, no. No, no, no.

I bug my eyes back at him, desperate to convey my insistence. He tilts his head and bites the inside of his cheek.

I mouth, *"What?"*

He lip syncs back, *"C'mon."*

I glower. Surely, he doesn't want to leave me alone with his mother for the entire day. Even he must know what a disaster that could be.

"*Please?*" he mimes, adding his praying hands to the act.

"*No!*"

Gloria lowers her phone and glares at us over the top of her glasses. "What's going on over there?"

Jet grins. "Huh? Nothing." He mops bacon grease from his plate with his toast and shoves the bread in his mouth. "I'm up for whatever," he says while chewing.

Gloria removes her glasses and smiles appreciatively at her son. "That's so sweet. You've always been so easy-going."

She holds up her hands and examines her nails. I try not to stare with loathing at the ginormous anniversary ring she nearly disfigured me with last year.

"You know, I could use a touch-up. It's already sandal season. Maybe Maura and I can leave you guys to your own boring guy stuff and go for mani-pedis. It'll give us a chance to gab."

"That sounds nice," Jet says stupidly before gulping the rest of his orange juice.

I hate you, I mouth at him, making him snort liquid.

While he mops under his nose, I pick up my own phone and quickly map our location. If I'm going to be stuck alone with Gloria, I'm going to control the setting, and I'm not going to be a hostage in side-by-side pedicure chairs with her.

By the time Gloria finishes fussing over her choking son, I've found a venue. "You know, mani-pedis are so blah. Let's go to the dry bar instead."

"Dry bar? I'm not one for day drinking, Maura. You shouldn't be, either. It's a horrible habit."

"It's not a drinking bar. It's a hair salon. It'll be fun!"

"Sounds trendy. I'm too old for trendy."

"It's relaxing. They massage your scalp and wash your hair, then they dry it and style it."

"Well, I suppose it wouldn't hurt to try it. What's it called again? A blow bar?"

Jet snickers, this time without any food or drink in his mouth to impede his airways.

I ignore him. "Dry bar," I say, my finger hovering over the link to the phone number of the closest place with the best ratings. "And leave it to me to make the appointments. Jet will clean up the dishes and the kitchen."

After some back-and-forth concerning my radical proposal that a guy would do such work on a day other than Mother's Day, she eventually capitulates and leaves with Ned to go upstairs and dress.

While I wait for the receptionist to pick up at Beach-comber's, I glare at Jet. "You owe me."

He stacks plates and gathers flatware on the top dish, then collects a glass on each finger, pinching them together with a clang to carry them into the kitchen. "How is this my fault?" he asks before escaping.

I follow him with the phone pressed to my ear but held slightly away from my mouth.

"If you have to ask, you owe me even more."

"You two are going to have a great day. You love blow jobs." He sets the dishes in the sink and the glasses on the counter.

I narrow my eyes at his back. "Keep laughing. After today, *you're* never getting another one."

"Tough talker." After rinsing his hands, he turns, and in one step is close enough to grab me around the waist.

Smelling of coffee and bacon, he brushes his lips against mine. "I'll make it up to you later."

"I already know that."

"All your favorite moves."

"Mm."

While he's specifying which moves, using the nastiest language possible in an effort to make me laugh, the ringing stops, and I hear in my ear, "It's a great day at Beachcombers! How can I help you?"

Blushing, I push away from him. "Uh, yes! I, uh, would like to book two appointments."

———

You know the best thing about dry bars? They're loud. So loud, there's no possibility of conversation. Oh, darn.

Bonus: my hair looks fabulous. Nobody stuck on a back patio for an evening of Yahtzee with her in-laws has had better-looking locks. I'm sure of it.

Jet stares at me between his turns. "It's so... shiny."

I laugh and pretend to fluff it. "Big, too, but I like it."

Gloria sets down the pencil after recording Ned's latest score and takes the cup of dice. Rattling it with her hand over the top of the shaker, she asks, "What about mine? You like it?"

Jet coughs. "Sure, Ma. It's nice."

In truth, it doesn't look that much different than it always does, since she blow dries, curls, and back combs the crap out of it every day. Maybe sleeker. Anyway, as long as she's happy with it and doesn't feel cheated from her afternoon of haranguing me, it's all good.

She spills the dice onto the table and clicks her tongue at

the mundane result. Leaving two fives in play, she picks up the other three cubes and rolls again. And manages to get three sixes. Damn her. I swear, she cheats. I just don't know how.

This is my life. Caring about Yahtzee.

Before I can despair too much about that, though, Gloria passes me the cup of dice and says, "I'm going to tell all of the ladies at church about that blow bar."

Jet snickers. I'd correct her, but we're talking about a woman who still calls Uber "The Boober." It's hopeless.

Almost as hopeless as my luck at this dumb, loud, annoying game. My highest scoring round so far has been fifteen points for a lame three of a kind involving twos, a five, and a four. Usually, like this round, I hand the dice to Jet after earning nada.

He pats my shoulder reassuringly. "It can only get better."

I stick out my tongue at him and laugh.

"Yahtzee!" he says when his casual roll produces five fours.

"You suck."

"Mwahaha." He passes the dice to his dad.

Gloria records his score. "Good job, baby boy."

While Ned shakes (and shakes and shakes) the cup, I add to the non-game-related conversation, "I'm glad you enjoyed your afternoon, Glo— Mom."

"Since we've become empty-nesters, I struggle to find ways to fill my days. I can only pester Gidget and her crew so much."

Poor, poor Gidget. I must remember to keep her in my prayers.

"What about friends?" I ask.

"I'm active at church, and I have friends there, but we're past the age of 'hanging out,' like all of you young people are so fond of doing. Seems silly and pointless."

Jet jeers at his dad's failed attempt to collect a straight, then says to his mom, "Friends aren't pointless."

"I didn't say they were, son." She shakes and rolls. Three threes. The other two cubes go back in the cup and come out as two sixes. Full house. Unbelievable.

"Nice one, Mom."

She blows him a kiss.

I suppress a gag and say, "Maybe you can go with one of your church friends to the blow bar."

Jet can kick me under the table all he wants; her hilariously mangled term is definitely going to be a thing from now on. I don't even care that I only got three ones this round. There's no way I'm winning this game, so I'll find my delight elsewhere.

"I suppose," she replies with a pout.

Jet starts his turn inauspiciously with a pair of fives. While he winds up for his next roll, he says to Gloria, "An afternoon of pampering with a friend would be fun, Mom. Having fun is a good enough purpose."

"Yeah," I concur.

His second roll yields two twos, which encourages more chair dancing, and the chant, "C'mon... Papa needs a five or two." But his third roll ends the streak with a one. "Doh. Put me down for fifteen in my combo category."

Gloria scoffs and writes down his score. "See, that's the problem with you two. All play and no purpose. You've ruined yourselves to it. That's why the thought of parenthood is so daunting."

Here we go. My contented smile fades, and my nerves wind tighter with each shake of the cup from Ned. Why does he shake it so long? Let it go, old man!

Ned finally does exactly that and says while picking up the

majority of the dice for his re-roll, "I don't know. I could have done with a little more playing when we were young and could still *do* things."

"Ned! Having children is the best thing we ever did."

"I didn't say it wasn't. But it wouldn't have been the worst thing if we'd held off longer than we did."

I try not to smirk too hard at his obvious defection from the Senior Knox party line.

Jet voices my sentiments when he says, "There you go, Mom."

"Ridiculous! What would we have done?"

Jet and I laugh.

Ned scowls. "Never mind. Your roll." He nudges the cup against her hand.

"What was your score?"

"You weren't watching? I rolled a Yahtzee on my third roll. It was a miracle."

She looks over the top of her bifocals at him. "If you don't tell me the truth, I'm going to give you nothing."

"Wouldn't be the first time."

Tightening her lips, she waits.

"It was a whole lotta nothin', so count it toward my fives, and give me ten points."

"Thank you." She writes it down on the scorecard and turns her attention back to Jet and me, holding the dice and cup hostage while she pontificates. "You're both too worried that having kids won't be 'fun' enough. Well, guess what? Sometimes it's not fun. It's hard work. But it's important work. Rewarding work."

"Mom, we're busy. Our life right now isn't all fun. Having kids would be stressful. It would be irresponsible! Not to mention unfair to both us and any children."

"Oh, boo-hoo. So entitled! You think you have all the time in the world."

"Not all the time, but there's a good chance we can spare a couple more years."

"Perhaps that's what Colin thought with his wife. Life has a way of proving us wrong."

At the mention of my friend and her use of his tragic history to prove her point, I stiffen.

Jet places his hand over my clenched fist on the table. "I'd rather not think about Maura dying, thanks."

Gloria, on the other hand, fantasizes regularly about it, I'm sure.

"We have to stop talking about this," I mumble as quietly as possible to my husband.

He nods at his mom. "Just play."

"'Just play. Just play,'" she mocks. "That's right; I almost forgot. No talking about anything un-fun."

Ned points out, "We *are* playing a game. Or were."

She turns on him. "Haven't you done enough?"

"What did I do?"

"Talking about how you wished we'd have had kids later than we did. What an unhelpful addition to the discussion!"

"As far as I knew, we were discussing hair salons; then it veered off to where it always does. Why don't you leave the two of them alone? They don't need your help deciding what to do with their lives."

"Guys, guys!" Jet gestures to the cup still firmly clutched in his mom's hands, against her bosom. "Let's finish the game and call it a night."

Ignoring his pleas, she holds her ground. "I don't want you to have regrets, that's all. I want you to have everything you want."

Jet sucks in his cheeks and bites down on them. Then he shakes his head and chuckles. "You know what we want? We want to stop having this damn conversation."

Gloria's eyes fill. "Jet!"

"Enough, Mom. Enough."

"I want you to be happy! Is that such a crime?"

"We are! Ecstatic. There. Wish granted. Now, drop it. Are you gonna roll, or what?"

She unceremoniously dumps the contents of the cup onto the table while simultaneously standing and walking away, entering the house and slamming the back door behind her.

To her retreating back, Jet yells, "You got a Yahtzee!"

I smile tightly at him when he looks back at me.

"What just happened?" he wonders aloud, fortunately not expecting an answer. Ned and I have none to give, anyway.

TWENTY

DEPARTURE

Four days later, I smile wanly at Jet across the tiny table in the airport bar and gulp the rest of my third piña colada. It was a long week, and I deserve to day drink.

He nods at the pineapple and cherry skewered on the pink plastic bayonet. "You gonna eat that?"

"Be my guest."

Snagging the garnish kabob, he slides the fruit off the sword with his teeth. "Starving," he muffles through chews.

"Get something to eat!"

"There's no time now."

"There was when we sat down in here an hour ago."

"I wasn't hungry then."

Who needs kids? I'm married to the biggest one on the planet.

He laughs at my pinched lips and folded arms. "I know! I'm an idiot."

"You're not an idiot, but you're going to be super-hangry by the time we land in Denver. And our connection is tight, so you might not have time to eat then, either."

"See, this is the problem with flying commercial."

I shoot him a dirty look. "You'd better be kidding."

"I am. Mostly. It's not fun running through airports, though. Or sitting at departure gates. Or waiting on the tarmac for takeoff, packed into a metal tube with two hundred strangers."

"You're spoiled."

"I'm not arguing that."

"And when you're hungry, you're crabby."

"I'll be fine."

"You're always fine. It's the people around you who have to worry."

"I'll be on my best behavior." Tossing some money on the table, he stands, shoulders our carry-on duffel bag, and bobs his head toward the door. "C'mon. Let's head that way. There's a duty-free a couple doors down. I'll grab something there."

Ten minutes later, seated at our departure gate, we wait for boarding, and he offers me my choice of candy bar after peeling open his own, but I shake my head and tuck the extras into my large tote bag for later. "No, thanks."

Outside the windows, the tarmac below teems with activity. Luggage trains, driven by rushed people in blaze orange vests and hearing protection, bustle back and forth to awaiting planes. Men and women drag fuel hoses from bulbous tankers and talk to pilots as they top off the planes' tanks. All sizes of jets taxi to and from gates. Some take off, others land, all at the direction of personnel guided by complicated schedules, computers, and radar.

Two uniformed workers take up their positions behind the tiny counter by the door leading to the jetway. While we wait for them to call first class passengers for boarding, Jet asks, "Who's picking us up from the airport, anyway?"

"Jake… and Torzi," I answer, scrolling through my texts to make sure I haven't missed any messages from the dog-sitter. I haven't. Or anyone else. Apparently, I could fall off the grid for days, and nobody would notice.

"Good old reliable Jake."

"Yes." I drop my superfluous phone into my bag and sit back in my chair. "He is." I ruminate for a while about all of the good people in our lives, which leads me to wonder aloud, "Do you think your mom warmed up a little more to Colin last weekend?"

Jet shrugs and studies the inside of his candy bar, as if the answer to life's biggest questions can be found in a peanut. "Dunno. Who cares?" He chomps down and chews.

"I care! He's our friend."

Around a mouthful of chocolate, nougat, nut, and caramel, he muffles, "No, I mean…" He pauses to finish chewing and swallows. After a swig of water, he starts over. "Who cares what Mom thinks about him? She needs to get over it. She needs to get over everything."

While I wholeheartedly agree, what Jet doesn't seem to get when he goes through these, "Mom-needs-to-get-over-it," phases is that those of us who live in that world full-time realize it's never going to happen. "Be that as it may—"

"'Be that as it may…," he mocks, polishing off the rest of the chocolate bar, licking caramel from his fingers, and wiping his hands on his shorts. He crumples his empty wrapper. "Don't get all Jane Austen on me. You know I'm right. Heaven forbid she doesn't get her way *all* the time. Then she becomes this passive-aggressive"—he struggles to find any word other than the one we're both thinking and eventually lands on

—"meanie and makes everyone around her miserable. I'm sick of it."

"If you'd let me finish…" When he waits, and I'm sure he's not going to interrupt again, I say, "That's all fine and good, but 'getting over it' isn't your mom's style. And I understand firsthand how miserable she can make someone. I don't want that for Colin."

As succinctly and unemotionally as possible, I relay to Jet a small sampling of the poison arrows shot my way during our visit when he wasn't around or was preoccupied with the kids, his siblings, or the dogs. When I finish, he blinks at me for a few seconds, then asks, "Why didn't you say something to me? Why didn't you tell me sooner, while it was happening?"

I pull a face. "I wasn't about to tattle on your mom and ruin the visit."

"She had already ruined the visit after her temper tantrum on the back patio!"

"Before, though. During the weekend, when everyone else was still there. I didn't want to ruin everyone's Mother's Day."

"But she says that shit because she knows she can get away with it."

"She'd say it, no matter what. I'd rather there weren't big blow-ups every time we're together."

He bites the inside of his cheek, shakes his head, and stares straight ahead. "Unreal."

"Who, me or her?"

"Both of you!" When his raised voice grabs the attention of some of the other travelers at the gate with us, he says more quietly, focusing on my face once more, "Honestly, Maura. I don't know what to do with the two of you."

"Why am I getting chewed out right now?" I cross and uncross my ankles.

"Because nothing is ever going to change if you don't let me know what's going on."

"Your knowing isn't going to change anything, either, except that you and your mom will always be at each others' throats, too. How does that improve things?"

He clenches his teeth while he thinks about it but several minutes pass without a response.

"See? That's not a solution." Quietly, I say what I've been thinking all week. "Maybe she's worried you and I want different things. And I'm bullying you into agreeing to what I want."

He considers it for a second. "Why would she think that, though?"

I shrug, not sure how to answer without getting emotional in public.

One of the gate agents picks up the handset at the counter and welcomes us, thanking us for flying Frontier and saving me from replying. Jet springs to his feet when she tells us first-class passengers can board. Still, despite him practically jogging to the line with me struggling to keep up, we're a few people from the front of the stationary queue.

He peers over everyone else's heads to see what the holdup is. Turning to face me, he whispers, "Seriously? Who rushes to the front of the line, then doesn't have their boarding pass ready? Who even uses a paper boarding pass still? Dude. Scan your phone."

"You'd better eat another one of your candy bars, or it's going to be a long day."

"As for Colin, you don't need to worry about him. He can take care of himself. Everyone, including Mom, likes him."

"He's tainted, because he was my friend first. I feel awful about that."

"Don't."

"Oh, okay. I'll magically not feel that way anymore."

He doesn't get a chance to respond to my snark, due to an approaching fan asking for an autograph. Low blood sugar be damned, Jet flips on his "charm" switch and signs the back of the fan's [paper] boarding pass. While they reminisce about last year's epic Super Bowl win and the vicious hit that scrambled Jet's brains at the end of the game, I stand by like a lump. An invisible lump.

Finally, we inch forward, phones at the ready to scan our boarding passes. We stride down the jetway and board the plane. At our seats, Jet hoists our duffel into the overhead compartment, and I tuck my tote bag under the seat in front of me. I settle near the window and give him the aisle, so he'll have an inch or two more leg room once we're in the air.

While we perform our pre-flight adjustments to the air vents and reading lights, and the other passengers file by, he leans closer and, head nearly touching mine, says quietly, "I'm sorry I snapped at you."

"You're forgiven. You should have eaten a better lunch."

"It's not just that."

"I know. But let's pretend it is, because it's the only thing we can do anything about."

He chuckles and fastens his seat belt. I buckle in, as well, and grab his hand.

Obviously surprised by my conciliatory gesture after our quasi-argument, he looks sharply over at me and grins, then gives my hand a gentle squeeze.

"Everyone needs to chill out, you know?"

I smile back at him. "Including you?"

"Especially me." He rubs his own neck. I let go of his hand and take over the job. Like Torzi, he thumps the foot closest to me. "Yeah. That's the spot."

Laughing at his antics, I continue kneading the tensest muscle, the one connecting his neck to his right shoulder, eliciting soft moans from him. When the flight attendant stands at the front of the cabin to perform the safety demonstration, I stop and pretend to listen, like I always do. I feel bad that nobody else does.

Case in point, Jet proceeds to blatantly ignore her as he continues to try to get comfortable, leans forward to look past me out the window, and checks his phone one last time before the crew tells him to turn it off for takeoff. As soon as they do, he obeys and sets the device face-down on his leg but seconds later says to me, "I'm bored."

Again I ask, who needs kids?

TWENTY-ONE

SEPARATION

Less than a month later, Jet stuffs a rolling suitcase full of casual clothes, shoes, and underwear as he prepares for another trip out west, this time to Culver City. There, he plans to do a series of interviews at NFL Network, plus take care of his upcoming season's headshots and introduction videos. Every year, he threatens to add something goofy, like a "hang ten" gesture or crossed eyes, to his intro, but he never follows through. He always smiles pleasantly and says, "Jet Knox, USC," like the obedient Boy Scout he is.

It'll be all work and no play, so I'm hanging back, choosing to oversee the last of the kitchen renovations, which are *finally* wrapping up after a series of delays due to complications. Who knew adding a staircase where there wasn't one before could be such a pain in the ass?

Okay, Sarah and Carl knew, but I was adamant about installing a more convenient (and stealthy) way to get from the main floor to the second floor when entering the house through the garage. Plus, now that it's almost finished, it looks fabulous, and it could be a huge selling feature someday. Kitchen staircases are cool. So technically, I was right.

But being right doesn't change the fact that we're one month and a few—give or take—thousand dollars over budget. And as much as I'd like to distance myself from those facts, especially right now, I'd also like to distance myself from my testy husband for a few days.

I'm hoping some time in his home state, jawing about football with experts and goofing off during photo shoots, will lift his spirits. Look at me, being optimistic.

"This is so dumb," he laments while retrieving his garment bag of nicer interview clothes from the closet and tossing it onto the bed. "Without a contract, I could be redoing all of this shit later for a different team. What's the point in parading around in my Chiefs uniform for pictures or sitting down to talk with reporters about 'the team,' if I'm not sure I'll be playing here in two months?"

"Obviously Tom and the team are confident you *will* be playing here this season. Otherwise, they wouldn't be sending you. This trip is a great sign, right?"

He grumbles something I can't hear.

"You're almost there. At least you've heard *something*. They want you to stay."

"They have a shitty way of showing it."

"They live for back-and-forth. And so do agents. Let Tom do his job. It'll be fine. "

I cuddle up to his back, wrapping my arms around his torso and resting my cheek between his shoulder blades. He stops packing, only because to continue would result in elbowing me. "I need to get moving," he says tersely. "Are you sure you don't want to come with me?"

Ha! Am I sure? I've never been more sure of anything in my life.

More diplomatically, I reply, trying to inject some regret into my tone, "Oh, I wish I could, but you know how crazy things are around here right now. I should stick close for Sarah and Carl. And I want to help Beau put everything away, so I know where things are." Placing a kiss on his shoulder, I add brightly, "When you get back, the house will be *done*."

He chuckles in spite of his black mood. "Until your next project."

"Nope. This is it." I pull on his arm to turn him around and look up into his face. "And your contract stuff will be resolved soon, too. The fact that you're still talking about it this close to the pre-season means you're here to stay. They only need to iron out the details: how long and how much. You don't care about the 'how much' part, and 'how long' is pretty irrelevant, too, since that can always be extended."

He chews his lip and chooses to stare at the floor rather than look me in the eye.

Since there's no convincing him, I let go of his arm and try a less direct approach. "Don't let this ruin your fun the next few days. You love this time of year. All that attention... Looking so much hotter than those other meatheads..."

He laughs. I tiptoe and kiss his lips.

Exhaling loudly, he closes his eyes. "I'd rather stay here with you."

"That goes without saying. But you can't."

He reopens his eyes and stares into mine.

After one more kiss, I say to his mouth, "Now, focus. Exude confidence. If you have a sour look on your face the whole time, you'll start rumors, and that'll only make things worse. Smile."

He grins to demonstrate he remembers how. It also proves he can still jigglify my insides.

I hug him, hard. "I'll miss you, you handsome goober."

"Not as much as I'll miss you."

When I release him, he returns to his packing. With a final smack to his butt, I say, "Go get 'em, Champ," and exit the room.

In the hall, I take a deep breath and duck into the brand new stairwell. Inhaling the fresh lumber and paint, I close my eyes and rest my back against the wall.

I believe all those things I told him. I have to believe them. Still... some niggling doubts gnaw at me. It worries me that the person who always tells me not to worry is worried. It's troubling that the veteran in the pro football industry doesn't see all of the things I've pointed out to him as positive signs that his contract will be renewed. It's scary to think that this time next year, we could be living in a totally different city, getting used to a totally different community and team.

I came into this marriage with my eyes wide open to the possible pitfalls of this lifestyle, so none of this should come as a surprise. Secretly, though—and stupidly—I thought it wouldn't happen to us. I've been cocky. I've let myself believe that Jet's irreplaceable on this team and in this town. Jet's always known better.

He's done this before. He knows what it feels like when an organization's confidence in you flags. Maybe this isn't unfounded insecurity on his part. Maybe he's privy to things I can't see.

There's only one remedy for this doubt and anxiety. I trot down the stairs and wind my way through the kitchen and dining room to get to the library. In there, I make a beeline for my desk, where I pull out my pencils and the custom coloring book I received for Valentine's Day. I carry both to my favorite reading chair and prop the tin of pencils on the wide, flat arm.

After a few minutes of deliberation, I choose one of the hilarious paparazzi shots of us that Jet impulsively included near the back. In it, I'm ducking my head, and Jet's holding out his arm, hand up, as if to block the shot—or pose like the Heisman trophy. We look guilty, as if we're emerging from a courthouse, prison, or rehab facility. If I remember correctly, though, we were simply leaving a restaurant after what we'd hoped would be a rare, quiet night out. I have no recollection at all as to why we were so uncharacteristically anti-social in this particular instance. Maybe the food was bad. Maybe we'd argued at dinner. Maybe we simply weren't in the mood to be bothered.

Regardless, it amuses me that Jet picked this picture, of all pictures, to include. And it speaks to me today. Some days, you're not in the mood. It doesn't mean life is bad or that the world is coming to an end or that you'll never be happy again. It simply means you're having a day. And the next day, you'll be back to your usual autograph-signing self, and everything will seem brighter and better and more hopeful. But you can't get to that day without slogging through the bad one. And the good days wouldn't feel as good without a few bad ones peppered in for perspective.

Chuckling to myself, once again, at the picture before me, obviously one of *those* days memorialized forever by some persistent photographer, I choose a dark brown for Jet's hair. What better way to get through this current crummy day than to color it away?

TWENTY-TWO

DAYMARES

The next six weeks offer more crummy days than not as contract talks continue to drag, but I've tried to stay busy to avoid full-on stir craziness. I've researched and planned and schemed more than I've done in my whole life.

Ask me about the laws for setting up and running a non-profit. I can recite them from seven states—all of which have large NFL franchises who *might* need a veteran quarterback next season. I've analyzed to death the differences between cloth, leather, Naugahyde, and vinyl movie theater seats. I've priced and selected—but haven't purchased... yet—popcorn machines, projectors, cash registers, and ticket printers. I've toured multiple properties, many of which will no longer be available by the time I can pull the trigger on this thing. Not to mention, they may not be in the right city. Or state. Or region. I'm confident I have the country right, though, so that's something.

Discussing any of this with Jet is out of the question, too. It will only make him more anxious, especially now that we're so close to the contract deadline. Therefore, I file everything away and stifle. When I'm around him, I try to keep things light. We discuss where we might like to travel next spring for our anniversary. We watch movies and binge-watch shows. We work out (him), color (me), and babysit to give our siblings breaks—and pass the time. We do our hospital volunteer work together, and I get out alone a couple of times a week to volunteer at the shelters.

As stressful as those activities were for me, initially, they've been my salvation lately. It's good to get out and help people with *real* problems. And I realize how awful that sounds, but it's true. It's not that I take delight in others' misfortunes, but they're an excellent reminder of how petty ours are. They're certainly not life-and-death. Having huge dollar signs attached to them doesn't make them more important. In fact, the opposite seems to be true. Gently, I tried to point that out to Jet, but it didn't go over well.

"They're still problems. They're still *our* problems," he snapped. "On top of everything else, don't make me feel guilty that I care about my career."

The cheerleader in me has fallen from the top of the pyramid and is lying on the ground. She's not hurt, but she's exhausted, and she doesn't want to do this anymore. She doesn't want to smile and hop around and yell encouragement from the sidelines while the team flounders on the field. What she wants to do is hit the showers, go home, wear baggy sweats, screen her calls, and pig out on Ben & Jerry's.

I can no longer muster the energy or enthusiasm to point out silver linings over coffee every morning. I don't want to end every day with a top ten list of the douchiest local jock talkers who are more obsessed with Jet's contract than Gloria is about his sperm count. I want to have fun again.

This morning, on the day of his departure for training

camp, Jet stares morosely into his bowl of Wheaties, probably to avoid the picture of current Super Bowl MVP and champion quarterback, Drew McKnight, on the cereal box. Finally, deciding I can't take his downer attitude anymore, I announce, "We're taking the kids to the toy store today."

As if drugged, he slowly looks up, finishes chewing, swallows, and says ever-so-eloquently, "Huh? What kids?"

"The ones whose parents are so desperate for some alone time that they'd allow two morons like us to take care of them. Our nieces and nephew."

"All of them?"

"The three who live locally, yes."

He shakes his head. "Uh-uh."

"Yes-huh. You're not going to sit here all day, staring at your phone, waiting for that call, until it's time to pack and leave for training camp. We need to get out of the house, take your mind off things."

I wait for him to finish drinking the milk in his bowl. When his only response is a burp, followed by wiping his mouth on the back of his hand, I march up the stairs. "You have one hour to gird your loins. This is happening."

"You can't make me!" he calls after me, but minutes later, he's upstairs, showering.

That's what I thought.

And as he shaves for the first time in days, he babbles about checking out the action figures associated with some comic book movie I don't care about but am suddenly grateful for. After all, it's the first thing my husband has enthused over in weeks.

Almost an hour to the minute later, we have all three kids buckled into the back of the H2, which they love, because it rides so high.

"Ice cream!" Meleah shouts before we've backed from her driveway.

Mikey seconds the motion, and Gracie squeals when they start to chant it.

"After the toy store," I promise them. Softer, to Jet, after redirecting the *Moana* soundtrack to the back speakers, I say with a snicker, "Right before we give you back to your parents."

"You're mean," he says with more than a hint of admiration in his tone.

"This is payback for decades of Greg's shit-giving."

"What have Colin and Cyndi done to deserve it, though?"

I frown. "Meh. Nothing yet. But there's nothing wrong with being proactive."

Jet laughs. "True. We can let Meleah have something extramessy to make it fair. You know, to get Greg and D back for that whole teething-slash-separation-anxiety thing on Valentine's Day. That was awful."

"Was it? For you? I seem to remember you bugging out."

"Only after she fell asleep. I was there for the worst part."

"Being held hostage by a sweaty, sleeping infant isn't much better than trying to soothe a crying one."

"It's quieter. You had it under control, and I was afraid I'd do something stupid to wake her up."

"Hmm."

Staring out the window at the passing streetscape, my present becomes my future: the kids in the backseat are ours. After hyping up our two toddlers with new toys and ice cream, we don't get to hand them off to someone else; we have to take them home and put their new toys together and feed them dinner and bathe them and attempt to get them all to bed at a decent hour so Jet and I will have time for each other.

When the kids are cranky or unmanageable, Jet disappears, claiming he's in the way and doesn't know what to do, anyway. If I complain too much about it, he suggests we hire a nanny or manny. Worse, he does so without consulting me. I'm mad at first, but since I'm overwhelmed, I eventually get over my discomfort at the bourgeois practice, and someone else raises our children. I pop out a new one every early spring, in the off-season, until all of the bedrooms at Fort Knox are full. Jet parades them out at big events, where people coo and say, "What a sweet family! What a great dad! You're so lucky, Maura." I smile vacantly and rub my huge belly.

After wins, on his one day off, Jet's a great dad. He crawls around and lets them ride him like a horse, teaches them how to hold and toss a football, bobs in the pool with them, and reads them stories. After losses, however, he retreats downstairs, leaving me to listen to the children cry and whine and say, "I want Daddy!" That refrain continues when he's on the road, playing, then following teams around the country to announce games in his "retirement."

Ned dies (sorry, Ned), and Gloria comes to live with us. She antagonizes the nanny/manny—the one I didn't want in the first place but have come to rely on—to the point of quitting, and she nitpicks everything I do, as well. Helen's allowed to stay, but Gloria overhauls the cleaning schedule and makes the housekeeper use more starch in all of the laundry.

She fires Beau so she can cook large, heavy meals every day. She sneaks the children sugary snacks, despite (or to spite) my requests to the contrary. Jet waves off my concerns about their health and says they can be linebackers.

We fight. Constantly and about everything. I rage and cry. He dismisses and pouts. These happy, early years of our marriage, with only the occasional argument while we adjust to living together or experience friction after losses or during contract negotiations, are foggy memories we won't trust are true, if we remember them at all. The only way we know how to be with each other is angry and resentful.

We lash out and spend money on unnecessary things to spite each other. He buys sports cars; I renovate the house over and over again, especially the living room, and throw out his chair.

Meanwhile, the entire arc of our relationship plays out in the insatiable media. People shake their heads and wonder what happened and how a couple who had everything could screw it up so badly.

"We're here," Jet says, then sings off-key, "'You're welcome!'" before shutting off the vehicle.

"Yay!" Mikey and Meleah shout.

I snap from my daymare and open my door almost before the car fully stops. Wiping sweat from my face and gulping fresh, cool autumn air, I turn my red eyes away from the others.

Oblivious, Jet ducks into the backseat and unfastens Meleah's car seat and Mikey's booster. I hurry to the trunk and frantically pull myself together while popping open Gracie's stroller. By the time Jet meets me at the back of the car with one kid on each hip, I'm relatively composed, and he's too busy making sure he doesn't drop anyone to notice or remark on my bloodshot eyes or pale complexion. I focus on situating Grace in the stroller so my stupid runaway imagination can't get the best of me again at the sight of Jet holding those kids.

Mikey squirms and demands to be let down, which Jet does, more to avoid being kicked in the junk than because he wants to relinquish his hold. He immediately snags his nephew's hand and reminds him to hang on until we finish navigating the parking lot.

I finally figure out the straps in the stroller that will ensure Grace doesn't fall through the leg holes, so we move forward as a drunken blob toward the doors. As Mikey drags his uncle forward, Jet maintains a running monologue with the two older children, discussing toy store strategy and laying the ground rules for today's visit. "Don't run too far ahead, okay? Stay with Mo-Mo and me."

"Okay, okay, okay!" Mikey replies with a sigh.

"Okay!" Meleah parrots.

"Nothing too huge this time, either."

"Awwww!" from both kids.

To Meleah, Jet says, "Your mommy got cheesed off at me last time with the walk-through dollhouse. It was totally worth it, and I'd do it again, but maybe we get something smaller this time. Let's look for something loud, though."

Our niece hugs his neck and stares adoringly into his eyes. It's obvious she doesn't care what the spree produces as long as he's part of the deal. I know exactly how she feels. And it scares me to death what I might someday agree to do to maintain my grasp on him and our life.

———

Our plan to hype them up and send them back to their parents goes slightly awry when I decide that being alone for the night is worse than living with a cranky husband or a sugar-crashing kid, so I invite Meleah for a sleepover. She doesn't need to be convinced, and neither do her parents.

Deirdre can't pack the overnight bag, complete with pre-printed instructions, fast enough.

Meleah's more disappointed to say goodbye to Jet than she was her own parents. Makes sense, considering her uncle spoils her rotten and has never uttered the word "no" to her in her fifteen months of life. The toddler reacts to his departure the way I always feel inside by crying her eyes out and saying his name over and over.

I croon, "I know, baby girl. It stinks." Then we soothe our loneliness in the usual way, with more ice cream and a viewing of *Tangled*. Flynn Ryder and the "funny hawsey" make everything better. By the end of the movie, our spirits are much higher.

When Jet calls to check in before he turns in for the night, our niece lies fast asleep in his usual spot beside me. I answer the phone barely above a whisper, expecting our call to be short.

Veteran players report to camp tomorrow, if they've been re-signed. If Tom couldn't come to a long-term agreement with the team, Jet can still play under a one-year tender, provided the two sides can agree on the terms for that. If they can't agree on anything, it's over. They have until three o'clock tomorrow to figure it out. It's crunch time.

There's definite tension in Jet's voice when he says, "Hey," and my shoulders sag.

Determined not to end the day on a sour note—I can be a cheerleader for one more night, smiling and bouncing on the sideline, as if the score doesn't matter—I say, "Hey yourself. All ready for some sweaty, public workouts tomorrow? Got your autograph pen juiced up?"

"Oh, yeah. You know me." He pauses. "Have you been watching any TV tonight? Sports Center? Football Network?"

Careful not to laugh too loud and wake up Meleah, I answer, "It's cute you think I turn on either of those things when you're not in the house." He chuckles tightly, putting me on my guard. "Why? Should I turn it on now?"

"Nope."

My hand hovers over the remote nestled between my thigh and my niece. "Are you sure? You sound like I might find something on there interesting."

"Oh, you will. In a while."

I sit up straighter against the headboard. "You have news?"

"Yep."

"Well?"

He clears his throat, and I hear paper snapping. "'Twas the night before training camp and all through the fields, / all the re-signing players were waiting for deals.'"

I giggle nervously at his theatrics. When his California shines through and baffles my Midwestern sensibilities, I always try to play along. His West Coast eccentricities are part of what I love about him, after all. At least, that's what I tell myself.

Either not sensing or not caring about my discomfort, he continues, "'The contracts were written by agents with care, / in hopes that team owners would stop splitting hairs. / Then up from my cell phone arose such a clatter, / as agent and media wanted to chatter. / A deal had been struck! At last! Hallelujah! / One-twenty for seven. That oughta do ya!'"

He stops, so I stifle my laughter and clap softly. "Magnificent. Very clever! Is there more?"

"More? After that last line, you need more?"

"Oh. No. But the original poem is much longer, so..."

"I didn't write any more, because I figured you wouldn't

hear anything else after that. Plus, I was sick of rhyming, and I wanted to call you before you heard it somewhere else."

"I see." I blink, and my heart stutters as I replay his poem in my head. "Wait. What? *That's* your actual deal?"

"That's it," he says, laughing. "So? What do you think?"

"Say the numbers again. I was distracted." *And I must have misheard, because they don't make sense.*

He sighs, but he sounds way too happy to be annoyed. "One-twenty over seven years, guaranteed fifty— That last part didn't fit into the rhyme scheme."

"One-twenty. As in?

"Million."

If I weren't already in bed, I'd need to lie down. "Jet, that's — I'm so..."

...sickened by that number.

...ashamed to be one of those *people.*

...astounded that an organization would give that much money to one person to play a game.

"...proud of you! And happy for you, too. That's... That's a lot of money, Champ."

"Not record-setting, but it's up there, yeah." He pauses, and I hear him swig and swallow. Gatorade cocktail, I'm sure, hydrating for his first day of training camp tomorrow. "It's a little embarrassing. I don't want to know what Tom had to say or do to get them there. I'm worried about the salary cap, too. But I guess that Super Bowl win went a long way. The ESPY awards might have helped."

"Must have. Wow. I'm speechless. Seven years."

"Right? Talk about your last-second Hail Mary! I'm getting too old for this."

"Yeah, you're ancient."

"Almost thirty-two! I'm a few years away from announcers

using my age as part of my name. 'Blah-blah-year-old Jet Knox…'"

"Stop it."

"I'll bet you anything they'll mention it every time they talk about the contract. 'By the end of the seven-year deal, Knox will be pushing forty, which is a huge gamble for any franchise.'"

"You're good at that whole announcing thing. You'll make a great commentator when you're too old and busted up to play—in a season or so."

"Laugh all you want, but it's true. I hope I'm good enough at it to get a job."

"You are. Now stop thinking so far ahead and enjoy this victory. I'm super-happy for you," I repeat, wondering when it's going to stop feeling like a lie. I mean, I am happy for him. But why do I have the urge to hide in this house for the rest of my life?

"Oh, and Maura?"

"Yeah?"

"Dust off your theater plans. Because that's happening. It's happening big. Nothing half-assed, all right? You go crazy on it." He's rendered me speechless again, but he doesn't seem to notice. "High-tech everything. Spring for that fancy popcorn machine you want, not the used one. Get the seats you *want*, not the ones you think you *should*. That place you loved near the Power & Light District is the perfect location and will be pretty easy to renovate. I know you wondered if it was too much, too big, but you're going to want room to expand when this idea takes off. It will. Because it's awesome. Maura? You there?"

I nod, then clear my throat. "Yes. I'm here. I'm— How did you know all that?" Unless I've been talking in my sleep, I never told him any of my plans, figuring they might not happen. I didn't want him to feel guilty that I'd done so much work for nothing.

He chuckles. "I had to hear it from Rae. Which kind of sucked. She totally bitched me out for not already knowing it. But I'm glad she told me. I... I'm sorry I've been so wrapped up in myself."

Sniffling, I say, "I understand. I understood. Sort of. It *has* been hard, though."

"Aw, don't cry!"

Like it always does, that command makes me cry harder. I pinch the bridge of my nose. "I can't help it. I'm sorry."

"Don't be sorry; be happy."

"I am."

"I am, too."

"And I *was*, before all this." To my dismay, he doesn't as readily echo my sentiments this time, so I prompt, "Weren't you?"

"Yeah. Yeah, obviously."

I snort skeptically.

"I was! But this is my life, too, ya know? A huge part of my life that I have to care about. If I don't care, then what's the point? Like any other professional... anything, it affects me when work is stressful. I can't help it."

"It's what makes you good at what you do."

"I hate the business side of it. I just want to play and train and... and win!" He pauses. "This contract is— I get that it's crazy."

My shoulders loosen with the relief that we're on the same page there.

"But it's about more than money. It's a statement. I've done it. I'm successful."

"You have a ring that already proves that."

"Well, yeah! Marrying you is the best thing I've ever done."

"I was talking about the Super Bowl ring, dingus."

He laughs. "Oh! That, too."

I shake my head. "You're something else."

"I'm tired. That's what I am."

"Another sign of how old you are."

Meleah stirs next to me, then rolls over, smacking her lips and mumbling something in Toddlerese. I sniff and blink furiously to clear the tears. "Listen. I'm going to text my family the contract numbers before they hear this somewhere else. You should do the same. And no pressure, but you're going to have to be better than ever this season."

"I plan on it."

"Have fun this week, though. See you in a few days."

"I can't wait."

TWENTY-THREE

EXTRAVAGANCE

Nearly two months later, the media is still obsessed with Jet's contract, and since they dictate the public discourse, nobody else will shut up about it, either.

I'm a golden pariah in the WAG Club. The other day, at the home opener, I discovered a fat deal for one player doesn't translate to joy all around. In fact, it likely means fewer earning opportunities for others' spouses, thanks to the salary cap. In some cases, it could also result in someone being *cut* from the team. This *is* a zero sum game. And Jet's hogging a big chunk of the change.

Between updates from my mom, who was keeping me informed on Deirdre's progress birthing my new nephew, I texted Colin at halftime.

Everyone here hates me

Did you wear a McKnight jersey by mistake? Poor form

WAGs

They don't hate you

They do

Haters gonna hate
It's not funny
You can't stop people from being jealous. Get them pissed
They already are
As in "drunk"

But it's going to take more than that. This isn't college. You can't host a kegger and call it good on a pay discrepancy of a hundred mil or so. Even if I'd pulled an "Oprah" and danced around the suite, pointing and singing, "You get a million, and you get a million!" it would have been viewed as patronizing, not generous.

There's nothing I can do to fix this. Being popular or well-liked has never been a huge priority of mine—until now, when it's completely out of reach because of something I can't control.

Who knows? Maybe I was being paranoid at that game, projecting my discomfort with our household income and misinterpreting their stares as glares. Tiffani Tiffenauer was her usual snotty self, but when I got the nerve to talk to a few of the other WAGs, like Keela Jackson, they seemed perfectly pleasant. To my face. And if people can't see past dollar signs, that's their problem.

I'm determined not to let anyone, including myself, put a damper on Jet's happiness. He's worked his whole life for this. The last thing I want is for him to think I'm ashamed of him, because I'm not. At all. Do I have some major issues with anyone making as much money as we're talking about here? Yes. Did I ever think I'd have to worry about being one of the top one percent vilified by champions of the middle class and poor? Hell no. But most of that money will find its way back into the community, thanks to the soon-to-be opened theater.

It's not like we're going to blow it on drugs or private villas. Or luxury cars.

"Well? What do you think?" His elbow hooked over the door of the shiny BMW sedan, Jet leans out the window to gauge my reaction, having summoned me to the driveway via text message. He slides his sunglasses down to the tip of his nose and looks over the top of them, wiggling his eyebrows. "The name of the paint color is 'jet black,' so I had to buy it, naturally."

Oh, happy day! Maybe he got rid of the H2.

I grin down at him. "It's gorgeous! Your new toy?"

"*Your* new toy."

My smile fades, and my chin drops.

He laughs and opens the door, pushing a button to close the window, and stepping out onto the driveway. "Come on. Get behind the wheel. Give her a whirl."

I remain rooted to the pavement, my thoughts pinging in time with the open-door alert sounding from the vehicle. "But I don't need a new car."

"Nobody *needs* a new car." He swings his arm as if to toss the key fob to me but hangs onto it when my arms remain crossed over my chest.

"Sure they do. Single moms with no reliable transportation need new cars. People with jobs and lengthy commutes and twenty-year-old vehicles with two-hundred-thousand miles on them need new cars. I have a perfectly good car in the garage that gets me where I need to go."

Pocketing the fob and his sunglasses, he says, "Yeah, but it's a tin-foil death trap, and this one is shiny and new and safe." He leans over and gazes lovingly down its side, from taillight to headlight. "And hot."

"Would you like a moment alone with the car?"

Straightening, he walks over to me and kisses my lips. "Don't be jealous."

"Don't worry, I'm not."

He returns his attention to the vehicle. "What else? Oh, yeah! It's a hybrid, because you've always wanted one. Consider it a new season celebration gift."

"I was thinking more along the lines of that cashmere coat I've had my eye on."

"I'll get you that, too. But look, Baby." He drags me to the open door and pulls me down to peer inside the cabin. "Nappa leather, sat nav, moon roof, Bang & Olufsen sound system..."

"Whatever the heck that is."

"Awesome, is what it is. Night vision, heated seats, parking assistant..."

"You bought me Kit from *Knight Rider*."

He laughs. "Almost as cool. Check out the doors." I step back and watch while he nudges the driver's door softly shut. A hidden mechanism grabs it and pulls it gently flush with the rest of the vehicle.

"Space-age stuff," I say flatly. "I'm sure you two will be very happy together."

His jaw tightens. "Why are you being like this? I special-ordered this car *for you* and have been keeping it a secret. I thought it would be fun."

I soften and kiss his cheek, then hug his arm. "I'm sorry, Champ, but... Look at this thing!"

"I know. Isn't it great?"

"It's amazing. But how the hell am I supposed to drive it?"

"Like any other car. It's an automatic."

"No, I mean, how am I supposed to roll up to the homeless shelter in this car? If nothing else, I'm afraid someone will steal it."

"That's uppity as hell. Being poor doesn't make people criminals."

"No, being desperate does. You can't dangle an eighty-thousand-dollar piece of cake in front of a diabetic. It's mean."

"Actually, it was closer to eighty-five."

"Oh, fabulous."

"Nobody's gonna know it cost that much!"

"It doesn't matter if they know. *I* know. We could buy someone a damn house for what you paid for this thing."

"Not a very nice house," he mutters.

"Better than the cardboard box they currently have."

He shrugs me off his arm. "What are you saying? We're never going to have nice things? We're not going to enjoy the money I've worked my ass off to earn, because others don't have what we do, and you feel bad about that?"

When I shrug, not sure, myself, what the answer is, he mumbles a string of profanity, then says more loudly for me to hear, "This damn privilege guilt of yours is beyond getting old."

I examine the cloudless blue autumn sky and bite the inside of my cheek.

"I give and give and give to this community—more than money. I donate my time and energy, too, outside of football. And sixteen weeks of the year, minimum, I sacrifice my body for the entertainment of millions of sports fans. It's my business, and I'm not going to feel bad if I want to buy my wife a fucking car."

Oh, so it can do that, too? I was wondering…

Yanking the door open, he plops behind the wheel. "I *earned* the money that paid for this. Nobody gave it to me."

"Where are you going?"

"I'm going for a drive in *your* new car."

"Jet, I'm sorry. I—"

Soft-close technology be damned, he slams the door on my apology and squeals the tires as he pulls through the horseshoe drive and down the private lane to the county road.

So much for not putting a damper on his happiness.

TWENTY-FOUR

GROWNUPS

The one person in my life who definitely has no problem with unequal wealth distribution whistles long and low as I alight from my new car in his driveway a couple of weeks later. "Nice wheels!" Greg says while he helps me load Meleah and her gear for our long weekend together. "Jet's already spending that money, huh?"

To save my marriage (and Jet's feelings), I've grudgingly agreed to drive the luxury vehicle the majority of the time. In exchange, Jet has promised to trade in the H2 for a more grown-up, reasonable SUV—although the one he's eyeing still sports more chrome than I'm comfortable with—and I continue to drive my "tin-foil death trap" on homeless shelter Wednesdays.

"It's just a car," I respond shortly. Annoyingly, the German import has had the nerve to be every bit as amazing as my husband promised.

Greg scoffs. "Yeah, sure, and your estate is 'just a house.' And your in-home theater is 'just a movie room.'"

I try to laugh off his teasing, like the old Maura would do, while giving it right back to him. "And you're 'just an ass.'"

"Hey, watch your mouth around my daughter. She repeats everything lately."

"She should learn early who her father is, so she's not as disillusioned later." I squint into the fall drizzle. "Anything special I need to know that's not in the three-page memo tucked in the diaper bag?"

He checks the car seat harness one more time and stands to face me. "No. Well, yes. If it's not too much of a pain, maybe you can take her to see Jack at Mom and Dad's once? Or twice? She's going to miss him."

If this is his way of making me feel bad because I wasn't comfortable taking both of his kids, one of whom is less than a month old, while he and Deirdre attend some hospital boondoggle in Barbados for the next four days, well... it's working.

Once again, I explain, "If Jet were playing a home game... But he'll be out in California, and—"

He waves me off. "I wouldn't want to take care of both of them alone, either, and they're my kids." Before he can slam the door, I gently close it, laughing when he stares, agog, at the whirring magic that occurs. "Whoa..."

"Fancy," I say drolly. "All right, then. We're off."

While I situate myself behind the wheel, he waves and blows kisses through the back window. Meleah whines, "Daddy!" a few times, but the minute he's out of sight, and we're on our way, her tears miraculously dry, and she squeals, "Ice cream!"

What a difference a few months of regular play dates and sleepovers with Mo-Mo makes.

In the garage at home later, I scrub the chocolate stains from her mouth with a raggedy napkin and water from a bottle in my purse and put my finger to her lips. "The ice cream is our secret, all right? Uncle Jet made us dinner, and I don't want his feelings to be hurt."

She grins and nods, but it's hard to tell how much she understands or if she's capable of the brand of deceit I'm inappropriately asking her to perpetrate. A mature, responsible adult would have told her to wait until after dinner for ice cream. A mature, responsible adult wouldn't ask her to lie.

Since I'm neither of those things, apparently, I have to hope for the best.

As soon as she bursts through the door and runs into the kitchen, where she finds Jet browning beef for tacos, she yells, "Ice cream!"

My blush and the chocolate drips on her shirt are all the clues he needs. "You took her for ice cream right before dinner."

"She was sad to leave her dad. I didn't want to bring a crying kid home. I know you like a quiet night before your first road trip."

He shakes his head and mutters, "Shameless," before turning back to his sizzling skillet.

"We'll still eat!"

Wooden spoon aloft, he whirls once more, eyes wide but mouth bemused. "You ate ice cream, too?"

"Ice cream!" Meleah confirms, hugging Jet's legs and hopping from foot to foot. "Up! Pick up!"

"A few licks," I lie. I detach the toddler from the hem of his shorts and swing her onto my hip.

He laughs. "Wow. Why am I bothering with this? I should have gone with you, and we could have all had ice cream for dinner."

"You don't eat stuff like that during the season."

"Maybe I'll start."

"No, you won't."

"No, I won't. It's not cool for you guys to do it, either."

With a fake pout, I say to him while looking at Meleah, who laughs and pulls on my bottom lip, "Don't be mad. We'll still eat your righteous tacos."

"You bet your ass you will," he says, draining the grease from the meat. "I've slaved over this meal. I sliced avocados and chopped tomatoes and mixed up a batch of strawberry margaritas."

"Babies can't drink, Jet."

He mock-glares at me. "They shouldn't eat ice cream before dinner, either."

Touché.

———

I whisper the last two lines of the picture book I was reading to Meleah before she zonked out next to me on the couch. Quietly, I close the book and set it on the cushion on the other side of me, then lean over and kiss her plump cheek. I tuck her flyaway blonde hair behind her ear and watch her sleep, wondering how I'm going to transfer her from here to the portable crib in our room without waking her up. Maybe it makes more sense to bring the crib down here to her.

I straighten and turn to mention the idea to Jet, who's sitting on the matching loveseat across from us, headphones firmly in place to drown out our voices, engrossed in his play book—or so I thought. He flinches when I catch him watching us and quickly looks back down at his binder. Licking his thumb, he flips the page and rubs his neck as if he had only been stretching, not staring.

Smiling slyly, I motion for him to lift one of the cans from his ears, so I can talk to him without yelling.

He complies, and I say, "Hey, creeper." At his feigned confusion, I decide not to tease him any further. "Would it be weird to bring the portable crib down here, so we don't have to move her so far?"

He shrugs. "Will she freak out when she wakes up alone down here in the library tomorrow morning?"

"Maybe." I wince.

"Let's stick to the original plan, then. I'll carry her up in a minute."

"Speaking of plans, are you going to be available this week to swing by the theater with me and check out the progress? The A/V equipment is going in, then the seats. I've been told Wednesday would be a good time to take a look."

He hisses through his teeth. "Tuesday would be better, but if you're okay with waiting until Wednesday evening, kind of late…"

"That's fine."

He stretches and yawns, removing his headphones completely and setting them on the coffee table between us. "Oh, man. I'm not looking forward to Sunday's game."

"You're already dreading games? It's going to be a long season."

"Not just any game. These West Coast match-ups are killer."

"I hate them."

"Not as much as I do. Especially Raiders games. The fans are such jerks."

"Are you breaking the story wide open that rivals are dicks to each other?"

"They take it to a whole new level. Throwing batteries? Come on! The stadium's a pit, too."

"Maybe that's why the fans are so unhappy."

He laughs. "Maybe. That, and their team sucks. I can't wait until they move to Vegas, so we can kick their asses a few hundred miles closer to home."

I moan. "I love it when you trash-talk."

"Yeah? Why don't you come over here and show me how much?" He pats the cushion next to him.

I giggle. "Like we're going to have sex with Meleah here? Gross."

"She's sleeping. Anyway, who said anything about sex? I only want to fool around."

"Not much better."

"You and your principles. Is this how it would be if we had our own kids? We'd never have sex again? That doesn't make sense."

Waving both hands at him, I click my tongue. "You're being weird."

"I'm being half-serious. Because that would be a major factor in the decision-making for me."

My only response is to tilt my head at him, look through the tops of my eyes, and flatten my lips into a straight line. This is hardly a conversation I want to have right here, right now. For one thing, it's ridiculous. For another, it's seeming more and more like a moot point. But that second thing will lead to a much longer discussion, and I'm way too tired for that.

His face relaxes into a smug smile. "Oh, who are we kidding? You can't resist me."

"You got me there." I stand and stretch, then pick up the picture book and put it on the low shelf where it belongs, at little kid eye-level. I move to collect Jet's stuff, but he distractedly tells me to leave it as he stands over Meleah and studies her, ostensibly to figure out how to pick her up without waking her.

I'm about to tell him to go for it, and we'll get her back to sleep upstairs, when he murmurs, "They're so sweet when they sleep, aren't they? Couldn't you watch her forever?"

Normally, I'd agree with him, but I desperately have to pee, so after a few more seconds, I nudge his arm. "She's adorable, Champ. Let's pull the plug on this day and get her up to bed."

He blinks from his reverie and slides his arms between her tiny body and the couch, like a human fork lift. Gathering her to his chest, he whispers, "It's cool," when she whimpers. She curls against him, burying her face in his armpit.

As I follow them up the stairs, he hums the USC fight song, and my heart melts. I'd say he needs to broaden his lullaby repertoire, but on second thought, that works just fine.

———

Today I keep my niece too busy to mourn the departure of her beloved uncle for long. I'm not gonna lie—the early morning was touch-and-go, and I'm not above serving the kid ice cream for breakfast, but I somehow found myself without any in the house. It's probably for the best. Jet will love me no matter how many meals I spoil with heavy cream and sugar; my mom is a different story. There was no way I was showing up for brunch at my parents' house with ice cream drips on Meleah's clothes.

After a perfectly adequate meal that I didn't have to cook, approve, or arrange, my niece and I spend a good part of the late morning and early afternoon snuggling her little brother and listening to my mom and dad's stories about their latest travels. I may have dozed off a time or two during the particularly long accounts, but Mom does a good job of mixing it up with pictures on the phone she keeps sticking under my nose, so I never sleep for long. Finally, my parents have mercy on me and let me snooze for about twenty minutes while Meleah and Jack take their early afternoon naps.

To ease the sting of separation from her brother, I whisk Meleah to City Market after we leave Mom and Dad's. I skip the clothing and home goods shops that would bore her stick to the open air farmers' market. In the fall, the vendors' stalls are festooned with chrysanthemums of nearly every color and warm-colored fruits and vegetables. We choose red, white, and yellow mums for the front porch and a fat pumpkin for carving later. I also pick up some local ingredients for a basic, home-cooked dinner. An artist paints matching "KC" arrowheads on our left cheeks. The dozens of selfies I snap will go to Jet later.

When Meleah starts to get crabby, I lug her and our purchases back to the car and get her home right as she's falling asleep in the backseat. She grouses about having to take another nap, but when I tell her she can sleep in Jet's chair with Torzi while I make dinner, she relents. The dog doesn't look as thrilled about it, but to his credit, he humors her until she falls asleep. As her limbs open like a carnivorous plant, he hops down with a huff and whines at the back door.

With the dog dispatched to the backyard and the child sleeping, I tiptoe into the kitchen, where I mix a spaghetti squash casserole for dinner, empty our carving pumpkin of its innards, rinse and mix up two batches of pumpkin seeds for roasting—one spicy, one sweet—and place the seeds and casserole in the ovens. I haul the empty pumpkin to the sun porch and plunk it on the table draped with newspaper and holding the carving tools.

Yeah, I'm a regular Martha Stewart, Suzy Homemaker, and Betty Crocker rolled into one. It's exhausting being three people.

Problem is, my day's only half over.

A cranky toddler doesn't hold back when she wants you to know how ticked off she is about being woken up from a nap she didn't even want. It's worse when the dinner you wake her up for isn't something she's particularly interested in eating. Kids shy of two years old aren't adventurous eaters, apparently. And she's not fooled by the pasta-like appearance of the squash. After only a few frustrating minutes, it's clear that Meleah isn't going to open her mouth for the food. Meanwhile, mine cools and congeals on my plate into something equally unappetizing to me, so I give in and heat up some of Beau's leftover mac-n-cheese. It has pureed cauliflower in it— the only way Jet will eat the white vegetable—so the joke's on the baby. She gobbles it up while I pick through my casserole, too tired to eat much.

And now, after carving a "unicorn" into a curved, bumpy, uneven surface; bathing a slippery, squirmy, splashy child; changing a horrific diaper—after the bath, of course; reading the same book as last night, plus six others; and uttering the word "no" approximately eleventy billion times in a house that's in desperate need of babyproofing, it's all I can do to keep my eyes open for Jet's goodnight call.

In fact, I can't. And I miss his first attempt altogether. The second time my phone rings—first time I hear it—I swim to the surface of consciousness with great effort and, dizzy and disoriented, slap at the device until my fingers figure out how to work it, independent of my brain.

"Herro," I slur.

Jet chuckles. "Oh, wow. Either you're drunk, or you were already asleep. Either way, sounds like it's been quite a day, and you might not remember this conversation tomorrow."

"Mmmph." I curl onto my side and burrow into my pillow, balancing my phone on my head, against my exposed ear.

"You're not drunk, right?"

"No."

"Okay. Just checking."

"Dude. I am 'zausted. You have no idea."

"You're right. I've been hanging out at the spa all day, gabbing with the guys." He laughs. "Now you know how I feel when I come home after a day of practice, and you're like, 'Let's go out to dinner,' or 'Let's run down to the theater and check out the construction,' or—"

"'Let's have sex'? Which you're never going to have to worry about again, if you don't shut up?"

"I'm just saying... You always make me feel bad when I'm too tired at the end of the day, but you're feeling now how I do most of the time."

"You're used to it, though! And there's a difference between working out and chasing after a kid all day."

"They're both draining."

"Did you have to try to force-feed any of your teammates?"

"Ha! No."

"Did you have to keep reminding Tiff not to touch the electrical outlets?"

"No."

"Did you have to read seven books to Jackson and change his diapers?"

"Yep."

We both laugh, me a tad less enthusiastically than him. Then he says, "I won't keep you long, then. I wanted to see how the day went and give you a long-distance goodnight kiss."

"Aww. The day was mostly fine. I made you some pumpkin seeds."

"Wow. You *were* busy."

"Shut up."

"I'm not being sarcastic!" He chortles, then says in a sultry voice, "What are you wearing right now?"

Eyes closed and feeling sleep wrap its warm blanket around me, I mumble, "Those matching Chiefs footie pajamas I got for Meleah and me."

"Not my first choice, but I can work with it. Are you going to wear a cheerleader outfit tomorrow while you watch the game?"

"No. Yoga pants and Knox jersey, like always."

"That's hot."

"Good. It's also comfortable and doesn't make me feel like an actor in a bad porno."

"Still hot."

"Fine. I can't help it that I'm unintentionally hot."

"No need to apologize."

We go back and forth a few more times, our utterances becoming more and more listless, until I say, "All right, Champ. Beddy-bye time for both of us. Get a good rest so you'll have a clear head and kick some Raider butt tomorrow. No injuries!"

He chuckles. "Don't you worry, Beautiful."

But I always do, and he knows it.

TWENTY-FIVE

RESPONSIBILITY

Jet's triumphant return disrupts Meleah's Sunday night bedtime routine, which isn't much of a routine at our house, to be fair. It's also undoubtedly hours later than her usual bedtime at home. (Have I mentioned I have no idea what I'm doing?) He mercifully interrupts our fifth reading of a saccharine-sweet illustrated book about acceptance and tolerance, so Meleah abandons me and scrambles for the foot of the bed. "Unca Jet!"

Still looking heart-stoppingly handsome in his post-game interview and travel attire, he trades his rolling bag for an armful of niece. "Well, hello there, Miss Priss. Did you watch me on TV today?"

She nods solemnly. I set the book on my nightstand and look on with amusement as Meleah strokes Jet's face, like she can't believe he's here with us.

"It took some convincing that the guy on TV was you, but they finally got a shot of you on the bench with your helmet off. I wish I had been recording it, because her reaction was hilarious."

He chuckles, then asks her, "Don't you watch the games with your daddy?"

Bored with the conversation, she rests her head on his shoulder and hugs his neck, so I answer, "It might be Greg's only alone time."

Jet clicks his tongue. "We need to fix this. How's she going to learn the game if nobody teaches her? She didn't even know who I was?"

"She knows you're her favorite uncle. That's all that matters."

"Did you teach her some new words today during the game?"

I laugh. "I didn't have to say any of those words. Nice butt-whoopin', Number Fourteen."

With the child still attached to him, he kicks off his shoes and joins me on the bed. Finally, I get my reunion kiss, albeit more chaste than usual. He nestles Meleah between us, but she immediately clambers back on top of him and curls up on his chest like an overgrown cat.

"Okay, then," he says, bemused.

I scoot closer to his side and pet her hair, continuing the cat act. She meows.

"Go with it," I mouth to a surprised Jet, who's nearly bursting with stifled laughter.

"Pretty kitty," he chokes, awkwardly patting her back.

I snicker at him.

"What? I'm a dog person." He scrunches his chin to his chest to get a view of her face. "She's falling asleep," he whispers.

"Good," I whisper back. "Tell me about your trip."

"Not much to tell. We went, we saw, we dominated, we left. Next week's game against the Steelers won't be as easy, because they're a better team. But we'll be at home, so I'm not worried."

"Don't get cocky."

"Never." His smirk tells a different story, so I roll my eyes, but before I can call him on it, he quickly changes the subject. "Other than watching football, what did you guys do today?"

I inhale a deep, contented breath and answer, "Not much. Swung by Mom and Dad's to give Meleah a chance to mother her brother."

"How's Cap'n Jack?"

"Adorable. Why are babies so darn cute?"

"So people will keep having them, and humans won't die out. Did he smell good?"

"Of course. Not as good as you do, though."

He laughs while I sniff up and down his arm, then rise on my knees to reach his neck. "That tickles. And I'm holding a kid here."

"Then put her down."

After tucking her under the covers in her crib at the foot of our bed, we slip from the room, and I lead him to a bedroom down the hallway. I remove his expensive dress clothes and strip for him while he reclines naked on the bed.

"Best weekend ever," he murmurs several minutes later, still on top of me with his face between my breasts.

He turns his head and exhales contentedly while I play with his hair, trying to finger-comb it into submission. It's hopelessly tousled, but I continue my efforts and say, "I have a name for the theater."

"Mm-hmm."

"I think we should keep it simple."

"Like me."

I chuckle and flick the top of his head.

"Ow."

"You're too hard-headed for that to have hurt. I'm being serious here."

"Tell me, then."

"Knox Theater."

"Bo-ring."

"Simple is good! Anyway, I'm not finished. The name of the theater will be our last name, but all of our marketing materials will have a slogan, too: 'Where opportunity knocks.'"

His silence could be interpreted two ways: disapproval or sleep. I wait. Just when I think it's the latter, he finally says, "That's cute."

"'Cute'? Oh, boy. You hate it."

"No!" With what seems like a greater effort than anything he displayed on the field earlier today, he rises on his arms and looks down into my face. "I like it a lot. But can we spell 'knocks' like our last name?"

"Maybe. Let's see how it looks written out."

He kisses my nose. "Deal. It might be too nerdy, on second thought." Searching my eyes, he asks, "Are you happy? Is everything turning out the way you thought it would?"

"Beyond my wildest dreams."

"Are you just saying that?"

"Nope."

"Okay, good. What's your first screening going to be?"

"Don't know. But we should get back to our room before we fall asleep in here, and Meleah wakes up alone."

He moans and collapses on top of me again. "A few more minutes."

I twist a lock of his hair around my index finger. "A few more minutes."

———

The higher we circle in the parking garage across the street from the theater, the more my excitement translates into anxiety. "There's a spot," I point out.

"I can see," Jet snaps.

Stung but determined not to take it too personally or snap back, I mutter, "Sheesh. Crabby much?"

He pulls into the space, jams the car in park, and jabs at the button to turn off the engine, but I don't release my seat belt or move to open the door.

He follows my lead, staring through the windshield. "Shit, I'm sorry, Maura. I'm tired and hungry. It was kind of a crap day." He smiles over at me. "But it's about to get a whole lot better, right?"

My nervous anticipation returns. "Yes! I hope so. I *think* so."

He laughs. "What are you so nervous about?"

"That it's going to fail," I say bluntly.

It's the most honest thing I've ever said to him, without major cajoling. In fact, he seems speechless that it was that easy to get an answer. "Uh... Well... What do you— I mean, what if it—"

"Who cares, right?" I say lightly.

"That's not what I said. I wasn't even thinking it."

I wave off his seriousness. "Bah. It's a silly little project to keep me busy and spend some of our ridiculous money in a way that doesn't make me feel guilty, right? If it doesn't work out, oh well. It probably *will* fail, in fact. Most of these pet projects do. And I'll be on to the next thing. Or ready to pop out babies. Or whatever." I brush my hair away from my face with a shaking hand.

"Hey." Jet unbuckles his seat belt and turns to face me, the leather seat squeaking under him. He reaches over and clicks the button to release me, too, then strokes my cheek with his knuckle.

I brush him off, my laugh brittle. "It's not a big deal. It is what it is. It'll be fun for however long it lasts. And it'll do a lot of good, I hope."

He continues to stare at my profile, so I inhale a deep breath and grab the door handle. Before I can get out, he snags my hand closest to him.

"Why do you think it's going to fail?"

I shrug. "I dunno. I've never run a business before, much less a non-profit."

"No pressure to make money," he says with a gentle smile.

"You still have to break even and cover operating costs, though. And there's more to all of it than I thought."

"That's why we hired Greg. Do you think your brother's going to let you screw this up?"

"No."

"What else?"

I smile in spite of my worries. "Who says there's anything else?"

He rolls his hand encouragingly. "What else?"

"This— Well, what if— This might not be something people around here are all that into. There's a multiplex two blocks from here that serves full meals and alcohol and—"

"Completely different niche. In fact, that's great, because people walking around down here will see that place and your place and have a choice between two different experiences, and I guarantee they'll be in the mood for what you're offering as often as that other place."

"What am I offering? One film at a time. Old films. Candy and popcorn and soda."

"It'll remind people of the good old days. Their money will go toward a worthy cause, too, which will make them even happier."

Closing my eyes and concentrating on regulating my breathing, I nod, hoping that by displaying an outward sign of agreement, I can convince the rest of me to listen to Jet.

"Come on. You're only freaking out, because it's going to be so much more real after this. Not just pictures and plans anymore."

I continue nodding.

"The same thing happened with the wedding, remember? But at some point, you have to master those fears and follow through, for better or worse. You have to put the game plan into action."

"Please. No sports metaphors. Not now."

He cringes sheepishly. "Sorry. Habit."

Before I can think any more about it, I open the door and practically bolt for the elevator that will take us down to street level.

Jet, laughing, scrambles to catch up to me. "Hey! Wait up!" When he steps into the elevator with me, I let go of the door and poke the "G" button. "That was Combine speed, Babe."

"Let's do this before I have a panic attack."

"It's going to be great. If there's anything—anything at all —you see in there tonight that isn't exactly how you imagined it, we'll fix it."

When the elevator opens to spit us out, I hesitate for a second, but Jet pulls me forward. "This is going to be awesome. I can feel it."

Since life rarely dares to disappoint Jet Knox, his declaration greatly reassures.

———

Standing before the front plate glass window, we stare at the two "Coming Attraction" posters framed in white lights that will chase each other 'round and 'round when turned on, drawing attention to the films we'll be promoting. Today, they simply say, "The Knox Theater: Where Opportunity Knox" and "Coming Soon," respectively.

Jet grins down at me. "Great idea. See? You've got this." He turns toward the door, but I remain rooted to the sidewalk, peering into the darkness beyond the window. Eventually, he returns for me and pulls on my hand. "The question is, do you have the key?"

"What? Oh. Yes. Somewhere." I dig in the huge shoulder bag that's a holdover from Meleah's stay, when I didn't want to carry a diaper bag everywhere, but I needed room for a few essentials. Pushing aside a sippy cup of tepid water and a travel package of wet wipes, I locate the key I haven't yet clipped to my key chain. "Here it is."

Jet bounces on his toes and rubs his hands together. "So exciting!"

His enthusiasm is contagious. The nervousness in my tummy morphs into an anticipatory fizz while I slide the metal into the final lock and turn it. "Here we go…"

The door swings wide with a swoosh when I pull on it. Jet grabs the edge and holds it open for me, waiting for me to enter ahead of him. Since it's still a construction site, it's not much warmer in here than it is on the chilly sidewalk, but there's no breeze. In the darkness, I can make out vague shapes where I assume the combined concession/ticket counter is. The antique popcorn machine and the glass-fronted cooler that will hold bottled drinks won't be delivered until closer to the grand opening, but I recognize the rectangular holes where they'll slide in. The distinct aromas of sawdust and fresh paint tickle my nose. I fumble on the wall for the light switch and finally locate it.

"Lookit this," Jet says breathlessly at the sudden illumination. "It looks great so far, don't you think?"

Now that my heart has started beating again, I'm able to breathe and nod. My eyes well with pride that this is *mine*. It's still unfinished and unfurnished, but I can see it exactly how it will eventually be, and it's magnificent.

Crossing to a tiny alcove in the small lobby, I say, "There'll be an area rug here with two sofas and a couple of chairs. You know, for groups meeting here or people who arrive before we're seating for the show."

"Yep. That's a must."

"And over here"—I skip to the glass and metal counter —"is where people will buy their tickets and refreshments."

"Naturally."

I mimic operating a cash register. Jet steps up to the counter. "Two for *Tangled*."

I toss my head back and laugh but quickly resume character. "Who's your date?"

He smirks. "This super-smart, funny, sexy chick who's way out of my league."

"I doubt that."

"It's true. But she hasn't figured it out yet, so..." He puts his finger to his lips.

"I won't mention it. Here are your tickets." I hand over the invisible stubs.

"Thanks. I'll also take the biggest, most obnoxious tub of popcorn you have. Oh, and Hot Tamales. Those are her favorite."

"She has great taste."

He takes the "snacks" from me then braces his weight on the counter and leans toward me, poised for a smooch.

I pull my head back. "I don't kiss men who are already taken."

Blushing, he freezes. "Oh. Well... But—" He sighs and forms a "T" with his two hands, tapping his left palm against the tips of the fingers on his right hand, in the classic "time out" signal. "I'm not smart enough to do this."

"I see. Well, since you're cute, I'll let it slide this time." He leans forward once more, and I peck his puckered lips, but he holds me in place with a hand to the back of my head for a much longer, deeper kiss that I'm happy to oblige.

He pulls back first and smiles lazily. "I think I'm going to like this place. Great service."

Dabbing my mouth, I round the counter to finish the tour, leading him to the door that opens on the facility's only auditorium. "Follow me."

Jet threads his fingers through mine as we stride up the narrow corridor with the slightly inclined floor. When the wall to our right ends, we find ourselves in a theater with terraced seating for two hundred.

Jet bounces into one of the seats to test its cushion. Then he lowers the armrest/cup holder and slouches like he would if truly here to watch a film. "Nice." He winks at me. "Why don't you sit down next to me, little lady?"

I caress the leatherette upholstery first, then follow his suggestion. "I wanted velour, you know, like the old-timey movie theater seats?"

"These are nice, though. Easier to clean."

"Exactly my thinking. Spills would be a nightmare on cloth seats."

Jet wraps his arm around my shoulders. "Gotta be practical." Nodding to the screen a few rows ahead of us, he asks, "When's the show start?"

I pop to my feet. "Oh, yeah. Hang on. The tech dude emailed me earlier today with instructions. He said the remote was in the cup holder of the first chair in the first row." I locate the device exactly where he said it would be. Since I tested the projector in the showroom, I only need to study the buttons for a few seconds to jog my memory. Locating the play button, I point the remote at the surprisingly small machine suspended from the ceiling almost directly above Jet's head. On the screen behind me, a test pattern pops up, followed by a countdown and the theme to *Indiana Jones*.

"Aw, yeah..." Jet says with a chuckle. "Is this going to be your first screening?"

I wince and pause the video so we can comfortably converse. "No, this is a test file. Sorry. I'm still not sure what the first film is going to be. Any requests?"

"*Indiana Jones*. No, wait. *Star Wars*. No, wait. *The Matrix!*"

"All worthy candidates," I say noncommittally.

"Nothing with guys wearing those neck scarf things."

"Cravats?"

"Yeah, those. 'Allo, Guvner."

"Don't ever let Colin hear you butcher his accent like that."

Jet ignores my criticism. "Promise me the first movie won't be some poncey period drama."

"Fine. As long as you promise never to use the word 'poncey' again."

"Make it something bad-ass."

I shrug and turn off the projector. "I was hoping to decide based on who the first charity was, connecting the movie to that. But I might not have any takers by the time we open in December."

"That seems so far away from now."

"I didn't want to cut it too close, in case there were delays. Plus, I still need to hire a couple of people, including a manager. Lots of meetings ahead with the board of directors..."

"I'll be there!"

"Me, too! And meetings with attorneys and probably a hundred other people I'm forgetting."

"It'll all come together," Jet reassures me for the billionth time. "Do you feel better now that you've seen it?"

I twirl in a circle to better examine the details: the faux balconies in the two back corners; the cathedral ceiling; the automated sconces programmed to dim and brighten based on a signal from the projector; the high-traffic, low-pile carpeting; the black walls; the runner lights along the rows and up the stairs. "Yes," I answer. "I do. It's exactly how I imagined it would be. Maybe better. And when the lobby's finished... It's going to be so cool."

Jet joins me in the side aisle and wraps me in a hug. "You know, with all the charities the guys on the team work with, I bet we can find one that would love to benefit from your opening weekend. Want me to ask around the locker room?"

"Sure. That's a great idea. Thanks!"

"I'll do it. Now, I don't mean to make this all about me, but I'm so hungry, I'm about to murder someone."

"Since I'm the only potential victim handy, I vote we go grab something to eat, then."

He steps ahead of me and holds open the door to the lobby. "Awesome. But first, I need to give the urinals in this place a test run."

Classy.

TWENTY-SIX

BOSS LADY

We have no conference room, and the manager's office can't comfortably hold ten people, so we've set a chair in front of the giant, dark screen in the theater, and the board members have each taken a seat in the front row. The house lights are at full brightness, which is still not overly bright or intimidating. It's an unconventional setting for interviewing potential managers, but it works.

Since volunteers from participating and benefiting charities will be providing the majority of the manpower, the Knox Theater will only employ two permanent people, in addition to me. Whomever we choose today for the manager position will be in charge of helping me hire a part-time attendant to help them coordinate operations and oversee the volunteers during benefit runs. In addition to tending to administrative details, like inventory, ordering, and maintenance, the manager will also help me with marketing. I'll fill in staffing gaps and represent the theater in the community. I'll also be in charge of screening and scheduling service groups who would like to volunteer for film runs and, subsequently, profit from those weekends' proceeds.

Suddenly nervous, despite being among family and friends, I clear my throat and make the mistake of glancing at Jet, who gives me a cheesy thumbs up. Stifling a giggle, I begin, "Thanks for coming, everyone. I hope this won't take long. We have four applicants. All of them have already passed background checks. You have the questions we agreed to in the folder in front of you. Feel free to chime in with any follow-ups. If, after all four meetings, there's no clear front runner, we'll discuss strategies for next steps. Hopefully, though, we'll have a manager by the end of the day. Ready?"

When I receive a full row of nods, plus a few grumbled wisecracks from Greg, I excuse myself to retrieve the first interviewee from the lobby, furnished just in time last week to serve as the perfect staging area. I push through the door that leads from the screening room and paste a smile on my face for the benefit of whomever happens to be waiting.

The first person I see, a pacing Derek, deadens the genuine emotion behind my expression. I halt a few feet away, but he closes the gap, standing directly in front of me. His eyes shift around the lobby. "Maura. How's it going?"

Good, until now. I reply with a wary, "Fine." When I called The Career Center to solicit candidates and set up this interview date, and my former boss told me she was putting her "best person" on it, I *almost* balked, knowing exactly who she meant. But I thought, *Don't be so petty, Maura. What's a couple of phone calls to discuss a job posting? Surely you can put aside your differences for that.* I also reassured myself that he would be extra motivated to do a good job, if for no other reason than to prove to me how superior a career counselor he is. Actually having to deal with him face-to-face wasn't part of the deal. I can count on zero hands how many times I showed up with a candidate to an interview.

I'm about to ask him if there's something wrong when he steps sideways, obviously with the purpose of blocking my view of the lobby. Of course, if I wanted to, I could see right over his head, but I'm almost afraid to look.

"Hey, uh, listen. I realize it's slightly unconventional for me to be here, but I thought it was appropriate, under the circumstances."

"Which are?"

His usual cocky smile makes an appearance at my nervousness. "Nothing earth-shattering, but there have been a couple of last-minute changes to the lineup."

If I weren't so caught off guard, I'd roll my eyes at the sports-speak, but I'm too numb from the rising panic that my precious theater's first official business isn't going to plan, which underscores my lifelong opinion that plans are dumb. "Such as…?"

He scratches the side of his nose. "To start, two of the applicants accepted positions at other companies since first applying. Which I warned you could happen when we discussed the lag time between the application deadline and the interview process."

I rotate my wrist, moving my hand in a circle at him. "Yeah, yeah. I get that. I still remember how it works. So, we only have two interviewees here today?" I crane my neck to see for myself, but he tiptoes, so I can't see over or around his big head. "Why do you keep blocking my view?"

He chuckles nervously. "I want your full attention while I explain things, that's all."

Biting my lip, I force myself to focus on his smug face. "You have it."

"One of the other applicants changed her mind at the last second—like, this morning—about working for a non-profit. Said she'd been there, done that— and hated it."

"Okay. Would have been nice of her to remember *before* submitting herself for consideration, but whatever."

"That left you with one candidate, which isn't much of a choice, right? What self-respecting career counselor would let that stand?"

I suck my teeth and begin a countdown from ten.

"Long story short, I sent you one of the original candidates and a last-minute substitute." He grins. "You're welcome."

Ignoring his self-congratulations, I say, "Fine, I suppose. Does the new person have a resume I can copy and give to the rest of the board of directors?"

"Yes! Of course." Finally, he steps out of my way so he can lead me to the pair of applicants waiting patiently in the lobby.

I smile at the first person I see, a young guy who looks like he sought fashion and personality advice from Derek before coming here today. We mutter greetings to each other, and I turn to the other candidate. For the second time in a short period, my insides turn to ice.

"Nina."

She stands and smooths her skirt, then shakes my hand. "Maura. Thanks for giving me this opportunity today. I realize it's a little weird, but Derek said it would be okay, and he'd explain things."

Nodding robotically, I take her resume from her shaking hands. "Absolutely. Life is about adjusting, right?"

"Yes! Which is why I'm here, in fact. Adjusting. To things." She glances at Derek, who frowns and shakes his head but tries to hide it behind a fake cough when I catch him. "Uh, anyway! There's my resume, and Derek's ordered my background check, although I have a pretty recent one on file already."

"Let me make some copies of this, and—" I turn when I hear the screening room door squeak open behind me and click shut again. *Must oil that thing before Opening Day.*

Jet beams a thousand-watter at us as he approaches and asks, "Hey, is everything okay out here?"

Before I can answer, Derek practically pushes me aside to offer his hand to Jet. "How's it going, my friend? I was discussing with Maura a slight change in today's starting roster."

Jet's smile shifts to one of bemused uncertainty as he shakes the job counselor's hand. "'Kay. Sorry, but have we met before?"

Somehow, I manage not to laugh when I jump in and say, "Jet, this is Derek, my former colleague at The Career Center."

Jet blushes. "Derek! Sorry, man. Didn't recognize you without the robe and hat. You were Gandalf, right?"

Derek's jaw tightens. He releases Jet's hand and bobs his head like he's working a kink from his neck. "Uh, yeah."

"Dude, that costume was the best." Finished with that conversation, Jet turns to me. "What's the holdup?"

I wave Nina's resume at him. "Last-minute changes. Not a biggie. I'll copy this, and we'll be all set to meet with Kirk, then Nina."

At the mention of his name, the first candidate stands and straightens his suit jacket. He shakes hands with Jet and says, "Stoked to meet you. Big fan. The team looks awesome this year. Undefeated season, you think?"

Jet chuckles. "One game at a time, I think."

I slip into the manager's office to photocopy Nina's

monster resume and try not to take too much delight in Derek's discomfort at being embarrassed, however inadvertently, by Jet. Sometimes my husband's bad memory is the greatest blessing.

———

The purpose of hand-picking the board members myself was so they'd agree with me. Even Greg, the proud contrarian, would see things my way the majority of the time, I figured, and the other times, he'd be outnumbered and outvoted. I had no idea our first official major decision would go so overwhelmingly against me.

"You guys don't understand," I say as we deliberate while munching ordered-in sandwiches from the pub down the street. "I know Nina. She's high-maintenance. And after she's made life difficult here for a few months, she'll leave us in the position of having to hire someone else. She's not a good choice."

Cyndi stares a potato chip down before popping it into her mouth and replying around it, "She seemed nice."

"She interviewed well," Deirdre adds.

"Of course she did," I say, abandoning my chicken salad croissant. "I trained her well in the art of interviewing, and she's had lots of practice."

Greg snickers. "That's ironic, then."

Ana Paula sips demurely through her straw and says, "What if she has never found her place? What if this is her place? She seemed comfortable with you."

"Because she knows me. Too well. Which is symptomatic of the problem. You're not supposed to visit your job counselor so often that you form a relationship."

A throat clearing down the row grabs my attention. Colin half-raises his hand, blushing. "I'm sitting right here."

Normally, I'd laugh, but I'm fighting for my life here. "You're different," I snap.

Dad balls his empty wax paper wrapping and squeezes it in his fist. "You're the one who has to work with her, Mo."

"Exactly!"

"But she seemed like the perfect candidate to me."

I grunt and nudge Jet, who begrudgingly turns his attention from his love affair with his roast beef on rye and says lamely while wiping his mouth, "Kirk was an okay guy, too."

"He wasn't the perfect person, either," I say begrudgingly. "Let's keep looking and hold more interviews later."

Everyone else murmurs their discontent at that suggestion.

Deirdre says, "Don't you think it's getting a tad late for that? Give Nina a chance."

Rae stifles a burp. "Frankly, I was impressed by how poised she stayed, despite you grilling her about her extensive job hopping. You were scary."

"That's saying something, coming from Rae," Jet mutters.

I shoot him a dirty look. "I needed you guys to hear it straight from her that she's a flake."

"But her answers made her appear anything but flaky," Cyndi says. "She sounded regretful, like she's learned her lesson and is a different person now."

"She's litigious," I say. "Litigious people don't change. She'll throw a hissy fit about something stupid and sue us. I've watched her do it countless times before."

Deirdre taps her nail on her arm rest. "She's never gone through and sued anyone, though, has she? Only threatened. We get people like that all the time at the hospital. That's their way of expressing their displeasure and making sure everyone's paying attention and taking them seriously."

"It's annoying," Greg says, raising my hopes only to dash them with, "but harmless."

"Colin," I beseech my best friend, "tell them about the repeat applicants you've seen for yourself at The Career Center. Explain how unemployable they can be."

"I was one of them, so I hardly think I'm the right person to explain," he says petulantly while pretending to examine his fingernails.

"Come on!"

He drops his act and smiles. "Fine. There are some people who don't have staying power."

"See?"

"But I don't believe this Nina person is one of them." At my exasperated grunt, he speaks louder and faster. "I think she's more like me before I landed at UMKC. Like Ana Paula said, she simply hasn't found that place yet. She's close, though. She admitted her last placement would have been perfect—she got along with her boss and her co-workers—but she felt a moral obligation to leave when she was asked to backdate those dog food recall documents. That's not flaky; that's ethical. Integrity is an important quality. She left a good-paying position that afforded her family much-needed stability."

"Yeah, yeah. She did the right thing."

"You'd be good for her."

I heave myself to my feet to collect everyone's trash in the delivery bag I hold out in front of me as I go down the row. "I need *her* to be good for *us*."

Jet leans back in his chair and stretches. "I may be just a dumb jock, but isn't the point of this non-profit to give people chances they might not get anywhere else? Wouldn't hiring someone like Nina, someone who's running out of chances, be the perfect way to walk the walk, right from the first snap?"

Glowering at him, I snatch Cyndi's proffered cup from her hand and jam it into the bag.

My husband chuckles nervously. "Right?"

"Do you want to come home every day and hear me complain about this woman? Because that's going to happen."

"Not if you'd have a better attitude about it."

I'm about to appeal to him with a locker room metaphor, something he'd understand, when Greg stands and jingles his keys in his pocket. "Come on. Let's take a vote already. Some of us have kids to pick up and lives to get on with."

I level an incredulous stare at his classless interruption, but before I can rip into him, Cyndi says with a wince, "Unfortunately, we have to get moving, too."

Rae says, "And AP and I don't have kids, but we have that 'life' thing he mentioned and a busy day of icing and wrapping body parts tomorrow."

"You sound like serial killers," Jet says, laughing.

I bite the inside of my cheek and drop the sack of trash at my feet. Raising my voice above the growing din, I say, "All righty. Let's officially piss me off, then. All in favor of offering the manager's position to Nina, raise your hand."

Jet's is the first to rocket into the air, followed by six others. Dad's slowly rises last.

"All opposed, raise your hand," I say, while lifting mine.

Greg says, "There you go. The 'ayes' have it. Make it happen, Mo."

I mock him behind his back, which gets a laugh from everyone else and breaks the tension. Gritting my teeth, I smile reassuringly in an effort to show there are no hard feelings. "Well, I guess that's that. The Knox Theater has a manager."

Jet claps, and the others join in. As we disperse, he winks and smiles at me through the mingling bodies. I glare back. His grin fades.

Yeah. If he thinks there won't be consequences for his treachery, he's a "dumb[er] jock" than he thought.

————

On the way home, my silent treatment isn't obvious, because I'm not technically silent. I stay busy on the phone, offering the job to an ecstatic Nina, who gushes, "I can't believe this! I thought for sure, and I told Derek, that there was no way you'd want anything to do with me, given my history, which you know so well. But I should have known you are such a good, caring person that you'd look past all that to my qualifications. I can assure you, Maura, you won't regret your decision. I really did learn a lot at my last job, and I took what you said to me at our last appointment to heart. It was the hardest decision of my life to quit there. It would have been so easy to change those dates and keep earning a paycheck and collecting those benefits, but I have to be a role model to my kids, you know, and…"

I let her prattle for the majority of the drive, not because I wanted to hear it, but because it meant I didn't have to talk to Jet, the traitor.

Also, by the end of the conversation, I have to admit, I felt much better about the situation. How could I not? She's so incredibly grateful that I'd have to be a robot to be unmoved.

Still… as soon as the call comes to an inevitable end, with Nina running out of steam and saying she has to go tell her kids the great news, I toss my phone into my purse and fold my arms across my chest.

Jet says, "See?" and I reply, "Shut up," before the word finishes ringing through the car.

He laughs. "I realize you're—"

"Put a sock in it, Knox." I turn my head and stare out the window at the side-by-side football and baseball stadiums as we pass them.

"It's just—"

"La-la-la-la-la!"

"Real mature."

Oh, I can only imagine the level of pouting that would be coming from his side of the vehicle if the tables were turned, but defending myself would require talking to him, and I'm not willing to do that yet. Plus, my biggest defense is something I'm not willing to admit to anyone else, even Jet.

Aside from the legitimate misgivings I have about Nina, I'm fully aware this is a challenge from Derek. Of course, he knows that he's setting me up with a bad candidate—we talked about Nina, specifically, in my office all those months ago. He's also aware that I'd rather eat the pet food Nina was asked to backdate than admit defeat to him. So, he gets rid of a repeat client and looks like a job counseling wizard—ha!—in the process. And if it does work out, he can legitimately claim that title and do what I couldn't do: place Nina permanently. With me. It's a win-win-win for him.

The only possible way for him to have lost is for us to have rejected Nina outright and picked the other guy. And he knew it was a safe bet I wouldn't allow that, considering the other candidate was someone just like him, the *last* person I'd ever want to work with again. Even then, if I'd called his bluff, he'd *still* get credit for the placement. Plus, he'd have the added satisfaction of knowing I was stuck with a manager who would question my every decision and presume he knew better than I did how to run a business, because he had a degree in it, whereas I was simply a film studies graduate. I suppose I could have rejected both Nina and Kirk, but then we'd be without a manager so close to opening, which could compromise our schedule. No, I was screwed the second The Giggler assigned Derek to my account. It's hard not to believe they're laughing at me right now.

We arrive home to a quiet house, since Beau has the night off. I startle Torzi with my effusive greeting, complete with full-on hugs and kisses as I carry him upstairs with me, but he quickly recovers from his confusion and basks in my affection, licking my face. "Were you a good doggy? I'm sure you were!" I set him on the bed, where he dances for a few seconds to keep my attention. I laugh at him and scratch his head. "Silly!"

"Are you going to stop using the dog as a distraction and talk to me?" Jet asks after several minutes.

My response is to stalk into the closet, where I peel off my uncomfortable clothes. When he tries to follow me, I kick the door closed in his face.

Mature? No. Nice? Hell no. Are either of those things a priority for me right now? That would be another "no."

"Fine! I have clothes out here, too!" Jet says triumphantly. I hear the dresser drawers slide open and shut, and he mutters something—presumably to the dog—which I pretend not to notice as I hang up my suit and quickly pull on a t-shirt and a pair of flowy palazzo pants.

I yank the closet door open and march up to him, jabbing my finger in his bare chest. "And another thing," I say in the middle of a mental rant I'm aware he's not privy to but don't care, "if this is how it's going to always be, everyone else voting the way they think is best for me and the Foundation, like they know better than I do, then... then..."

He waits, eyes wide, eyebrows raised.

"Then... Well, that sucks!"

He wraps his hand around my pointer finger and lifts my knuckles to his lips, his eyes never leaving mine. "It seemed like you were being unfair, not giving her a chance. The rest of us could tell we're not going to find someone more qualified or more eager-to-please than her."

I snort. "Puh-lease."

"She hero-worships you, Maura. Trust the guy who sees it all the time. I can spot it from a million miles away."

"That doesn't mean she'll do a good job."

"It means she'll try, and that's just as important. She'll do anything to impress you." He transfers his grip to my upper arms, backs me to the foot of the bed, and presses down gently to force me to sit. He sits next to me and drapes his arm around my shoulders. I shrug him off, but he persists until I give up. "That guy, Kirk, was too busy kissing my ass to care what you were asking him during his interview. He acted like I was the one he needed to win over. Same with that oily twerp, Derek, in the lobby. But Nina barely looked my way. Or at the other board members. She wanted to prove herself to *you*."

I flap my lips on a massive exhale. My shoulders slump under the weight of his arm. "She's such a pain in the ass, Jet. I thought I was done with her." Blushing preemptively, I take a deep breath and finally say, "Derek sent her to me out of spite."

"Oh, come on."

"No. I'm sure of it." I turn my head and force myself to

make eye contact with him, so he'll take me seriously. "He knows about my challenging past with Nina. He knows I wouldn't want to hire Kirk, either. He's done this to prove a point and torture me."

Jet laughs. "Make this work with Nina, and he'll look like an idiot."

"He still wins."

"How?"

"Because that means he was able to do what I couldn't: permanently place Nina."

"So what? Shit, that's petty as hell."

"Yeah, but—"

"Nina is a person." His eyes flash. "With kids to support. Who the hell cares if Derek wins some stupid job counseling contest between the two of you?"

My blush deepens and shame blooms in my stomach and chest. Tears sting my eyes and nose. "You think I don't realize that? That's part of the torture."

"Well, fuck him and his mind games." He moves to stand, but I grab his hand and pull him back down with me.

"You're right. You're right."

He takes a deep breath and releases it slowly before saying, gently, "Maura, you're better than this."

"Maybe I'm not."

"I *know* you are. I've seen you cry in the bathtub after feeding homeless people for an afternoon. I've seen you read books to kids who won't live long enough to read to their own children. I've seen you call everyone in your cell phone to try to find a home for a cat or dog you know is about to be put down, because they've been at the shelter too long. And *I* know about Nina, too."

I swipe the tears off my cheeks.

"You might think I don't listen or remember things, but when they matter to you, I do. I remember all the times you came home from work after another session with Nina, hopeful that *this time* you'd found her the perfect job." He rubs his thumb against my knuckles. "This could finally be it. It won't be down to Derek, either; it'll be down to you. You know her and how to make this work. Anyway, the last thing she wants is to disappoint you."

"I hate you."

"No, you don't," he says, pressing his lips against my head.

I pull back. "Yes, I do." My eyes drop lower, to his mouth. "I hate you and that stupid mustache you're already starting for 'No-Shave November' and—"

He silences me with a thought-erasing kiss and follows it up with, "Well, I love you. And I can't wait to see this blow up in Mini Gandalf's face."

TWENTY-SEVEN

PROMISES

Nina and I, while still trying to get used to each other, have made a surprisingly efficient team in our first month of co-employment. We've hired and trained a part-timer, a college student named Henry, to help out on the weekends; we've passed building and fire inspections with aplomb; we've even scheduled our first dress rehearsal.

After that comes the invitation-only screening night we're holding as a wedding gift to Rae and Ana Paula, which will take place the weekend before our official grand opening. Trying to pin down the almost-no-longer-newlyweds to a date to throw them a party was proving impossible. Rae finally admitted they weren't comfortable with a gathering like Jet and I had when we returned from Belize. They didn't want to be the center of attention with a cake and speeches and toasts to their happiness. Although I could relate, I was *this* close to reminding my friends what I was told a billion times by Gloria: weddings and receptions aren't really about what the couple wants. They're for family and friends. Then I realized I was about to quote Gloria and would rather cut out my tongue first.

I was prepared to let it go and was instead brainstorming extravagant gifts for my best friend and her bride when it hit me that the two of them would hate that just as much and would probably rather Jet and I donate to their favorite charity. When I ran the idea past the couple, they jumped on it and chose the Malala Fund, co-founded by the Pakistani woman of the same name who survived a murder attempt by the Taliban when she was just eleven years old and is now one of the world's most ardent activists, particularly for young girls. We're hosting a screening of *He Named Me Malala*, the documentary about this amazing woman, her family, and their cause. So far, it's worked out perfectly.

Planning for the grand opening is going well, too. Our first beneficiary is a cause close to all of our hearts, the children's hospital where Jet and I both volunteer and where Nina's third child spent a week with pneumonia when he was less than a year old. We'll be showing *Patch Adams* for that.

In addition to that first movie being open to the public, we've sent special invitations to local leaders and celebrities, as well as some of the families whose loved ones have recovered, thanks to the hospital. We've written and transmitted countless press releases—with one specifically addressed to a certain Kendra Johnson, ace gossip reporter wannabe.

Buses, billboards, and buildings display The Knox Theater's logo, website, and motto all over the city, like I dreamed of doing with Jet's cheesy smile to promote our fantasy trinket shack in Hawaii. We've also purchased some sponsorships on public radio, figuring community-service-minded folks will be listening during their morning and evening commutes. I'm praying it all works, because our advertising budget for the month of December is gone, and it's only mid-November. Our accountant reassures me that's how all the big companies operate.

While taking inventory as Nina stocks the concession stand for the first time, I lament that we're not a big company, and that I'm still worried.

"It can be scary," she acknowledges. "But if it makes you feel better, it was the same at the pet supply headquarters. With spending, you're always a month or two ahead—or behind—however you look at it. Sometimes a full quarter. I'd imagine it's crazier when you're first starting out, because it's all outgoing. But that's why it's more important than ever that everyone in this whole town knows about this place and wants to check it out."

"We have to keep them coming back for more, too," I say.

"Yes. And we will." She slides a row of Mike and Ike boxes into place, and I check them off the list. "What are three things people love? Nostalgia, celebrity causes, and feeling like they're making a difference. We have all of it wrapped up here."

"Now we need to book more children's charities, and they'll be all over it."

She grins while reaching into the shipping box for more candy. "That reminds me. I've made first contact with The Boys and Girls Club, Boys and Girls Town, the YMCA, and Head Start. The names of their outreach coordinators are on my desk; I haven't had a chance to email them to you today. But they're waiting for a call back from *the* Maura Knox." Motioning for the clipboard in my hands, she says, "I can finish this up. You go call them before we lose track of time. None of them will be around after five."

For about the thousandth time, I'm blown away by how

wrong I was about my former difficult client. She's anticipated my every need and has brought a knowledge to the table I doubt I would have found in anyone else, considering they wouldn't have possessed her varied work experience.

Later, she joins me for a brainstorming session about seasonal decor, and struck once again by one of her great ideas, I blurt, "Hiring you was the best decision I never wanted to make." When her focus remains on her notepad, where she's doodled arrows and hearts, I blush and stutter, "That's not— I didn't— It was nothing personal."

"Right." She swallows audibly.

"I'm sorry, Nina. That came out wrong."

"No, I get it." Finally, she lifts her eyes, but they find a spot just over my shoulder as she says for the umpteenth time, "I can't tell you how grateful I am that you took a chance on me, knowing what you know. I'm different now, though."

"I've noticed."

"Walking around offended all the time is stressful, ya know?"

"Yep."

She chances eye contact. "Plus, something you said to me at my last Career Center appointment with you hit me here." She taps her gut.

I tilt my head and wait, trying to remember what part of our conversation could have had such an impact.

"You pointed out how I was teaching my kids to be victims. I couldn't stop thinking about that. It was harsh, but true. I want my kids to be a lot of things. 'Victim' isn't on that list. Thanks for having the guts to say that to me." Rapid clicks of her pen punctuate her speech.

I wave off her appreciation. "Ah. I thought I'd never see

you again. When you showed up here for the manager position... Awkward!"

We both laugh at that. Then she notices the time. "Oh, shoot! Speaking of kids, I need to meet them at the bus stop!" On her way from the office, she pauses and, keeping her back to me, says, "I won't let you down, Maura. I promise."

———

If only the Chiefs were as simpatico. While Nina and I have been kicking ass and taking names, the city's football team has had its ass handed to them by the Giants. Hardly any team goes an entire season unbeaten, but this first loss broke an eight-game winning streak with authority. In Prime Time. On Monday Night.

Still, it's only one loss, no matter how widely watched. You'd think, judging by the fans' and sports analysts' grumblings, that we're suffering the worst slump in team history. I suppose when you get used to winning, you become spoiled, and every loss feels like the beginning of the end of a Golden Age.

Whatever the logic behind it, morale was low when the team returned home late last night. Instead of shaking it off and sticking to the big-picture plan, Jet and some of the other guys have made the mistake of listening and giving credence to the critics, who are always waiting to pounce.

"Knox hasn't been the same this season, after knee surgery. He's slower, he's tentative, and he's too quick to throw it away."

"Once a guy starts using his off-season for things like surgeries, it's all over but the cryin'. The Wise brothers were complete morons throwing all that money at Knox."

"Earning that fat paycheck is about more than showing up and winning the easy games."

"Ease of schedule has been a huge factor so far. Going into the harder part of their season, we're about to see just what the Chiefs are made of, and I'm afraid the fans ain't gonna like it."

"Poor Draft choices are coming back to haunt the Chiefs now. Didn't make as big of a difference in the easy games, but they're going to seriously regret not going for some of those stout Arkansas and Nebraska players to beef up that O-line as they head into these matchups with such dominating defenses."

"The Chiefs implode when they fall behind. They can't come back from a deficit to save their lives. And you're not always going to be able to score first and stay in the lead."

The post-game shows were brutal, as commentators leapt from the team's bandwagon like it was on fire.

So despite all of the exciting momentum Nina and I have made with the theater, I've found myself tempering my enthusiasm around Jet, taking my cues from his sullen mood.

I'm not sure if the Bye week falling right now is a good or bad thing, either. It could be a great time to regroup and recharge; or it could provide Jet and the rest of the team too much time to stew and brood.

"Milk or *A Single Man?"* I say this morning while sipping a cappuccino and watching Jet shovel eggs under his ridiculous —and extremely temporary—No-Shave November mustache and down his throat.

Foot braced against the rung of the bar stool, his leg jiggles like he couldn't keep it still if he tried. He swallows the three bites he's crammed into his mouth at once and grumbles, "I don't understand the question."

Beau shoots a knowing smile at me over his shoulder from

his position at the fridge, where he's standing, planning the week's grocery run.

"Films. LIKEME Lighthouse is the charity our second week. We're still trying to decide which movie to show."

"Both are kind of depressing, aren't they?"

"They won GLAAD awards, though."

"If you want to really depress people about gay rights, go full *Philadelphia* on them."

I sigh. "We're not *trying* to depress people."

"Are there any comedies on the list? How about *The Bird-cage*?" He wipes his mouth but misses a dangling piece of egg in the hair above his lip.

I motion for him to keep wiping, so he does, although he seems annoyed that I would dare point out the lingering food. Maybe I should have let him walk around like that all day. Instead of calling him on his bad mood, I persevere with the current conversation. "We don't want to appear to be making fun or reinforcing stereotypes. We want people to think. 'Uplifting' would be okay, though. That's why I'm leaning toward *Milk*."

Tossing his napkin on his empty plate, which he pushes away, he crosses his arms over his chest, both legs pumping now. "I don't know. You're the expert. Why are you asking me?"

"I was mostly making conversation."

"So you'd already decided, but you thought you'd ask me so you could make me feel like an idiot when I chose the wrong one."

I pull my mouth sideways and raise an eyebrow. "There is no 'wrong' one. I was mostly seeking validation."

"I don't ask you to validate the playbook."

"Maybe you should. I'd tell you to throw away that garbage

slant pass play that never works."

"It keeps teams guessing."

"And wastes a down. And risks a turnover, because Tiffe-nauer can never get into position in time." A staring contest ensues, before I yield and say, "Whatever. Never mind."

He leans forward and plunks his forehead against the counter, nearly putting his head in his dirty plate. Beau moves it just in time and quietly places it in the sink. "I'm sorry," Jet says with a whine. I assume he's talking to me, not his personal chef/trainer.

Rubbing between his shoulder blades, I reply, "It's all right."

But it's not all right. He needs to cool his effing beans. I'm sick of him taking his shitty moods out on me. I'm not a sports commentator or know-it-all blogger. I'm not an entitled fan. I'm not one of the New York players who humiliated him and his teammates in front of a national audience. I'm his wife, and I'm killing myself trying to be there for him, because he's there for me when I'm struggling, and that's what you do. But since he already seems to have come to that conclusion on his own, I refrain from saying all of that out loud.

Beau widens his eyes at me over Jet's head and mouths, *"See ya,"* on his way toward the door with his shopping list.

Great. The one morning I'd rather not be alone with my grumpy husband, everyone makes themselves scarce. Not that I blame them. I respect their intelligence and envy their right to be absent in times like these.

I don't even have the theater to use as an excuse to put some distance between us. I've purposely structured the non-profit's schedule to coincide with Jet's so we'd both have Tues-days off during the season. The whole day yawns before us. If only Jet had hair long enough for a "blow bar" outing…

Hopping down from my stool, I grasp the top of his shoulders and knead more aggressively. "How about massages?" I suggest. "You liked that couple who made house calls."

"Only because it sounded like the setup for a cheesy porno."

"They were actually good, though!"

"I got a rubdown yesterday before my ice bath. But you go ahead if you need a massage. I have some video I should watch."

"It's your day off!"

He sits up and shrugs off my manhandling. "I don't deserve a day off after that pathetic performance last night."

"After a loss is when you *most* need a day off." I squeeze between his seat and mine and cuddle up to his arm. "You need some separation so you can move on to the next opponent with a clearer head. What's the point in dwelling on mistakes?"

Gazing forward, as if already watching the videos in his head, he answers, "You learn from mistakes."

"Okay. Then learn from them tomorrow, when you're not so mad about them."

Helen enters the kitchen. He blinks, then beams at her, but she immediately bustles about, wiping down counters and loading the dishwasher. Beau must have tipped her off that things were weird in here.

"Hi, Helen," we say in sunshiny unison, earning us a wary glance and "Hello…"

When both of us simply watch her for a few seconds, she asks, "Is everything okay?"

Is it? Not really. I haven't felt this out-of-sync with my husband in a long time. But that's nothing she needs to concern herself with. My job isn't making beds, and hers isn't providing a distraction when Jet and I don't know how to be around each other.

I laugh off her question. "Of course. We'll be out of your way in a sec—"

Jet rises and exits the room.

"—ond. Well... now, I suppose." I toss a nervous chuckle at her on my way out.

He trots downstairs, ostensibly to watch that video he's so obsessed with, so I leave him alone, retreating to the library.

A few hours later, we leave together, as usual, for our volunteer work at the hospital. I figure the kids will put things in perspective for him, and he'll come home ready to act like a normal human being. But while he puts on a good show for the patients, he's nearly silent again on the way home, answering me in grunts and monosyllables when I dare to address him or try to draw him out.

What. A. Turd.

I might as well have gone to The Knox to accomplish my own tasks today. Heaven knows there's still plenty to do and seemingly not enough time to do it. But I've been disciplined about down time, if not for myself, then for Nina. She deserves a weekend free of wondering what I'm getting up to without her and dreading the piles of work waiting on her desk or in her email inbox as a result. We've agreed to stay away for two days every week, barring emergencies, knowing it will be a mental benefit to both of us.

But I'm not benefiting mentally if I'm stuck at home, pissed off at what a brat my husband is.

Before he can rush back downstairs to work out or pout or both, I snag his arm on our way through the living room. "Hey."

Surprised at the contact, he half-turns and looks down at

my hand on his sleeve as if it's the most offensive thing he's ever seen. "Yeah?"

"What the heck is your problem today?" When he opens his mouth to answer, I interrupt, "How about you get over yourself?"

I'm relieved when he actually laughs at that and self-consciously strokes his mustache. "I don't know! It's not that easy."

"Make it easy. We get one guaranteed day together each week from August to February, and you're ruining it by being an ass-face, pouting over a loss that doesn't even really mean anything. It's not like the Giants are division rivals, or something."

"Every game matters."

"Oh, puh-lease. If you were going to lose one, that's the one to lose, and you know it. But odds are, you're going to have at least one or two more shitty games this season; important ones, even. How you recover from setbacks says a lot more about you than winning ever could." When he seems unmoved by that, I add, "You know, I could be doing a million and one other things today."

"Go do whatever you want."

Softening, I say quietly, "I *want* to spend time with you."

He sighs. "I'm not very good company."

"Let's change that."

"Can I get in a quick workout and a shower?"

"Sure. That'll be the perfect opportunity for you to reset and figure out how you're going to redeem this day."

With a lopsided grin, he salutes me. "Yes, ma'am." Continuing on his way, he stops at the bottom of the stairs and shouts up, "This whole scary-boss-lady thing is kind of hot."

Now, that's more like it.

TWENTY-EIGHT

BUSY

Time has proven me correct. The Bye week did wonders for public opinion, and by the time play resumed for the team, the loss was being explained away as a fluke. A home win against the Jaguars, followed by an away rout of the Ravens cemented that opinion. Now we're facing a Thursday night matchup at home, and confidence is higher than ever.

Fans love Thursday night games. The players, coaches, and WAGs hate them, although nobody's allowed to come out and say it. The short week throws off everyone's schedule, and it's a pain to cram the usual six or seven days of preparations, injury recovery, and travel into four. But Thursday games are here to stay, because the NFL money-making machine loves 'em.

When I was a casual fan, I, too, enjoyed a good mid-week matchup. I'd pick up some dinner on the way home, change into my most comfortable clothes, and settle in with a glass of wine or a beer. Depending on how tired I was (or how boring the battle), I'd often fall asleep in the third or fourth quarter, but I'd wake up in time to see the final score and listen to the commentators give their last thoughts. Then I'd drag myself to bed, sleeping well in the knowledge that a full day of football was only three days away.

Nowadays, the sport consumes my life every single day, whether I tune in or not. It's the other woman in our marriage, always there in the background (and sometimes not-so-background), reminding me she came first and will always be my husband's first love. Before I met Jet, she was a high-society name, someone I admired from afar, someone I thought I could be great friends with, if given the chance. I've found out she's an attention- and time-stealing hag, half a relationship that's often unhealthy and co-dependent. I'm jealous of her, and my resentment is impossible to hide.

Then again, she keeps Jet happy and busy and a roof over our heads, so it's selfish to dislike her. It's not her fault she's so high-maintenance. It's the only way she knows how to be. And I knew exactly what I was getting into when I married him.

All this to say, unless the Chiefs are one of the teams playing in the Thursday night game, I don't watch it. And even then, I have it on in the background while I do other things, merely monitoring the action on the screen for information that allows me to speak intelligently about the match when Jet inevitably wants to discuss it in detail later.

Tonight is no different, considering we're playing the lame Titans. I want to care more about the game, but we're less than a week away from The Knox's grand opening and only two days away from Rae and AP's private benefit, so I'm more than the usual amount of distracted.

To say I don't care about the game isn't accurate, either, though. In uneven matchups, announcers tend to exaggerate the excitement to keep people watching. More than once, their

raised voices have caused my eyes to snap up from the obses-
sive checklists (yes, I've become *that* person) spread out on
the bed in front of me. The Tennessee defense is playing the
part of annoying mosquito tonight, swarming Jet, seemingly
harmless and easy to kill, yet always holding the threat of
blood-borne illness. Once again, our O-line has decided to
half-ass the first half.

I focus on the TV for a few seconds, and when the scare is
over, I return to my papers, muttering, "Where was I?" until
the next instance of Jet's name spoken in panicked tones.
Repeat three thousand times, to the point of exhaustion, fall
back on the pillows, and pass out.

I wake up to Jet's chuckle and the sound of rustling papers.
Blinking and smacking my lips, I sit up and guess, "Hey, good
game."

"Like you would know. Looks like you had an orgy in here
with Georgia Pacific." He hands me the neatened stack of
pages I'm sure he's gotten hopelessly jumbled.

I laugh. "Nice one."

He grins proudly. "Adrenaline. I'm still high and firing on
all cylinders."

Glancing at the TV, I hope for some clues, but the late-
night infomercial isn't offering any. Pretending to check the
time on my phone, I say, "It's late," while thumbing to the app
that will tell me the score and a few relevant details.

"Might take a while for me to wind down."

Finally, I find his personal stats: sixty-six-point-seven
percent completion, two-hundred forty-three total yards, and
three touchdowns, for a quarterback rating of one-eighteen-
point-six. I blink a couple of times to make sure I've read that
correctly, then say, "You were on fire." *Must have been in the
second half.*

"Hell yeah, I was. Would have had a higher completion percentage, too, but you know…"

"Tiff still having trouble?"

"Tiff, O'Doyle, Palmerton… I had to recover a dang fumble —of my own—off Livermore's ass, because his snaps were so bad tonight."

"Not a butt fumble!"

He giggles. "Yes. But because I'm awesome…"

"And humble."

"…it worked out okay."

"I'd say one-eighteen-point-six is more than okay. And we'll take that seven-point win, too." I shuffle through the papers for a second but realize I'm too tired to make sense of them now and toss them and my phone on the chair on my way to the bathroom.

Jet intercepts me between the foot of the bed and the bathroom door. Hands on my hips, he lowers his chin to my shoulder and says near my ear, "Now I have ten days to recover," while brushing his blessedly post-November naked lips against my lobe. "I'm glad you got a nap, even if it does mean you didn't catch one of my best performances of the season."

"Hmmmm."

"I plan to give a better performance right now, anyway."

Patting his face and hoping it conveys an appropriate amount of regret in conjunction with my tone, I pull away from him and continue into the bathroom to prepare for bed. "Oh, gosh. I'm not sure I'd be able to fully appreciate that. I'm so tired."

"But Maura! I'm jacked!"

"Then jack… off."

He laughs miserably and slumps on the foot of the bed, kicking off his loafers. When he bends over to pick them up, I worry he'll poke out his own eye, and I regret not having the desire to satiate him.

For a second, while brushing my teeth, I contemplate humoring him, but that's not a precedent I want to set in our relationship. Either we both want it, or we don't do it. There are no obligatory hook-ups here. Then again, there's never been a need for them. We're usually pretty in-sync. And if anyone's doing the rejecting, it's him—for professional reasons.

I try not to take any satisfaction that I'm the one saying "no" for once. It's not about control, after all; it's about honesty. I'm honestly too exhausted to enjoy it, and what a shame it would be to waste his predicted amazing performance on someone half-dead.

I rinse my toothbrush and smile sadly at him in the mirror as he joins me at the vanity. "Sorry. Maybe tomorrow morning, when we're both more rested?"

"I don't want to have to negotiate it," he grumbles, squirting toothpaste onto his electric brush. "Forget it."

That's a relief, because as soon as I suggested it, in an effort to appease and reconcile, I remembered I have to get up early and meet Nina at The Knox for our post-final checks and a long day of other preps before our final-final rehearsal in the evening. Sex is going to be the last thing on my mind when my alarm beeps in four hours.

Since Jet was so pumped, for lack of a better word, only a few minutes ago, I'm surprised when he slides into bed at the same time I do. I pat and kiss his arm while settling on my pillows. "Goodnight, Champ."

"Goodnight, Beautiful."

———

"This is really happening," I say to Henry and Nina, as we stand behind the ticket/concessions counter, observing Nina's wild children, our "customers" for tonight.

Six kids, ranging in age from three to twelve, have taken over the lobby. I watch in hopeful dread as they carelessly run in loops, jostling the soda in their bottles, dropping popcorn all over the floor and treading on it, and shaking their boxed candy like percussion instruments. Part of me hopes for a minor disaster, so we can test our contingency plans, but I don't want anything huge. Spills are okay. Blood, puke, or other bodily fluids are not.

In the chaos, the youngest finds himself on his bottom on the concrete floor, where he thinks about crying for a few seconds but ultimately decides it would detract from his hedonism for too long. He returns to his feet, retaliating with a punch to his seven-year-old brother's crotch.

"Oh, my gosh," Nina mutters. "I'm so sorry."

I wave off her apologies. "They're excited."

"They're hellions. Foster! Beckham! Stop beating up on each other and say you're sorry!"

They grudgingly grumble something in each other's direction before returning to the bedlam.

"Stop it right now!" Nina bellows at the hyped-up kids, who freeze. "Get in line at the door, behind the red rope. Geez!" Without pausing a beat, she softens her voice and says to me, "Tomorrow's going to be great."

If this dress rehearsal is any indication, it *will* be great. Or, at least calmer. These gap-toothed wonders have put us through our paces, buying tickets and ordering concessions in the most chaotic manner possible. When Nina implored them to be still in line or order one at a time and they only obeyed for a second or two before reverting to their excited behavior, I secretly rejoiced, glad for the challenge. I would have never contradicted their mother or asked them to ignore her directives, but I was glad for their shenanigans. If we can manage them, we can handle anything.

I've schlepped popcorn while covertly observing both Henry's and Nina's customer service. Considering her kids are the rude customers, I've given Nina a pass a few times, but I've noted a couple of times when twenty-year-old Henry has become flustered, so I've made a mental note to give him some strategies for keeping cool under pressure. As soon as our customers settle in for their movie, I'll do a debrief with both of my employees, and we'll reset everything to be ready for Rae and AP's benefit tomorrow night.

Before Nina's children ramp up their antics again, I say while rounding the counter, "We're now seating for *Home Alone.*" I unclip the red rope and position myself to the side of the open screening room door, where I hold out my hand for ticket stubs. As each child stands before me, I rip their stub, keeping one half and handing them the other. When the last one passes, I follow them into the screening room and take my position in front of the screen.

Henry and Nina peek around the wall while I wait for everyone to find their perfect seat. I rock on my feet and clear my throat to get their attention. I may as well be invisible. Nina blushes, and I can sense she's about to step in, so I insert my index fingers into either corner of my mouth and blow as hard as I can, whistling the way Jet's been trying to teach me since we first met. I've never achieved it. Until tonight.

All six children whirl to face forward, butts in seats, eyes wide. One of them (Swift, maybe? Or is that Madonna? I can't keep them straight) covers her ears with flattened hands.

Acting like I had complete confidence in my mad skills, I pluck the remote from its perch on the screen ledge and say, "Welcome to The Knox Theater, where 'opportunity Knox.' See what I did there?" They stare back, unimpressed. "Right. Okay. For helping Henry, your mom, and me tonight, The Knox will donate one thousand dollars to the charity you chose with your mom, Toys for Tots. Thank you for being so generous!"

"I want toys!" Foster yells.

I stifle a chuckle. "I'm sure you'll get some for Christmas. If you're a good boy."

"There goes that dream," pre-teen Winona mutters.

"But thanks to you, some other kids who wouldn't get any toys for Christmas will," I soldier on. "You can feel good about that. Give yourselves a round of applause."

They clap uncertainly at first but the younger ones get into it after a few seconds.

"All right, then. Before we start the movie, I'd like to tell you about some other events coming up here at The Knox. Tomorrow night, we're holding a special benefit for the Malala Fund, an international effort to expand women's rights, especially focusing on the education of young girls. Next weekend, we're screening *Patch Adams*, with proceeds benefiting Children's Mercy Hospital. And the weekend after that, we'll be showing *Milk* to benefit LIKEME Lighthouse. We hope you can join us again soon and continue to support worthy causes in our community."

"When do we get to watch the movie?" someone whines.

Nina covers her face and shakes her head.

"Anyway! Without further ado, tonight's feature, *Home Alone*. Enjoy the show!"

I point the tiny remote at the projector box on the ceiling

and press "play," then scurry down the side aisle to get to my cohorts.

"How'd I do?" I ask. "Is the speech too long? I want to make sure our visitors know about upcoming events before they leave, and posters in the lobby might not be enough, you know?"

"You did great," Henry says somewhat dully.

"I said, 'Knox' too much, though. The motto needs to go. It's fine on stationery and promotional materials, but I'm taking it out of the introduction script."

"It's fine," Nina replies, patting my arm. "Other audiences won't be so... bratty."

Henry laughs. "You ever thought of spanking them?"

She looks down her nose at him, "We don't believe in corporal punishment in our house."

"Maybe you should."

Before the argument can escalate, I hand the remote to Nina. "Here. Normally I'd leave it by the screen, but maybe that's not a good idea tonight."

She smiles while pocketing the device. "Good call. Sting loves to press buttons."

With one more glance over my shoulder at the temporarily (I'm sure) rapt audience, I say, "Let's discuss improvement areas while we straighten the lobby and get the posters and standees set up for tomorrow's benefit."

Nina hisses a command to Winona to keep her younger siblings in line and follows Henry and me to the lobby, where we unexpectedly find a six-foot-four occupant staring at one of the promotional posters on the far wall.

Jet turns at the sound of our voices, and my delight at his unannounced visit immediately dissolves when I see his pale face and pinched mouth.

"What's wrong?" I say, instantly frozen to the concrete, popcorn-strewn floor.

He glances at Nina and Henry, nodding a quick hello to both of them before swallowing and saying, "My mom. She had a heart attack. A big one."

Nina says to me, "We've got this," and immediately pulls Henry away to start cleanup and reset efforts.

I finally figure out how to make my feet move and cross the lobby to my husband, whose chin puckers as he hopelessly fights a frown and says, "I'm on the way to the airport. I packed a bag for you, too, but I get it if you can't leave right now."

Brushing off logistical talk for the moment, I grab his hands, then pull him in for a hug. After a few seconds, I step back and ask, "What happened? Why didn't you call me?"

He shakes his head. "I don't know any details yet, and I knew you were busy here tonight, so I... I started throwing stuff in bags and finding a charter and making reservations and calling Coach Bauer. It was easier to come by here on my way to the airport."

"You don't know anything else about her condition?"

"Only that it's bad. Gidget was crying too hard on the phone for me to understand much. Something about emergency open-heart surgery."

"Oh, geez." The surgery seems par for the course; Gidget crying is another story.

"I have to go," he says, edging toward the door.

I glance over my shoulder at Henry and Nina, who seem to be quietly bickering while wiping down the counter and straightening the candy display, respectively. Gulping, I decide, "I'm coming with you. Hang on."

"Hurry," he says as I trot over to my employees. "Cyndi's waiting in the car."

Henry takes the news of my unexpected departure with barely a shrug and a simple, "We've got this. I hope everything's okay."

Nina echoes Henry's sentiments, but the panic in her eyes is unmistakable. Still, when I bite my lip, my internal dithering paralyzing me, she says, "We'll be fine. Go, go, go."

Finally, when the draft from Jet holding open the front door hits my back and legs, I mobilize. "Right. Okay. Well, I guess I'll be in touch. I'll email you both some of my thoughts about how we can improve customer service, and Nina, I'll call you tomorrow. I need to let Rae know she'll have to do more talking than we'd planned."

"Or I can. Email me your scripts."

"Will do."

Jet beckons me with an impatient wrist roll, to which I reply, "Sorry. I'm coming."

As I cross the threshold into the cold night, I pause for one more second to gaze back at all of my hard work come to fruition. The human in me disregards every other aspect of the situation and allows herself to experience the disappointment in not being present for its debut. It's like a parent missing a child's first word or first steps. It happens, but it's not ideal. No parent wants to watch that on a video or hear about it secondhand. Nobody wants to relinquish that joy to someone else.

Nina smiles reassuringly at me. I wave one last time and jog after Jet.

TWENTY-NINE

CRISIS

Not every charter jet is fancy. Puttin' that out there, in case anyone didn't know or thought that a fourteen-million-dollar annual salary meant pure luxury all day, every day, in all situations. It doesn't. Sometimes that money gets you the last flight with the last available pilot in the last puddle jumper in the hangar and saves you from spending the night at the airport, but it doesn't guarantee comfort. Or survival. Several times during the three-hour flight, I thought, *Well, this is going to be a tragic write-up,* and, *Gloria surely won't survive this news. She won't shed a tear for me, but losing two of her kids, including her favorite? Fuhgeddaboutit.*

Somehow, by some miracle, we made it, though.

There's no rental car desk or taxi service at this tiny private airport (imagine that), so Jet initiates "game plan" mode. While he calls Gidget's husband, Rick, to pick us up, Cyndi and I huddle together in the light of the vending machines in the smoky-smelling "lounge" and nervously giggle, like you do after a near-death experience.

When Cyndi's giggles turn to sobs, I squeeze her shaking

shoulders and block out the vivid memories of all the times I've speculated about how much easier my life would be without Gloria in it. Now that it could be a real possibility, I'm filled with shame. So many people I love would be devastated. And I realize that for all my joking and grumbling and petty complaining, I would be sad, too.

I never wanted her to die; I simply wanted her to leave me alone.

Jet disconnects with Rick, both guys confident in the GPS to finish the job, and turns his attention to the two of us. I swipe the guilty tears from my face and ask, "All set?"

He stands behind my plastic chair and, massaging my shoulders, replies, "Yep. We're going straight to the hospital." He leans down and over to kiss Cyndi's head. "It'll be all right," he tells her, sounding more like he's convincing himself than either of us.

She manages a soggy nod, and that's the last the three of us say until Rick arrives. We let him do most of the talking, too, despite his not having much new information. He's at least familiar with hospital procedure and protocol, telling us there are no set visiting hours, but only two people at a time can go into ICU, where Gloria's recovering from surgery and will be for a couple of days—if all goes well.

In the ICU waiting room with our special late-night badges, we watch as Rick approaches the door and presses a button to alert the nurses' station to visitors. Gidget and Ned currently sit by Gloria, despite the wee hour. "We can't get Ned to leave," Rick explained in the car. "The nurses are going to have to kick him out."

Cyndi yelps when Gidget slips through the heavy doors and walks toward us as if she's underwater. She tries to smile a hello to us, but it falters at the sight of her two youngest siblings. Catching her face before it crumples completely, she straightens her back and blinks rapidly, summoning that strong big sister she's always been.

After prolonged hugs, she asks, "Who's first?" and I almost laugh that she includes me in her question.

Jet defers to Cyndi, who says to her big brother, "No, you go. She'll want to see you first."

Nobody argues with that, although Gidget warns us, "She's pretty out of it. Don't expect her usual sparkling conversation skills."

Jet chuckles nervously. "But she's going to be okay, right?"

She pats his arm. "Go in and see her for yourself. You'll feel better."

He doesn't wait for further encouragement. Gidget escorts him to the doors and introduces him to the nurse who has the unenviable job of playing ICU bouncer, on top of keeping seriously sick and injured people alive.

Cyndi inhales shakily and says, "I need to use the bathroom and freshen up." Gidget offers to go with her, but the youngest Knox waves her off. "Sit. Rest for a second. I saw the restrooms on the way in."

After she departs, Rick says he's going to head home before the kids have to get up for school and ask too many questions of the neighbor staying with them. "You gonna be home soon, Gidge? At least get a couple hours of sleep?"

Gidget shrugs. "In a while, maybe. I want to wait until David gets here." She looks at the clock on her phone and adds for my benefit, "He's flying standby on the first morning flight out of Minneapolis."

Rick kisses and hugs his wife, then gives me a quick hug and a wave goodbye.

I turn to my sister-in-law as she watches her husband turn

the corner to take him to the exit. "Jet, Cyndi, and I can hold down the fort here."

She nods and smiles gently. "I know. But I need to be here."

"Okay."

She lowers herself to a chair and taps her fingers on the wooden arm. Another group of traumatized-looking folks enters the waiting room, whispering and standing in a cluster as close to the ICU door as possible while still being in the waiting room.

Gidget nods at them, then murmurs, "New members of the Bad Day Club."

Perching on the edge of the chair next to her, I say, "You're doing great. And Glo— Mom's recovering, right? The surgery went well?"

She pauses, which makes me swivel toward her so I can glean some information from her expression. It reveals nothing. Finally, she answers carefully, "As well as can be expected. They didn't have the necessary surgical facilities at the hospital closest to Mom and Dad's house, so they had to fly her here." Glancing nervously toward the hallway leading to the bathrooms, she clears her throat and says so softly I have to nearly lean into her lap to hear, "She coded in the helicopter. They almost couldn't get her back and stabilized enough to do the surgery."

"Oh."

Gidget's eyes flash, and her usual bossy spunk returns. "Don't you dare tell Jet or Cyndi that."

"Okay, but... why not?"

She dabs impatiently at the tears collecting on her lashes. "Because. They're just kids."

I chuckle. "No, they're not! They're grownups."

"They'll always be little to me. And I don't want them to know how close we came to losing her."

"They can handle it. Besides, they deserve to know, don't you think?"

She hops to her feet and paces to the black windows. "Don't make me regret telling you, Maura."

I slump and stare at her rigid back. "Fine. I won't. But they're going to find out eventually. And they'll be mad that you and I didn't tell them right away."

"I guess I'll deal with that if it happens. I won't implicate you, either. You can pretend you didn't know. I had to tell someone, though." She drops her head, and her shoulders shake.

I rush to her side, folding her in a hug. "You don't have to be strong for me, you know?" Her ear rubs mine as she nods through her sobs. "You're not my big sister... or the boss of me." Feeling her smile against my cheek, I continue, "I'm not taking my cues from you, so you can be a scared kid, too."

"What if she doesn't make it?" she rasps. "What are we going to do? She's... She's everything in this family. Good and bad. Who's going to be that when she's gone? Me? I'm not ready. I don't want to make sure Dad's eating right and taking his blood pressure medicine. I don't want to ask Jet about turf toe and nag Keith and David to get more exercise, or help Cyndi plan a wedding, or host big holiday get-togethers. I'm drowning in my own life. I can't be her, too."

She pulls back, and I search her flushed face, but I don't say anything.

"I sound so selfish."

"Not at all. I get it. As well as I can. I don't have kids of my own, so I don't know that stress firsthand, but I can imagine."

"This is happening too soon. My kids were supposed to be grown before I had to be a parent to our parents."

"You have four other siblings, you know. And they're *not* babies. They can do things, too."

"Nobody else lives *here*, though."

What can I say to that? I can't fix this. The circumstances are what they are; we've all made the choices we've made, and this is where they've brought us. Imagining the responsibility this drops on Gidget nearly triggers a panic attack.

"Let's breathe and take things one step at a time, okay?" I say to both of us. "Come on. Sit down. You're exhausted and scared."

I lead her back to our chairs. She snatches a tissue from the nearby table and mops her face. "I need to get it together. It's bad enough I lost it on the phone when I called Jet to tell him."

"You need to do what your husband suggested and go home. Watch your kids sleep. Kiss Rick. Let him hold you. Sleep. Take a shower. Eat some breakfast. And come back here, refreshed."

Before she can accept or reject my suggestion, Cyndi returns, hiding her splotchy face as she digs for something in her purse. Gidget sniffs, stands, and smiles. "Better? Let me go tell Jet to stop being a Mom hog and give you a turn."

Cyndi smiles gratefully at her sister's retreating back. "I don't know how she does it," she says, locating a tin of mints that she offers to me. Paranoid that her offer is of necessity, not manners, I readily accept one.

"You do what's expected," I reply, sucking on the candy. "Somehow you find the strength and do it."

———

Jet's been excused from practice this week on the condition that he mentally prepare for the game against the Chargers on his own during this time. He's been instructed to meet the team in Los Angeles on Saturday.

I doubt he'd be given this much leeway for any other situation, even for the birth of one of his own children. Many a player has missed his child's entry to the world because there was a game to win, and... priorities. They're not paid to be present at any huge life events that dare to happen from August to February. The NFL feels no obligation to accommodate their poor planning.

This is a favorite topic of Gloria's. Colin once observed in private to me, "She's put way more thought into baby conception schedules for NFL players than is probably healthy."

Fluttering my eyelashes and pursing my lips, I said in a perfect impersonation of my mother-in-law, "'I will never understand these players' wives due to give birth in the middle of the season. Do they not understand how these things work? You conceive in mid- to late-summer, so that you give birth in the off-season. It's hardly nuclear physics. All these women, distracting their husbands, going into labor and having babies when the focus should be on winning games! It's downright selfish! Seems like a pathetic bid for attention and a shout-out on national television.'"

Instead of laughing with me, Colin had stared, horrified, at me during my uncanny performance. When I finished, he said, "That was scary. Never do that again."

The point is, the NFL's public relations campaigns over the years to prove how family-focused it is don't translate to a league-wide family leave policy during the regular and post-seasons. Most situations are left to the head coach's discretion. Since Coach Bauer has a heart and the utmost faith in his quarterback, he's put Jet on a long leash, almost to the point of off-leash.

Jet has made no mention of leaving before he absolutely has to, and I refuse to ask. My selfishness has some limits. And since his schedule permits him to stay until Saturday, I've assumed that's when I'll leave, too, having missed the Friday night premiere at the theater. Helen texted me to tell me my evening gown had been delivered and that she removed it from its plastic to hang it in the closet. Chances of my wearing it the day after tomorrow: nil. It sucks, but dwelling on my disappointment isn't going to change anything, so I've tried not to think too much about it.

Instead, I've tricked myself into believing this is the way it's always been planned, with me overseeing things long-distance and Nina executing the orders. With the success of the Malala fundraiser last Saturday, she's much more confident. At least, she's wisely not let her panic show during our talks.

My presence won't be missed Friday night; Jet's is another story. We haven't made an official announcement or sent out a press release that he won't be attending, which seems disingenuous. But we can't risk people deciding not to come because of that one, small detail. I didn't want to use his name on the invitation and original press release, but the rest of the board insisted. The only thing saving me from major guilt is that there will be other players and local celebrities there to sign autographs—just not the main one they were expecting. Still. I've agonized over the decision to keep our absence quiet, and I continue to go back and forth on it.

To clear my head and get some distance from the rest of the family, I periodically take walks around the huge hospital campus. Sometimes I find a quiet waiting room; other times, I sit in the bustling cafeteria. Still other times, I venture down to the emergency room, where the best people-watching opportunities await. It's not quite the same without Colin, but I've texted him a few of the more bizarre goings-on. Like the guy who dragged himself across the floor while his dispassionate wife (girlfriend? sister? friend?) and an equally unimpressed nurse trailed him. Studious eavesdropping on my part helped me deduce that this behavior was a frequent occurrence for this particular patient, a regular in the ER, although I never did figure out what the whole story was. It was disturbing enough for me, though, that I stopped visiting that waiting room, having realized how twisted it was to seek entertainment—however subconsciously—from other people's troubles.

These excursions are mere distractions from the decisions I have to make, decisions that need to be made and won't be made until I make them. A business venture can't be paused because other facets of life suddenly become more pressing. I'm still not comfortable misleading guests about Jet's presence at the opening, but I'm also not prepared to announce his absence. It's only Wednesday, so I still have time.

In a sunny courtyard, I text Rae.

Nina told me the Malala fundraiser was a success. Did you & AP have fun?

While I wait for a response, I close my eyes and tilt my face toward a sun that's too warm for December. California is so weird.

My phone dings, so I shade the screen and read:

It was great. Raised a lot of money.

Excellent

People are pumped about the theater, too. Lots of folks planning to come back when it's officially open.

Yay!

When are *you* coming back?

Not sure

Has almost dying made Gloria a better person?

Not sure

What are you sure about?

Nada

Come home.

I stare at her suggestion, although knowing Rae, it's more like a command. It's tempting to take it as such, no matter what, and pretend like I have no choice but to follow orders. That's not true, though. I'm my own boss, and I have capable people taking care of business at home. My place is with my husband and his family—my family—at this critical time.

While I think of a concise, text-friendly way to convey this to my bossy friend, she loses patience and types:

You're not gonna, are you?

I will, eventually

But not in time for the big night you've been working so hard for?

It's not looking likely

That's dumb.

I can't help but chuckle at her characteristic bluntness. When I want to hear what I want to hear, I text Colin. When I want to hear the truth, I text Rae.

Yeah, I know

But it doesn't change anything.

Nope

Tell Jet I said he better appreciate you.

I'm not going to say that. It'd be weird

Okay, then just tell him to be ready to play Sunday. Has he been doing his yoga?

Yes. I'm definitely not about to be honest on that score.

I don't believe you. Tell him to do his yoga. I don't want any dumb muscle strains from him because he thinks he's too cool to stretch and stay flexible.

Fine. Whatever you say

Gosh, you two are annoying.

Love you, too, Rae! Give AP a hug for me

Yeah, yeah

THIRTY

SHOWDOWN

When I return to Gloria's room, the cardiologist, a guy who looks like he plays a doctor on TV, is at her bedside, finishing his daily rounds visit. I quietly step inside the door and stay out of the way while he gives Gloria's foot a final, reassuring pat and says, "You're doing great, kiddo. A veritable miracle, all things considered."

Gidget and I exchange nervous glances, but fortunately, the doctor doesn't go into further detail, likely figuring everyone in the room is aware of how miraculous her survival is.

While my heart rate recovers from the close call, he addresses the rest of us more directly. "She's going to need some extra help at home for a while after her release. Not live-in care, or anything that drastic, but home nurse visits, for sure."

Gloria sighs. "If you're going to talk about me like I'm not here, can you do it out in the waiting room? I'm so tired..."

Everyone, except me, rushes to apologize. I'm sorry she had to say it, but she doesn't need our regret; she needs us to shut up and be more thoughtful.

When the room finally quiets, the doctor smiles. "If that's what you want, then that's what we'll do."

He motions for the family to lead him into the hallway and down to the waiting area. As usual, I bring up the rear. Ned hesitates.

"What's the matter?" I ask him.

"I don't want to leave her alone, but I need to know what the doctor's saying."

Since everyone else is already gone, I'm the lone candidate for staying behind. And I don't need to know about in-home care, so I pat his arm and lower myself into the chair he had previously occupied, right next to the bed. "Go on."

Gloria groans weakly. "I don't need anyone to stay in here. Go. Both of you."

Ned shakes his head. "No. Maura's staying, and that's final. I'm in charge now. You better get used to it." He shuffles his feet. "If that's okay with you."

I cough to cover my laugh.

"None of this is okay with me," my mother-in-law says so pitifully, it brings to mind one of her previous guilt trips from healthier times. "So, do whatever."

I motion for Ned to go, and I settle back in the chair with my phone. When he's gone, I say, "You don't have to talk to me. Sleep."

Her response is to close her eyes.

After a few minutes, when I'm sure she's napping, she startles me by saying, "I have no idea what day it is, but it feels like I've been here forever. Doesn't Jet have a game?"

"Today's Wednesday. Jet has to report to LA Saturday morning." I finish my latest email to Nina, a simple confirmation about what time Henry should report to work on Friday.

"Your theater opens on Friday night, though, doesn't it?"

I swallow. "Yes. But that's all taken care of. We don't have to be there."

"Don't be a martyr."

"I'm not."

"You'll never forgive me if you miss your big night. I don't want any part of that resentment. Don't do me any favors."

I bite my lip, inhale, and count to three. "Jet wants to be here."

"Well, *you* don't have to be."

Pressure builds in my head and behind my eyes, but I take a deep breath and merely say, "You should rest."

"I don't need you to tell me what to do, thank you."

"Ditto."

"You know, you and Cyndi are the only ones who consistently defy me. You seem to delight in contradicting me, sometimes against your own self-interests. And now you have Jet doing it." The beeps quicken on the machine next to her head.

I don't reply, for fear of bringing on another cardiac event.

"If it weren't so infuriating, I'd respect you for it," she says, her fingers twitching against the sheets on her legs.

Keeping my voice low and steady, as controlled as possible, I reply, "I don't defy you to be difficult. I do it because you overstep and try to dictate things that are none of your business."

She snorts. "My children are always my business."

"Jet and I make decisions based on what's best for our lives, because we're the ones who have to live with those choices. If our choices make you happy, great. If they upset you, that's unintentional. We're not doing anything to spite you."

After rolling her eyes, she closes them. "On second

thought, maybe we shouldn't talk. I'm in no condition for you to pick on me."

I clench my jaw, glad she's not hooked up to life support. It would be way too easy right now to simply unplug a few things and be free. Dismayed by that homicidal thought, I take a deep breath and count to thirty. It doesn't work.

When I'm still seething after several cycles of counting, I contemplate leaving the room, but I promised Ned I'd stay, and I like Ned. I like Gidget, Keith, David, and Cyndi, too. I love them, in fact. And I love Jet more than any other person I've ever loved, more than I ever thought possible. This woman will not push me to say or do hateful things to her, someone *they* love.

I chase after my tangled thoughts, following the string from one point to the next, until I catch up to the wayward, rolling ball of yarn. What I'm left with in one hand is a snarl of hurt and frustration that I have to somehow tame and wind back into some semblance of order with the truth, a tiny, tight pellet in my other hand.

When everything is packed neatly together again, I say, "You know, just once, I'd like you to be proud of me, no strings or caveats attached. I don't *need* you to be proud of me —I have my own family and friends and Jet for that—but it would be nice. I'd like to know what it feels like. It must be amazing, because so many people practically kill themselves to earn your approval. You even have Colin doing it. He's bending over backward to prove his intentions with Cyndi and the kids. For you."

She snorts. "He has no idea what he's in for."

"Show me a first-time parent who does."

"He'll get tired of sharing Cyndi's attention."

"He's not like that. He's one of the most selfless people I know. He changes diapers and cleans up puke and cooks dinner and... and... shops for minivans!"

"It's hard to maintain that for children who aren't yours."

"He loves Mikey and Gracie. It doesn't matter to him that he's not their biological father. I doubt it crosses his mind."

She fakes sleep in order to end the conversation, but her fluttering lids and erratic monitors betray her.

"Colin is a much better person than I am. Of course, you've probably already figured that out. You're just arguing with me now for the sake of arguing. And because he's my friend. Heaven forbid you give me credit for anything, even having decent friends. The dumb thing is, I keep hoping the day will come that I manage to do something that coincides with what you want. That way, I can get a taste of that approval without sacrificing my own happiness. But it's never going to happen, is it?"

I give her a chance to respond, but she remains silent and still.

"It's never going to happen, because you don't want what's best for anyone else; you only want what's best for *you*."

She opens her flashing green eyes. "I want what's best for my son."

I roll my eyes. "Oh, puh-lease."

"I do! I want what's best for all of my kids and grandkids."

"Don't worry; he still believes that. But I know better, so save your energy."

"Stop twisting things to make me sound selfish."

"But you are. For your pride and joy, you wanted a subservient mate, another walking womb to help you collect more grandchildren, to build *your* legacy. You thought you had that. When you first met me, you saw someone who was perfectly aimless." I tick off on my fingers, "I loved football, and I loved your son, but I had no idea who I was or what my life should be. You thought you had it made. Then I had to go and figure shit out. I'm so sorry."

"The only thing you're sorry about is that I'm still alive."

Oh, how I want to agree with her, if only to shut her up. I would gladly give her the satisfaction of confirming the worst of me, but she doesn't deserve it. She does deserve the whole truth, though.

After a bitter chuckle, I say, "That would make my life so much easier on so many levels—except for the most important one: someone I love more than life itself would be devastated. And his happiness is more important to me than mine. That's how *real* love works."

She blinks skeptically at me, so I shrug. "Believe me or don't believe me. It's true. So, shut up, get some rest, and do everything the doctors tell you to do, because if I never again see the look on Jet's face that I saw when he thought you were going to die, it will be too soon. Why don't *you* earn *his* devotion, for once?"

She opens her mouth to speak, but I put up my hand and return to my buzzing cell phone. "I'm busy. And you're resting. Everyone else will be back soon, and you can go back to pretending like I'm not here."

Her begrudging grumbling is the most satisfying sound I've ever heard.

———

It doesn't take me long to figure out that in order to prove a point, I've truly committed myself to missing the debut of the biggest project I've ever seen from conception to fruition. And that sucks so much harder than I ever imagined. My moral bedside victory is small consolation when I realize what a wretched corner I've painted myself into. Life was so much easier when I didn't care about anything.

On the way to our hotel for the night, Jet taps my wrist. I turn my attention from the moving landscape outside the window to the spot he's tapped and say to it, "What?"

"You've been so quiet all week."

Ha! If he only knew. Surely, I blew my word quota with his mom earlier today.

I swallow hard and return my eyes to the window so I won't have to lie to his face. "Just trying to stay out of the way."

He laughs. "Out of the way? How could you be in the way?"

"You know what I mean. I'm here to support, that's all."

And tell off your mother the minute I get some time alone with her. You know, how any normal, sane, rational person would act toward a sick woman.

He returns both hands to the wheel. "You're going home Friday morning, though, right?"

My head snaps around.

Glancing over at me, he grins uncertainly at my expression. "What?"

"*Are* we?"

"*I* hadn't planned on it, but I'd assumed you would be, considering…"

"Considering what?"

"Well, you need to get back. For the grand opening."

"I'm not going without *you*."

"Why not?"

I try to conceive of a great reason but can only come up with, "Because."

"That's silly. You have to be there. It's your big night."

"It's not that big of a deal. Nina has it covered."

"That's beside the point. And it *is* a big deal. You've worked hard for this. It's bad enough you missed Rae and AP's thing. Mom would want you to go."

She wants me to go, all right.

"Well, I don't want to do it without you, okay? It's bad enough that you attended the ESPYs without me. I don't want to set a precedent that you do your thing, and I do my thing, and we never do anything together unless it's convenient. I see that with the other WAGs, and that's not what I want for us."

"This is a one-time thing. An extreme situation."

"That's what they all say the first few times. Then it gets easier and easier to handle everything alone. And I don't want to."

"I don't want you to, either. I want to be there, but I can't."

"Then neither can I. We're a package deal."

He grunts. After a few seconds' pause, he says, "So, if I don't go, you won't go at all? Do you realize how awful that makes me feel? Like it's my fault? What if you had said you weren't going to go to the Super Bowl with me, and I said, 'Then I'm not going to play in it'?"

"That's different. You had an entire organization counting on you. Not to mention the fans."

"You have the same thing."

"Hardly."

"Maybe on a slightly smaller scale, but they still matter."

"Whatever. It's not the same. At all. But if it were, you'd be so hurt that I wouldn't be able to follow through."

"Then I'm a bad person who doesn't care enough?"

"No! This is a completely different situation. That's what I'm saying."

"It's not. This is your Super Bowl."

"Your family needs you."

"They do need me."

And with those four words, it sinks all the way in. "Ah. Yes. I see. What you're saying is that they don't need *me*."

"That's not—"

"No, I get it." I laugh mirthlessly. "Of course, I get it. Everyone *wants* me to go."

"Maura!"

"Wow. I'm sorry I made you practically come all the way out and say it. How embarrassing for both of us."

"What are you—"

"Forget it. If that's what you want, I'll leave."

"I don't *want* you to go. But it's not fair to ask you to stay."

Pulling up a travel app on my phone, I jab the dates into the fields to search for flights back to Kansas City. "Unbelievable," I mutter, choking back tears and nausea. Great. I'm probably getting sick from hanging around at the hospital for the better part of a week.

Jet rubs his forehead and hooks a right to pull under the canopy and hand over the car to the parking attendant. As soon as he puts the vehicle in park, I jump out and hurry ahead of him to the elevators, where I jab the button. I hear him behind me but don't turn to look at him as the doors slide open, and I step inside.

"Maura! Wait! Hold the elevator!"

I push the button for our floor. Jet's hand flies into view, but he misses the two-inch gap, and the doors kiss together, leaving him on the other side. I keep my finger firmly pressed on the "close door" button until the box begins its ascent. He wants me to leave him here? Done.

THIRTY-ONE

OPENING

This isn't the way it was supposed to be. I was supposed to be happy. I expected some degree of stress and nervousness, but I didn't expect it to be mixed with such disappointment. And nausea.

By the time I boarded the plane early Thursday morning after spending the night in the airport, paying an ungodly amount to fly standby, and miraculously winning a seat, I had finished crying. Mostly. The occasional rogue tear or two still leaked down my face when I allowed myself to think too much about Jet's dejected posture on the side of the bed while I threw clothes into the same bag he'd hastily packed for me nearly a week ago. Or how he kept saying my name over and over again in that sad, hopeless tone. Or how he merely sighed and looked down at his feet when I said the only thing I uttered before leaving: "Don't follow me to the airport." He knows I don't make idle requests hoping he'll ignore me and do the opposite. Most of the time. This was one instance where I may have been bluffing a tad. But I meant it when I originally said it, and he complied.

Since returning to a geographic area with one hundred percent fewer real palm trees, I've attempted to focus on the grand opening, not the black cloud hanging over it and my personal life. Tonight is about the kids and the hospital. It's also about an amazing new chapter in my life, one devoted to public service on my own terms, where I'm most comfortable.

But I've never been more uncomfortable in my life. Physically or mentally.

Hours before people will start arriving, I stand behind Nina's desk in the manager's office of The Knox with my blown-out hair and makeup professionally applied, taking in the bad news she's just told me: "Everyone still thinks Jet's going to be here tonight."

"I thought we agreed to send out the press release, announcing the change."

She stares at me as if I've lost my mind (I have, possibly), then says slowly, "No...The last I heard from you, you still weren't sure, and then you disappeared from the conversation and never said anything else about it."

Oh, man. That does sound familiar. The week is such a blur.

"Shit!" I yell, more at myself than at her, but there's no way for her to know that.

She cowers on the other side of the desk. "I can send it now."

"It's too late now! Forget it. Everyone will have to be disappointed. They'll get over it. I have to."

"Are you going to fire me for not reading your mind? Because that's not legal grounds for termination." She backs toward the door.

"I'm not going to fire you, Nina." I plop into the chair behind the desk and plunk my elbows on the surface, cradling my head in my hands. Remembering my makeup and hair, I gingerly place my forehead against the desktop and let my arms dangle at my sides. "I think I caught something out in California. Probably at the hospital. Or on the plane. Flying germ chambers."

"Are you going to be okay?"

"Yes. I'm dizzy, my head's all fuzzy, and I'm queasy. Too much stress, too much travel, not enough sleep. I need a couple minutes alone to rest my eyes, that's all."

"Fine. I'll, uh, double-check the concessions inventory, or something." She pauses at the threshold. "Maybe you're pregnant."

"Not funny, Nina."

She laughs maniacally on her way out, shutting the door behind her.

I'm allowed three minutes of peace before there's another knock. "So help me God, Nina, if I didn't like you so much, I'd fire you and figure out a legit reason later."

"You're awfully grumpy for someone about to have such an exciting night."

I straighten and try to smile for Rae, but my face crumples.

"What the hell is wrong with you?"

I laugh miserably at myself and her characteristic impatience. "I don't know! Actually, I do know. But I don't know why." I frantically pull tissues from the box on the desk and hold one under each eye to absorb any wetness before it can damage my face.

"You're deranged."

"This sucks," I whine. "Jet's not here, and I can't do this without him."

"Pathetic. And not true."

Whether it's literally true or not, I need him. And he needs me. Our lives before we met are testaments to that. Neither of us worked to our full potential until we became whole, together. Maybe that sounds cheesy, but I believe it. And I'm okay believing it. I'm not arrogant enough to think I could have gotten to this place on my own, running a cinema that benefits so many different causes. I didn't have the means, financial or emotional, to make it happen on my own.

But Jet has made me *me* in so many other, more subtle ways, too. And I've influenced his personal growth. We've changed each other. For better *and* worse, in some instances. Change we have, nonetheless, though. And we'll continue to evolve—as partners, as (gulp) parents (maybe), as friends, as companions, as helpmates.

"Of course, it's not literally true," I snap at Rae. "But I don't *want* to do this without him. I got married so I wouldn't have to do shit like this alone. Ever again."

She clicks her tongue. "You're still the hopeless romantic you've always been. Good to know this life hasn't changed you that much."

"Knock, knock!"

Both of us swivel toward the door, where Colin stands, knuckle poised but not quite touching the wood.

"Who's there? Nerd," Rae asks and answers in response.

"What are you doing here?" I ask. "Where are the kids?"

"The children are still at nursery, and I'm here as part of my duties as a board member, checking to ensure you don't need anything before I pop home to get suited and booted for tonight's festivities."

"I see."

"What are *you* doing with those tissues?"

Rae turns to Colin. "Our friend here was just telling me how she can't do anything without her snookie wookums."

Colin chuckles. "Ah, bless."

I sniffle and blush. "It's not a popular sentiment nowadays and makes me sound like a co-dependent ninny, but I don't care. We're a partnership, and we do things together. I would hope he feels the same way I do."

"Trust me; he doesn't," Rae says. "Guys don't think that way. They take all the credit for their success and assume they can do everything by themselves."

"Not true," Colin intones.

"You're hardly a typical guy, so your experience doesn't count."

"Has anyone ever told you you are the most sexist person on the planet?"

"You've never been in an NFL locker room, obviously."

He flutters his lashes at her. "You don't have to rub it in. Any chance you could sneak me in someday?"

I slap the surface of the desk and rise. "Do you two mind?"

Colin looks at me as if he's forgotten I'm here. Then he shakes his head and says, "Anyway, isn't this a moot point we're discussing, now that Jet and Cyndi are home?"

"What?"

Rae laughs. "You're kidding."

Drawing a cross over his heart, Colin says, "On my word. Cyndi texted me minutes ago from the airport, saying she'd landed."

"But Jet's not with her," I guess.

"Not now. He went home to dress for tonight. He's here in this state, though. This city. You had no idea? I hope I didn't speak out of turn and ruin a big surprise."

Hope, joy, and elation crash land when I realize, "Gloria must have given him permission to come home early."

Colin shrugs. "I wouldn't know. Haven't had a chance to get the full story from my love."

"Barf," Rae grumbles.

He ignores her. "Does it matter why he's here? He's here. The team is back together!"

It makes a difference to me, but it won't to the rest of our "team" or the fans who will show up tonight for autographs. Gloria's found a way to give me what I wanted while also spoiling it for me. Gotta hand it to her—the woman is talented.

Tossing the tissues in the trash, I say in a dead tone, "Nope. I suppose it doesn't matter."

———

The lobby of The Knox Theater sparkles and twinkles with Christmas lights, and a huge Douglas fir stands tall, proud, and fragrant in the corner, its branches weighed down by massive baubles and strings of shiny beads. Light beams through the plate glass windows, giving the appearance of broad daylight on the section of sidewalk directly in front of the building. The old-fashioned sign blinks and flashes, directing people to the front door and beckoning them forward.

Another shiny object inside the lobby, I pace in front of one of the leather sofas in my black, sequined floor-length dress, mumbling the short speech I've prepared and practiced ad nauseum to welcome our guests and introduce tonight's feature film. Occasionally, I lift the heavy material away from my legs and above my feet to prevent treading on the dress, then resume pacing and whispering, "'Welcome to The Knox Theater. We're so glad you could join us tonight for our inaugural public screening—' I am so going to screw up that word. In-aw-gyer-all. Is that how you say it? It sounds weird. Keep it simple. For the kids." I clear my throat. "'...our first-ever public screening.' Yes. Better. Simpler. Simple, simple, simple."

"Thinking about me?"

"Gaaaaaaaaaa!" The pointy toe of my shoe catches my dress and sends me catapulting forward, face-first into the neighboring sofa. Leather creaks, and the sequins rasp as I slide against the surface, falling toward the floor, unable to use my dress-encased legs to catch myself. As I twist and hit the area rug on my back with a thud, Jet's panicked face hovers above me.

"Maura! Oh, my gosh. Are you okay?"

I blink away humiliated tears. "I'm fine, I'm fine! Help me up before someone passing by sees me."

He tosses aside the enormous bouquet of red roses in his arms and yanks me to my feet, brushing me off while I pat my hair to make sure it hasn't moved. It hasn't, of course. When he kisses my forehead, then searches my eyes and asks again if I'm okay, I will them to dry and whiten.

"You scared me," I say, which doesn't help with the drying and whitening.

He laughs, probably at the replaying mental image of me flopping around like a bedazzled seal, then pulls himself together with a tiny cough and says, "I'm sorry. I came through the back, in case there were already people lined up outside."

I snort at that concept, and he looks over my shoulder to verify the sidewalk is empty of all except the usual foot traffic.

"Oh. Well, they'll be here soon. It's still early. The board members aren't even here yet. Where's Nina? And Henry?"

He pushes the roses aside to make room for me on the couch.

Hiking my skirt, again, I sit carefully on the front edge of the sofa and cross my feet at my ankles. I flatten my palm against my unsteady stomach. "Nina's in her office; Henry's quadruple-checking under all of the seats in the screening room to make sure he didn't miss any trash after last weekend's show."

Jet lowers himself next to me, his tuxedo-covered knees touching mine. "You're stunning."

"Thanks. I went to the blow bar." He chuckles. "You look pretty spiffy yourself."

"It's my wedding tux."

I can't help but giggle at his sheepish expression as he pulls on the ends of his sleeves and brushes a few rogue flecks of dandruff from his lapels.

"How unfair. Women can't do that. Can you imagine if I'd showed up tonight in my wedding dress?"

He raises an eyebrow. "That would be pret-ty weird."

"Yeah. So..."

"So..."

I want so much to ask him why he's here, and why he didn't call or text to tell me he would be, but I don't want to get into it right now, especially if it will trigger a fight. I'm at a loss for anything else to say, though, other than a quiet, "Thanks for the flowers." Then I motion to the lobby around us. "The place looks great, huh?"

"Fantastic." He looks around. "I can't believe how *shiny* everything is. And festive. People are going to love it. When they walk in, they're going to feel like they're somewhere special."

I duck my head. "How's your mom?"

He leans back, spreading out, his arms stretched along the back of the sofa, his ankle resting on his knee. "She's fine. Better. They're going to discharge her tomorrow, if everything holds." His suddenly casual, curt tone makes me look up, but he's focused on the Christmas tree, jaw slack, eyes unfocused.

"Good. That's great," I say, trying to convey sincerity and none of the resentment I still can't help but feel. I *am* glad she's recovering and that she'll be home, but probably not for the most altruistic of reasons. I want everything to return to normal so Jet won't have as much on his mind during this weekend's game. Also, her recovery doesn't absolve me of my guilt.

We sit in uncomfortable silence for a few seconds. Jet clears his throat and says, "Hey, uh, listen. I'm sorry I didn't give you a heads up that I'd be here. It was kind of a— Well, it was a last-minute decision."

"It's okay."

"No, it's not. It shouldn't have taken me so long to figure out that doing what I wanted to do—be with you tonight—was also the right thing to do."

"Your mom—"

"Is fine." His neck flexes. "Back to her old self—and then some. And everyone else is still there with her and dad. Me leaving a day earlier doesn't matter. To them. But it matters to us."

I smile and whisper emotionally, "I'm just glad you're here." I hold up one of my shaking hands. "I'm so nervous."

He grabs my hand to stop its trembling. "That's normal. This is a big deal. But you're going to be great." He kisses my fingertips. "Can I say something quick to the audience before you start the movie?"

Narrowing my eyes, I say, "Only if it's not sappy and embarrassing."

He pretends to be crestfallen. "Oh, darn."

"Yes, you can say whatever you want."

"Just, like, two minutes. It's something that really needs to be said."

"I trust you."

Movement out front snatches Jet's attention—the man's peripheral vision is damn-near robotic—and he jumps to his feet. "Your parents are here." He helps me stand without another accident, then strides to the front door to hold it open for Mom and Dad. "Hey, guys! Lookit you! Bruce! I forgot you cleaned up so nice."

"Wedding clothes," Mom says with a guilty giggle.

Jet and I laugh harder than likely seems natural, but there's no time to explain, because Greg and Deirdre arrive next, bickering all the way in, barely pausing to greet the rest of us. "...told you it was black tie!"

"I couldn't fit in that tux if I tried, anyway. This is fine! Lots of other guys will be in regular suits. Do you think the little kids are going to be in tails? No. Chill out, D."

Jet and I exchange bemused glances and stifle more laughter, especially when Rae actually does show up in tails, her hair slicked back like a 1920s movie star. Deirdre hisses something fierce at my brother then stomps away to commiserate with my mother.

It's going to be a fun night after all.

THIRTY-TWO

REVENGE

One minute, Jet and I are alone in the lobby. The next, it's heaving with people. Loud people. Excited people. I direct the volunteers to Nina and Henry and greet guests. Jet remains at my side, his hand on my lower back. We chat up hospital board members, local television personalities, and reporters. A few of Jet's teammates arrive, taking advantage of a rare excuse for a Friday night out before an away game.

Keela and Demarcus Jackson pause on their way into the theater to say hi and congratulations. Keela leans close and says, "Thanks for the night away from the kids."

"You could have brought them," I say.

She laughs and pats my arm, edging away to follow Demarcus. "Why would we do that? See you after. We need to get together when the season's over and catch up. I've missed you!"

While I nod and wave my agreement, watching her and Demarcus depart, I hear Jet greet another guest. "Hey, man. Glad you could make it."

I turn with a warm smile still on my lips, expecting a friend. Instead, I'm shocked—and dismayed—to find Derek.

"Oh! What are you—"

Jet tweaks my waist. "—drinking?" he finishes for me, beckoning the nearest adult volunteer with a drinks tray. "We have complimentary champagne, wine, and beer for one night only, since this is a special occasion."

Derek accepts a beer and raises his bottle toward us in a mini-salute. While the job counselor takes his first sip, Jet says, "We, uh, invited you, since you had such a big part in tonight's success."

I tense and swallow, my smile becoming painful.

With what can only be described as a simper, Derek replies, "Happy to help. How *is* Nina working out, Maura?" He tries to hide his smirk by taking another swig, but there's no doubt he's gloating.

I manage to say, "Great. Wonderful. We make a great team. Who knew?"

"Well, *I* did, obviously."

I tilt my head. "See, I don't think you did. But it all worked out, so that's all that matters."

"I know it's hard for you to admit it, Maura, but I'm damn good at my job."

Jet chuckles. "If you say so yourself, right?"

Derek shrugs. "Confidence is a huge part of success. You of all people understand that. There's no point in guys like you and me pretending to be humble, is there? I mean, that just comes off as phony."

"Hm. My humility is always sincere. That's how *I* avoid sounding phony. But you do you, man." Before Derek can respond, Jet pats him on the shoulder and says, "Enjoy the evening. Oh, and..." He pulls a folded sheet of paper from his inside tux pocket. "I have a little something for you later. You know, to show our appreciation."

Derek beams. "Oh. Wow. I wasn't expecting that."

"That's what makes it even better," Jet says magnanimously. "But I need you to sign this release." He flattens the paper and holds it out.

"Sure," Derek replies, somewhat warily, taking the document. "But what's it for?"

Jet scoffs and waves a hand dismissively, producing a pen. "Ah, just something saying we can use photos from tonight on the website and social media. Blah, blah, blah. Legal crap. Feel free to read it."

"Nah. I'm sure it's all standard." He signs with a flourish and hands the pen and paper back to Jet.

"Thanks, man. See you in a bit." With that, Jet steers me toward another group of people and busies himself signing autographs before I can ask what the hell is going on and why he thought it was okay to invite Derek, much less give him an appreciation gift.

That opportunity never arrives. The chime sounds, alerting our guests that it's time to file into the theater. They obediently do so, and I turn to where I think Jet is, hoping we'll have two seconds to ourselves, but he's gone, disappeared into the crowd. Figuring he's using the bathroom before his "two-minute" speech, I hang back while the lobby clears. Then I address the volunteers and Nina and Henry.

"You guys have all done a magnificent job tonight. Give yourselves a hand." They clap and give each other high-fives. "Thanks to you, more kids will get the quality care they deserve, and many will live longer, healthier lives. That's huge. And it's something you can be proud of." My glance lands on a little girl with no hair and sunken eyes, and I have

to take a minute to compose myself. "Anyway!" I say brightly.
"Thank you! There are prime rows reserved for each of you
and your families in the theater. Nina and Henry will hold
down the fort out here during the movie. Afterwards, we ask
that you help us check for trash in the theater, but then you're
free to go." I locate and say to the hospital representative,
"We'll deliver and present a check of the entire weekend's
proceeds first thing Monday, as we've discussed." With a deep
breath, I say, "And now... the film. I'll see you inside in five
minutes."

After our volunteers have gone, I say to Nina and Henry,
"Okay, guys. You know what to do. You can get started
clearing up out here, if you—"

"Hey! You guys coming?" Jet says, poking his head
around the edge of the screening room doorway. The rest of
his body emerges, and he jabs a thumb over his shoulder.
"Everyone's waiting for the MVPs." When Nina, Henry, and
I exchange blank glances, he sighs. "That would be you
three." He beckons us to follow him, so we do, to the front
of the theater, where we stand awkwardly in a line next
to him.

A hush gradually spreads through the room.

"Hey, everyone," Jet begins. "Thanks for coming tonight.
Welcome to the Knox Theater."

Oh, my gosh. He's stealing half my speech! I grit my teeth and
smile.

"We're super-pumped you're here. And actually, I'm not
supposed to be saying any of these things, because this isn't
my show. This is one hundred percent the brainchild of
Maura, my wife, who amazes me every day and humbles me
by using my name for herself and this place. Before she officially welcomes you, she's generously let me speak—some-

thing she's probably already regretting." He pauses for the gracious chuckles.

"I just wanted to take a minute to make sure everyone here knew how hard she's worked to make this a reality, because she's never going to tell you. And it's not just about the usual hard work you put into opening and running something like this. She fought hard for this place. She fought hard for each and every person The Knox is going to help." He takes a deep breath. "And I should probably stop talking, because I can actually feel her boring a hole in the side of my head." He fingers the exact spot—his temple—I've been focusing on throughout his remarks, and I can't help but laugh.

He half-turns and beams at me. "I knew it." Still looking at me, he says, "She's a better person than she gives herself credit for."

If he only knew... I flash to myself at his mom's bedside, taking advantage of her weakened state to say my piece. Like a coward. Everyone here thinks my blushing is about what Jet's saying. It should be. But it's more about what *I've* said. And although I feel shame for it, I don't regret it. I'd say it all to her again, given the chance and the exact same circumstances. That's what makes it even worse.

Just when I think I can't take it anymore, that I'm either going to pass out or poop my dress, Jet swivels back to the audience and says, "The Knox board of directors and I wanted do something a little extra for some very special people who have also made tonight possible: Nina, The Knox's tireless manager, and Henry, the theater's only other paid employee. Plus, I'd like to invite up here Derek Duggan, job counselor with The Career Center. While he's making his way up here, let's give them all a big hand."

Oh, Lord. What is this? This is all Derek's already-huge head needs.

Sure enough, he looks as though he's approaching the stage at the Oscars to accept an award he knew he had in the bag. Supporting role, of course. I hope he knows that.

While he walks down the slanted side aisle, two of our volunteers also appear from the shadows, near the emergency exit by the screen, where I didn't notice them before. One, a teenager in his electric wheelchair, holds a stack of nine shirt boxes in his lap. The other, a slightly younger girl, carries something flat and covered by a cloth under her arm. When she arrives at Jet's side, he takes it from her and stands it up next to him, adjusting the cover to ensure what's under it stays concealed. It's just a little taller than she is. Jet thanks Ty and Opal for their help and asks them to stay with us.

"Okay, I'm totally going over the amount of time I asked for, so real quick..." Taking the top three boxes from the stack, he checks the names written on the bottom and hands them off to Derek, Nina, and Henry. Meanwhile, an image fades onto the screen behind us: a front and back view of a white jersey with maroon accents and lettering. It bears a "1" on the front and "Knox Theater" across the chest. On the back, it says, "MVP," across the shoulders, above another huge "1."

The audience claps. Jet says to the recipients, "You can open them later, when it's convenient, but that's what's inside each box, plus a little note from the board and me, thanking you for everything you've done. Nina, I have one for each of your kids, too. I guessed on sizes, so if any of them don't fit, let me know." He turns to Henry. "Henry, my man, in your box I've slipped VIP tickets for you and a guest for the New Year's Eve game against Philly. Let's hope it's a winner, huh?"

Derek rocks on his feet while Nina and Henry hug their

thanks to Jet and me—even though I had nothing to do with this—and the crowd claps again.

Finally, it quiets, and Jet focuses on Derek. "And Derek. In addition to your jersey, we have a very special honor for you. Opal, do you mind taking off that cover?" She does, revealing a cardboard standee of Derek in gray robes, pointy hat, fake beard, and long wig, holding a long pipe.

The real Derek quickly masks his annoyance with what he must think looks like a good-natured chuckle, but the red creeping up his neck suggests otherwise. The audience bursts into laughter. Jet laughs, too, but quickly mock-sobers and quiets everyone with a hand up. "Now, now. No laughing at The Knox's official mascot, Mini Gandalf. This is a very serious honor." He stifles another giggle. "This is what Derek looked like the first time I met him, at one of The Career Center's job fairs. A very convincing grey wizard, right? I have to admit I judged him based on my first impression, and I never would have guessed that he was such a wizard at job placement, but he sent us Nina, who has gone above and beyond to get us here today. His instincts were right on the money. And such a talent should be rewarded. So here he is. He'll guard and protect The Knox, so make sure you say hi and get a picture with him each time you visit. Post your pics on social media and tag us or use the hashtag, 'KnoxTheater,' and you'll get a free drink or snack on us your next time here. We'd absolutely love for Mini Gandalf to go viral. Wouldn't that be awesome?"

The crowd cheers and chants a mixture of "Gandalf" and "Derek."

I pivot and grin at Derek, who blinks and reflexively smiles back.

"Thanks," he says robotically, shaking Jet's hand.

Jet squeezes tightly enough to produce a grimace from the smaller guy. "You totally deserve it, man."

Then my husband steps back and chants my name, coaxing the crowd to follow his lead.

I edge forward and clear my throat, not sure how to follow that. The speech I've prepared definitely won't work. Time to improvise. Welp, here goes.

THIRTY-THREE

AFTERGLOW

A few hours later, when the movie is over, I stand behind the concessions counter, my throbbing bare feet concealed under my dress, and survey the stragglers and remaining minglers who don't want the night to end. I can't blame them. Well, I blame them a little. I'm exhausted. It's a good tired, though. I say as much to Cyndi when she joins me and gives me the hug she hasn't had a chance to give me all night.

"This has been amazing."

"Right?"

"You sound surprised."

I turn my back to the lobby and say, "Earlier today, I didn't have much hope. About anything. Nothing was going the way I'd imagined it would go, and I... I was being a pretty big spoiled brat about it."

She laughs. "We all have our moments."

"I felt lousy all-around. Still don't feel one hundred percent physically, but a good night's sleep will fix that, I hope."

She studies my face. "You're pale."

"I believe it. But everything worked out. I'm so glad this night is over. Almost."

She bobs her head over my shoulder. "Is Jet forgiven then?"

I turn my head and look sideways at her while smiling. "Hmmm. How much of that Derek stuff did you know about?"

"Considering 'Mini Gandalf' has been taking up residence in a corner of my garage for nearly two months? All of it."

"And if Jet had decided to stay in California and skip the opening?"

"That was never going to happen. But he had asked Colin to make the presentation from the board in his absence."

"That turd."

Cyndi laughs. "You forget that Jet's a schemer. He takes after Mom like that."

The mention of Gloria dims my mood, but I'm surprised that it seems to have the same effect on my sister-in-law. "What? What's wrong? Did your mom say something to you before you left?"

She shakes her head. "Not to me. No."

"To Jet?"

"Mm. They exchanged words."

I grip her forearm. "Tell me everything."

"There's not much to tell," she says with a tiny shrug and paranoid glances behind me to ensure the subject of our conversation isn't in earshot. We both spy him talking to a person I don't recognize, a tall red-faced guy who seems wobbly on his feet and is laughing too loudly to be mistaken for sober. Perhaps unlimited free booze wasn't the best idea.

Cyndi leans closer to me and says barely above a whisper, "He told me this morning he was coming home, and I was welcome to join him or fly back tomorrow, as planned. Of course, I said I'd kill him if he left me behind."

"And he came to this decision because your mom gave him permission to leave?"

She snorts. "Hardly. When he told her, she faked chest pains."

"How do you know they weren't real?"

"She's still hooked up to a bunch of monitors. They were steady, and no nurses or doctors came running."

I roll my eyes. "Geez."

"Yeah. He coddled her but reminded her that she's going home tomorrow and doesn't need him around. Then he mentioned the game Sunday, and she was more receptive to his leaving. And when we thought we were home free—we were practically in the hallway, saying our goodbyes—she said, 'Make sure to send me pictures of *Maura's* theater. I suppose it's the closest thing to a grandchild I'm ever going to get from her.'"

I squeeze my eyes shut and grip the counter behind me.

Cyndi chuckles at my reaction. "Uh, yeah. The good news is, Jet didn't feel guilty leaving. The bad news is, he said something you should never, ever, ever say to your mother. It does, ironically, have the word 'mother' in it, though."

"Oh, no. This is awful. This isn't what I wanted. At all."

"He knows that. He doesn't blame you for her behavior."

"She's not well, though."

"She knew exactly what she was saying."

"I still feel bad."

"Don't."

I pause and consider what I'm about to say. On the one hand, I don't want anyone to know; on the other, I need to unburden myself and tell *someone*. If anyone will understand how far that woman can push a person, it's Cyndi. I stare down at my unpolished toes, peeking out from under my dress's hem. "I yelled at her. When you guys were talking to the doctor Wednesday afternoon, and I stayed in the room with her." Cyndi gasps theatrically. "Well, I didn't *yell* at her. But I did tell her off. Quietly."

"You did? Why?"

"Because I'd had it. And I took advantage of her helplessness and inability to storm from the room, like she usually does, and I told her everything I've been thinking and feeling for months. Years."

"Holy crap."

For a split second, I weigh mentioning specifics, especially about Colin, but decide that will only make things worse. "I let her have it. About her need to control people, her passive-aggressive behavior, her inability to truly want what's best for others and not just what's best for her. And"—I say the last bit on a squeak—"I told her to shut up."

Cyndi giggles.

I look up. "It felt amazing, too. I... I snapped."

"Good."

"Good?"

"Yes. I'm glad someone finally had the balls to put her in her place."

"But it wasn't an appropriate time. She'd just had a heart attack!"

"It's never going to be a *good* time."

"But that was the *worst* time."

"Sounds like it worked out just fine. Jet's exactly where he should be, out there schmoozing and signing autographs and reminding everyone what an incredible woman he married."

"Don't tell Jet."

Her eyes sparkle. "That you're an incredible woman? He already knows, based on that cringe-worthy speech he gave before the movie."

I slap her shoulder.

"Ow!"

"Don't tell him I told off your mom. Days after she almost died."

"She didn't almost die!" When I return my attention to my feet, the amusement fades from her voice, which becomes small, like a child's. "Did she? Who told you that?"

"Gidget," I mumble. "It happened in the medivac. Twice. Your mom coded. They almost couldn't operate on her, because she was so unstable."

Cyndi stands silent for so long I can't resist looking up at her, expecting to finally see the disapproval I deserve. But she smiles through her tears and pats my arm. "Well, she doesn't get a second chance at life only to come back and be the same jerk she was before."

"Just don't tell Jet," I repeat. "I'm not proud of what I did."

"I'll respect your wishes, but I believe you deserve a medal. You're officially my hero, Mo."

"I don't know about that."

Metal hits glass as Jet sneaks up behind me and rests his flat palms against the counter, tapping his wedding ring against the surface. "Have you two finished solving all the world's problems over here? Or are you gossiping?" Before we can answer, he lowers his voice and asks his sister, "Did you tell Maura what Derek's jersey says?"

She smiles indulgently at him. "I was leaving that for you. The piece de resistance."

"There's more?" I gasp, eyes wide.

He pulls a face. "Of course. Just in case he didn't get the

message here tonight, when he opens his 'gift,' it's not going to look like the one I flashed on the screen, the ones that Nina and Henry got." He pauses for effect. "His says, 'DICK.'"

My mouth drops open. "Micah Edward Knox!"

Cyndi claps her hands rapidly, like a little kid getting exactly what she asked for on Christmas morning.

He laughs at our reactions. "It had to be done."

"You said I was better than that."

"*You* are. *I'm* not."

I imagine Derek opening the box and can't help but feel vindicated. Then again... "Let's hope he doesn't take it as a compliment. Guys like him are usually pretty proud of being jerks."

"He knows it's not a compliment coming from me. And in case he *still* doesn't get it, I placed a handwritten note in the box, too."

I gulp, almost afraid to ask but also dying to know, "What does *that* say?"

Jet shakes his head. "Nah. It's best you don't know. What's that called, when you can't be guilty, because you don't know what happened?"

"Plausible deniability," Cyndi says.

"That's it! That. You should totally have that."

I sigh. "Tell me you didn't threaten him or say anything that could get you in trouble with the league... or the law."

Hand over his heart, he closes his eyes and says, "I promise. No threats. No cuss words, even. Just a clear message that he and I are not and never will be buds."

Cyndi pulls me in for one last hug while I'm still distracted, wondering about the specifics of Jet's message to Derek. "On that *note*," she says, "I'll leave you guys alone. I have some kids to get home to, anyway. I'm sure they're still up and terrorizing the babysitter. Now, if I can only find Colin..." She lets me go and rounds the counter, searching the thinning crowd.

I blow her a kiss. "Thanks for listening. Last time I saw him, he was in the middle of a bunch of linemen, saying words for them in his accent. Ever think of renting him out for weddings and mitzvahs?"

She shakes her head and chuckles, heading for the knot of very large laughing men in the center of the lobby.

Jet sneaks around the counter and takes his sister's place. I push away from the structure, ready to use my final energy reserves to close out the night, but Jet holds me still with one hand on each of my upper arms. "You're done."

"No, I— There are a few people here I want to thank personally, and—"

"Send them a pretty note in the mail on that fancy stationery you have but never use."

Another peek behind me reveals an emptying lobby. Even the most steadfast guests are heading for the doors.

I move down my to-do list. "I have to clean up. We're open tomorrow night, too, you know."

"That's why you pay that strapping college guy. I'm assuming that's why you pay him, anyway." I glare at him, and he laughs at himself, then says more seriously, "You've done enough. Let's go home."

"Okay." I rise on my tiptoes and peck his lips. He pulls me in tighter and holds the kiss longer, giving me a faint taste of the Twizzlers he ate during the movie.

A few minutes later, Nina breezes through the lobby with a spray bottle of cleaner and a rag. Henry follows closely behind with his broom and dustpan, plus the rolling trash can that normally sits outside the screening room door to collect refuse after the show.

"Hey, love birds," Nina says. "Why don't you go home and celebrate?"

Henry fake scowls. "Yeah. You're blocking the register, and we need to close that thing out. I have places to be."

"Do those places pay you?" Nina retorts. "Remember who you're talking to."

"I was only kidding!"

Jet widens his eyes at the manager's strictness, but I simply laugh and say, "Henry's right. If we're in the way, we should go. I'll be back tomorrow."

He beams at me and sticks out his tongue behind Nina's back.

"I saw that!" she yells on her way to the restroom with her cleaning supplies.

Staring incredulously after her, he whispers, "How the...?"

"She's a mom," I say. "Three-sixty vision and six or seven extra senses. It must be exhausting." I stifle a yawn. "Speaking of, my five senses and I are beat." It seems safe to finally admit that. More importantly, it seems critical to do so.

Jet pushes me gently toward the office and pats my butt. "Get your stuff and let's go."

I'm too tired to argue, even if I wanted to.

————

Even though I'm not in the mood, the attention is nice, and I can't deny what he's doing feels good. Plus, how do you say no to someone who insists you are a queen and should be treated as such—right now? Personally, I'm not strong enough to do that. I try to turn off my thoughts and ignore my bone-weariness so I can enjoy what he's doing to me under the covers.

It's no use, though. Obviously not getting the physical response from me he's expecting, Jet surfaces and kisses my lips. When I peck back distractedly, he asks, slightly out of breath, "What's the matter?"

Where to start? I can't stop thinking about what Cyndi told me. I can't stop seeing the sadness in his eyes all night as he played the jolly host, signing autographs and bragging about me to anyone who would listen, especially to the ones who only wanted to talk to him about football. I can't un-know the fact that while he was delivering his speech—and Derek's comeuppance—he most certainly had the events from earlier in the day nagging at the back of his mind too. No, as pleasurable as this is, there's no way it's going anywhere with me as long as I'm thinking about a certain person.

"Call your mom." I answer simply.

Raising his eyes, he looks over my head at the tufted wall that serves as our headboard and bites the inside of his cheek.

"It's not too late out there. Call her and tell her you love her. Send her those pictures she asked for."

His jaw tightens, and his nostrils flare. "Cyndi blabbed."

My silence is all the affirmation he needs.

Flopping onto his back next to me, he runs his hands through his tousled hair. Palms still bracketing his head, he says, "I hope you never tell my little sister anything important that you don't want the rest of the world knowing, because she sucks at keeping secrets. Always has."

I gulp and try not to worry about what she has on me, as of a couple of hours ago. Cuddling up to his side, I trace curlicues around his nipple. It twitches. "It's no secret your mom is a master at hitting nerves. And that she doesn't like me." My throat closes, but I clear it. "She's your mom, though. And she's earned your respect over the years. You can't deny her devotion to you."

He presses the heels of his hands into his eye sockets and groans. "That's why I feel so awful. It was out before I realized I was thinking it. Then I was too mad—and super-embarrassed—to care or to stick around for her reaction. I basically said it and ran, like a dumb, scared kid. It was stupid, but... you know what? She deserved it." He shakes his head drops his arms, slapping his thighs. "Damn it, she pisses me off sometimes."

"I know. I get it. Trust me." I reach over and grab his fingers. He stares at our hands. "Call her anyway. Be the bigger person."

He nods. "Yeah. I will. Like I always do. But tomorrow, huh?"

"Fine. Maybe you're right. Maybe you both need to sleep on it."

With a mischievous grin, he flops onto his side and props his head on his hand. "Yes. Please. Let me forget about it for a few, blissful hours." He walks his fingers down my throat and chest, then under the covers and all the way down the length of my torso. They slowly disappear into me, stroking me to distraction.

I suddenly feel much more in the moment.

He rolls over and pulls me on top of him. My tummy quivers when he brackets my waist in his hands and strokes me with his thumbs. "Ah, Beautiful."

"Champ," I whisper back.

"What would I do without you?"

Rather than answer verbally, I show him what he'd be missing.

THIRTY-FOUR

SHOCKER

But he doesn't call her the next day. Claims—legitimately, perhaps—that he's too busy traveling and preparing for Sunday's game. Or the day after that—game day. Or any of the four days after that, when he surely has no excuse and plenty of time.

Now, another busy weekend and a Division match-up are looming, with Christmas only a few days away, too.

The NFL is in the running for Grinch this year. Since the holiday falls on a Sunday, the full slate of games will be played, as usual. That's pretty standard. The guys and their families are used to that. It's a rare Christmas that falls on a team's rest day, anyway, and it's so close to the end of the season that nobody can afford to sacrifice practice or prep time.

The Chiefs' game against the Broncos, however, is the night game. And it's here at home. And we're so far ahead in our Division, it would take a meteor strike to change that. Which means, technically, *our* guys *could* spend the morning with their families before reporting for duty. But no. The

Commissioner has declared it just another day in football, and all of the owners and coaches have agreed, so the standard routines, complete with Saturday night hotel stays away from family, apply. Happy birthday, Jesus.

My convenient and newfound piety isn't the only reason I'm disappointed. Inexplicably, I had some mad hope that this year would be different. I *needed* it to be different. So I'm downright devastated.

In fact, when the final itinerary for Week 16 was handed out, and there were no provisions for the holiday, there might have been some players' *kids* who took the news better than I have.

"This is bullshit!" I rage, pulling leftovers and other food from the fridge willy-nilly on Beau's night off. Hard boiled eggs, fajita mix, hothouse strawberries, hummus, black cherries, sliced cucumbers, chicken curry and rice, chili, blocks of cheese…

"Yeah, it's a bummer," Jet says, watching each item hit the island counter and slide to its final resting spot. He catches a few containers before they sail off the opposite edge. Torzi waits on the other side, hoping Jet's reflexes fail us. "But we'll have our Christmas on Christmas Eve, before I have to leave for the hotel." He lifts one of the glass containers. "These are my eye cukes."

"Are you telling me I can't eat them? Are you seriously that vain? I'll slice some more for you."

"Or you could slice some fresh ones for yourself to eat." When that suggestion meets with a glare, he chuckles. "Or… *I* could slice some fresh ones for you to eat."

I wave him off. "Never mind. I don't want them enough for all that trouble. Or for you to lose a finger."

He surveys the collection of containers arrayed in front of

us. "Are you cleaning out the fridge, or are you going to eat all of this?"

"I'm hungry. But not. Nothing looks good." The frustrating but recently familiar phenomenon triggers panic, but I try to hold it together.

"This is a lot of nothing."

"I can't decide, okay?" Must. Not. Explode.

He stealthily slides his "eye cukes" back into the crisper, flinching when I whirl on him and say, "Stop changing the subject. This is going to be the worst Christmas ever."

He laughs. "Oh, come on. At least I'm not traveling."

"May as well be. What's the difference? You'll be sequestered in some hotel, away from home."

"If you want to do something on Christmas Day, we can do it after the game Sunday night."

"After the game? It'll be so late! It won't technically be Christmas by the time you get home."

"I don't know what you want from me, Maura. It is what it is."

"It is what it is," I mock under my breath.

"What's your deal? Is everything okay at the theater? You and Nina getting along all right?"

I unclench my clenched muscles (all of them; I've read that's important to practice) and adopt a lighter tone. "Everything's fine. Better than fine. We didn't have enough seats for the last weekend's showings of *Patch Adams*, so we're going to have to consider adding some matinees to future runs for the more popular causes."

"That's a good problem, though, right?"

I bite into a hardboiled egg but move to toss the rest of it when the rubbery texture grosses me out. Jet intercepts it and eats it himself while I answer, "Yeah! Absolutely! It's good." I tap my lips. "It's a shame this weekend's charity is getting the shaft because of the holiday."

We'll be open Monday, to try to make up for it and to capitalize on the day-after-Christmas crowd—people who are still off work and school and sick of their families—but it's still only two days of proceeds, as opposed to the usual three.

Jet says around a mouthful of egg, "They knew that going in, though."

I wrinkle my nose. "Please, don't talk with your mouth full. Disgusting."

"Yes, Mommy."

My stomach lurches. "Speaking of..." I survey my next choice of food to try, landing on a strawberry, the tip of which I nibble, then bite the whole thing away from the stem when it passes the test. After swallowing, like a civilized human, I continue while selecting the next berry, "Your family isn't coming here this year for Christmas, right? I'm not going to have to entertain a houseful of guests without you, am I? Because that was okay last year, but this year, with... everything else going on, it would be seriously stressful." I flap the front of my shirt to give myself some air and dry the sweat that's popped at the mere thought of repeating that experience, especially now. Especially when...

"No. Mom's not up for traveling. And everyone else blew their vacation time out in California when Mom was in the hospital."

"Right. Whew." He shoots me an incredulous look that makes me blush and giggle. "Sorry! I don't mean, 'Whew! I'm so glad she had a heart attack.' I'm just not up for it, either," I explain, cramming things back into the fridge.

Jet rushes forward. "Hey! I still haven't eaten."

"Oh. Sorry." I pause for him to choose the chili, then

continue my cleanup job so I don't have to witness him dumping globs of saucy, glistening ground beef into a bowl. It's bad enough I can still hear it and smell it.

He slides his dinner into the microwave and pushes the buttons to get it started. "A bite of egg and two strawberries? That's your dinner?" he asks, leaning his lower back against the counter while he waits for his food to heat.

I shrug and bend over to pick up Torzi, who allows me to nuzzle my nose against his furry head. "I guess I wasn't as hungry as I thought."

After the grand opening, I spent all of Saturday in bed, feeling hung over, although I'd only had one sip of champagne to toast the night before. I tried to help out at The Knox that evening, but Nina took one look at me and sent me and my "cooties" home. "There may be recovering children with compromised immune systems here tonight. Get the heck out of here. And don't come in tomorrow if you still feel like you look."

So, I didn't. Sunday, I watched the football game in bed with Torzi, where I avoided any scary reflecting, and I made frequent trips to the bathroom, where I avoided my scarier reflection. By Monday, I was feeling stronger, physically. Yesterday, I was almost back to normal, minus an appetite. And today, I actually got dressed and was productive, more as a distraction than anything else. We have charities lined up through February, thanks to my hard work today. But I hit the wall at about three o'clock, and food still isn't my friend.

Now, seemingly unable to help myself, I continue to pout about my latest disappointment, one that I'd rather focus on than the *huge* worry eating at the corners of my consciousness. "This Christmas is going to suck."

The microwave beeps and darkens. "With an attitude like

that, I guess it will." Jet shakes his head and retrieves his food, poking a spoon through the pile and sticking his tongue against the utensil to determine how hot the chili is in the middle. Hot enough, apparently, so he closes the appliance and relocates to the island, where he straddles a stool and starts digging in.

Torzi squirms in my arms, sniffing and licking the scent wafting toward us. Normally, I'd set him down and shoo him from the kitchen, but I need his fur to filter the smell for me, so I hold him more tightly and bury my nose deeper.

Wolfing down food in double-time, Jet chews and swallows, then shovels another bite, his jaw and neck muscles working angrily. Eventually, he stops eating long enough to say, "You're that pissed off that Santa has to come a day early?"

"Forgive me for wanting to spend the most important holiday of the year with my husband!"

"Go stare at our bank balance. It'll make you feel better."

"This isn't about money."

"It's always about money!"

"What good is money if you're not here to open the presents I buy with it?"

"I'll be here! I'll open presents! Just a day earlier!"

"It's not the same."

He pushes his half-empty bowl away. Torzi redoubles his efforts to spring from my arms. "Would you let the poor dog go?"

"No."

Jet stands and tries to make me, but I hold tighter. "Let go," he commands through clenched teeth.

"No! Stop it! You're going to hurt him!"

"*You're* hurting him!"

Torzi yelps and nips at my hand, surprising me enough that I drop him. He lands on his feet and skitters from the room.

My eyes fill. "He... He bit me!"

"I don't freaking blame him! Geez. What the hell is wrong with you?"

Sniffling, I examine the tiny indentations in the heel of my hand and repeat in a whisper, "He bit me."

Jet cranes his neck to verify the bite is nothing serious. "It was only a warning snip. Because you were holding him too tight." He returns to his chili and takes one more bite, then carries the bowl to the sink, where he rinses the rest down the garbage disposal.

"You were grabbing him, too. And pulling on him. You don't know your own strength sometimes."

Dropping the bowl and spoon with a clank, he turns slowly to face me. "Are you listening to yourself? You sound like a bratty kid. 'You were grabbing him, too,'" he mocks in a high-pitched voice. "'You started it!' 'I want Christmas on Christmas!' 'I'm—"

"I'm pregnant!"

He blinks and licks his lips. "What?"

I bury my face in my hands, one of which still tingles, and cry pitifully. Loudly. Wetly. My shoulders bounce up and down with every sob.

Hands still damp from rinsing his dishes, Jet skirts the island and pulls me to his chest. His heart booms so fast and loud against his breastbone, he may as well be on the field, sprinting for the end zone. Or his life. I drop my hands so I can press my forehead harder against him and count the beats through my skull. One, two, three, four, five, six, seven, eight. One for every half-second or so.

"Uh, it's okay," he finally says, patting my back.

"It's not okay!"

"Yeah, it is. It is. Uh... Wait." Having no idea what I'm waiting for, I nevertheless painfully stifle a sob and hold my breath while he continues to pant and mutter something to himself. After a few seconds, he says, "Okay. Yeah. This is... It's okay," so I allow myself to breathe again, which allows me to think, which brings back the tears, full-force.

"Shhhh," he says, his heart slowing slightly. "We've got this."

"No, we don't. Look at us! We're idiots, not parents!"

His Adam's apple bobs against the top of my head as he gulps audibly, and his heartbeat quickens once more. Gently, he pushes me away and says down into my face, "Are you sure?"

"That we're idiots? Yes."

"That you're... pregnant."

"Same answer."

"Sure-sure? Like, 'missed-your-period' sure or 'took-a-home-test' sure or 'went-to-see-a-doctor' sure or?"

"The first two." He nods encouragingly, so I explain, "In all the excitement with the theater renovations and your mom's heart attack and the opening, I didn't think much about being late, but Nina jokingly suggested Friday when I didn't feel well that I might be pregnant. At first, I dismissed that, because... well, I didn't want it to be true, and it was more likely that I caught something during our travels while I was stressed out and my immune system was vulnerable."

"You *were* pale Friday night, but I thought the same thing. And that you were nervous."

"Yeah. All those things. I couldn't stop thinking about it, though, so after Nina sent me home Saturday, I stopped at a pharmacy. I took a test, mostly to rule it out. Then I took three more tests when I didn't like the answer the first one gave me. But they said the same thing. And then I went to bed and tried not to think about it. But we have to think about it, right?"

"Yes, we do." He's quiet for a few seconds, then asks, "You've known since Saturday? Five days? Why didn't you tell me? I would have sat with you."

"On the toilet?"

He laughs. "Sure. Or maybe next to you. Or on the phone, since I was probably in L.A. by then."

I bite my lip. "I wasn't brave enough to take the tests right away, so I did it on Sunday, right before kickoff. I assumed you were busy."

He chuckles. "I may have been, now that you mention it."

"Don't be mad at me for not telling you right away."

"I'm not mad. Not at all."

"Are you sure? I'd be mad. And I've been so out of control, such a bitch."

"I *am* a little worried about you. You seem really upset."

"Oh, gosh. I know. I'm... I'm a hideous, horrible mess!"

"No, you're not, Babe."

"Yes, I am! You said it. I'm a brat. I hurt the dog. And he bit me." I dissolve into wracking sobs again, painfully aware this is the ugliest cry he's ever witnessed from me but, at the same time, not able to do anything about it.

He hugs me, wrapping his arms around me, crossing them over my back, and cradling the back of my head in his palms. Chuckling, he says, "Oh, Babe. It's okay."

"St-stop calling me 'Babe.' I h-hate it. You only call me that when you're drunk—or you want something."

"I do want something, though. I do."

Pushing me away so he can look down into my face, he says, "I want you. And I want this baby. And I want— I want all of this."

I hiccup and still while I let that sink in. "You do?" I whisper, not believing anyone would want *this*.

"Yes. I do." He swipes my cheekbones with his thumbs.

I sniffle.

A soft smile lights up his face. "This... This is a surprise. And unexpected. Because it's a surprise. And everything. But it's a good surprise."

"It is?"

"Sure!"

"I'm scared."

"Me, too." He laughs in a way that sounds like it could be followed by vomiting. "I feel like my heart is going to explode."

I stack my hands over my lower abdomen and whisper, "It's starting."

He widens his eyes, looking more alarmed than ever. "What's starting?" Dropping his attention to my hands, he places his over mine. "You can already feel it? Wait. No. That's not— Really?"

I shake my head. "No, I just mean..." I breathe deeply a few times to muster the composure to continue. "I finally figured out what I want to do with my life, and now... Now I have to do this instead. Babies. And I one hundred and nine percent don't want to. I hope it can't hear me say that, because it's so selfish and awful and—" I collapse against Jet.

He lets me cry for a while, then kisses the top of my head. "Baby."

"Please, don't call me—"

"No. 'Baby.' As in '*one* baby.' Not bab*ies*. This is one baby."

"We hope."

"Oh, gosh, yes." He steps away for a second and comes back with a clean dishtowel that he uses to wipe the tears and snot from my hot face. "Let's focus on this one, all right?"

I nod, grabbing the cloth and taking over the job of cleaning myself up.

"You can do this. *We* can do this."

I nod again and inhale a shuddering breath. "Okay."

"It's going to be great, Maura."

"You think so?"

"I know so. Because I love you. And now I know you're not crazy. You're… You're a mom."

I laugh.

He laughs more nervously. "Okay?"

"Okay."

"Tell me we didn't screw this up so that you're due at some stupid time, like September or October."

"Beginning of August, if my calculations are correct."

He whistles through his teeth. "Not great. But not awful. Pre-season baby is better than a post-season baby, right?"

"I guess. Still kinda sucks."

"Kinda. But we'll make it work. My mom can come stay with us and help out."

I stiffen.

He laughs. "Kidding! Kidding! Oh, man. We need to find your sense of humor again, or it's going to be a long nine months." He tweaks my hot, red nose. "I love you."

"I love you, too," I whine, cranking up the tears again, "but I can't stop crying."

"Maybe this will help. C'mere, Mama." He lowers his lips to mine.

I sink into his kiss, then pull back.

"My breath smells like chili and green onions, doesn't it?" he says with a playful grin.

I wince. "Yeah. And please don't call me 'Mama.' Ever."

His laughter shakes me while he holds me in a crushing embrace, my face smooshed against his shoulder.

Eventually, I laugh, too. What else can you do?

THIRTY-FIVE

ANNOUNCEMENT

I always imagined when this day came that Jet would want to take out ads in the paper, rent a billboard, and buy TV commercial time. At the very least, I figured he'd want to make one of those cutesy announcement videos that always go viral—and make me want to puke (even more than usual lately). But he's been strangely—and disconcertingly—taciturn since I told him the news. Sure, it's only been two days, and it's admittedly still way too early in the pregnancy, but I never thought that would matter to him. In my dreams—okay, nightmares—I was the one holding him back and begging him to keep the secret as long as possible.

His uncharacteristic behavior about this is making me nervous. More than nervous. Paranoid. Because I need to be able to count on him to act predictably while everything else in my life feels so upside down.

"When we Skype with your family later, I think we should tell them."

He wrinkles his nose at my proposed plan but doesn't look up from the owner's manual to his new electronic personal assistant, Geoffrey. "I don't know if I'm ready for that level of attention to the, uh, situation."

I blink back my ever-threatening tears and choke, "Okay. It's a baby, not a situation, but…"

At the timbre of my voice, his head snaps up, and I only glimpse a nanosecond of irritation before he softens and says, "Oh, Maura. That's not what I meant."

I wave him off with one hand and fan my face with the other. "This would be the best Christmas present I could *ever* give your mother. Ever. And after—" I stop myself, remembering at the last second that Jet still doesn't know about my abominable bedside manner.

He tilts his head and waits. Then realization—and chagrin —pass over his face, when he assumes I'm talking about his parting words to his mom. Before I can recover and finish my sentence with something feasible, he says, "Don't remind me."

Grabbing his out, I wheedle, "Oh, come on. It'll get you out of the doghouse. You know it will."

"That's… not right."

"Yes, it is."

"It's not okay to use that," he nods at my still-flat tummy, "to manipulate her. That's something *she* would do."

Because she's smart.

Apparently thinking that's the end of the discussion—silly man—he returns his attention to the black and red cylinder in front of him on the coffee table. "Geoffrey, who was the MVP of Super Bowl LVII?"

"The MVP of Super Bowl LVII was Micah 'Jet' Knox, quarterback for the Kansas City Chiefs," rings out a deep, posh English voice. *"Now, try asking me something* not *about you."*

"Oh, my gosh! Did you hear that? It knows I'm me!"

While he continues to play with his new toy, I chew my lip and watch him, desperate to figure out how to get him to agree to my scheme—without calling it such.

Begging is the only option.

I crawl across the living room floor and kneel in front of his chair. "Jet. Champ. Baby."

Eyes wide, he stares down at me, his expression clearly stating he thinks I've lost my mind.

"I need this," I say. When he appeared unmoved, I continue, "I need this bad. Your mom, she... she hates me."

"No, she doesn't!"

"Yes, she does. And all she's talked about since we came home from our honeymoon is babies. She signed me up for a prenatal vitamin delivery before our first anniversary. She sends me two or three articles—a day!—about reproductive health and fertility. For my birthday, she gave me a member-ship to a prenatal yoga class, which has already expired, because we've 'waited so long.' When we were in California last Mother's Day, she asked me if I was 'barren' and how long I'd known. She offered to call around the greater Kansas City area to find the best reproductive specialists and book an appointment for you and me to have your sperm and my eggs counted."

He winces.

"See? This is what I'm telling you. I'm telling you we need to get this monkey off our backs."

"But what if— I mean, it's early. Something could happen, and then..."

"Who cares?" I shake my head, immediately regretting that outburst. "That's not what I—" After a deep breath, I say, more calmly, "I care, obviously, if something happens. But so what if we have to give her bad news later? The important thing is the good news today. She needs this as much as we do. She's been blue since she came home from the hospital, frustrated by her recovery. Don't you think this will be the perfect motivation for her to eat right, exercise, and listen to her doctors? Surely she wants to live long enough to see her precious Jet's offspring."

His shoulders slump, and I know I have him.

Giddy, I say, "It doesn't have to be a big production. In fact, the smaller the better. We come out and say it. No biggie. And we let everyone know it's early, but it's such a perfect Christmas gift, we couldn't keep it from them. Then we swear them to secrecy, because, you know, I don't want this to be a filler story on ESPN's twenty-four-hour 'news' cycle."

He whitens at that thought, and I kick myself for bringing it up. "Never mind. It'll be fine. They'll keep it quiet."

"Greg, too?"

"Especially Greg." I pull from my mental catalog at least four things my brother doesn't want Deirdre to ever know and plan to hold them over his head as insurance. With my winningest smile, I check, "Okay?"

He slumps with resignation. "Fine. You do realize how naive it is to think this will get the monkey off our backs, though, right? That monkey's going to hang on even harder now."

I wave off his dire prediction. It can't be worse than it is right now. Impossible. He'll see. This isn't her first grandchild. She'll chill, knowing that she's gotten her way.

————

Not much later, my entire family and Colin, Cyndi, and the kids arrive to do a quick gift exchange before Jet has to leave for the weekend. We've also scheduled the Skype four-way call during this time, so everyone can wish each other a happy holiday—if technology cooperates.

When the pre-arranged time for the call comes, my stomach burbles, and I have an almost irresistible urge to run up the stairs and hide in my closet until this is over. I'm not sure I can handle Gloria's smug face when she finds out she's getting her way, that in fact, she wins.

No, *I* win, I remind myself for the ten billionth time this week. If it's about "winning" at all. Which it's not (says every loser ever). More accurately, it's a draw. She may feel vindicated, because she'll know based on my rant at the hospital that this was most definitely not planned, not my idea, not my ideal. But I get the last laugh, because in the end, if all goes well (still not a given, I understand), Jet and I will have a child to love and nurture—and hopefully not screw up too badly.

Jet props the tablet on the mantle and zooms it in on the group while we wait for the call to connect us criss-cross-country to his parents and Gidget's gaggle in California, Keith's clan in Texas, and David's tribe in Minnesota and says, "Here we go," at the series of beeps that let us know others are coming online.

Mikey hops up and down in front of Jet, who hurries to stand behind the couch where we're all gathered, some sitting on the floor in front, some standing behind, some on the sofa itself. "Make me tall!" the youngster demands, prompting his uncle to swing him onto his shoulders and shush him.

The call starts lightly enough with everyone figuring out how not to talk over each other. Then we share our favorite gifts and what we're planning to eat later. Jet makes everyone laugh by saying, "Protein bars and salad, if Rae has her way."

Then the conversation starts to wind down, so Jet steps

closer to me and rests his hand on my shoulder. I reach up and grasp his fingers, hoping I can make it a few more minutes without barfing. With one less hand supporting him, Mikey leans forward and rests both of his palms on Jet's forehead to hang on tighter. "Hey, uh, before we hang up, Maura and I have something to tell everyone."

A tense hush falls.

Not able to stand the silence for another second, I blurt, "I'm pregnant!"

Pandemonium breaks out. Babies cry, grandparents cry, siblings laugh, nieces and nephews take their cues from their parents and use the moment as an excuse to burn off some of their stocking candy. The people in the room with us rush us, making me glad nobody has a barrel of sports drink. Because if they did, Jet, Mikey, and I would be drenched.

As it is, Mikey says in the deep voice he uses when imitating his favorite uncle, "Whoa, whoa, whoa, peeps!"

Jet hands him over to Colin for safekeeping and succumbs to the hugs and handshakes foisted on us. When the crowd clears, Jet pulls me by the hand closer to the tablet, so we're the only ones in the frame. His siblings congratulate us in turn, as does Ned, but when Gloria says nothing, Jet prods, his voice shaking, "Well, Ma? What do you say?"

The room around us silences.

"Are you expecting a thank you?" she asks with a chuckle.

"No! I mean, what do you think?"

She pauses, and we all wait. I say a thousand prayers in those seconds, hoping she doesn't ruin this moment, for Jet's sake if nothing else. Finally, she says, her voice thick with pride, "You are going to be an amazing daddy."

My smile dies in my eyes but remains glued to my face.

Mom sidles up to me and side-hugs me. Jet says, "And Maura will be an amazing mom."

"Darn tootin'," my own mom adds.

Dad places his hands on my shoulders from behind me and squeezes.

Gloria sniffs. "Of course. That goes without saying."

"It's still nice to say it," Jet says coldly.

Cyndi steps in to diffuse the tension. "You guys! How did this happen?"

Keith laughs. "Your life is making a lot more sense now, Cyn."

She glares at him and sticks out her tongue. "Shut up. You know what I mean." Turning back to Jet and me, she clarifies, "You two were actively *not* trying to get pregnant, right?"

I blush and shrug. "Turns out, it *is* important to take those pills every day at the same time, even when you're busy and distracted."

She laughs. "*Especially* when you're busy and distracted. Oh, my gosh! I'm so glad you're a scatterbrain!" She pulls me into a suffocating hug, and I'm vaguely aware of Jet ending the call to a chorus of, "Merry Christmas!" "Thanks for the presents," and "Love you!"

He turns off the tablet and closes the cover on it but keeps his back to the room.

Greg clears his throat. "Uh, what's for brunch? I'm starving!"

The group, minus Jet and me, shuffle into the kitchen to see what Beau pre-made for us yesterday and that I've had heating in the ovens while we've opened gifts.

When we're alone, Jet pivots.

I shake my head. "Don't. It's okay."

"No, it's not."

"Right, but if we make a big deal about it, I'll start crying." The telltale prickle of tears enters my sinuses and tightens my throat while I pick up a few stray balls of wrapping paper and toss them toward the large black trash bag in the corner. "Let's go eat. Or, in my case, try to."

He tugs my arm while simultaneously tossing the tablet onto his recliner. His voice softening, he says, "C'mere you." Backing me up to the wall, he soothes me with a long, lazy kiss, reminding me what got us into this situation to begin with. "Do you think they'll miss us if we go upstairs for a while and skip brunch?"

"Yes," I manage to rasp in reply.

"Darn."

I pull him back for more. "I didn't say I cared."

THIRTY-SIX

RESET

Not recommended: watching your husband play in the Super Bowl—and lose—while still in your first trimester of pregnancy. In fact, I wouldn't recommend doing anything in your first trimester of pregnancy, except floating for twelve weeks in a sensory deprivation tank.

When you're married to an NFL quarterback, you can buy and install your own tank in your basement gym. So I did. When you run a non-profit, however, it's not feasible to spend your whole life in one. So I don't. There are people to be helped, marketing to be done, and the press to be courted. (Little Miss Kendra's effusions about The Knox's debut were almost as embarrassing as her article about my final job fair—on the opposite end of the spectrum.) And when that NFL QB husband of yours is the best in the league, December through February tends to be pretty busy, too. Granted, the biggest defeat of his life barely features as a footnote in *my* life story. To him, though, it's devastating.

And what can I say to the guy? "Sorry you lost the game. If it makes you feel any better, I lost my lunch—and breakfast—

and yesterday's dinner—while watching that nightmare on the field"? No. Because it's not about me. It's about him. It's about his heartbreak. I have a new appreciation for the losing team's pain while celebrations are swirling around them. In a word, it sucks.

Although it seems unsympathetic to put a time limit on it, I've decided I'm going to give Jet a week to mourn the loss. At some point, we have to seize control of the things we have the power to choose. Since that doesn't include my body at the moment, I choose to take charge of the attitude and general atmosphere in our house. I have a week to develop the perfect pep talk.

The speech is still pretty rough at the moment. Something about blessings and new beginnings, blah, blah, blah. I'll edit out the "blah, blah blah"s later.

I do my best thinking in "the tank," but apparently that's where Jet does his best moping. We've been taking turns in there for the past three days. Jet beat me down here this morning, so I'm lying on the bench press, patiently waiting, when he emerges, already changed from his wet trunks into dry shorts, but still shirtless.

Toweling his hair, he grins down at me. "'Morning, Beautiful."

"Hey." Twelve weeks into this epic gestational adventure, I merely look like someone who indulges in too much junk food and beer and not enough exercise, rather than the preggo I am, but sitting up by myself is a struggle, thanks to Bump. (Yeah, we're creative like that. It's Jet's fault. He's the one who started calling it that exclusively, and now it's stuck.)

I strain for a few seconds, trying to use my legs as leverage, but Jet quickly drops his towel and offers me a hand. "Easy there. Don't hurt yourself."

Before I can stand, he straddles the bench, facing me so our knees are touching.

"How are you feeling?" I ask, figuring he can take the question however he wants and answer accordingly.

"Right now? Amazing. Relaxed, content. That thing's almost better than sex."

"Wow."

"I said *almost*."

"Good. I'd hate to be replaced by a water tank."

He sobers. "No, but seriously. I'm okay."

"Yeah?"

Grabbing my hands, he breathes all the way in and releases it before saying, "Yeah. I mean, I'm not going to lie; it sucked a century egg to lose that game."

"Duh."

"But this rotten week has been better than some people's best weeks."

"Well, I guess."

"For sure. I have you and Bump and Torzi and a great life."

"Yes. You do. We do."

He brushes a knuckle against my bikini-exposed belly. "I have everything I've ever dreamed of or could ever want, and then some. I have a job I love, and even on the worst of days, it's still a game—a game they pay me an embarrassing amount of money to play, although I'd do it for free. Because I love it so much, and it's all I know how to do. Besides, I already have one of those rings, and to be honest, it's pretty ugly. Why would I want two ugly rings?" Lifting my legs over his, he pulls me closer and knits his hands behind my lower back to support me. "The most important ring I own is the one I wear proudly every single day. It tells the world I'm a winner, because I'm married to you."

I pull back and feign annoyance. "You're developing a nasty habit of stealing my speeches."

He laughs. "Sorry-not-sorry." Kissing my nose, he rests his forehead against mine and proposes, "Let's get the hell out of here for a week or two."

I crack up, then realize he's serious. "Jet, I— We can't. Aren't your parents coming for their usual visit? I can't believe your mom would skip that after missing Christmas, too, and—"

"No, I've told them not to come."

"Oh."

"It's not a big deal. Just... I need some space. *We* need some space."

"Okay, but the theater. I can't—"

"Yes, you can. That's the whole point of being your own boss and hiring dependable people."

Chewing my bottom lip, I stare at his shoulder while imagining how this could work. Nina would have to work a Sunday —or two, depending on how long we're gone. But she could take an extra weekday to make up for it. Henry's schedule wouldn't change. I have partner charities lined up for the next several months, so unless someone cancels on us last-minute, we're set there...

"Please," Jet says, interrupting my logistical musings. "I need to get away. We both do."

"Where do you want to go?"

"Anywhere. I don't care. You choose."

"Somewhere warm."

"That goes without saying."

"Somewhere neither of us has been."

"That shouldn't be too hard." We chuckle at our collective

lack of international travel experience. "Somewhere private," he adds.

"Yes! But not too remote," I say, thinking specifically of our honeymoon, where we had to take a boat to get anywhere populated. That was nice, at the time, but I don't want to be too far away from civilization and modern medicine right now. I loop my arms over his head, resting my wrists on his neck and leaning back to watch his eyes sparkle as he plots.

He taps his lips. "I'm thinking… a villa."

"Oooh! In Australia? I've always wanted to go to Australia."

"I was thinking Greece, but Australia sounds even better. So… You're in?" He grins hopefully.

"Let me clear it with Nina first, but yeah. I'm in."

Leaning forward, he brushes his mouth against mine. "Later, though, huh? After your float—and maybe some other things."

I press my chest to his and wiggle in his lap. "The float can wait, Big Guy."

"Told you my life was amazing."

Let's hope he never forgets it.

———

Sydney Harbor. Infinity pool, balconies galore, harbor views from every bedroom, clean, modern architecture and interior design, fully-stocked kitchen. I'm in love. In fact, permanently relocating here seems like a perfect idea.

But Kansas City is our home. For now. For the next six years, presumably. I often try to picture what life will be like six years from now, but more than half the time, it leads to me sitting with my head between my knees.

It took us three weeks to get ourselves organized—and to wait for the perfect villa to become available, thanks to a last-minute cancellation that Jet may or may not have "helped along." I can't get him to admit to it, but I'm pretty sure money changed hands under the table. We're here now, though, and it was worth the wait.

Our first couple of days were rougher than I expected, thanks to jet lag. I even slept through most of my birthday, but thirty-two is hardly a big deal, so no loss there. Who knew flying fifteen hours into the future would mess so horribly with your body clock? Of course, Jet recovered sooner than I did. My days and nights are still a bit off, but since it's vacation, I'm not too worried about it. No reason to get up early each morning, so staying up late into the night and the wee hours of the morning watching the boats in the harbor, set off by the lights from the city, is not only acceptable but romantic as hell.

I breathe contentedly in Jet's arms on the lounger. He scoots down to rest his chin on my shoulder, so we're cheek-to-cheek, gazing through the glass balcony wall. "You okay there?"

"More than okay. Fantastic. You?"

"Same. You feeling all right?"

"Amazing." And it's the truth. By the time we left the States, my morning sickness was gone. I'd read about such miracles but never thought it would happen to me. I thought I was destined to be one of those women who has to keep a toilet close by for all forty weeks. But no. I'm as ordinary in this experience as I've been in nearly everything else in my life, only this time, it's a major relief.

"I can tell. You look..." He stops and winces. "Gosh, I hate to say you're glowing, because that's so cheesy. But you kind of are!"

I laugh. "It's the harbor lights."

"Oh, okay." He kisses my cheek. "I'm so glad we're finally here. This was the best idea ever."

Leaning sideways, I turn my head to look at him. "You're not sorry we're doing this rather than hosting your parents, like usual?" (Translation: *"Your mom's not making you sorry we canceled on them?"*)

"Hell no! It's..." He squints out at the harbor. "It's time for some changes. Past time."

I carefully roll so I'm curled sideways against his chest and can look up more easily into his face.

He presses his chin to his chest. "What? What's that look for?"

My smile broadens. "Nothing. Only I'm pretty relieved you're ready for some changes, because..." I pull his hand to my belly. "Ready or not..."

He chuckles but his expression is earnest when he distractedly strokes my pooching abdomen and says, "I'm gonna get it right from now on."

"You already get plenty of things right."

"Not everything, though."

I laugh and return my attention to the twinkly lights and the boats. "I can't wait to have a perfect husband. That'll be neat."

His chest puffs out as he breathes in deeply. My head falls as he exhales. "Not perfect, but better. It's time to choose us, to stop worrying so much about what everyone else thinks."

"Hmmm..." I murmur skeptically then say, "Hey!" when he pushes me gently into a sitting position and spins me to face him, my back to the view.

"This baby is an opportunity to learn, to grow up, to step up."

Reaching out, I cup his face in my palms. "Oh, Champ. That sounds scary."

He jerks his face away, so I drop my arms and settle my hands in my lap. "I'm being serious."

"Yes, and that's not allowed on vacation."

With an agility I can only vaguely remember having—probably in my teens—he springs from the lounger. I follow his progress over my shoulder as he crosses to the balcony window. "While you were sleeping off your jet lag, I did some thinking," he says, staring out at the boats.

I resist the urge to make any jokes about avoiding off-season injuries. Instead, clamping my mouth shut and heaving myself from my seat, I join him at the window.

He runs his hand through his hair. "You know, we got married, and I thought as long as you were allowed to do your own thing, I could continue to do everything the same way I'd always done things. Until recently, I hadn't changed *anything*. I sort of slotted you in wherever you fit and let you make all the changes and adjustments to your life."

"My job was a whole lot more flexible. It made sense."

"I'm not talking about our careers. I'm talking about drilling down to the smallest details, from what we ate to when we had out-of-town visitors to what freaking brand of laundry detergent we use. I've called all the shots. And I've been so resistant to change. Like a little kid."

Although I disagree with him, to a certain extent, a part of me sees what he means, so I ask, "What changed?"

Wrapping his arm around me and pulling me closer to his side, he shifts his focus from the harbor to my face and says, "You."

I snort. "Oh, whatever."

"You don't see it, because it's you, but you've definitely changed." Before I can make another joke, he turns me so we're front-to-front and arrests me with that intense gaze I've never been able to resist or break. Tonight is no different. He cups my face in his hands. "I know I've been a shit."

Since I was expecting a more romantic declaration than that, I can't help but giggle.

He smiles, too, briefly, but quickly regains his fervency, so I try to follow his lead and stifle my mirth while he continues, "I've been so whiny and hard to live with. Moody. Mopey. Pouty."

"Sounds like you had all of the depression dwarfs."

"But you hung in there. And better than that, you called me on it. I needed that."

"Good. Because you're going to get it. Every time."

"You're the first person who's ever challenged me, who's ever called me out and told me to get over myself."

"What a charmed life you've led, Jet Knox."

He chuckles. "Spoiled. Entitled. Privileged."

"All that, too."

Grabbing my hands, he weaves his fingers through mine. "The past few months, you've rediscovered that Maura I met at the Christmas party. Snarky, funny, take-no-shit Maura. The Maura I fell in love with. And it wasn't until you found her again that I even realized she'd been hiding."

"'Lost,' more like," I say in a near-whisper.

"Nah. She's still been around. Stifled. Overwhelmed by our lifestyle's stupid demands. You were rebuilding."

I laugh at the inevitable sports metaphor. "Here we go."

"I'm serious."

"I know. That's what makes it even cuter."

"I'm not trying to be cute, I'm—"

"You don't have to try. You just are." I lean forward and kiss his chin. He purses his lips, clearly frustrated by my inability to take a compliment.

The problem is, I know exactly what he's talking about. And I know exactly when I fully "rediscovered" myself. The last thing I want to do is talk about it. It's best—if not a little cruel—for him to continue to think he's the only one who kicked Gloria while she was down. So I offer an equally plausible explanation:

"It's The Knox. I finally figured out my purpose. Everything else has fallen into place since then."

He nods. "That makes sense." Stroking Bump, he says, "You've taught me how to think differently about life. It's not a set-in-stone plan that only works one way."

I pat my pooch. "This little one's going to teach us that lesson over and over, I have a feeling."

"But it's not scary, right? It's… it's wonderful. The opportunities are endless."

Since it sounds like he's trying to convince himself as much as me, I find a way to agree with him. "It's more exciting than scary. Like a rollercoaster. I'm ninety-nine percent sure I'm safe, but that doesn't mean my heart's not pounding. That's what makes it fun."

Laughing, he pulls me into a crushing hug. "You're so much better at metaphors than I am."

"Clichéd similes. But yeah."

While he rubs my back, we stare out at the harbor. If we could stay here, like this, forever, the three of us, that would be bliss. At the same time, I'm just as curious to see what the future holds. It's such a foreign feeling, this ambition, that I don't know what to do with it at first. Then I relax into it and say, "We've got this, Champ."

With a kiss to the top of my head, he says against my hair, "Absolutely. It's going to be super-awesome."

I can't wait for life to prove him right, like it always does.

————

ACKNOWLEDGMENTS

Thank you, thank you, thank you to patient readers. It was a long wait, but you hung in there. At least, I'm assuming you did, if you're reading this.

Thanks, too, to beta readers Heather McCoubrey, Bethany Dodson, Erin Baker, Lynda G., and Natasha Walsh, and proofreader Gilda Sebenick. I wouldn't dream of publishing a book before seeking your eagle-eyed reviews and insightful perspectives.

Thanks to my husband, my kids, my mom, my siblings, my friends, and my pastor (who's also my friend and fellow writer). Your encouragement, optimism, and wisdom were sometimes the only things keeping me plodding toward the finish line. I have all the best people. Really.

Love you all.

ALSO BY BREA BROWN

The *Secret Keeper* series:

- *The Secret Keeper* (Book 1)
- *The Secret Keeper Confined* (Book 2)
- *The Secret Keeper Up All Night* (Book 3)
- *The Secret Keeper Holds On* (Book 4)
- *The Secret Keeper Lets Go* (Book 5)
- *The Secret Keeper Fulfilled* (Book 6)

The *Underdog* series:

- *Out of My League* (Book 1)
- *Rookie of the Year* (Book 2)
- *Opportunity Knox* (Book 3)

The *Nurse Nate* series:

- *Let's Be Frank* (Book 1)
- *Let's Be Real* (Book 2)
- *Let's Be Friends* (Book 3)

Stand-alone novels:

- *Daydreamer*
- *The Family Plot*
- *Plain Jayne*
- *Quiet, Please!*